SHANGHAI BRIDGE

They reached a port at last. Yokohama.
The stop was not long enough for the
Valentines to disembark. From the deck
of the ship Laura stared at her first
glimpse of the Orient. The Japanese
women on the pier in their bright silk
kimonos and high-soled wooden clogs
seemed like toys to her—charming,
living, breathing toys of human size.
She was enchanted. Even their move-
ments were tripping and toylike, she
thought.

Then the vessel slid away into the
waters of the China Sea and Yokohama
disappeared like a vision. The *China*
was about to reach its final port of call.

Shanghai.

SHANGHAI BRIDGE

Dore Mullen

Hamlyn Paperbacks

A Hamlyn Paperback

Published by Arrow Books Limited
17-21 Conway Street, London W1P 6JD

A division of the Hutchinson Publishing Group

London Melbourne Sydney Auckland
Johannesburg and agencies throughout
the world

First published in Great Britain
by Hamlyn Paperbacks 1985

© Dorothy Mullen 1983

Printed and bound in Great Britain by
Anchor Brendon Limited, Tiptree, Essex

ISBN 0 09 935410 1

BOOK ONE

A Pair of Golden Lilies

CHAPTER 1

The mahogany door of the library opened noiselessly and eighteen-year-old Laura Canfield entered the room. Her tread was strong for so slender a girl, and her chin was lifted firmly. But her pulses were throbbing in her temples. She fingered the golden locket at her throat: a birthday gift from her parents in 1893, two years before. She saw her father seated behind the library desk and knew he was hoping she had changed her mind. She steeled herself.

"Papa, I must tell the truth," she said in a low voice. "My decision remains as before."

Her father objected immediately. "No, Laura, we must discuss it. Please, dear, come and sit down." He gestured toward the chair beside him.

Laura moved to the chair and sat down with a rustle of bronze-colored taffeta silk as her skirt swept the floor. The shade picked up the highlights in her hair. She could smell the aroma of brandy in the room, the lingering odor of cigar smoke and the mingled fragrances of bookbindings and leather furniture and her father's bay rum cologne.

Henry Canfield plunged directly into his plea. "You cannot cling so stubbornly to your choice, Laura darling. Not when it means fighting against your own family. Your sister and I are opposed to your taking this step, as I am sure your mother would have been if she were still alive."

"I know that, Papa. But you always told me that if something is worth having, it's worth struggling for."

They gazed at one another. They had almost identical hazel eyes. Laura's were clear and filled with the certainty of youth;

Henry Canfield's expressed puzzlement and growing unhappiness. His second daughter had never before made him unhappy.

Laura knew she was doing that now, but she felt she had no choice: she had committed herself to the red-haired young man waiting in the foyer to say good night.

His name was Michael Valentine. He had promised to take her to Szechuan Province in China, as soon as they could be married. As soon as it could be arranged, and Laura hoped it would be within the week.

Henry Canfield passed a hand over his forehead. "My dearest Laura—why are you so sure this is what you want? You are choosing a life of hardship and uncertainty in a foreign country with a young man of unknown character and a totally different upbringing from your own."

"I cannot explain it to you, Papa. Except to say that I love him." Laura's face was alight with the intensity of her feeling. She did not wish to cause her father pain, but fate had placed her on a one-way road and she could travel only in that direction— with Mike Valentine to China. She was too young, too alive, and too brimming with a passion to investigate the strange corners of the world to refuse that invitation.

Middlebury, Connecticut, could not confine her spirit.

"You hardly know Mr. Valentine," Henry Canfield said.

"We have been corresponding for over a year, since we met in Oregon the summer you took us out West, Papa. I haven't kept it a secret. You know he has been writing to me from China. And now he has come to claim me."

"Letters, Laura! How can you decide to marry based on letters!"

Laura averted her eyes and kept silent.

Mr. Canfield folded his hands on the desk. His look of anxiety had deepened. "Laura dear, I am going to speak frankly," he said. "I believe Mr. Valentine is unreliable, in many ways."

Laura lifted her chin, her gaze no longer averted. "What ways?" she demanded.

"For one thing, the young man drank six glasses of wine with dinner. That is entirely too much."

"He was nervous and ill at ease! You were all so polite to him you were like icicles! Why wouldn't he try to relax with glasses

of wine? Anyone would!'' Laura caught her breath. ''Be frank,
Papa. Say that you think he is a common fortune hunter, the son
of an Irish immigrant lumberjack from Oregon trying to marry
the daughter of a wealthy man, and that he is not good enough
for me.''

''Very well, Laura. That is exactly what I think. Call it
snobbish if you like, but I am much older than you are and much
more experienced in the world. I see aspects of this young man's
character you do not perceive.''

''Oh, Papa, how wrong you are!''

''My dear Laura, how young and innocent *you* are! You have
been dazzled by a handsome face and the promise of adventure,''
he said with an air of melancholy. ''That is far too flimsy a
foundation on which to build a life.''

''It will be my kind of life,'' Laura whispered. ''The sort I
have always dreamed of. I know Mike and I will be happy.''

''You will be very far from home.''

''I am prepared for that.''

''So you believe.''

They were going around in circles, too much alike to
compromise. One of them would have to submit. Eventually it
was Henry Canfield. He said at last in a weary tone, ''I will
consent, because I have never refused you anything. Perhaps to
my cost, Laura. But there will be no fortune. You will go to your
bridegroom empty-handed.''

''I agree to that, Papa.'' Laura looked at him pleadingly.
''There is something we want more. Will you give us your
blessing? Will you wish us well?''

''I will always wish you well and pray for your happiness.
You are my daughter. That will never change.''

It was not what Laura had asked, but she knew that it would
have to suffice. At least their marriage was possible.

She rushed to the foyer to say good night to Mike Valentine,
aware that she had kept him waiting long. He was standing by
the door in his overcoat, for there was January snow on the
ground outside.

Laura went to him and looked up into cornflower-blue eyes
and the square-jawed, strong-planed face she had thought of so
often as she had written letters to China in her rose and white

bedroom upstairs. Now there would be no more letters. There
would be Mike himself. "It is settled, Mike," she said. "Papa
has consented to our marriage. But he says he will not give us
any money."

"Oh, lord, Laura. Do you think I want your father's money? I
want you." Mike placed a hand against her cheek.

Laura sighed and pressed her face against the warmth of his
palm. "I am so glad. Although I don't really understand why."

Mike's expression became pensive. His voice, a low and
musical baritone, grew slightly husky. He dropped his hand and
put it in his pocket. "Laura, I have never known anyone I could
really depend on until I met you. You are foursquare. It shines in
your eyes. That's why I love you. One reason, anyway. All my
life I have known people who have made promises and broken
them. I left Oregon for China because of disillusion."

Laura gave him a steady gaze. "It won't be that way with me,
Mike," she said.

"No, sweetheart. That's why we'll achieve our goals."

"We will, won't we?"

He nodded. They were both silent, filled with their belief in
each other.

Laura hesitated then, remembering something about the conversation with her father. She wondered whether she should tell
Mike. Yes, she decided. They would tell each other everything.
"Papa said you drank too many glasses of wine with dinner,"
she said.

"And three whiskeys before I got here. It's called Dutch
courage." Mike smiled crookedly. "I won't need that kind of
courage any longer. I won't be alone. I'll have you."

"Always," Laura assured him in a fervent tone.

Before Mike left, he spoke to Laura of Szechuan and the city
of Weichang, where they would be living. He wanted her to face
reality, he said. To know what she was in for. It would not be
easy. He could not offer her the comfort of her family upbringing.
He could only offer himself and his love and his resolve to make
her happy. And China, where he and his partner, a young man
named George Henderson, were attempting to make a go of a
steamboat service on the upper Yangtze.

"It all sounds thrilling," Laura said.

Mike glanced around at the lovely Canfield foyer. "Weichang is not like this. Not even Shanghai is. We'll have to love each other a lot."

"That will be the easy part!" Laura cried.

He took her in his arms and kissed her good night, and any doubts Laura may have harbored about her decision melted in the strength and promise of that embrace.

The next day Laura approached her father about a wedding.

It would be very simple, Henry Canfield informed his daughter stiffly. It would not be in a church but in the Canfield parlor. Only the immediate family would attend.

Laura consented gladly, knowing Mike cared as little about pomp and circumstance as she did.

"Will you ask Reverend Woodruff to perform the ceremony?" she asked.

"Perhaps Mr. Valentine would prefer a Catholic priest," Henry Canfield answered, tightening his jaw.

The idea hadn't occurred to Laura. "I'll find out," she whispered as a wrinkle appeared between her eyebrows. There was much she didn't know about Mike.

With hesitation she brought up the question when she saw Mike that evening in the parlor. He refused curtly and immediately, saying he wanted nothing to do with priests ever again. Laura was startled by the black scowl on his face.

Mike saw her reaction, and his face softened. "We will invoke the spirit of Kwan-Yin, the Chinese goddess of love and mercy. She will preside over our wedding."

"I've been reading about Chinese gods and goddesses," Laura said. "There are so many."

"Don't forget about demons. They exist too."

"I suppose there must be demons if there are gods," Laura said slowly.

Mike agreed. "That's why buildings in China have curving roofs. Demons can only fly in a straight line."

Laura laughed. "We won't encounter any demons."

They were married the following week. Laura wore an ivory lace dress that frothed beneath her chin and an ivory brooch pinned at the hollow of her throat. Mike wore a dark broadcloth suit with a high collar. Around the room were bowls of pink and white camellias, their creamy pastels lightening the dimness. Only Laura's father and sister were present.

The Reverend Mr. Woodruff took as his texts the words of Matthew, chapter 19, "they are no more twain, but one flesh," and Proverbs, chapter 31, "the heart of her husband doth safely trust in her. . . . She will do him good and not evil all the days of her life," and Malachi, chapter 2, "let none deal treacherously against the wife of his youth."

The words dropped into the silence of the Canfield parlor like snowflakes into still air, punctuated only by the hearers' soft breathing, a tiny sigh from Julia, a low throat-clearing from Henry Canfield, and the steady ticking of the ship's clock on the mantelpiece with its miniature clipper ship in full sail behind shining glass.

After the ceremony Michael and Laura Valentine boarded a train for San Francisco where they would embark on the vessel S.S. *China*. The sun had set at four o'clock, and now it was ten. Laura was with Mike in the smoking car. Connecticut was behind her. An unknown exploration lay ahead. She did not even know what state they were passing through or what city they were leaving behind as lamplight flashed and disappeared against the glass. The train was a small world of its own. As the ship would be.

She had come this far, Laura thought. She had left everything of her life in the past. She was alone with Michael Valentine. That was her name now, too, Laura realized with wonder. She nervously watched her own reflection in the window.

Mike crushed out his cigar in the metal ashtray, then stood up and held out his hand. "Laura sweetheart, let's go back to the compartment."

She rose to join him.

Inside the compartment Mike locked the door. He turned to Laura and took her into his arms. He could feel her trembling as he began to help her out of her dress. He stopped to kiss the hollow of her throat. But soon the trembling stopped and Laura

found herself responding eagerly as her husband continued to
undress her, then led her toward their bed as the train rocked into
the night.

Days passed. Honeymoon days on a smoky, gritty, swaying
train in a small compartment with a locked door. Days of love for
a young wife who had abandoned a life of sheltered comfort for a
leap into an uncertain destiny, and a young husband who had
found his bulwark against loneliness in the person of the girl he
held in his arms.

San Francisco. Gingerbread houses and steep hills and sunlight
glittering on blue water. The Pacific. The S.S. *China*. A small
cabin with one porthole and narrow bunks, but for Laura and
Mike it was all they needed. Embarkation on a vast ocean. A
rolling deck and moonlight on the waves and the two of them
alone when the cabin door was closed.

There were so many things Laura didn't yet understand about
her husband. She knew only that he had experienced many
betrayals in his life: he had told her that much. But he never
described them to her or spoke of his parents or his family. Laura
didn't care; she loved him as he was. They had so much to share:
laughter and passion and plans for the future. They would build
their own life and fortune in China, Mike had promised Laura,
and she was willing to hurl all of herself into that endeavor by his
side. The future was what counted, not the past. Someday, Laura
was certain, she would learn Mike's story.

They reached a port at last. Yokohama. The stop was not long
enough for the Valentines to disembark. From the deck of the
ship Laura stared at her first glimpse of the Orient. The
Japanese women on the pier in their bright silk kimonos and
high-soled wooden clogs seemed like toys to her—charming,
colorful, living, breathing toys of human size. She was enchanted.
Even their movements were tripping and toylike, she thought.

Then the vessel slid away into the waters of the China Sea and
Yokohama disappeared like a vision. The *China* was about to
reach its final port of call.

Shanghai.

*   *   *

Laura's first impressions of Shanghai were confused, excited, bewildering, and contradictory. At dawn they anchored in the muddy waters of the Whangpoo River, where people on houseboats offered trinkets to the passengers on deck. Later in the morning they reached the docks. Lines of coolies trod the gangplanks here, their backs bent under loads of packing cases. Mike and Laura climbed into separate rickshaws for a ride through the International Settlement, and then across the bridge over Soochow Creek. Still in their rickshaws they entered the walled Chinese section of Chapei, where their hotel was. White banners with red characters streamed overhead as they traversed narrow alleys. The rancid smell of the river mingled with the fragrance of boiling noodles.

CHAPTER 2

Three evenings later Laura was alone in the Shanghai hotel room. Tallow candles in lanterns of thin oiled paper were making splashes of yellow outside against the sidewalk. Laura could see them as she looked down from the window. She and Mike had been spending their days investigating Shanghai: the curio shops, the East Gate, the Temple of the Ten Immortals where women prayed for fertility. They were still awaiting the departure of the steamer to Weichang.

Mike had gone out to keep an appointment. "It's about buying spare parts for our own steamer," he'd told Laura. "You might be bored by the conversation; it will be technical. Do you want to stay home and read?"

"That's a good idea."

"Fine. I won't be very long."

Laura had been studying *The Globe Magazine,* a local publication by an American missionary named Dr. Young Allen. She was interested to learn that so much of Shanghai was English-speaking, including the street vendors. But as she stood by the window with the magazine in her hand, reading suddenly lost its interest for her. Too much was happening on the sidewalk below. Street peddlers were appearing from the alleys and laying out merchandise on the pavement. A ragged man was sitting cross-legged by the curb playing music that was thin and wailing and pleasingly dissonant on a bamboo flute. Laura was charmed by the scene and decided to join it.

She quickly discovered that the street bazaar was called the "night market" and offered a variety of merchandise: broken pieces of old bronzes, pewter pots and cups, spectacle frames without glass, brass bowls and candlesticks, bone and ivory chopsticks, secondhand pocketknives, German silver watches with broken works, snuff bottles, plaster Buddhas, wooden back scratchers, ear cleaners, towels, glassware, glazed tiles from an old temple. Laura browsed happily, not buying anything.

Then she came upon a little cloisonné dish that seemed beautiful to her, with deep glowing colors and a perfect shape. She bargained for it, wondering how it had come here among all the junk, and finally bought it. As the vendor wrapped it in a scrap of old newspaper, his face with its myriad wrinkles and leathery skin broke into a sweet smile. "You have made an excellent purchase. Not many would have noticed the little dish. Have you studied antiques?"

"No," said Laura. "No, I haven't."

But maybe I should, she thought.

The vendor nodded a trifle skeptically. Laura's spirits lifted. His words sounded sincere. "An excellent purchase."

She tucked the dish into her purse and wandered off. Looking away from the night market she could see the lights of the Bund across the bridge that spanned Soochow Creek. The Bund was the wide street that ran along the riverfront. It was lined with stone office buildings housing the Shanghai branches of shipping and banking and export companies from England, America, France, Holland, and Germany, Mike had explained to her on their arrival. Now the buildings were dark. The river was full of shipping, however. Lights bobbed on junks, sampans, freighters, and tugs.

Laura told herself she could cross the bridge on foot and stroll beside the river. It would not take long.

She made her way to the bridge. Then she paused on the rise, startled and confused. She saw Mike. He was standing beneath a lamp, his red hair and broad shoulders unmistakable. He was talking to a young woman. His head was bent, his face preoccupied and serious. The girl was absorbed in what he was saying.

Laura could see that the girl was beautiful. She was slender and Chinese, and she was wearing a turquoise silk gown. Her black hair was sleeked into a bun at the nape of her neck.

Laura's thoughts tumbled in bewilderment. Why had Mike lied to her? Had he left the hotel in order to meet this Chinese girl? He had arranged for this rendezvous on the bridge, she whispered to herself, not a discussion about engine parts at all. No wonder he had told her to stay in the hotel.

She shrank back onto the sidewalk, wishing she had stayed away from the bridge, asking herself why she had come, why she hadn't stayed in the hotel room. With a sudden sense of abandonment and betrayal she remembered a comment made to her and Mike by their hired guide at the Temple of the Ten Immortals. The guide had remarked, "We have a theory in China regarding happiness. We believe that there is only so much happiness possible in a person's lifetime, and an early abundance brings a later scarcity."

Suppose that were true, Laura thought. Suppose she, Laura, had already squandered her lifetime of happiness in these early blissful days with Mike? She knew so little about him, when all was said and done! She covered her face with her hands and turned away to block out the sight of the two figures on the bridge. Then, trembling, she dropped her hands so that she could see her way back to the hotel.

The Chinese girl on the bridge was named Li-san.

"I am wearing this gown for the last time," she said to Mike Valentine. "It is from my old life. After today I will have no more use for it."

"So you married your woodcutter," Mike said.

"Yes, in my native village."

"Felicitations on your marriage."

Li-san bowed.

She had been Mike's concubine in Weichang. He had purchased her in a saloon, shortly after his arrival in China. He had been lonely, and Li-san had been scared and young and appealing, the property of a Chinese "mama" who had taken her from her country village in exchange for money to be a "traveling girl," a prostitute. Li-san's family had been desperate and starving and for that reason she had gone willingly.

In Weichang with Mike, Li-san had been quiet and obedient. One night, however, she began to cry silently before they fell asleep. "I was not always a traveling girl," she whispered when Mike asked her what was wrong.

The story came out in halting phrases punctuated by tears.

"I was to have another life, at home in my village. I was planning to be married. My future husband was a woodcutter. We were in love. I was to have my own house, my own husband and children. Not this life of disgrace. My mother was widowed, and the landlord took away our farm. I was sold to the old woman you saw in the tavern, so that my brothers and sisters could have rice to eat."

"Why didn't the woodcutter help?"

"He wished to pay a dowry, but he needed time to save the money. My mother couldn't wait." Li-san made a gesture. "That is nothing to you."

Mike frowned uneasily.

A few moments later, out of the darkness, he heard Li-san say in a timid voice, "If I could find the money to buy my freedom, would you release me?"

"Maybe. Ask me when you've got the money."

Six months later Li-san approached him with a formal bow. She was wearing a fresh gown and she had a fresh flower in her hair. There was a man from her village at the kitchen door, she explained to Mike. He had come a long way. He wished to return to the village with an answer.

Li-san's woodcutter had sent her a message. By next month he would have saved enough money to buy her freedom. He still wanted to marry her. He offered her a life of poverty and respectability.

"You'll have nothing in that one-horse town," Mike told her.

"You'll live in a shack. No silk dresses. Rice instead of meat—if you're lucky."

"I know that. And I will give up other satisfactions as well. My husband is a simple man. He will not be able to delight my body and rouse my senses as you do. Yet the price for such pleasures of the flesh is too high." Li-san folded her hands and looked at the floor. "For a woman like myself it is too much to pay. It is death to the spirit. I was not born to be any man's toy. I am not a plaything."

Mike realized he would have to let her go.

Li-san said finally, trying to suppress the joy in her eyes when he consented, "I will come back from my village and pay you the money, Taipan."

"Forget the money."

"I must pay my debt." She was quiet, polite, and stubborn.

Mike objected that it was too far from her village to Weichang.

"It is not too far from Shanghai. Sometimes you are in Shanghai."

He agreed that that was so.

"I will meet you in Shanghai on the bridge that spans Soochow Creek. Six months from today."

"I may not be able to make that date, six months from today."

"I will wait for you on the bridge. Every day for two months, just after sundown." Li-san folded her hands before her. "Please do not destroy my dignity. Please let me pay the debt."

Mike finally consented to the appointment.

Now, on the bridge, Li-san held out an oilskin-wrapped package. "Here is your money. From my husband and myself. With our deep and humble thanks." She bowed.

"Please keep it," Mike said. "Consider it a gift."

"No. In order to be completely free, I must pay my debt."

Mike was silent for a while. Then he nodded. "All right. To save your face. But I'll hold it for you in safekeeping. If ever you're in trouble, tell me and I'll give the money back to you."

"Very well," replied Li-san.

"Don't forget."

"I will not forget." Li-san bowed again and said good-bye. Looking small and straight in her blue silk gown, she moved off and disappeared at the end of the bridge.

Mike, watching her, thought about how lucky he was. He had the girl he loved, and he would have her from now on. The lonely, edgy days were over. He would not need a concubine any longer, or whiskey either. Laura had given him an anchor; she would always be there when he reached out his hand. Li-san had not satisfied his hunger for love; she had only provided an outlet for physical desire. Laura made him happy. There were continents of difference.

In the hotel room that night Laura sat at the dressing table brushing her hair and wondering how to bring up the subject of what she had seen. Mike was lying across the bed with his arms folded under his head, waiting for her to join him. Silence was choking her.

Slowly she put down the hairbrush and looked at her hands in her lap. "Mike," she said after a moment, "I saw you this evening on the bridge."

Mike paused before he answered. "Did you?"

"Yes. You were talking to someone. A girl."

He paused again. Then he said in a voice that was brightly cheerful, "Oh. Sure. Li-san. I met her once in a restaurant. She used to work there as a waitress."

"Were you seeing her for some special purpose?"

"Why . . . no. I just happened to meet her by accident."

"It didn't look that way."

"Well, it was that way." Now his voice was growing irritable. "Come to bed."

"Mike—you said you were meeting someone to talk about engine parts."

"That's so. We finished early."

"Then why were you on the bridge?"

"I told you. I ran into an old acquaintance. Purely by accident. What's the matter? Don't you trust me? Why would I be interested in anyone else when I have you?" Mike held out his arms. "Laura, come to bed. I need you."

Laura stood up. He was right. She had to trust him.

"Take off your nightgown."

Laura pulled off the nightgown and moved to the bed. Mike tugged her down beside him. She moved closer. She was Mrs.

Valentine, she thought, loving him with all of herself, and she
was in China. Those facts were irrevocable. It was best to forget
the bridge and put the Chinese girl out of her mind. Soon they'd
be leaving for Weichang.

CHAPTER 3

The steamer's side-wheel churned its way through the broad
reaches of the lower Yangtze.

In the wide stretches of the lower river muddy waters flowed
to the sea, the water colored yellow by the mud. Rice paddies
extended on either side, black and shiny with marsh water.
Farmers trudged home from the paddies with sickles over their
shoulders. Night fell. A solitary junk bobbed like a shadow on
the swell from the steamer, and from across the water came the
creak of the junk oar in its lock. It was time for the evening
meal.

In the saloon the first-class passengers were dining. A dozen
kerosene lamps swayed on chains from the ceiling; hot light
flickered on the table and the food. The conversation was about
Japan. People were discussing the war the Japanese had just won
against China. The victory had awarded them Korea. "Japan is
the real power here in the Orient. She's strong, ambitious, and
determined." The speaker was a Catholic priest who was returning to his mission in Hankow after a trip to Japan.

Mike glowered at the man. After a moment he shoved away
from the table and left the room. Laura sighed, knowing why but
not understanding. For some reason he couldn't abide Catholic
priests. She debated whether or not to join him, finally staying
and finishing her dinner alone.

The steamer pushed through caramel-colored waters. On the
shore grave mounds swelled over the land like blisters of earth,

some bearing prow-shaped coffins. Walled cities of crumbling stone with watchtowers and parapets looked down from clifftops. The steamer churned upriver, leaving the watchtowers behind. Pagoda temples stood on hillsides, their rooftops curving to the sky.

This was not Shanghai, thought Laura. There were no office buildings, there were no European faces. This was truly China. This land, she thought, was old and secret and hostile, austere and strangely beautiful. She was stirred and challenged. She must learn to know this country. Then she wondered how one could know China, not being Chinese? That was the challenge.

"I'll be away from Weichang a lot of the time," Mike said to her before they docked. "I know I've told you that before, but I hope you won't be lonely."

"I'll do my best to keep busy. It should be easy. There's so much for me to learn."

The river was narrow at Weichang, and steep cliffs rose on either side. The water was silver now as it tumbled from the high gorges of the west. Weichang loomed on the clifftop, walled and closed, protecting a maze of winding alleys crammed with shops.

"Be careful on the street," Mike warned Laura. "You can get into trouble for the most trivial reason. If you have a foreign face and just brush against somebody by accident, you can collect an angry mob. Especially with Boxers in the area."

Laura promised to be careful, but she did not anticipate any trouble; she was just deeply excited. At the dock they climbed into rickshaws for the trip to the house, through the narrow streets. Shortly afterward she was being introduced to her new living quarters in Weichang. George Henderson, Mike's partner, was waiting to greet her and Mike in the courtyard of the house. The Chinese cook stood smiling beside him. He spoke no English. Chen, the houseboy, appeared on the run; he had been shopping and was breathless and startled to see his employer and his new mistress. Chen was young and polite and soft-spoken, and his English was good. He would interpret for the cook. Laura saw kindness in Chen's narrow black eyes and gentle intelligence in his smile. She took his hand and pressed it.

"Welcome, missy." Chen made an embarrassed gesture at his gown, which was rumpled and unbuttoned at the collar. "Not knowing when to expect you, not truly prepared. Many days since a woman has been in the house."

"I understand," Laura said.

"Tomorrow will be different, missy."

"Of course."

George Henderson, a lanky, fair-haired man, stood bemused. He moved his hands awkwardly, trying to put them in his pockets, then finally extended his right hand to Laura. "Welcome to Weichang, Mrs. Valentine."

"Please call me Laura."

"I'll do that, ma'am. Laura." George had light skin that colored easily. He was blushing now. "You're not what I expected."

"George." Mike gave him a warning frown.

The blush deepened. "What I mean is, we're not used to a real lady around the place. I guess you'll straighten things up a little bit."

"I'll try."

"We'll all get used to each other," Mike said heartily. "Starting with dinner tonight."

"I bring you tea now," said Chen.

"Wait a minute, Chen," said Mike. "I don't want tea."

"Whiskey for you," Chen amended quickly, "and tea for the missy." He bowed and withdrew. Laura gazed about her with a brightly cheerful air when he had gone. "What an interesting structure the house has," she remarked after a moment. She couldn't think of anything else tactful to say.

"It was built by a prosperous Chinese merchant," George volunteered. "A prominent citizen of Weichang."

"To live in?" Laura blurted, unable to stop herself.

Mike provided her with the history of the house. The Chinese merchant had built it to entertain his wives and concubines in the afternoon. Then he got bored with it and leased it to the two foreigners.

Laura saw that the house would be the project to keep her occupied for a while. As it stood, it was not really livable. Three narrow rooms stretched under a thatched roof. Stovepipes ran out through the windows because there were no chimneys. One room was used as the parlor–dining room, one was George Henderson's bedroom, and the last was the bedroom that would be used by Mike and Laura. Its stovepipe, she found later, when clogged, puffed soot all over the room. The servants' wing, across the court, was as big as the house, a gesture made by the Chinese landlord to save face for the tenants.

Chen served them tea and whiskey in the parlor as Laura tried to realize she was a resident now of Weichang. Mike stretched and relaxed, swallowing his whiskey, feeling its comforting warmth in the pit of his stomach, gazing at Laura and reflecting with amazed happiness that he had established a home for himself at last. Why did he want the drink? It eased him, increased his sense of well-being. But he would not overdo it when he had Laura. He did not need to.

When they were alone that night, Laura asked Mike if she could attempt to make improvements in the house.

"I'll try not to spend much money," she said.

Mike thought that was a good plan. Since labor was cheap, he informed her, she might be able to hire carpenters and painters at a reasonable rate.

Laura wondered how much difference painting the walls would make, just before she fell asleep watching shadows on the ceiling.

Mike and George left on their own steamer the next morning. They were going downriver to pick up cargo. The vessel, a small wooden craft painted gleaming white with a pilothouse on the upper deck, was docked in the river at the foot of an immensely long flight of stone steps on the cliffside edge of Weichang. Laura stood at the top of the steps and waved as they departed, although she knew she was only a tiny figure as seen from below. Water carriers with poles over their shoulders and buckets balanced on both ends of the poles passed her going up and down, their bare feet slapping on the stone. Chinese women stared at her curiously as they went by, carrying babies or baskets of laundry. No one had stared in Shanghai, Laura thought. Here in Szechuan, however, a foreign face was an oddity.

She returned to the house. Then she thought: *My first home. In China.*

The same excitement seized her that she had experienced on her arrival in the Orient, that she had felt on glimpsing Weichang. She was embarked on a great romantic adventure. Mike would be at her side battling the Yangtze. Together in this exotic country they would find success and love and fulfillment because they were strong and young and hopeful and they could not lose.

She turned her mind to improvements in the house. She began to pace the room, taking long strides.

Chen, the houseboy, peered at her from across the court in the servants' quarters. He asked himself what the new missy was thinking. She was only a child, he reflected with surprise. Perhaps she was not much younger than himself in terms of years, but how different their lives must have been. Certainly she could not have had his terrible childhood.

Great floods had come to his district, and there had been hunger in the countryside. Farmers had slain their oxen, put down their plows, and taken to the hills and mountains, banding together in groups to pillage, steal, and murder. They became robbers instead of farmers, and when they entered Chen's village and burned his father's cottage and stole his father's savings and killed his whole family, Chen became an orphan at age eleven. He had saved himself by running away in the darkness.

He wandered along the road, a skinny starving boy, a beggar with fearful memories.

He found himself in the great city of Chungking on the upper Yangtze, bewildered and frightened. Such a big city! Such a huge river! Shops everywhere, selling copper vessels, chinaware, furniture, precious stones, fans made of silk, paper or palm leaves. He heard shouts and running feet. "Make way for the mandarin! He comes!" Then the palanquin of the mandarin was swaying through the streets to the sound of gongs and firecrackers. The mandarin was within, his retinue trotting alongside, his standard-bearers shoving people into the gutters and beating them with sticks. "Make way!"

Chen gazed at the fruit merchants selling orange slices, a juggler performing his tricks by the puppet theater, a vendor of noodles selling hot delicious food. Chen could afford nothing. He was starving.

He was taken at last to the Christian orphanage, where the missionaries fed him and clothed him and gave him a home and taught him to read Chinese and speak English. The only price was that he worship the Christian god. Chen paid it gladly. He never forgot that he was Chinese and wore his queue with pride when he became a man, but he was always grateful to the foreigners for saving his life.

Yes, the missionaries were foreign devils and barbarians and could not tolerate the ancient Chinese gods, but they did not steal Chinese children in order to tear out their hearts and eyes to grind up for drugs. That was a foolish and evil rumor and led to killing. Chen detested killing; his soul was gentle.

Now he was a fine houseboy and worked for foreigners.

Would the new missy think he was a fine houseboy? He had been wondering, Would she like him? Would he keep his job? Chen had been frightened all over again. He knew one could always starve and be forced to beg on the roadside. There was always that chance. He had been awaiting the new missy's arrival with apprehension.

Without being asked he decided to bring her tea as he watched her pace the rooms of the Weichang house.

Laura, in the parlor, was considering building an additional room. It would have to be directly behind the others, she decided, since there was no space to build on either side. That would make the house look even more like a line of railroad cars.

With stovepipes. She laughed helplessly.

"I have brought you tea, missy." Chen had entered the room with a tea tray. Laura had already become accustomed to the handleless cups and the liquid awash with loose tea leaves. The tea itself, when the leaves were pushed aside, was the best she'd ever tasted.

Chen was wearing a spotless white silk gown, freshly ironed. Laura observed him with approval as he set down the tray.

"Chen," she said, "I need some advice. Will you help me?"

"Yes, missy." The houseboy folded his hands in his sleeves.

"I must think of a way to improve this house. It's very ugly, don't you agree?"

"Oh, yes," he said at once. "Only foreigners would live here. It is a very bad house."

"Then how can I fix it?"

"There is no way."

"There must be," Laura said. "There must be something I can do."

Chen said, "Only one thing, missy." Laura waited. Chen paused, then inclined his head. "Find another house. If you like I will send word to a house broker. For a commission he will seek you out a better place to live."

Laura recognized the idea immediately as the solution to her problem. She decided to act upon it at once.

"We will find a new house before my husband returns from his latest trip," she declared to Chen.

The houseboy did not contradict her. However, he knew better. In Weichang affairs did not move so quickly. He marveled silently at the missy's impetuous optimism.

CHAPTER 4

When Mike returned to Weichang from his river trip, he agreed with Laura's decision to find a new house. But since he and George would be leaving again in less than a week, he knew he would have to move quickly to help her.

Laura was already enmeshed in the Chinese house-finding ritual, which involved dealing with a house broker, inspecting and discussing dozens of unsuitable prospects, pretending to be interested in them, and even opening negotiations before finding an excuse to break them off. Somehow this process saved face on both sides. Mike decided, however, that enough face-saving had been done. He would take matters into his own hands.

He spoke to Chen in the servants' quarters.

"Have you heard from the broker about new houses to look at?" he asked.

"I believe there are three," the houseboy responded. "They are available to inspect tomorrow."

"I would like to see something today," Mike said.

"You, master?"

"Yes, by myself. Something unusual, that I can survey without the missy. To surprise her."

"Unusual?" Chen repeated.

"Something out of the ordinary." Mike paused. Then he added casually, "The house that the broker has been saving for last."

"Ah," said Chen. The master had learned the ways of China, he thought. He bowed. "I will inquire if there is an inspection for today."

"If so we will plan to leave at two o'clock," Mike told him. "We will make an excuse to the missy. I'll say that I need you for chores on board the steamer."

Chen assented.

There was indeed something unusual to see at two o'clock. The broker took them to a secluded house in a Chinese residential neighborhood, at the end of a long empty road. High walls flanked the entrance gate. Within all was neglect and disrepair. The woodwork was splintered, the paint was peeling, the doors were missing, and the rooms were filigreed with dust and spiderwebs.

"Needs only cleaning and painting and a good carpenter," Chen whispered to Mike. "I have a friend who is a carpenter."

"He may come in handy," Mike said.

He was making discoveries as he prowled around. Space. Three courtyards, four bedrooms, servants' quarters, a stone terrace in the rear leading off a huge sunken area three steps down, which would become the dining room/parlor. Beautifully constructed brick pathways in what would be the garden, now a jungle of weeds. Then the most unexpected discovery of all hidden in the central courtyard: the remains of a Chinese temple, with a pagoda roof of red and gold tiles (many broken), a black and white mosaic floor, equally dilapidated, and four carved stone pillars holding up the ceiling, each pillar chiseled with twining patterns of dragons and lotuses. The pillars stood serenely in the light filtering from the broken roof, surrounded by swirling motes of dust.

"This was the house of a rich man," Chen whispered to Mike. "He built his own private temple."

Many rich Chinese did that, as Mike was aware. *Laura will be crazy about it,* he thought.

"If you like it, I must negotiate with the broker," murmured Chen.

"Maybe I can't afford it."

"With clever bargaining, perhaps it will not be much more than the other house. Maybe even less. Perhaps you and Mr. George were not terribly clever with present landlord."

Mike gave him an ironic glance. Chen chuckled to himself. *The missy will be very happy,* the houseboy thought.

Laura was delighted with the house. She was overwhelmed by the temple. She smiled at Mike in their bedroom before he left Weichang for the river. "A new place to live," she said. "I'll be able to do it over. That will be my task while you're gone."

"How about your Chinese lessons?"

"I'll do that as well. Chen has found me a teacher, Mr. Fu. He's coming the day after tomorrow."

"I guess you'll be busy," Mike said contentedly.

Laura plunged into her new activities in the following weeks. She supervised the house repairs. She greeted Mike each time he returned to Weichang and saw him off from the top of the long flight of stone steps by the cliff. She studied Chinese.

Her teacher, Mr. Fu, was an elderly man with a wispy beard who wore a black cap with a red button to indicate his standing as a scholar. Often he quoted Confucius. One day he explained to Laura in a severe tone why he quoted the old texts.

"We must keep to the customs of our ancestors. Foreign ways are not suitable for China. The young people of today do not understand that. Fortunately the Dowager Empress understands. She protects us against foreign influence."

"Some people say the Manchu Dynasty must reform," Laura said carefully, quoting Mike and others who spoke of China as the sleeping giant. "They claim China must enter the modern world or there will be trouble." She volunteered the opinion with exceeding respect, befitting the attitude of a pupil to a teacher.

"There has always been trouble in the Middle Kingdom. Rebellions come and go but China remains. Our nation is like a decaying mansion which is constantly patched and repaired from roof to walls. Yet it stands for century after century."

"Yes, Honorable Teacher," Laura said obediently.

"There are those who would tear down the mansion. They talk of revolution; have you heard such talk?"

Laura nodded.

"If such a thing happens," Mr. Fu declared, "it will be of and by the Chinese people. Not foreigners. Thus the mansion will continue to stand."

Laura agreed respectfully. "I venerate your wisdom," she said with lowered eyes.

"Repeat the sentence in Mandarin Chinese," Mr. Fu commanded severely, but there was approval on his face for the correctness of her response.

Laura repeated the phrase in Chinese, stumbling, but accomplishing it at last.

The Peony Moon arrived. The Budding Moon had passed and so had the Sleeping Moon (sleeping because of the drowsiness of spring). Now it was almost summer, by Western reckoning the beginning of May. Summer came early to the Yangtze valley.

Laura made rapid progress with Mandarin Chinese, for she pored over her lessons in all her free time. She made notes in English using phonetic spelling, and she practiced with .Chen. Soon she could even talk to the cook. In spite of the activity, however, she was lonely when Mike was gone from Weichang. She consoled herself with the remodeling of her house.

When the house repairs were completed, after months of work by dozens of chattering workmen, Laura wandered through the rooms with a glow of happiness. The temple had been restored to its former beauty, its mosaic-tile floor gleaming and polished, its glazed tile roof once more an unbroken red and gold. The walls of the temple were white marble and red lacquer, with columns and trelliswork and papered windows. In the garden was a natural rock formation that pleased the eye with its twisted shape. It was surrounded by stunted pines. The massive entrance gate was black lacquer centered by an old bronze knocker. Laura had found the knocker in a shop in a Weichang alley, stroking it until her hands knew its contours and she was sure it was proper for her gate. She had learned that from a shopkeeper. In order to understand a piece of craftsmanship, he had told her, you must touch it and study it with your fingertips.

She was left with the problem of loneliness. Now that her beautiful home was finished, Laura wished she had a friend. There was an American missionary couple in Weichang, the Petersons, who had invited her to dinner, but apart from their nationality they had little in common. The Petersons were simple people from Iowa who read nothing but the Bible and had no interest in Chinese culture. They considered Laura's house eccentric. They told her so when they came to visit.

"Why don't you have some real furniture, instead of all that lacquered wood?" inquired Mrs. Peterson kindly. "You can have your husband bring it from Shanghai on his steamer. And a nice homespun rug, instead of that grass matting. And some flowers in the garden."

"I have lotuses in the pond. And a plum tree that blossoms."

"I mean growing flowers. Some nice hollyhocks instead of that ugly piece of rock."

"The Chinese admire the shape of natural rock," Laura said shyly. "My gardener suggested it."

"But why would you take his suggestion?" asked Mrs. Peterson in genuine puzzlement. "After all, he's Chinese."

After a fumbling attempt at an explanation Laura realized it was useless, and she was relieved when the subject changed. They discussed social problems.

"I hope this summer is better than last," said Mrs. Peterson anxiously.

"What happened last summer?"

"We had a cholera epidemic. It was ghastly. Especially when the children died. So many of them. All those tiny coffins."

"Oh, how terrible!"

"Sometimes I dream of home," Mrs. Peterson said with a wistful expression. "I dream of clean white farmhouses and big cornfields and healthy children with fat on their bones, and no cholera, and no floods, and no starvation." She sighed. "But our work is here."

Laura thought that her work was in Weichang too. She had to maintain a home in China for herself and Mike and guard their happiness. Until they went home in triumph.

*   *   *

She wished she could get to know her neighbor. The house next door was one of many pavilions and courtyards, and it was surrounded by a high stone wall. Only the pavilion roofs were visible over the top. Sometimes she could hear the servants chattering at their work. The house was owned by the most important family of the city, the Weis, who had given their name to Weichang. Occasionally a sedan chair borne by four servants would halt at the gate, and a small exquisitely gowned woman with tiny feet would be lifted out and carried within. She was almost unable to walk, Chen told Laura, for her feet had been bound in childhood to enhance her beauty. She was Madame Wei, the matriarch of the family.

Once Laura had paused at her own gate as the sedan chair arrived and watched the pale hand with the long jeweled fingernails emerge from between the silken curtains. Then she had smiled timidly at Madame Wei. The Chinese woman had not smiled back. There had been a flicker of her eyelids, though, and a lift of her slim arched brows.

"The Weis are much too grand for me, Chen," Laura had sighed.

"Madame Wei is a very clever woman. She speaks English. She reads books, English books and Chinese books. I have heard that Madame Wei's father was angry with her when she was a girl because she learned to read. Not necessary for a woman, he said."

"She sounds fascinating. I wish I could meet her."

"I don't think it is possible, missy. You are a foreigner. The Weis do not associate with foreigners."

"No, of course not," Laura said sadly.

"I will think of something to entertain you, missy. During the Peony Moon there is a temple fair in the next village. It is called the Fair of the Five Fierce Gods. It is very amusing. Would you like to go?"

"Yes, Chen. I would like it very much." It would be something special to look forward to.

But before it was time for the fair, Laura received a letter. Her spirits rose as she saw the return address: Middlebury, Connecticut. She held the envelope against her breast for a moment before she broke the seal. She had written home every two weeks, long letters describing all her experiences and activities in China, but this was the first answer she had received.

To her amazement the letter was from Julia. Of all people, Julia! She and her sister had never been close.

Julia was going to be married to a wealthy suitor from New Haven, but she was delaying the nuptials until December so she could have a Christmas wedding and be married in white velvet, with the bridesmaids in red velvet and the church decorated with red poinsettias.

"You would have been my maid of honor, if you hadn't run off to the land of the heathens," Julia wrote. "But maybe it's just as well. You always looked terrible in red."

The letter closed with regards from Papa. "He says you're welcome to come home at any time. Write at once and he'll send you passage money. You're not to hesitate."

Laura placed the letter in her sewing box where she wouldn't lose it, where the sight of it made her happy and lonely at the same time.

The Fair of the Five Fierce Gods spread out over a field on the outskirts of a village near Weichang. Booths and stalls and vendors covered the ground, splashing color beneath a hot summer sun. Acrobats tumbled on mats; peddlers cried their wares. Candy-sellers dispensed sticky sweets to children. Family groups laughed and strolled and pointed at the sights. The highlight was the Parade of the Gods. To the wail of pipes and the clash of cymbals it wound through the lanes of stalls. Figures dressed in red and green silk robes, with their faces painted blue and their cheeks adorned with designs of fish scales, leaped and capered, shaking steel tridents with clanging rings. Chen explained to Laura that they were ghosts.

"They are the attendants to Wu Chang, the King of the Ghosts. He dresses all in white and walks on stilts and has a tall paper hat on his head and carries a palm-leaf fan in his hand. Soon he will make his appearance."

In the distance Laura could see Wu Chang's tall paper hat. Children were screaming excitedly and clapping their hands.

"Wu Chang! Wu Chang!" Silk robes swirled as the ghosts bounded and capered.

"This is mostly for children," Chen remarked, smiling at Laura's obvious enjoyment. "It is a treat for small children and old grandmothers who still believe in spirits."

"It's all new to me, Chen! I'm like a child at this parade! Or maybe a grandmother!"

Then Laura began to feel dizzy. The sun was beating down on her head and people were pressing her on either side. Waves of odors were washing over her, the heavy smells of pork and garlic and fried dumplings making her stomach heave.

"Let's go into one of those little shops, Chen," she said. "The sun is too hot for me."

Concerned, Chen led her into a stall that sold brass oil lamps. Afterward Laura was never exactly clear about what had happened in the shop. Had she stumbled into someone by mistake? Mike had warned her about foreigners in Chinese crowds. She could recall only that a hostile group had been hovering in the doorway and that Chen was suddenly being shoved and slapped by a muscular six-footer with a red scarf tied around his head. *The Righteous Harmony Fists*, Laura thought confusedly. *The Boxers*. She tried to protest. *Leave my houseboy alone*. The crowd began to advance, moving into the stall, bearing down on her with growls in their throats. Laura felt peculiar. She put a hand to her head as she sensed her vision fading, darkening to blackness, dwindling to a tiny pinpoint of light. Then there was nothing.

She became aware of confused voices and shouts and above her a blue sky. *Doesn't this shop have a roof? Am I lying down?* It was too bewildering; she closed her eyes again.

She opened them to movement. Swaying, heaving movement. Dim light, coming through silken curtains. The delicious fragrance of jasmine perfume. A small shape opposite her, with folded hands and long jeweled fingernails.

"Madame Wei?" Laura heard her own feeble voice.

The figure gave a regal nod of assent.

Laura struggled to sit up. "Why is the ground moving?" she said weakly.

"You are in my sedan chair. You fainted in the lamp-seller's shop."

"The Righteous Harmony Fists . . ."

"They are rabble." Madame Wei lifted her chin disdainfully. "They were dispersed by my servants."

"Chen! My houseboy!"

"He is unharmed."

Laura sank back, fully awake at last. "Oh, Madame Wei, how good of you! I am your neighbor, Mrs. Valentine."

"Yes, I know, You are studying Chinese with Mr. Fu. You are a very good pupil; he is pleased. You restored the temple in your courtyard to its former beauty, and your house is furnished in excellent taste."

"You know all this."

"Certainly. One of my maidservants, Plum Blossom, has a romantic attachment to your houseboy."

"Chen never told me about it."

Madame Wei laughed, a sound like the tinkling of wind chimes. "He does not know it yet. Sooner or later, however, he will marry Plum Blossom, for she always gets her way."

Laura smiled in answer. She was feeling much better. Even the swaying of the sedan chair wasn't upsetting her. "It was foolish of me to faint," she said. "I'm not usually such a coward."

"You are expecting a child."

Laura blushed. She had thought so but was not yet sure.

"I am never mistaken," Madame Wei said calmly. "Your child will be born during the White Moon."

Madame Wei explained that she had taken her grandson as a special treat to see the Parade of the Gods. Fortunately she had observed Mrs. Valentine's predicament in the lamp shop. Her grandson was in the following sedan with his amah.

"Now you will come home with me and drink two cups of bitter tea," she continued. "It is the best thing in your condition."

Obviously she was a woman accustomed to being obeyed. Laura had no inclination to rebel. She sat back feeling very happy. She would see the house of many pavilions. "Madame Wei, how can I thank you for your kindness?"

Madame Wei answered promptly. "You will tell me stories of the exotic land across the ocean from which you come. I have a great curiosity to hear of it." She raised an inquiring eyebrow. "For instance, is it true that women look into men's faces in the street, without causing the men to feel shame? Is it true that people congratulate one another on looking young, instead of complimenting one another on their happy age?"

"Yes, Madame Wei, it is true."

"How very odd." Madame Wei looked politely amazed. "We have much to talk about."

CHAPTER 5

Laura regarded her gift to Madame Wei with love and anxiety. Madame Wei might think it a hopelessly ridiculous object, and Laura would be aware of that opinion, for during the last weeks she had come to know Madame Wei. The woman was autocratic, egotistical, and charming. Laura considered herself fortunate to have become her friend, and Chen assured her that was true.

Madame Wei avoided spending time with Laura's husband when Mike was in Weichang. Men in trousers offended her. Trousers were for workingmen and peasants; gentlemen wore gowns. Of course no foreigner was ever a gentleman. Then, too, she remembered Li-san's presence in Mike's household, for she was aware of whatever happened in Weichang. She never mentioned the fact to Laura; she was too wise.

Laura reached out and stroked her completed gift. It was a rocking chair. She'd had a Chinese carpenter copy it from a picture in an old *Delineator Magazine*. The carpenter had been baffled at first but then had done his best, and Laura had nagged and criticized and supervised until she had achieved her vision. It had Chinese touches—a black lacquer finish and mother-of-pearl insets on the arms and back. Otherwise it was a classic Boston rocker. Surely, Laura thought, Madame Wei had never seen such a piece of furniture. It was truly American. She wanted to express her gratitude to Madame Wei for their friendship, and she had pondered for days on the problem of how to do so until she had hit upon this idea.

"Say, Laura, what's that? A Chinese rocking chair?"

George Henderson had entered the terrace where she was standing by the rocker.

"Yes, George, I had a local carpenter make it as a gift for Madame Wei. Do you think she'll like it?"

"She ought to; it's real pretty." He gave her a shy smile. "I thought it might be for you, to ease your back, now that you're in an interesting condition."

Laura glanced at her middle, which was barely expanded. "Nothing shows yet," she murmured with a frown.

"You won't be saying that in a couple of months."

Laura laughed. "Maybe I'll have the carpenter make another rocking chair for me. If we're still on speaking terms."

"You'll win him over. You always do."

Laura was reminded of a comment of Madame Wei's. "If you give birth to a daughter, you will no longer be the sole goddess in your house."

"I? A goddess?"

"Yes. You have four worshipers to burn incense at your shrine. Your husband, Mr. Henderson, Chen, and the cook. If you bear a son, there will be five."

Laura, of course, had not taken that comment seriously.

"Mike's a lucky guy to have found a girl like you," George said after a moment.

"Thank you, George."

"Mike's always had a way with girls. Not like me. I never know what to say. Except . . . except with you."

"Well, I'm glad of that."

George was silent for a moment. Then he burst out, "Mike doesn't deserve you!"

"George! That isn't true!"

"See? I made the wrong remark again." He blushed. "Even with you, I put my foot in my mouth. And I wouldn't hurt you for . . . for . . ."

"All the tea in China?" Laura supplied gently.

He laughed in relief. "That's about it."

They both laughed, and the little moment of tension evaporated.

Laura sent her rocking chair to Madame Wei, still uncertain of its reception. The house of the Wei family contained so many treasures that Laura thought of it as a place of enchantment. In the main pavilions were curved vases of deep yellow glaze, a color so intense that it was almost tangible, color that filled not only the eye but the brain so that *yellow* pierced the mind like a sword. They had been created during the Ming Dynasty. In the courtyards were great bronze water jars as high as Laura's head— very, very old, flawless in shape, with curved lips and round bellies, their patina the greenish-black of antiquity. There were huge incense burners that had been standing in courtyards for ten centuries. There were porcelain lion-dogs as blue as the vases were yellow. There was a Han horse's head stylized to conveying the idea of horse, with a snarling lip and rolling eyes. There were lacquer-and-gilt chests with cubbyholes to contain a scholar's scrolls and wells to hold his brushes and ink, intricate and elaborate, built during the craftsman's era of the eighteenth century; hanging above them were parchment scrolls covered with graceful calligraphy, the characters brushed by the scholars who had owned the chests. There were too many treasures to comprehend. Laura had been forced to stop looking on her first visit, for her eye was surfeited.

The Weis had great landholdings in Szechuan Province. They were of the class of mandarins and landlords who were the target of radical discontent. Laura and Madame Wei, however, on Laura's subsequent visits, avoided the topic of politics. They had long conversations about other things in Madame Wei's private pavilion, beneath her favorite willow tree, as Madame Wei poured cups of bitter tea from an exquisite porcelain pot. Madame Wei was fascinated with tales of America. Some of them she could scarcely credit. She was particularly amazed by Laura's description of Mr. Alexander Graham Bell's celebrated invention. Telephones had not yet come to Weichang.

"How is it you can hear your friend's voice through the machine?" she demanded. "From a distance? How is this possible?"

"It has something to do with sound waves, Madame Wei.

Invisible waves of sound in the air." Laura gestured apologetically.
"I don't really understand it myself."

"Invisible waves in the air!" Madame Wei laughed shortly.
"And we ridicule peasants for believing in Wu Chang's ghosts!
Perhaps they are the wise ones and we are the fools."

The warm golden afternoons passed into lavender twilight
above the arch of the willow tree and the curves of the pagoda
roof. The Peony Moon drifted into the Dragon Moon, and Laura
built her rocker and sent it to her friend.

The next day she received her answer. Two of Madame Wei's
servants arrived at Laura's gate and were admitted to the courtyard by Chen, who was wide-eyed with astonishment. They were
bearing an answering gift: a pair of bronze vases. Not ordinary
vases, but wine vessels inlaid with gold and silver and covered
with a green-black patina of age. They had a savage splendor of
form that Laura recognized at once; she had been studying bronzes.
She gasped and put her hand to her mouth.

"Chou Dynasty!"

The wine vessels were two thousand years old.

"I cannot accept them," she said later to Madame Wei, with
tears in her eyes.

"Certainly you can," said Madame Wei serenely. She was
rocking gently back and forth in her rocking chair, her fingers
clasping the mother-of-pearl arms, her jeweled nail guards glinting in the sun. "You have given me something I could never find
in Weichang, or even in Szechuan Province. Something invented
in your own country. I have given you something from mine."

"They are too valuable! They are priceless!"

"I will not be argued with," said Madame Wei in the same
calm voice. "No one opposes my will, not my sons nor my
daughters-in-law nor my grandchildren. Nor you. So let us speak
no more about it."

As far as Madame Wei was concerned, the subject was closed.

Laura was about to object again when she caught the glance of
Plum Blossom, Madame Wei's maidservant. Plum Blossom said
nothing as she stood by her mistress's chair, but her eyes counseled silence. Laura smiled to herself and kept silent. Plum
Blossom's advice, she knew, was worth taking. Finally she bade

Madame Wei a quiet farewell and departed, going home to her wondrous vases.

Plum Blossom, as she observed that her unspoken suggestion had been followed by Missy Valentine, felt satisfied. Someday soon, the girl was resolved, she would join the Valentine household as the bride of Chen.

Plum Blossom was the sort of young woman who was apparently suited to be a kitchen helper, not maidservant to the mistress of the house. She had qualities, however, that were evident to the discerning eye, and Madame Wei had noticed them. She was not beautiful, but she was extremely handsome, with erect posture, a fine complexion, and clear black eyes. Her brows were arched, thick for a woman yet perfectly formed. She was intelligent and decisive and she had capable well-shaped hands.

She was like her grandmother, a steel-willed woman who had ruled the household in her village. Plum Blossom remembered her village and everything about it. She could recall the red-earth landscape of west Szechuan, with its shattered mirror of rice fields that reflected every mood of the sky. She could see the old feather fan swinging in the field to scare the birds. She could hear the peddler crying ''pears'' in the autumn, making farmers' children start with fright, for pears meant winter was coming, and winter meant hunger and hardship. She could remember how the oil lamp lit her grandmother's face in the room with the string of dusty red peppers on the wall, and the baskets and hooks for gathering grasses piled helter-skelter in the corner. Especially she could remember the struggle to pay the landlord's rent: half their grain crop every year.

''A farmer like my son,'' Plum Blossom's grandmother had said over and over, ''is a man who stands with his head in someone else's sky and his feet on someone else's land.''

All the tenant farmers of China knew that proverb. But what could anyone do against the landlord? He lent money at interest, he held mortgages, he collected rents. His ''dog's leg,'' the bailiff, collected extras as well: chickens, eggs, pigs. Every animal, every harvest, every grain of wheat, carried a tax for the landlord and his bailiff.

Plum Blossom was no longer living on a tenant farm, but she

remembered. She would marry Chen, she thought, and never worry again about a landlord, but she would not forget. She would pass on her memories to her children.

In Plum Blossom's village there had lived a gentle young man called Peng the Mender of Old Shoes. He'd had a smile like that of Chen, tender and kind, which was why Plum Blossom was drawn to Chen.

Peng had once grown terribly angry at the landlord. Famine had come to the district, and the people were boiling bark to make soup. Yet the landlord and his bailiff were hoarding grain in their storehouses.

"In a time of famine," cried Peng, "the landlord must share grain with the people! It is the traditional way of compassion!"

He had roused the farmers and the villagers. Led by Peng, an angry mob stormed the landlord's courtyard with scythes and pitchforks. They demanded the bailiff, the "dog's leg," and when he appeared, they beat him to the ground.

The landlord grew frightened.

"Come back in two days!" he cried. "Peng, listen to me! Disperse the mob and in two days I will give you grain from my storehouse!"

"Now!" the mob demanded.

"I am too frightened! You are too angry! Go home, go home! Let there be a peaceful distribution of grain!"

Peng believed him and dispersed the mob, smiling with relief. Such a lovely smile, Plum Blossom recalled. He had come to take tea with her grandmother later that night and spoke in his gentle voice about a farmer's justice. He was not a man of violence, yet this was famine. Grain must be given.

But in two days, instead of receiving grain, the people of the village heard the sound of bugles on the nearby slope. Soldiers on horseback galloped down into the village street, soldiers of the provincial governor who had been summoned by the landlord.

They found Peng in the shop where he mended old shoes. They tied his hands in front of him and bound him to a horse and dragged him to the landlord's courtyard. There they forced him to kneel and chopped off his head and tied it to a tree branch by its long black hair, where it twisted in the wind, the gentle smile transformed to a grimace of death.

Plum Blossom would marry Chen, she thought, and tell her children this story.

According to the Jade Calendar it was the waning of the Dragon Moon and the approach of the Lotus Moon. Laura, however, realized something more significant. It was almost the Fourth of July.

"Mike, we must do something," she told him one night. "We can't just ignore the Fourth of July."

"Fireworks?" he suggested sleepily.

"Yes, but that's nothing new. The Chinese invented fireworks." Laura lay back against the pillow. "We should have a party, and serve pink lemonade, and toast marshmallows, and hire a band to play 'The Star Spangled Banner.' "

"Marshmallows?" Mike looked dubious. "Where would we find marshmallows?"

"Well, we'll do without the marshmallows."

"Pink lemonade?"

"You can spike it with whiskey."

"You really have your mind made up. I guess I'll have to go out and look for a band that knows 'The Star Spangled Banner.' "

"And, Mike . . . the Maryknoll Fathers at the mission . . . may I invite them?"

"No." The reply was curt.

"But they're Americans. There are so few of us in Weichang, it seems unfair to leave them out."

"I made a compromise about the mission hospital, Laura. I want you to have good medical care when you have the baby, so you'll go there. But I won't have priests in my house."

"Why do you bear a grudge, Mike? Whatever it is, whatever happened in the past, can't you forgive?"

"No," he said shortly. "I don't believe in forgiving my enemies and doing good for evil. I believe in remembering wrongs."

"Like an elephant. You know how an elephant never forgets an injury? That's you. Nursing a grudge for years and years and never letting it die."

"It's probably in my blood."

"A Celtic elephant."

Mike laughed, and they went to sleep friends. He wouldn't relent, however, about the priests.

The Fourth of July party symbolized to Mike and Laura their first months together in China. Their own courtyard and lotus pond and flowering plum. Their own friends. A Chinese band playing a strange, screeching, out-of-key version of "The Star Spangled Banner" while fireworks exploded into roses of light against the sky. Mrs. Peterson pressing Laura's hand and saying, "Laura, what a good idea, why didn't Tom and I think of it?" Mike strumming a banjo while the Americans sang "Home on the Range" and their voices rose ragged and emotional in a quiet Chinese courtyard.

Madame Wei listened attentively to the song, holding a grandchild on her lap.

Laura asked her later what she had been thinking.

"What is an antelope?" Madame Wei asked politely.

Laura laughed and explained. Then Madame Wei added, "I also asked myself how it would feel to be an exile in a strange land, as you are. I would be longing for my own country."

"Surely it will never happen to you."

"Probably not, for I am sixty-five now, and I will not see change in my lifetime. If I am fortunate."

Sixty-five! Laura was astonished. She had assumed Madame Wei to be in her early fifties.

After a moment she said, "I am happy in China."

Madame Wei looked pensive. "Do not be complacent."

"Am I?"

"Perhaps only young. We have a saying: A pair of golden lilies must be bought with a water barrel of tears." Madame Wei paused. She glanced at Mike, who had a fresh whiskey-and-soda is his hand. "Your husband, too, is young," she added. "And the Yangtze River is very old. It has drowned many hopes over the centuries. And it does not like foreigners. Take heed, dear Laura."

Mike had been speaking to George about that very subject, the Yangtze River and their troubles with the steamer. Repairs were expensive, and the cargoes he and George hauled were not bringing in enough profit. The whiskeys were relaxing Mike and calming his worries. He was grateful for the effect, but he promised himself again he would not drink too much.

Finally he and George dropped their conversation and Mike picked up the banjo again and began to sing Irish songs in a husky light baritone, accompanying himself with strumming chords. He sang about taking Kathleen home again; he sang about crossing an ocean deep and wide.

Home, thought Laura, listening dreamily. Across the ocean. No, this was home now. Her child would be born here.

CHAPTER 6

Mike desperately needed a drink. He sat on a hard wooden bench in the corridor of the Maryknoll Fathers' hospital. It was called a hospital, but it was really just a big shabby house converted by the missionaries into a medical facility. It was the only hospital in Weichang. Laura was in the room at the end of the corridor, and he could hear her moaning. Beads of sweat broke out on his forehead as he listened. Just as Madame Wei had predicted, it was the White Moon—December—and the baby was arriving. *Let it be soon. Let this be over*.

He reached into his jacket pocket and felt the hard glass of a whiskey pint. The bottle was empty. Christ. He couldn't stand to see or hear Laura suffering in any way; it terrified him. The whiskey helped to blur the edges of the terror, but he didn't dare leave to buy another.

He avoided looking at the priests who passed in the corridor. Laura was being attended by a young Chinese, Dr. Tao, who had been educated in London. Laura seemed to like him. In the previous month he'd given Mike a rather pedantic lecture on childbirth.

"We define natural labor as one where the child presents by the head and the labor is terminated within twenty-four hours."

Mike had nodded impatiently.

Dr. Tao had continued earnestly. "The element of time has this importance: It is found that the mortality both to mother and child becomes greater the longer the duration of the labor."

Mortality. Laura couldn't die, oh, no, oh, no. Not possible. Ever.

The young Chinese doctor finally came to the point: he suspected breech presentation, the infant appearing feet first. He could then attempt a forceps delivery or resort to a cesarean section: an operation to remove the infant.

It all meant danger to Laura, and that was what terrified Mike. He couldn't do without her. He loved her and depended on her. He put his head into his hands.

A touch fell on his shoulder.

"Mike, what is happening?" said a low voice.

Mike raised his head. George Henderson had arrived. "Oh, Christ, George, I don't know. It's going on too long." He gazed up at George imploringly. "Did you bring anything with you?"

George removed a pint of whiskey from his pocket and handed it to Mike. Sighing with gratitude, Mike uncapped it and took a long swallow. He offered it to George, who shook his head. George took a seat on the bench.

"Madame Wei said to tell you she's burning incense at a shrine."

Madame Wei disapproved of the hospital. She considered it a place where people died and thus unlucky, but she hoped her prayers to the goddess of childbirth would counteract the ill fortune. Outwardly she scoffed at superstition, being an educated woman who could read and speak English, but the old beliefs were strong in her, and she knew in the depths of her mind that the ancient gods still wielded power. Burning joss sticks could do no harm.

George himself had just spent half an hour on his knees in the Peterson house, with the Reverend and Mrs. Peterson, praying to his own God. "O Lord, help us to know Thy will, and to accept it. Aid Thy servant, Laura." George's faith was simple and firm. He had been raised a Methodist.

Mike Valentine was the only unbeliever. Without Laura he was a dead man, he thought despairingly. He would smash himself up within months.

The steamer venture was still faltering. They needed new parts more badly than ever, but money was still short. River bandits were demanding extra squeeze, and they would have to be paid. It was a necessary expense. Although Mike's inclination was to fight the bandits, he understood it was not sensible. For once he listened to George. *Pay the protection.* Tribute was an ancient tradition in the Chinese interior. When the money was paid, the bandits honored the agreement.

But with a baby coming, Mike could not take financial risks. He and George would have to keep the steamer going any way they could. His dream of wealth had receded; now it was a question of survival.

He groaned to himself. George, knowing nothing else to do, advised him to take another drink.

Time wore on. Mike's terror dwindled with the second pint of whiskey. He could no longer hear Laura moaning at the end of the hall.

The baby had presented feet first. Since it could not be removed with forceps, Dr. Tao was performing a cesarean. Mike had consented.

"Anything. Just don't let her die!"

"Easy, man," muttered George. "Pull yourself together. Where's your courage? I saw you take that steamer over Yellow Cat Gorge with iron nerves."

"That was different."

Physical courage, thought George. *Yes, it was different.* If it came to a bar fight, a struggle with the river, a bare-fisted combat against heavy odds, Mike would never hesitate. He had plenty of guts for that. Life, though, presented sterner and more complicated challenges. Mike would have to face them someday without his glass crutch.

Or would he? He had Laura. She was safe. Out of danger. Recovering.

"Her vital signs are excellent," said Dr. Tao, smiling with relief, his face beaming above his bloodstained gown. "You have a daughter, Mr. Valentine. She, too, is well."

"Oh. A daughter."

It didn't matter to Mike one way or the other. As long as Laura was safe. He felt like crying. And he did.

* * *

"Mike?" whispered Laura, tired and radiant in her hospital bed. "We'll name her Eileen, after your grandmother. Just as we planned."

"Whatever you say." Mike's voice was hoarse.

"Maybe next time we'll have a boy," Laura said sleepily, still struggling out of the ether.

"There doesn't have to be a next time, Laura. Not if we're careful. Once was enough for me." He had never meant anything more sincerely.

"Oh, no. Eileen needs a brother or a sister."

Mike sighed. He was already forgotten.

Laura reached out and touched his hand, sensing his feelings. "You will always be first, Mike. It wouldn't matter if we had ten children. I pledged myself to you, and no one else."

Comfort washed over him. She was still his. He bowed his head, feeling her touch on the back of his hand like the benediction of the sun, the mother's love he had always craved, the father's strength he had been denied, his wife, his love, his Laura. If there were any gods, Mike thanked them.

The baby was small, red, and disagreeable. She squalled and complained when she was awake, and then she slept. Mike wondered why people became parents; it was an unrewarding experience at best.

Then Eileen opened her big blue eyes and gurgled. She bestowed toothless grins upon her parents. She recognized Mike when he approached and raised her arms to be lifted from her cradle. Her hair grew out golden and silky and her face became plump; a dimple appeared in one cheek.

"In fact she's adorable," Laura declared, holding Eileen in her arms. "Admit it!"

Mike was happy to admit it.

Although she was delighted with the baby, Laura was worried about her own physical inadequacy. She wanted to be a wife to Mike; she could not keep denying him the comfort of her body.

"Dr. Tao, when may I resume my marital duties?" she had inquired anxiously in his clinic.

"Mrs. Valentine, we must be patient. You have not experienced ordinary childbirth, but a major operation. You must allow yourself a full recovery.''

She thought he was being too cautious. Mike had not reproached her, but she sensed his restlessness.

''There are times,'' Madame Wei remarked, ''when our ancient custom of concubines has merit. Just before and just after childbirth, for example. One may select an obedient and dutiful young woman to comfort one's husband at such a time. One need not worry about a scheming usurper or a loose-living wanton. The matter is supervised by you yourself, the Number One Wife. And of course it is good to have help with the housework.''

Laura did not approve of concubines, and besides, they couldn't afford one. There was no money for an extra person in the household; it was a struggle to maintain the amah for Eileen. Laura had not wanted a baby nurse but ''face'' demanded it. Chen had provided her. George Henderson was taking less than his fair share of the steamer profits, which was distressing, but George insisted. He claimed that as a bachelor he was entitled to less. Anyway he was only the engineer; Mike was the pilot.

One night Laura donned a fresh silk nightgown after a jasmine-scented bath. She moved close to Mike when they were in bed and ran a hand over his bare chest.

He frowned. ''Did you get permission from the doctor?''

''Yes,'' she lied. ''He said I'm fully recovered.''

''Well . . . in that case . . .'' He pulled her close. ''Oh, Laura, I've missed you so,'' he muttered against her cheek.

''Me too,'' she whispered, arching her body against his, and knew it was the truth.

When Eileen was sixteen months old, Laura became pregnant again. Dr. Tao warned her that this baby must be the last.

''Two cesareans are allowable, but three is too dangerous.''

''Many women have three!''

''Each case is different.'' He looked slightly offended. ''Of course you need not accept my advice.''

''I will accept it, Dr. Tao,'' she promised. ''I trust your judgment. After this baby, we will take precautions.''

Their son Michael was born in November 1898, at the waning of the Chrysanthemum Moon. He was a quiet baby, as reserved as Eileen was extroverted, with a sweet smile and Laura's hazel eyes. The Moon Years began to wheel.

The Moon of the Hungry Ghosts. The Harvest Moon. The Chrysanthemum Moon.

In 1900 they were frightened by the Boxer Uprising. It was in far-off Peking, hundreds of miles north of the Yangtze valley, but the shock waves rippled as far south as Canton and as far west as Szechuan. An angry mob, incensed at foreigners, pounded on the Valentine gate in Weichang and stormed the house of Reverend and Mrs. Peterson. All of them were sheltered by Madame Wei and her family, kept safe in the lovely pavilions for two days and three nights of terror. Only Eileen was unaffected, bubbling with her customary mischief as she raced around the courtyards.

"She will be a handful, Laura," observed Dorothy Peterson.

"Yes, I know." Laura sighed. "I won't worry about it yet."

Dr. Tao bravely protected the clinic of the Maryknoll Fathers during the Boxer terror, reasoning with the mob on the doorstep until they dispersed and went home.

The Holiday Moon. The Budding Moon. The Sleeping Moon.

Mike and George Henderson battled against the river, scrambling for cargo and fighting the gorges and rapids, keeping the steamer afloat. The months slipped by.

The Peony Moon. The Dragon Moon. The Lotus Moon.

Chen came to Laura and shyly asked permission to marry.

"Is it Plum Blossom?"

"Yes, missy! How did you know?"

Laura suppressed a smile at his astonishment. "I am very wise."

There was a traditional Chinese wedding, with the bride in red, and then Plum Blossom and Chen settled into happy domesticity in the Valentine house. Only one shadow fell on their contentment: They were not blessed with children. Plum Blossom patiently burned joss sticks at the shrine of the goddess of childbirth.

The Kindly Moon. The White Moon. The Bitter Moon.

It was 1903, and Mike was thirty years old. He was happy with his wife and family—Eileen adored him, he was wonderful with the children—but other things disturbed him. The ambitious dream was receding; China was too vast and too stubborn to be conquered.

"We're not getting anywhere, Laura. We need more than one steamer. It's the only way. Otherwise George and I are just going around in circles. When I'm an old man, we'll still be stuck here in Weichang, the back of beyond."

"I'm happy here," Laura said wistfully. "I like Weichang. I have all I want. You and the children. My courtyard and my flowering plum and my temple."

"They're not enough," said Mike. "One disaster on the river could wipe us out. We've been lucky so far, but we need another vessel. I'll talk to George about finding a third partner, maybe in Shanghai. That might be the answer."

He and George began to look into it.

The Dragon Moon wheeled around once more with its choking heat. Rain began and did not stop, hot, steaming rain that fell day after day. The river was rising; Mike and George could not operate the steamer. Weichang's water supply was being swollen by streams and torrents from the village above them on the gorge. Laura worried that the weather was unhealthy. Everyone had upset stomachs. The children were suffering from diarrhea, and little Michael looked pale. One night he threw up his supper.

"If it would just stop raining," Laura muttered in the nursery, wiping Michael's head with a damp towel. "There's something I don't like about this rain. So humid, so unnatural."

She caught the glance of the amah, who was sitting by Eileen's bed. The Chinese woman looked frightened. She averted her face.

"What is it?" Laura demanded immediately. "Why are you looking away?"

"Nothing, missy. It is nothing."

"Tell me! If there's something you know, please tell me at once!"

"Only a rumor, missy. It may not be true."

"What rumor!"

"The village above us," the Chinese woman whispered after a moment. "They say there is illness. It washes down with the water."

"What illness!"

"I cannot say the name."

"You can say it! Tell me!"

The woman hung her head. "Cholera," she muttered very low.

Laura stared down in fear at Michael's little face. He opened his eyes and smiled at her. She caught her breath.

"What are the signs of a cholera epidemic?" she asked of Mrs. Peterson.

"It's hard to say, dear. . . ."

"The sickness starts with vomiting and diarrhea, doesn't it?" Mrs. Peterson nodded unhappily.

"How did it begin the last time in Weichang?"

After a moment Mrs. Peterson whispered, "Like this, Laura. It rained and rained. . . ."

"Dr. Tao—tell me what causes cholera?"

"It is a microorganism, sometimes infecting the water supply, sometimes traveling in the sewer system. What causes it to flare and erupt with sudden vicious energy, we do not know. Perhaps a factor in its reproductive cycle. They are investigating the organism in the Pasteur Institute in France, but so far they have found no answer."

"Has cholera come to Weichang?"

He bit his lip. "Possibly." The look on his face was like that of the amah. Like that of Mrs. Peterson.

"Michael has been vomiting!"

"It may be just a childish upset," Dr. Tao said in a gentle voice.

"He's only five years old!"

Dr. Tao paused. "Just as a precaution," he said in the same gentle tone, "move your daughter to another room. I will give you a prescription for calcium tablets, to clear Michael's digestion. Then we will see."

"Oh, God!" Laura put her knuckles to her mouth.

She ran out to the courtyard and stood in the hot hissing rain. The drops pimpled the surface of the lotus pond like tiny blisters. The great stone walls of Weichang were not even visible in the rain, but Laura sensed them looming around her like ancient evil. Old, old stones, soaked with blood and war and illness. Smelling of death.

I'm happy here, she'd said to Mike. *I like Weichang.*

The demons of China must have heard her and chuckled with cruel amusement at the presumption of the foreigner. *We have many ways to teach you humbleness, foreign devil. You will learn to fear us. You will learn.*

CHAPTER 7

From all the alleys of the walled city of Weichang came the wail: "Save life! Save life!" In anguish the mothers of stricken children raised their arms to the sky and begged heaven for mercy. Each alley resounded with the coughs and gasps of the dying. The stench of death mingled with the smell of burning incense. All night long the hammers of the coffin-makers pounded nails. In the morning death-carts rattled over the cobblestones. Dr. Tao and the Maryknoll Fathers went sleepless. Weichang was a city in agony, groaning with pain, battling death, losing too often.

Laura turned in terror to her husband. "Mike, our son is dying!" she cried wildly. "We're losing him! What will we do?"

"He won't die," Mike replied, as terrified as Laura, perhaps more so, but unable to show it. They sat in their dining room, across the table from one another. Mike had a whiskey bottle and a glass in front of him, the only escape he could depend on in these hideous days. He was trembling within.

"Mike, talk to me! Don't leave me alone! Our son is dying of cholera! I can see him growing weaker every hour!"

Mike had nothing to say to her. He could find no words; they were clogged in his throat. Laura's pain was intolerable, worse than his own. She was his strength, but suppose that strength failed? Michael would die, and then what would they do? There was no bottom to this panic. He shoved the glass of whiskey at Laura. "Take a drink, Laura. It will help."

She swallowed some whiskey, coughed and choked, then pushed the glass away. "It doesn't help; how can you say it does?"

It does. Oh, Jesus, it is the only thing that does. It gets you through the days and the nights. It erases the memory of little Michael and Laura's anguished face. It stops the trembling.

Mike had risen to his feet. "Don't go away, Mike!" Laura cried. "Talk to me!"

"I can't sit here any longer," he said hoarsely. "I'll be back." He picked up the bottle and the glass and left the room, as Laura's head sank to her arms on the table and Mike heard her begin to weep. He had to get away from that sound. It was tearing him apart.

"Save life! Save life!" cried the mothers of Weichang.

"Mike, come back," Laura whispered brokenly into her arms. "Help me to face this. Don't let me do it alone."

She sat by her son's bedside in the days that followed, spending hours that she never remembered later, never wanted to remember. The child grew weaker, could not eat. His eyes grew sunken; his skin turned gray. After a while he did not recognize Laura or his amah but only tossed weakly in fever.

Laura was alone as she endured these hours. The doctor could not help her. Mike could not bear to watch what was happening. She was an exile in a strange land, longing for her own country.

Longing to take her children and go home.

One of those children would never go home. Five-year-old Michael's physical resources were exhausted by the cholera and he succumbed, ending all the fear and hope.

As she stood beside the grave of her son, Mike was next to her. Laura was numb. She no longer spoke to Mike; she knew he was drunk anyway. She could not understand the pain that wrenched her chest or the tears that poured silently from her eyes. It was not possible to endure such agony of the spirit without dying oneself. It must be better to die. To rest, to be at peace. To sleep in a quiet coffin. Like darling Michael. *I will join you, sweetheart. We'll rest together.*

No, there was Eileen. She must look after Eileen.

Such a tiny coffin. Such a little boy. Is he frightened, does he need me? God, let me die, stop these tears.

How strong was her yearning for death. As strong as the hatred of suffering. Suffering and death walked together, hand in hand. Death was sweet, suffering was bitter. Simple.

Laura thought only of that simple idea as they led her back to the house after the funeral.

Days passed that were still haunted by terror. Eileen came down with cholera. Once again there was the dreaded routine in the Valentine house: the vomiting, the cool cloths, the coaxing to swallow soup, medicine, the coughing of a desperately sick child, the agonized prayers, and the fear. Eileen, however, had a sturdier constitution than five-year-old Michael had possessed. She reached her turning point and survived.

"Eileen is out of danger," said Dr. Tao wearily at last to an exhausted Laura. "She will be weak. You must be very careful of her diet; her stomach is tender. Only rice broth until I change the instructions."

"I will see to it," Laura said in a low fierce tone that trembled slightly.

"Laura, you must look after yourself. It is not only children who die of cholera."

"I am aware of that, Dr. Tao."

Yes, Laura was aware that the elderly succumbed as well as the young, for her friend Madame Wei was dying. It was again time to say good-bye to someone she loved. Laura went to the Wei house and knelt by the dying woman's bedside, gazing into the ravaged but still beautiful Chinese face as the terrible silent tears poured again from her own eyes.

"Madame Wei," she whispered, "I am here."

Madame Wei was tiny and frail against her pillow. "My dear friend," she gasped, "our country has been cruel to you. Forgive us."

"You have been kind and good." Laura clutched the slender hand that lay across the sheet. "Don't leave me, Madame Wei. Don't die."

"But it is time. I am old and sick and weary. Would you have me stay?"

"No," Laura said hoarsely, tasting the salt of tears in her mouth. "I would like to come with you."

"Nonsense," said Madame Wei, with a flash of her old spirit. "Heaven is not ready for you yet. You know I am never wrong."

"I know that." Laura tried to smile through the tears that were raining across her cheeks. "I have always known that." She bowed her head. "I will never forget you, Madame Wei."

Madame Wei feebly stroked Laura's hair. "You have been almost like a daughter to me," she murmured. "My foreign daughter."

At that Laura burst into sobs. She had not sobbed since Michael's funeral. Not even during Eileen's illness. She laid her head across the sheet, her body wracked with weeping. "Oh, Madame Wei!" she cried in the voice of a heartbroken child. "I want to go home!"

"I know you do," Madame Wei said softly. "I know you do. My dear foreign daughter. But you cannot. You have buried your son in China. You must stay here."

Two of Madame Wei's grandsons led Laura out at last. She was blinded with tears.

"Where did my brother go, Uncle George?" asked seven-year-old Eileen. Four months had passed. They were in the nursery.

"You know where he went, sweetheart."

"To heaven, to live with the angels."

"That's right."

"But if Michael's happy with the angels, why does Mama look so sad?"

"She misses him."

"Why doesn't she talk to Daddy anymore?"

"She does, Eileen. At night when you're sleeping."

Eileen looked dubious, but she said nothing. George sighed and rose to his feet. He had been sitting in one of Eileen's little chairs. Laura was doing something or other in the kitchen with the cook. She was always busy these days: she had a thousand trivial chores to accomplish, none of them with her old love of life. She was a rigid and unsmiling ghost. Did she talk to Mike at night in their bedroom? George did not know. She hardly spoke to anyone during the day. Briefly to Chen and the cook. Eileen, with a visible effort. And that was all.

He had to find Mike. He had to talk some sense into the man, for Laura's sake. Mike was the only one who could help her.

It was Mike Valentine's fault, thought George, that Laura had not recovered from her grief. They should have comforted one another, sharing their strengths, helping one another through their bereavement. George's own parents had done that, upon losing a child. Mike would not offer strength. Instead he was retreating into a bottle, taking his old escape route.

"You damned fool," George said through his teeth. Mike was sprawled in a chair in the courtyard with a half-empty bottle of whiskey on the table before him. "You'll lose your wife if you're not careful. She needs you, damn it! She needs you to sober up!"

"I lost a son too, remember? Where's your sympathy for me? I'm entitled to a drink now and then."

"Stop making excuses, Mike. Nobody believes them. You're deserting Laura when she needs you most."

"Where'd you read that pretty phrase? Some pulp novel?"

"If you don't like the way I express myself, I'm sorry! I'm just a lousy engineer, not a poet! But I can see what's happening, and I'm telling you to wise up!"

"Oh, George," Mike said with a sigh, "I believe Laura should have married you." He was extremely drunk and spoiling for a fight. George recognized the signs. "You're such a nice, steady fellow; you'd make a perfect husband."

"Maybe I would," George said tautly. "And maybe she should have."

"Aha. The truth appears at last from out of hiding."

"But she happens to be in love with you. More's the pity."

"I guess," Mike said musingly, pouring himself another drink, "the time has come for me to knock your block off."

"The same old drunken hooligan from a one-horse lumber town," George said.

"That's right. And a bastard to boot."

"For the way you're treating Laura, I agree."

"No, George, you don't understand." Mike smiled sunnily up at George. "I mean a real bastard. With a whore for a mother and a liar for a father." He paused. "So how about it? Shall we fight? Shall I start knocking your block off?"

"I don't want to fight with you or talk to you," George said in disgust. "You're too drunk. God help you, because I don't know who else will."

He left the courtyard. Alone, Mike put his head in his hands and cried weak tears.

"Nobody will," he whispered aloud. "Nobody will help."

He could not reach Laura. She had gone away; she had withdrawn to a place somewhere within herself where Mike could not find her. He considered the thought that she did not love him any longer. Could it be true? The idea cast him into a state of panic. Grievous to lose your son. But he could have struggled through it with Laura. Without her—Mike stretched out his hand for the bottle, his remaining solace.

"Damn her!" he growled, whipping his anger to calm his panic. "Damn her! She ran out on me!"

"Mike? Did you quarrel with George? He left looking so stormy."

It was Laura's voice, cool and aloof as always these days. She had entered the courtyard. He hated that cool aloofness. It turned her into a stranger.

"To hell with George," he muttered.

"Why are you drinking so early?" Laura picked up the whiskey bottle from the table. "You said you wouldn't." Laura's cool exterior was a pose. She, too, was panic-stricken. She didn't know this Mike Valentine, didn't know how to reach him.

"Put that bottle down," said Mike.

She frowned and held it against her chest, covering up her fear. "I'm going to take this away from you. You've had enough."

"I said put it down."

"Please, Mike. I insist."

"And I'm going to give you until I count to three to put it down."

"Is that a threat?"

"One."

"What do you think you're doing?"

His eyes were glaring with hostility. Laura had never seen him look that way before. "Mike, stop staring like that."

"Two." Mike rose to his feet and clenched his fist. He raised it in front of his face. "I'm about to count to three, Laura."

The action and the words goaded Laura, turning her fear to anger. In a single sweeping motion she hurled the bottle to the ground where it shattered on the flagstones. "Hit me, then! Hit me with your fist! Like a drunken animal!"

"I—"

"Go on, Mike! Prove what my sister said was true!"

"Your sister?" He faltered.

"Yes, my sister Julia! And everyone else! They said you would make me miserable, and maybe they were right!"

"I—I wouldn't have hit you, Laura."

"Look at your fist!"

He stared at his clenched fist and slowly, with an effort, opened his fingers. "I'm sorry," he muttered. "I'm a little drunk."

"A little! You haven't been sober for weeks!"

"I know, sweetheart, and I'm sorry. I'll quit. Right now. No more whiskey, I promise."

"It's too late, Mike." Laura passed a weary hand over her eyes. The angry note left her voice. "I want to go home." That was all she wanted. She had given up. On China, on Mike, on everything. It was all too much, and she was so exhausted.

"To visit your family, I understand. It's been a rotten time for both of us, and you need some space to recover. When you come back—"

"I won't come back." Laura sounded very tired. "I can't live here any longer, Mike. This country has too many evil memories. And I can't bear to watch you drinking yourself into a stupor whenever you're in the house. I'm taking Eileen and going home."

There they were. Spoken aloud by Laura. The words Mike had been dreading for weeks. In desperation he tried to stave them off. "I told you I'll quit," he said, feeling his heart pound against his ribs. "I know I said that before, but this time I mean it."

"A drunken promise isn't worth anything."

"I'm sober now."

He was. If only Laura would recognize it. No, she wouldn't relent. She was determined to leave him, that was suddenly, horribly clear, and he couldn't change her mind. No smile, no charm, no jokes, would shake her resolve. It was all over. He had cut his own throat, and now he was bleeding to death. He tried to grin jauntily. "Can I stay here tonight, or am I banished?"

"I'll have Chen make up a room for you across the courtyard," Laura said quietly.

"Don't bother," he said. "I'll find a room in town."

Maybe now she'll change her mind.

"All right, Mike. If you prefer."

No use no use no use. All over.

"Well, look, before I go," he said, reaching into his pocket, attempting to be casual, "I'd better leave you some money."

"Keep it, Mike. You'll probably need it. I have some household money."

Let me have my pride, goddamn it!

No, nothing, nothing, nothing. Finished. No pride no love no Laura. She didn't care. He smiled to cover up the void in his chest. "I'll find out from George how you're doing. Maybe you can write from Connecticut once in a while."

"Oh, Mike, of course I will."

"I'll—I'll just say good-bye to Eileen before I go."

Tears flooded into Laura's eyes, and she turned her face away. She knew how much Mike loved Eileen, how close they were. Mike stared at her averted cheek, aching to bridge the space between them. Yearning to embrace her. Kiss her mouth. He didn't dare; he couldn't risk being repelled or he would shatter.

He could smell the aroma of the spilled whiskey following him like some evil perfume as he left the courtyard, and he held himself together through sheer will.

CHAPTER 8

Laura wandered through the empty spaces of her house. She had loved it so. Now it was a memory of pain, every room a reminder of Michael. He would always be five years old. Until she, Laura, went to her own grave. Maybe they would be reunited then, in some vague fairy-tale heaven, but she didn't really believe it. She had lost her little boy.

She caressed the bronze knocker on the gate, saying good-bye. She bade farewell to the temple in its quiet serenity.

It was harder saying good-bye to Chen. He wept.

"Missy, I would like you to stay!"

"I must go home, Chen."

"This is your home now!"

"I will write you letters, Chen. In English, but Mr. Fu will read them to you. I'll tell you all about America."

He turned away, unconsoled.

It was hardest of all explaining to Eileen why her daddy had gone away.

"I don't want you," she objected. "I want Daddy."

Laura tried to distract her with tales of the wonders of America.

"We'll stay in a big beautiful house in Connecticut with your aunt Julia and your uncle Charles."

"I don't know Aunt Julia."

"You will, dear."

"Does Aunt Julia have children for me to play with?"

"Well . . . no . . . but she'll love you all the more."

"I want amah to come."

"She can't come, Eileen."

"Uncle George?" she quavered.

"Eileen, darling, Uncle George must stay here."

Eileen started to cry. Her world was collapsing. Laura desperately promised her a roomful of toys. Julia, wealthy and childless and unhappy about the fact of her childlessness, was eager to welcome Eileen. She wrote that she was already making trips to Fifth Avenue to buy little girl's frocks. Laura was sure she was paying horrifying prices, but Julia could afford it.

They would take a junk to Hankow and the train to Shanghai. Then a ship to San Francisco. America. Home.

Laura closed her eyes, feeling tears well beneath her eyelids. She was always crying these days. She couldn't seem to stop. She had thought when she made the decision to go home that the tears would cease. They had not, however. She was more desolate than ever.

How will it be, she asked herself, *when you are separated from Mike by an ocean and thousands of miles?*

She had to stop thinking of Mike. Her marriage had failed, and she must accept that failure and begin again. The laughing, exuberant young man she had met in a muddy road in Oregon was no more. She didn't want to remember the stricken look on Mike's face in the courtyard when she'd seen him last, the hollow misery in his eyes, the way his hands had been shaking.

"You have made a wise decision," Julia had written. "Thank God you're coming home, Laura. Father can't wait to see you. Charles has a wonderful friend I want you to meet, but first we'll arrange for a divorce. You're still young, and you can put this mistake behind you."

A divorce!

Yes, naturally. Wasn't that what she wanted? A divorce? A fresh start? If only things could be as they once were between her and Mike! The tears were spilling over her cheeks.

Laura had done everything, said all her good-byes, made all her explanations, completed her packing. Amah would leave in the morning. Chen would remain, waiting for instructions from George and Mike. Perhaps they'd still need him.

Laura was in the parlor. She wandered to the window that looked out on the flagstone terrace. Rain was falling, not the steamy rain that had preceded the cholera but cool, silvery drops blown by the wind. She could smell moisture through the window. Fresh, damp, breeze-laden—stirring up yearnings and longings that she did not want to feel. She covered her face with her hands. Lines of poetry drifted in her head.

> Western wind, when wilt thou blow,
> The small rain down can rain?
> Christ, if my love were in my arms,
> And I in my bed again!

"Laura," said a low voice behind her.

She turned. Mike was leaning against the doorway. He was very thin. She saw that he was freshly shaved and was wearing a clean white shirt. Although his eyes were red-veined, he was sober. He had taken pains—she knew it immediately—to be sober and presentable before he came. An ache spread through her chest as she stared at him.

"I didn't expect you."

"I came to say good-bye," he said.

"Eileen is sleeping."

"Don't wake her. I just want to say good-bye to you."

She turned back to the window. "I . . . don't think I want to."

"Do you hate me that much?"

"I don't hate you. But we've said good-bye. I'll write you a letter when I get to Shanghai."

"You're good at writing letters."

She didn't answer.

"Would you like me to give back the letters you wrote from Connecticut? I have them in my room. I took them with me when I left."

"No, I don't want them."

"Well. Okay. Don't trouble to write, though, until you have my new address."

She turned back to face him. She couldn't read his expression. "Aren't you staying here?"

"No. I'll be leaving Weichang. So will George. He's going to Shanghai. He's got a job in a shipyard."

"What about the steamer?"

"I smashed it up, Laura. Tore a hole in the hull on a rock. It can't be repaired."

"Oh, Mike!"

"Sorry, but that's how it is. It was just a matter of time anyway."

"Where will you go? What will you do?"

"I haven't decided. Find a job, I guess. George is lucky; he's an engineer. I don't know what work there is for a washed-up riverboat pilot who drinks too much. Here or at home, it doesn't make much difference. Hell, Laura, I'm not twenty years old anymore."

"Mike, don't talk that way about yourself!"

"Why not, it's true." He grinned crookedly. "Without you I'm not much use."

"That isn't so!"

"Yes, it is." He gave her a puzzled glance. "Don't you know that? You've always kept me straight. You were my anchor. My safe harbor, my port, my rock in the ocean, my candle burning in the window on a stormy night. All those things."

"Stop, please!" She was close to tears.

"If you don't understand the way things are with me, and the way they always have been, I don't know how to explain. Maybe you'll realize it someday. When you're back home, and have a little distance." He gave her a sad, rueful smile and raised his hand. "Well, so long. Kiss Eileen for me, and tell her her daddy loves her." He turned to go.

"Mike!"

He paused.

"Don't go! Don't go!" The cry was wrenched from her throat. Hope lit up Mike's face.

"I want you to stay," she choked out, past the tightness in her throat. "Just for a while. A little while."

The hope faded. "Sure," he said after a moment. He shrugged. "I have nothing better to do."

"Would you"—she forced out the words—"like a drink?"

"No, I've quit."

"Were you drunk when you smashed up the boat?"

"Yes," he said quietly.

"Oh, Mike! I'm so sorry!"

They stared at each other across the vast distance of the room. Laura could hear herself breathing. She twisted her hands together.

"Would you come over here and tell me that?" Mike said very low. He paused. "I can't go to you, because if you pushed me away, I think it would kill me. But I want you so much, I feel like dying anyway."

"Don't die, Mike. Please don't die."

She was crossing the room, taking one slow step after another, until she reached him in the doorway. Then she was clasped in his arms. She was weeping. Mike was crying too. They were kissing with heartbroken passion, tasting salt, filled with love and regret and desire. They were uttering broken words that made no sense. They were fumbling with their clothes, but there was no time. He took her on the floor, both of them almost fully dressed, straining for a unity of the flesh that would be deep and searching, compounded of lust and sorrow, joy and regret. They found it in the depths of Laura's body.

Finally Mike raised himself up. He made a wry face. "Well, I never did that before."

"What?" She laughed. The tension was dissolved.

"Took you with your clothes on."

"No, you never did."

He began to do up his buttons. "Let's go into the bedroom." He stood up and held out his hand. She took it and rose to her feet. He led her to the bedroom. This time he undressed her carefully and then shed his clothes. They began again. Now there was no urgency, no need for haste. He understood exactly what pleased her, his sexual instincts were almost perfect, and he had observed Laura closely over the years. She lay panting across the bed, her lips parted, her eyes heavy-lidded, her nipples hard and taut between his fingers. He was throbbing within her, but he did not move. He was watching her, narrow-eyed, intent. When he moved, it was with deliberate calculation. He heard her gasp, felt her shudder, felt her hips and breasts straining against him.

"Laura, listen," he said between his teeth.

"Yes . . ."

"Don't leave me."

"No, Mike."

"Ever."

"No . . . no . . ."

"Ever again."

"No . . ."

"I can't stand it if you leave me."

She gave a long shuddering moan. "Oh, my God! What are you doing!"

"Loving you."

"Dear God . . ."

"Easy, baby. Easy. Lie still. Let me love you."

"Mike, I'll never leave you. I promise. . . ."

CHAPTER 9

"Mike, let's go home together," Laura said the next day. "Home to America. The steamship venture is wrecked, and so there's nothing for us here. Only war and disease and terror."

"I thought you loved China."

"I did, but no longer. Not since the cholera. And not since—" *You began to drink.* The words did not need to be spoken.

Mike did not want to go home. China still gripped his imagination, and it did so more strongly than ever. In spite of everything. He could sense that the Manchu Dynasty was crumbling, and with the death of the Dowager Empress, which was surely not far off, there would be new opportunity in this bewildering, fascinating country. His manhood was challenged, for he had failed in the steamship attempt, but he could redeem that failure if he persisted in China. Somehow. He knew it. No, he did not want to leave. Their Chinese life could begin again in Shanghai, he thought with ineradicable hope.

He attempted to persuade Laura. He had the chance of a job selling cigarettes, he told her, for an American tobacco company. He would be traveling in the interior if he got the job, but the family could live in Shanghai, using the city as a home base.

"The family will be increased before too long," Laura told him quietly.

Mike gave her a startled glance.

Yes, she was pregnant.

"Oh, Christ. When did that happen?"

"It doesn't matter, Mike. It is a fact."

Mike talked of abortion, with Dr. Tao's consent, but Laura would not consider it. She wanted the baby.

"At home. Not in China," she said to Mike.

They argued briefly about the baby, but Laura was adamant. She wanted the child. Still Mike clung to his dream of China.

"Please, Laura," he said. "There are good hospitals in Shanghai. We can give it one last try."

Laura was oddly torn. She did want to go home, yet another part of her did not want to leave China. There was too much here. Much too much. Unlike Mike, she saw not the future but the past; she envisioned centuries of beautiful objects covered with the grime of the years, waiting to be unearthed, discovered, cherished; she could close her eyes and imagine exotic loveliness beckoning to her; and somehow she did not want to sail for home and leave it behind.

Why not give their marriage another chance, she thought, in a different city, instead of running home to her father? Mike was right. They could try their luck in Shanghai.

Seven-year-old Eileen snuggled in Mike's lap in the parlor. They were always happy in each other's company.

"Will I like Shanghai?" she inquired.

"Sure. Uncle George found us a nice place to live."

"I'm glad we're not going to Aunt Julia's."

"Believe me, so am I," Mike said feelingly.

"Probably I would throw up on the ship," she said with a frown.

"You'd better not throw up on the junk to Hankow."

"Oh, no. Demons would get me, because it's a Chinese boat."

"Who told you that? Amah?"

Eileen nodded.

"She's absolutely right," Mike declared.

"Daddy, why don't you smell nice the way you used to?"

"How do I smell now?"

"You don't smell anything. Before it was kind of . . . spicy. When you kissed me."

"Oh." Mike cocked an eyebrow. "You'll have to find yourself a whiskey-drinking man, Eileen. If that's what you like."

"No, I guess I'll stay with you for a while," she replied.

George had found the Valentines a place to live in the Chinese quarter of Shanghai at a rent that suited their circumstances.

Chen and Plum Blossom were going with them. Plum Blossom would look after Eileen.

Laura had looked helplessly at Mike when she told him. "It's absurd to have an amah and a houseboy when we're so poor. But Chen thinks we'll make our fortune in Shanghai, so he wants to come along."

"Who knows, maybe he's right." Mike had regained his good looks since he had stopped drinking. His confidence was back; his hands were steady. He felt he could lick the world again. He knew he would get the tobacco job. He would take it temporarily until another chance came along. George was earning good money at a Shanghai shipyard. They'd both bide their time and then look for another venture.

Once more Laura was approaching a day of farewell. This time it was truly farewell to Weichang, to the ancient walls, the gorges and cliffs, the flowering plum in the courtyard, the temple and rock garden, the grave of Michael and the grave of Madame Wei.

She paid a final visit to the clinic of Dr. Tao. He had given her the name of an English doctor in Shanghai, a man Dr. Tao had met in London and trusted.

"We will see one another," he said. "I come to Shanghai now and again."

"I'll write to you," she promised.

"Oh, I will have news of you anyway," he said with a smile in his eyes. "I have told Dr. Fortescue all about you."

She said farewell to Mr. Fu, her teacher, very old now and fragile, his bones shining through his flesh like light through thin fine porcelain.

"The Great Wall of China still stands," he said in a voice like the sighing of wind through ancient pines, "but Ch'in Shih Huang, who built it, is no more. Soon I, too, will be no more. Remember me, Honorable Pupil, and remember what you have learned."

"I will, Venerable Teacher."

"Good. Good."

Hao. It is good.

Young Mr. Wei, Madame Wei's oldest grandson, who was

twenty-four and the father of two children, came to the riverfront to see them off the day they left, along with Tom and Dorothy Peterson. Mr. Wei was in a Western business suit with a polka-dot necktie.

"You look very modern," Laura said.

He touched the knot of his necktie. "This is a modern age. We must change with the times, must we not? My grandmother left me an inheritance. I plan to use it to construct a large modern house, with electric lights and plumbing and telephones. Three telephones." He looked both proud and nervous.

"I am sure your grandmother would be pleased."

"Perhaps not. In order to build my house I must sell the treasures she left me."

"Treasures?"

"Yes, the statues and vases and paintings and scrolls."

"Sell them!" Laura was shocked. "They belonged to your ancestors, Mr. Wei."

"But this is the twentieth century, Mrs. Valentine. My father and my uncles possess all the landholdings of the Wei family. I have only the art objects with which to move forward."

"Well, you must do as you think best. Do you have a buyer?"

"Not yet. I must consider carefully." He dropped his gaze, abashed. "It is still not completely settled in my mind."

Laura thought of all the magnificent possessions of Madame Wei, now in the hands of this young man, so dazzled with the glamour of the twentieth century and the Western world, and she sighed. She thought of her own bronze vases, the most precious things she owned, then pressed his hand and said good-bye.

The sails of the junk filled with wind. The Valentines stood on deck. The Petersons were waving from shore. Eileen held tightly to Mike's hand. Her fair curls were tucked into a woolen tam, bright red to match her coat. Her little face was alive with excitement. Plum Blossom and Chen stood shoulder to shoulder, Chen looking anxious and a little frightened. Plum Blossom stood straight and sturdy, taller than her husband, with a firm jaw that bespoke the strength of her will. She was wearing a long padded tunic and silk trousers. She was thinking that her mistress's pregnancy was a good sign for herself. This year, next year, some year, she would bear a son, a strong and healthy boy to gladden her and Chen's old age. Changing residences would change their luck. Laura watched Weichang slip away until tears blurred her eyes as she whispered good-bye to five-year-old Michael. *Sleep well, my son.* She thought of his grave beneath a Chinese willow and had a yearning for the quiet hills of Connecticut, but the river was bearing them on, south along the Yangtze to Hankow. Connecticut was only a dream. China was a living presence all around her, moving in the depths of the water and rising from the hollows of the earth, beautiful and cruel, mysterious and loving. She would not go home. *This is your home now, missy.*

BOOK TWO

Bitter Tea

CHAPTER 1

Chen and Plum Blossom walked wide-eyed, hand in hand, along the crowded streets of Shanghai.

"We will never learn our way here," whispered Chen to his wife.

"Yes, we will." Plum Blossom's voice was calm. "They are only people like us. There's nothing to be afraid of."

Not like us, thought Chen. Those who lived in Shanghai were a different breed—quick, impatient, self-confident, and discourteous. The Chinese and the Westerners both. What was this new world of the city? He feared he would never learn it.

They were strolling in the International Settlement. This section of the city, Chen knew, belonged by treaty to foreigners. Here Western businessmen were the rulers. Here they maintained their own police force. Here they lived by their own laws, not that of the Chinese government. They drank whiskey, socialized, and conversed in their own clubs served by Chinese bartenders and waiters. In the great office buildings along the Bund, where Chen and Plum Blossom were now walking, they conducted shipping and exporting and banking and real estate businesses. They were knowledgeable about ways to own property in Shanghai, with a "perpetual lease" and a Chinese agent to act as middleman. They were making money. Chen sensed much of this without being told. He was a Chinese from the interior; he did not belong in the International Settlement; he understood that clearly enough.

Too, he observed that the Chinese of Shanghai seemed desperate to imitate the West. They attired themselves in cheap Western clothes. The girls wore skirts; the men wore trousers. The most valued possession in their homes, he had discovered, was a cheap loud-ticking clock or a gimcrack mirror with a tin frame. The ancient lacquer rice bowls and porcelain teacups were scorned as old-fashioned and worthless by these Shanghai residents. *Change is coming,* thought Chen, *but what sort of change?* China was colliding with the West and something would come of it. He could not fathom what it would be. There was a strong and determined military men in Peking whose name was Yüan Shih-k'ai, and there was an idealistic physician in the South called Sun Yat-sen, and all this boded something. Revolution?

He and Plum Blossom stopped on the Bund, on a grassy patch of ground by the riverfront. A foreign lady was seated there with an easel before her, sketching the ships in the water. She wore a large hat with a drooping plume, a high-necked white blouse with lace at the chin, and a sweeping skirt. Chen and Plum Blossom paused to watch her, along with some other Chinese who had gathered curiously. Then the foreign lady spoke. One young man was in her way, and she asked him in English to step aside because he was obscuring the view.

Chen was astonished at what followed. The young man, who was a Chinese in ill-fitting Western clothes, refused to move. He said in English in a high clear voice, "This is China. I am Chinese and I stand where I please. I stand on my sovereign rights."

Seeing the anger on the foreign lady's face, Chen turned uneasily to Plum Blossom. "Let us go back to our house," he said. "This is a strange city."

Plum Blossom had no such anxieties about Shanghai. One day not long after their walk she brought home a sheet of paper to their Chapei flat. Chen was in the kitchen at the stove. He was acting as cook as well as houseboy. Plum Blossom was maid as well as amah.

"Read this to me, my husband," she demanded. "A young man gave it to me on the street. He said it was important. He was handing it to all who passed by."

"I have no time to read to you," Chen said impatiently. "Can't you see I'm busy?"

"Take a few moments. Your pots will not explode." Plum Blossom was illiterate; she depended on Chen.

He snatched the paper from her hands. "What a turtle's egg you are," he muttered. "The curse of my existence."

She laughed; he laughed too. Then he read the paper, his lips moving as he interpreted the characters.

"It's a political manifesto," he said finally. "It tells of the ideas of a revolutionary leader called Sun Yat-sen."

"I have heard of him. He has good ideas."

"He's from Canton," Chen said, frowning. "What good ideas can come from the South?"

"Don't be so provincial, my husband. We're city people now. We're no longer country bumpkins."

"Yes, we are," Chen grumbled. He still wore his gowns and braided his queue every morning. Secretly Plum Blossom thought he looked very handsome in his gowns, but she didn't tell him. She wanted him to be more modern. But not too modern.

"What are his thoughts?" she inquired. "This person from Canton?"

"We must drive out the barbarian dynasty of the Manchus," reported Chen. "The northern barbarians have ruled over China too long."

Plum Blossom nodded in agreement. Manchuria was not China. The Manchus were not Chinese.

"We must establish a national revolution, not just a revolution of heroes. A *kuo-min-ko-ming*. A revolution of all the people. We must equalize landownership, so that the value of the land can be shared by everyone, not just the privileged few."

"Excellent," said Plum Blossom. "I like his thoughts. They have justice."

"Oh, you! A woman from the hill country who can't even read! What worth are your opinions?"

Plum Blossom took back the manifesto from Chen's hand. "Nevertheless I'll keep it," she said. "Someday our son will read it." She folded it carefully and put it into her tunic pocket.

She still had faith that Kwan-Yin would send them a son. She decided she would add the name of Sun Yat-sen to her prayers.

The Valentines were living on an alley called Stealing Hen Street, in the Chinese district of Chapei. The streets all had picturesque names: Chessboard Street, Beaten Dog Street, Iron Street, Big Street. In this neighborhood vegetable stalls spilled over the pavement in a profusion of cabbage and lettuce and red peppers, and children raced and laughed in the road between the rickshaws and horse-drawn carts. Everything was overlaid with the mud-flat odor of Shanghai, rancid and pungent but after a while so familiar it ceased to be noticed.

Laura had enrolled Eileen in an English day school, the first formal schooling Eileen had known. She had learned to read and do sums from Laura herself, in Weichang. Eileen was not very happy with the academic aspect of her school, and Laura thought wryly that she would never be a student. She did like being with the other children. It was important for her to attend this school, Laura and Mike both agreed, and they willingly paid the money. The fees were high. But their rent was cheap, and food in Chapei was abundant and not very expensive, if one shopped carefully. Plum Blossom was an expert and vigorous bargainer and Chen was a skillful cook.

Mike had been given the job with the tobacco company. Now he was traveling in the North, around Peking and Shansi Province. He was visiting small-town merchants, owners of little Chinese shops, taking orders for cigarettes and making sure the merchandise was sold, displayed, and advertised. It was not difficult, if one didn't mind living on the road for weeks at a time. What Mike did not like was the idea of supervision, even from a distance, and reporting by letter to the branch manager in Shanghai. He was not cut out for taking orders.

What he did like was the dry, clear air of the North, the brilliance of the northern sun, and the way the sunlight often threw black shadows of tree branches on the plaster-beige walls of village houses, making filigree patterns of light and dark. That exhilarated him. It almost gave him back his ambition to waken the sleeping giant; but not quite. He was now too wise in the ways of China. He knew better. In fact he realized now that China had never been sleeping at all, only dozing. Waiting. He wasn't sure what for, but he knew he would stay around and find out, and that made him happy.

One night he was in Peking, at the Hotel Wagon-Lits. It was a quiet evening, and Mike was nursing a gin-and-bitters at the bar. He decided to move on for his nightcap; he limited himself to two drinks a day and a glass of wine with his meals. He finished his gin and paid up.

He strolled through the lobby. A Chinese magician was doing his usual magic act by the door, making scarves and flowers appear and disappear, crying out a meaningless phrase as his fingers flashed, *I ko leng feng, I ko leng feng*. He was hired by the management to provide atmosphere.

Outside, moving at a leisurely pace, Mike reached Hatamen Street. Peking was still fascinating, the smells in the air a mixture of burned camel dung, coconut oil, spicy food, human sweat, and animal refuse; the glitter in the distance was the blaze of the starlight on the gilded rooftops of the Forbidden City.

He came to his destination, a little bar on a side street, and pushed through the door. He was almost knocked over by two brawny employees dragging a limp figure to the threshold. They were about to throw the man into the gutter. He was a pitiful-looking creature. He was a white man, but not one of the lords of creation who wielded power in the East. He was red-eyed and unshaven, his cheeks sunken, his hands shaking, his knees like rubber. "Give us a break, mates," he was pleading. "Give us a break. One more drink for the road. I'll pay you tomorrow."

Mike felt a surge of pity for the fellow. He knew what it was like to need a drink that badly.

"I'll buy him a drink," Mike said. "Leave him alone."

The two Chinese dubiously retreated. Mike put a hand on the man's shoulder, steadying him.

"Come on, old-timer," he said. "Let's sit down."

The man took a ragged breath. He blinked. "Thanks, mate. Thanks, good old cobber."

"Australian?"

"That's right." He attempted a grin. "Haven't been home for a while, though."

"Me either."

At the table the Australian made a valiant effort not to gulp his second whiskey. "When did you come out, Yank?" he asked, trying to ignore the fresh glass that was set in front of him.

" 'Ninety-four."

"Christ. Ten years. Why do we stay?"

"Beats me. Maybe after a while you're scared to go home. Then you get too old and you're afraid you can't compete and it's easier to knock around China."

"Too right," the Australian said feelingly. "What made you come to my rescue like that?" he asked after a moment.

"Just a good-hearted chump, I guess."

"Don't drink much yourself, I notice."

"Who, me?" Mike raised a mocking eyebrow. "Drink is the curse of the workingman, you know that."

They both laughed. There was no need for Mike to explain himself; one drinker always recognized another, even when one was reformed.

"Let me do you a good turn, mate," said the Australian, wiping his mouth with the back of his hand. "I picked up a bit of paper at Frisco Sam's one night a long time ago. Got it off a legation guard, and been saving it ever since for old age. But it looks to me like I won't be having any ruddy old age, the way things stand now, so I'm offering it to you."

"Offering it, huh? For how much?"

The man looked apologetic. "Thirty dollars Mex. How about it, cobber? Do a bloke a favor."

"What is this piece of paper?"

"It's a treasure map. It shows you where to find a certain cave in Shansi Province stuffed with loot. Pinched from the Summer Palace in 1860. Hidden away till the bloody British soldier who took it could get back, but he never got back—he died in a singsong house on Telegraph Lane. So it's all there waiting. Clocks, music boxes, vases, jades, rubies, the lot."

"Sounds like a cock-and-bull story to me."

"Oh, no, Yank. It's true."

The man embarked upon a story about the British soldier under the command of Sir Hope Grant, who had helped to loot the Summer Palace during the Opium Wars. How the soldier had hidden his booty in a cave to protect it against mountain bandits. How he had later died in the arms of a singsong girl in Peking after bequeathing her the map. How she had fallen in love with a legation guard and hoped to make their fortune with the treasure. And so on. The tale wound through adventures. The singsong girl met a bad end; the legation guard turned to drink to drown his sorrow and landed up one night in Frisco Sam's on his uppers looking to raise some money, and here was the map.

"Why didn't you ever go and get the treasure, old-timer?"

"It's in a ruddy fucking cave!" the man replied indignantly. "You need to hire mules and Chinamen and go up into the mountains! Fighting off bandits! I'll never do it. I never did do it. Now I haven't got the nerve."

The story was a fable if he ever heard one, Mike thought. But it was worth thirty dollars Mex, it was a good yarn, and the Australian needed the money.

"Don't spend it all in one night," he said, handing over the cash.

The man glanced at Mike with gratitude and shame mingled in his eyes. He fingered the tattered map he was holding, then passed it to Mike. "This is yours now, Yank," he said. "May it bring better luck to you than it did to me."

Mike tucked it into his wallet. How many hands, he wondered, had grasped this dirty piece of paper, passing it back and forth over whiskey-puddled tables and telling that improbable story? It didn't matter. It would be a souvenir and reminder to keep sober.

CHAPTER 2

Laura was spending time browsing through the antique shops of Chapei. Sometimes she took a rickshaw across the bridge and over the dividing line of Avenue Edouard VII to the International Settlement, where the French Concession began. Her schoolgirl French began to return to her memory as she listened to the conversations on the streets and in the shops.

The antique dealers were Chinese, however, even in the French Concession. In that district of Shanghai the shops were expensive and stocked with gimcrack Chinese export ware, polychrome porcelain birds, and gilded Coromandel screens: objects selected to appeal to tourists. Laura considered them overpriced. She had been told that the experienced French antique dealers from Paris did not purchase in these shops. They bought at auctions or had their own agents in the countryside.

She discovered a handsome calligraphy scroll in a French Concession shop, with characters brushed on beautiful old silk, but the dealer's price was too high.

"I will go away and you will think it over," she said to him. "Perhaps you'll change your mind."

He bowed politely. Chinese dealers were always polite. "It is possible I will do so, Honorable Customer."

She was happier in the narrow alleys and open-fronted shops of Chapei, where cheap bamboo knickknacks were jumbled together with antiques of authentic beauty, and you never knew what you might find.

The shop owners were wary of Laura in the beginning. Then they discovered she spoke Chinese. They soon grew to know her and joked and teased when she appeared.

"The foreign lady has come to steal our treasures! She takes the rice from the mouths of our children!"

"Your children are fat and happy," Laura retorted. "Your son has rosy cheeks. I saw him in the road."

"Behold! We can keep no secrets!"

She bought sparingly, but what she did buy was of high quality. The merchants respected her taste. They learned to set things aside for her inspection. The days passed quickly.

She returned one afternoon to the French Concession shop to look at the calligraphy scroll. Another customer was in the shop that day.

Pierre-Marc Daniel, a Parisian who was visiting Shanghai, was in a state of dramatic despair, standing not far from Laura. "The auction, for me, was a total calamity!" he cried with a sweep of his hand. "A disaster! A catastrophe!"

"Pierre-Marc, you treat every tiny disappointment as a catastrophe," remarked his companion, a well-dressed middle-aged man in a homburg hat.

Pierre-Marc was a small dark man in his early forties, with a wryly humorous twist to his mouth and shrewd black eyes. "It is true!" he cried to his friend. He lifted one hand to his forehead with the palm outward in a gesture of desolation. "I was not able to make a single purchase! *Mon cher ami*, what hell it is to be poor!''

"You manage to eat," his friend observed. "You stay alive, Pierre-Marc.''

"Consider my filthy rich family, however," said Pierre-Marc darkly. "All those cousins and second cousins wallowing in wealth from making gloves. Living in Passy. While I—I—the cleverest of them all—must work for a living. *Quelle bêtise.*''

Pierre-Marc was the art critic for the Paris newspaper *Le Temps*. This was his first visit to Shanghai.

"One must have an entrée," he said more thoughtfully. "One must have a companion who speaks Chinese, as I do not, and understands the Oriental mind. And of course, appreciates art.''

"Find yourself a Chinese guide.''

"A professional guide? No, no, not the thing.''

"Ask your cousin to find you someone.''

Nathan Field, Pierre-Marc's mother's cousin, a member of the South African branch of the family, was the owner of a chain of hotels in the Orient. He had expanded his interests in the 1800s from Johannesburg to India to China. Now a millionaire, he lived in Shanghai, in a mansion on Hungjao Road.

"Nathan the Rich?" said Pierre-Marc disdainfully. "He disapproves of me. He is my last resort.''

"Well then, I cannot help you," said his friend. He raised his shoulders in a Gallic shrug. "You never take advice anyway.''

"Do you see that lady over there?" said Pierre-Marc suddenly. "She has selected the best thing in this shop.''

"What, the scroll with the Chinese writing?''

"Yes, it is eighteenth century. Beautiful quality. She must have excellent taste. And she speaks Chinese.''

"She is rather *enceinte*," remarked his friend.

"What things you notice!" exclaimed Pierre-Marc impatiently. "What difference does that make! Pregnant! Not pregnant! I will enchant her with my unparalleled charm and she will lead me to hidden treasures. I have just decided.''

"You are the most complete egomaniac I have ever met," sighed his friend.

"But seldom wrong," Pierre-Marc reminded him.

"She may not speak French."

"*N'important.*"

Pierre-Marc adjusted his jacket on his shoulders and approached Laura, who was gazing wistfully at the scroll. She was thinking that it was still too expensive.

"Pardon me, madame," Pierre-Marc murmured. "Do you speak French?"

Laura gazed at him. "Not very well, I'm afraid," she said.

"Ah! You are English!"

"American."

"But how delightful!" Pierre-Marc favored her with a radiant smile. He had the sort of smile that lit up his face. "Americans are my favorite people! So unspoiled! So enthusiastic!"

"That's very nice," Laura said, a little bewildered.

"We will speak English," Pierre-Marc declared. He bowed deeply from the waist. "Allow me to introduce myself. Pierre-Marc Daniel, of *Le Temps* in Paris. That is a newspaper."

"Yes, I know." Laura hesitated. "My name is Mrs. Valentine."

Pierre-Marc seized her hand and raised it to his lips. "An enchanting name for a most charming lady!" His English was fast, fluent, and heavily accented.

Laura was still bewildered. Pierre-Marc started to laugh as he released her hand. "I see you are puzzled, madame. You are asking yourself, who is this madman?"

Laura began to laugh too. "Why, no. Well . . . maybe a little."

"But of course! It is only natural! I will buy you coffee and pastry and explain my lunacy. Let me say now that I am the art critic for *Le Temps* and I admire your taste." He gave her a mischievous glance. "Are you not flattered?"

Laura couldn't help smiling. "I am, Mr. Daniel. But I must return to my family. I'm afraid I can't stop for pastry."

"Nonsense. You must take nourishment before you go home. Otherwise you will faint on the street and cause a large commotion. Your family will then be very upset. I cannot allow such a thing to happen." He waved his arm. "We will discuss the wonderful scroll, and other matters of artistic interest. You will be enthralled by my conversation. One moment while I bid au revoir to my friend. He has another errand."

Laura suppressed a smile. She saw that she had no choice but to come.

"You have practically kidnapped me, Mr. Daniel," she said over coffee and pastry in a nearby shop.

"You are so lovely and so charming I could not resist," he declared.

"Do you always pay such extravagant compliments to women?"

"Only to you. I have fallen in love. It has struck me like a clap of thunder."

Laura observed that it was unusual for a lady in her condition to inspire such instant devotion.

"Love does not take note of such trivial obstacles."

Her companion was even laughing at himself, Laura saw, although only his eyes gave him away.

"Won't your wife object?" she asked.

"I am not married. Nor likely to be, Madame Valentine."

"Don't be so certain. You never know when you'll meet the right woman."

He was amused. He sat silent for a moment. Then he said, "I perceive that you are quite innocent concerning matters of sex."

Laura could not deny it. "I married very young, and I've never been interested in anyone but my husband," she said. "I'm certainly not a sophisticated Frenchwoman."

"Certainly not. Quite refreshing, too. Do not fear, Madame Valentine. I will not invite you to have an affair with me. My talk of love is only of the spirit, not the flesh. Your husband has no worries with regard to myself. I am no threat to any woman. Do you comprehend?"

She felt foolish. He was telling her something she did not particularly want to believe.

He was even more amused, reading her expression. "So," he said, "you have understood. You have met a wicked Parisian, a practitioner of vice. You are shocked. In fact, repelled."

"I should be but I'm not," she said honestly. "I like you."

He started to laugh. "The beginnings of sophistication! You have discovered I am a human being, and we can be friends!"

She started to laugh too. "I suppose I have."

"Excellent." He leaned forward across the table, his eyes sparkling. "Now let us discuss Chinese art."

They discussed painting on silk. Laura had not studied painting very thoroughly, having concerned herself with porcelain and bronzes, and there'd been so much in those areas to learn that she had been daunted. Pierre-Marc Daniel, she thought in wonderment, must have been a child prodigy to have acquired so wide a background. She did not really discuss anything after a while; she only listened. Pierre-Marc was a fascinating speaker.

He talked of the painters of the Sung Dynasty. The Sung masters were anonymous for the most part, preferring to let their works speak for them in the halls of posterity. They were famous for their birds, flowers, and landscapes.

"To an artist steeped in the Zen philosophy of contemplation," said Pierre-Marc, serious now and not flamboyant, "a flowering branch is the symbol of the infinite harmony of nature. The Sung masters were artists of landscape. They painted mountains, mists, waterfalls, torrents, a solitary fisherman in his boat on a quiet lake, a flock of wild geese soaring above a reedbed. Consider the titles of their paintings. *The Moon Above Raging Waves. Curfew from a Distant Temple.*"

"Poetry," said Laura.

"Exactly. A century later, in the Ming Dynasty, the glory faded. Alas, alas. Ornament replaced simplicity and poetry. Everything became complicated, elaborate, rich with decoration." Pierre-Marc sat back and sighed.

"Mr. Daniel," said Laura suddenly, "I am glad I met you."

"I too," said Pierre-Marc. "It may turn out to be a valuable friendship." He gave her a droll glance. "But bear in mind, my dear lady, that *I* met *you*."

Laura could only smile and agree.

CHAPTER 3

Mike Valentine was entering an open-fronted shop in a small Shansi village. He had arrived on ponyback along a dirt road that ran beside a drainage canal. Behind him was a hired coolie carrying two boxes, one of sealed cigarette cartons and one of advertising handbills. Behind the coolie was a trail of curious townspeople, many of them children, who had come to see the foreigner. This was an entertainment that never lost its appeal. Mike was well used to it. The shopkeeper was coming to greet him, bowing in the doorway in his long blue gown. Mike knew what would happen next. These calls followed a pattern, inside the shop as well as without. The shopkeeper, in this case Mr. Wong, would offer him tea. Then in a roundabout way, in fluent but ungrammatical Chinese, Mike would inquire why he had seen no stocks of his cigarette brand on Mr. Wong's counter. What was the trouble?

Mr. Wong would throw up his hands. He had none.

Why? Mike would wonder aloud in a puzzled tone.

Mr. Wong would explain sorrowfully. He was burdened with too many brands already. Only two or three ever sold well, yet the company was always asking him to take on a new one. He could not afford to; he had too much money tied up in stock.

Mike had learned not to launch into a direct sales appeal at this point. He could not extol the virtues of his own brand of cigarettes, as a salesman would do in America, for that was crude. It was not the Chinese way. Instead he would suggest. He would hint. He would drop delicate little allusions into his conversation and ask for more tea. Sooner or later, Mike knew, Mr. Wong would capitulate. He would even allow Mike to paste up an advertising handbill on his wall.

The call went exactly as expected. During the course of the conversation Mr. Wong shook his head in wondering disbelief. "So many foreign brands of cigarettes," he murmured. "So many. Where do they all come from? One pictures foreigners in their own lands totally occupied with making cigarettes, to the exclusion of all other activities." Mr. Wong sighed. "Of course we see you here in China doing many kinds of things, so we know better."

"We must have learned it somewhere," Mike agreed.

"So it appears."

Mike grinned. "Tell me more about your opinion of foreigners in China, Mr. Wong."

The shop owner assumed the bland, polite, deliberately dense expression that signaled a Chinese unwillingness to answer a question. He could possibly be discourteous and lose face. Up till now the conversation had been urbane. He raised an eyebrow and looked blank.

"My opinion?"

Stalling for time, thought Mike. He felt like hearing a reply, however, since the topic had come up.

"Yes, your opinion of foreigners like myself."

"Ah. Like yourself." After a moment Mr. Wong decided to comprehend. "Most helpful," he said with a nod. "Aware of our needs. Wakening the sleeping giant, is it not so?"

"I wonder if you believe that, Mr. Wong."

Mr. Wong suddenly gave Mike an impish grin. "Perhaps yes and perhaps no," he replied. "In some ways I do and in some ways I do not. There are lessons you can offer us, Mr. Valentine. You foreigners. If we are clever enough to learn them. Mr. Sun Yat-sen is learning them, isn't he? Planning a revolution with American advice? Does that answer your question?"

Mike bowed gravely. "In some ways yes and in some ways no," he said with a straight face.

They both laughed, and soon the call was over. Then Mike was free to shop for Eileen. He would buy her a silk butterfly kite for her kite collection, he told himself. Mike had created the collection for Eileen, and she adored it. But everything Mike did was perfect in Eileen's estimation. She was increasingly important to him as well. He looked forward to going home to his wife and daughter.

"And so is this Shanghai?" said Pierre-Marc Daniel to his new friend Laura Valentine. "The Europeans live isolated in the International Settlement and the Chinese live crowded and poverty-stricken in their own section of the city?"

"Across Soochow Creek, yes," replied Laura. They were seated in a café on Avenue Edouard VII.

"And how long can this state of affairs last?" said Pierre-Marc.

"Forever, it would seem."

"I think not forever," Pierre-Marc commented. "There will be a revolution made by Sun Yat-sen. Everyone expects it."

"The revolution will be directed against the Manchu Dynasty. It won't affect foreigners in Shanghai. Everyone expects that too. Status quo."

"Ah, the inscrutable tranquillity of the Orient," said Pierre-Marc with a sardonic smile. "We plunder her of art and antiquities and there is no one to tell us nay. A robber's paradise. A thieves' market and we are the thieves. Shanghai."

"What can we do?" asked Laura with a worried expression. "My husband wanted to modernize China, but he has given up that dream; it's beyond us. We can't get involved in Chinese politics. Especially me. Even living here, I don't know enough about it."

"You are not a revolutionary. But what of your children? Your children's children? Will they grow up in China? How will they feel in years to come?"

"Good lord, Pierre-Marc, I can't think that far ahead."

"No, of course not," said Pierre-Marc, soothingly. "Tell me instead, dear Laura, about this discovery you have unearthed."

Laura's face grew serious and she leaned forward across the table. "It is in an antique shop in the Chapei district, Pierre-Marc. It is a small painting on silk. Very simple, very beautiful. Perhaps Sung. I dismissed it from my mind when I first saw it, because I can't afford paintings, and I am more knowledgeable about porcelain and bronze. As you know, I have been buying bronze cylinder seals, which are not expensive. But you might be interested in the painting." She still had hopes of buying the calligraphy scroll for herself someday.

Pierre-Marc's eyes kindled. His dark, clever face lit up. "Can one bargain with the owner?"

"He only speaks Chinese, but I could help you. This is Shanghai. Everyone bargains."

"Laura, I am most interested! You must take me there at once!" Pierre-Marc's face changed, and he gave Laura an appealing, apologetic glance. "Naturally if you have time. I do not mean to bully. It is a failing of mine, forgive me."

Laura smiled. She was well accustomed to Pierre-Marc by now; they had become good friends in a very short time. "Of course. I'll take you to the shop this afternoon. It's on my way home."

"Let us hope," Pierre-Marc breathed, calling for the check, "the painting is not sold."

The painting was titled *Parakeet on a Blossoming Pear Branch*. The bird's plumage glowed with softly iridescent color, surrounded by an aureole of blossoms. The bird and branch were carefully placed in the lower left of the painting, in beautiful proportion to an expanse of empty silk.

"It is lovely," said Pierre-Marc, holding it between his palms. "I believe you are right; it is southern Sung. Perhaps by a follower of the Emperor Hui Tsung."

The owner was gazing at Pierre-Marc's face, standing by his shoulder. Pierre-Marc frowned and shook his head, assuming his bargaining expression. The owner grinned. Bargaining was an ever exciting game of wits, and when played correctly, both sides won.

"Speak to him, my dear," Pierre-Marc said softly. "Be clever and be brave. I depend on you."

Laura nodded. She turned to the owner, who was waiting with his hands folded, having assumed his own wooden face.

"Perhaps we would be willing to take this worthless bit of fabric off your hands," she said carelessly.

He was offended. Deeply offended. He drew himself up. "I have changed my mind, Honorable Valentine. I cannot sell this precious object. It is priceless. Nothing will persuade me to part with it.'' He bowed from the waist in a ceremonial kowtow. The game had begun.

Forty minutes later Pierre-Marc and Laura left the shop. Pierre-Marc was carrying the painting under his arm, wrapped in brown paper. He was smiling.

"Marvelous!" he exclaimed. "Astonishing! A sensational performance!" In his elation he had lapsed into French. "The world is suddenly *couleur de rose!*"

"I am glad you are pleased."

"Even with your ten percent commission it is a bargain."

"Ten percent commission?"

"Yes. Naturally. When I send you my friends from Paris, of course, who are rich, you will charge them twenty."

"I cannot take a commission, Pierre-Marc."

"Don't be idiotic, my dear. Of course you can." Pierre-Marc gave Laura a shrewd glance from the corner of his eye. "You live in Chapei, right? And you have a family? Therefore you can use the money. Or are you too proud?"

"No," said Laura slowly. "No, I am not too proud. I just never thought of it."

"Then I have given you an excellent idea."

"Yes. Yes." Laura frowned, considering this new development. It would help with Eileen's school fees. "But from you, Pierre-Marc," she added after a moment, "I can only accept five percent commission."

"Agreed," he said promptly.

She laughed. "Thank you for the advice."

He adjusted his jacket. "You will learn always to take my suggestions, dear Laura. In some ways I am a *poseur*, it is true, but at bottom I am extremely sensible. You, on the other hand, are romantic. You require guidance." He paused thoughtfully. "You must improve your French; that is imperative. Start to study at once. Then you will have three languages at your command: English, French, and Chinese."

"Very well."

Laura felt bemused. She had the strange sensation that she was in the company of a small Gallic version of Madame Wei, and she started to laugh.

"What is so amusing?"

"I have the curious feeling I have met you before in another shape."

"One often feels that way about people," he said loftily. "In my case it is probably true."

CHAPTER 4

Pierre-Marc Daniel lost no time in sending Laura friends with whom to shop. They were people he knew in Shanghai. Pierre-Marc had a wide circle of acquaintances in a variety of countries. He had told Laura the truth: most of them were well-to-do. Before he sailed for France at the end of his visit, he promised to send her clients from Paris. She in turn promised to write faithfully and keep him informed.

"I will come back to Shanghai before long," he warned her, "and see how you are progressing. You are my protegée, and I always keep close watch on those whom I have adopted."

"I will try to justify your confidence, Pierre-Marc," she said solemnly.

He laughed and kissed her on the cheek. "I cannot wait," he exclaimed, "to display my *Parakeet on a Blossoming Pear Branch*. I will hang it in my bedroom. In the place of honor, over my bed!"

Laura told Mike all about it when he returned from his trip.

"It seems that I am in the antiques business," she said, "in a very small way. I've come in by the back door, so to speak. Pierre-Marc must think my French is good enough to get by, at least for now."

"Who is this person Pierre-Marc?" Mike asked. "What is he like?"

"He is somewhat like . . . Oscar Wilde."

"Tall and fat with a lily in his hand?"

"Well, no. He is small and slender. If he carried a flower, it would not be a lily."

"Oh?"

"Think of another flower. One that grows in borders."

After a moment Mike suggested, "A pansy?"

"Yes, I suppose that's what I'm trying to say."

Laura sat down at the kitchen table and explained about Pierre-Marc, how much she liked him and what an odd and interesting person he was. Mike realized, as did Laura, that the extra money would prove to be useful. Especially when the new baby arrived.

Eileen was not at all sure that she would welcome a new brother or sister. Anyone who threatened to come between Eileen and her beloved daddy, including Laura, was a possible enemy. She decided on a plan.

"The new baby can have Chen and Mama," she explained to Plum Blossom. "You and Daddy are mine."

"You do not share people like playthings," Plum Blossom scolded.

That brought up a new and unpleasant idea. "Will I have to share my clothes and toys?" Eileen asked.

"Certainly."

"My clothes will be too big."

"Not your clothes, silly girl. I didn't mean that."

At least she would be able to keep something of her own, Eileen thought in relief. What would it be like, she wondered, feeling worried, to have a baby in the house? She couldn't remember her brother Michael as an infant, she'd been too small.

"Mrs. Valentine," said a soft voice with a French accent, "you have a son."

Laura struggled awake and forced open her eyes. She had left the recovery room and was back in her hospital bed. A blood-pressure tourniquet was strapped around her arm. She was looking into the countenance of an elderly nun, the rosy wrinkles of the woman's face framed by her white coif. *There are no nuns in Weichang*, she thought blurrily, *only Maryknoll Fathers*. No, she was in a hospital in the French Concession of Shanghai. And she had a son.

"Where is my husband?" She wondered if she'd said it aloud.

"He is right here, waiting to see you." Yes, she had spoken the words.

Mike was beside her then, holding her hand.

"He won't take the place of little Michael," Laura whispered anxiously.

"No, sweetheart, of course not."

"He will have his own place." Laura sighed in drug-blurred vagueness. "Every baby makes his own place." The world was fading again. "We'll call him David, after my grandfather. Won't we, Mike? This time it's my turn to name the baby."

"That's what we agreed."

"David Canfield was a clipper captain. He came from Scotland to New England when he was only . . . ten years old. . . . Did I ever tell you that?"

It was too late to hear Mike's answer because her eyes were too heavy to keep open, and she was falling asleep again.

Plum Blossom was delighted with little David. At two months he was quiet and self-reliant and happy in his own company, lying in his cradle and playing with his wooden rattle, a hand-made gift from George Henderson.

"Such a good infant," Plum Blossom murmured, leaning over the cradle. "He never cries. Just like a Chinese baby! Except for this." She patted the infant's corn-silk blond hair.

Eileen, beside her, was disgruntled. "I never cried either," she said with dignity. "I was a perfect baby."

"You were a mischief-maker from the day you were born," Plum Blossom retorted. "I heard all about you from your amah in Weichang." Then she softened. "But now you're different. You're a big help to your mother and me." She picked up David in her arms.

Eileen's face grew brighter. "Am I?"

"Of course. And from now on you'll have to be a grown-up girl and look after your brother, because your mother will be busy."

"You mean helping people to shop for antiques?"

"Yes, as soon as she's stronger, very shortly. Many people want her. She is most clever and has good taste."

Eileen considered that remark thoughtfully. "How do you get good taste?"

"You study your schoolbooks and listen to your teachers."

No help at all. Eileen thought that Plum Blossom sounded just like her mother when she talked that way. She couldn't wait to grow up and close her schoolbooks forever. She sighed, contemplating the long years ahead. *Hurry up, hurry up. Make the time go faster, God. I want to be a woman.*

Laura informed Mike that she had received an unusual communication from a person in Shanghai.

"It's a letter from Nathan Field," she told him.

"*The* Nathan Field? The one who lives in a mansion on Hungjao Road?"

"Yes, isn't it crazy? He wants to meet me. He's interested in buying antiques that are—and I quote—'off the beaten track,' and he was told I have 'an uncommonly keen eye for selection.' That's another quote."

"The guy must have a houseful of antiques."

"He does, so I've heard. All priceless."

"I wonder how he got your name?"

"From Pierre-Marc. He's some kind of relative. I'm going to see him tomorrow. I'll travel in Mr. Chow's rickshaw, so it won't be tiring for me." Mr. Chow was a neighbor on Stealing Hen Street. "Mr. Chow will wait for me and take me home," Laura added. "I'm curious to meet Nathan Field. It might lead to something important."

"Don't count on it," Mike said. "Millionaires are usually hard to get along with. They have whims."

"Well, dealing with him will be good experience for me, in case I meet other millionaires in the future."

Laura dressed carefully the next day. She was able to wear fashionable clothes since her figure had returned to normal. She selected an ensemble that had just been made for her by a dressmaker on Avenue Edouard VII. Ordering it had been an act of courage on Laura's part, for the fashion was extremely new. Once more she had followed the advice of Pierre-Marc Daniel.

"I have another new protegé," he had written in dark purple ink on lavender paper. "His name is Paul Poiret, and he is a genius at designing clothes. He is disgustingly young, still with adolescent spots, but in five years he will be the rage of Paris. You know my intuition is always correct! I am enclosing a sketch of Paul's. Have it made up at once, dear Laura, now that you are slender again, and you will look at once chic and avant-garde and make me proud of you. Don't forget, I have ways of supervising you from a distance!''

Laura had laughed when she read the letter, seeing and hearing Pierre-Marc himself, and then had taken the sketch to a dressmaker. The woman had been both shocked and intrigued by the design.

"So short, madame! Only to the middle of the ankle! And so narrow around the calf!"

"I know."

It didn't look anything like the full-skirted ground-sweeping dresses Laura's acquaintances were wearing. Nor did the dress have a normal waist. Instead it hugged her body just below the bosom.

"This waist is called Empire," the dressmaker informed Laura. "It will look very, very new. You must have a new hat to go with it. Wide in the brim and flat on the crown, with a sweeping feather." She was getting into the spirit of the sketch.

Now the dress was completed. It was lilac-mauve wool, with a deep-red Empire waistband, and the hat was black felt with a black ostrich feather. Laura didn't recognize herself in the mirror. She might have stepped straight off the Champs-Élysées, she thought, admiring herself. Where, she wondered, was plain Laura Valentine of Stealing Hen Street in Chapei? The new friends she had made in Shanghai would be astonished.

She thought perhaps Mr. Nathan Field would be impressed too. He wanted something "off the beaten track" and suddenly she looked like the woman who would find it.

Mr. Chow, when he arrived with his rickshaw, was struck with admiration. "Who is this elegant, fashionable lady?" he exclaimed. "I will travel only the main avenues! It will give me much face to be seen with you! Assume a haughty expression," he added. "Do not speak to me except to give me orders." He grinned. "Where are we going?"

"To Hungjao Road," Laura said with a haughty lift of her chin. "To the mansion of Mr. Nathan Field, one of the foremost businessmen of Shanghai.'' She swept out of the door and into the street. Chuckling with amusement, Mr. Chow followed.

In spite of her new clothes Laura felt a sag in her confidence when they turned into the driveway of Nathan Field's mansion. The driveway was long and winding, bordered with willow trees. A pond stretched serenely behind the lacework of willow trees. The house came into view. It was of French Palladian architecture, with a circular portico, glittering windows, and a curved staircase with shallow stone steps leading from the driveway to the door. Everything was in perfect proportion.

''This is not very Chinese,'' Laura said with disdain, to bolster her courage. ''It could be located anywhere in Europe.''

''The honorable Mr. Field is not Chinese,'' Mr. Chow pointed out.

''Nevertheless, he lives in Shanghai; he should have better judgment.''

Laura's objection was denied in the entrance hall. The tables, the vases, and the watercolor paintings were all Chinese, and all were of museum quality. Just inside, flanking the door, were two seven-foot-tall bronze water jars. Laura recognized them as Shang Dynasty, for they had the savage and splendid authenticity of 1500 B.C. Her courage sank lower.

In the library, where she was ushered, she found more magnificent bronzes and porcelains. Laura forgot her unease in fascinated admiration of the objects. She wandered around the room absorbed by them. Sometimes she stroked an object with the tips of her fingers, to be in touch with its soul. Sometimes she sniffed at it. With bronzes and porcelains one had to touch and smell, for the inner truth of such things resided in the feel and the scent, not the look. Old metal and fine ceramics had their own special fragrances; she had learned that from the dealers of Chapei. Orientals knew it but Westerners seldom did. They were content only to look. Seeing was not enough, however. ''It is like making love,'' one dealer had remarked.

''Aha!'' cried a booming voice behind her. ''A woman who appreciates value!''

''I beg your pardon?''

''Expensive goods! The real stuff!''

''Oh. They certainly are.''

"You are Mrs. Valentine."

"Yes," said Laura, "and surely you are Mr. Field."

"Of course, who else would I be?" He gave her a mischievous glance. "Do I look like the butler?" He pulled his eyes into a slant.

It was an absurd thing to do, but Laura had to laugh, because he looked so funny. His appearance was not at all what she had expected. She had pictured Nathan Field as old and wizened and crotchety. Instead he was tall and husky with very pink cheeks. Despite his age (surely he was in his sixties?) he had an air of boyish playfulness.

He advanced into the room and tapped the head of an ivory statue. "Do you know how much this piece cost me?" he asked with a serious expression.

"A great deal, I am sure."

"A fortune, my dear lady! A small fortune!" Nathan Field paused. "In fact, not so small. But do you know something else?" He laughed heartily. "I can afford it. I'm a rich man."

"So I've heard," Laura said in a faint tone.

"Everybody's heard! Look at this." He strode to a lacquered desk and pulled open the drawer, then withdrew a small piece of paper. "It's a check. I'm negotiating for a hotel in Hong Kong, and this is the amount I've decided to pay." He snapped the check open between his hands. "Have you ever seen so many zeros?"

Laura glanced quickly at the paper, then shook her head.

"How many people do you know could write a check like this?" Nathan Field waited rather anxiously for her reply.

"None," Laura answered. She thought it best not to mention the Weis.

"Now you do," he said proudly. "You know me." He replaced the check in the drawer and waved his hand. "See this room? Total up the value of it in your head. Then think to yourself, Nathan Field made it all himself. From nothing! Bloody nothing! Just this"—he tapped his forehead—"and these"—he held out his hands. "How is that for a bloody fine achievement?"

"Bloody fine," Laura agreed.

He grinned. "You have a sense of humor, that's good. It

shows brains. And you're also damned attractive. I like that.
Turn around so I can see your dress."

After a moment's hesitation Laura turned around.

"Makes all the other women look like frumps. Something
about a trim pair of ankles, eh what?"

"If you say so, Mr. Field."

"Good, keep on agreeing with me and we'll get on like a
bloody house on fire."

Laura suppressed a smile. There was definitely a family resemblance between Mr. Field of Johannesburg and M. Pierre-Marc
Daniel of Paris. At least in temperament. She should have anticipated that, she told herself.

At Mr. Field's invitation she sat down, and he joined her.

"So you're a friend of Pierre-Marc's," he commented. "Ruddy
little nance, isn't he? Never mind, he knows what's what. Thinks
I don't like him. He's wrong; I do. Don't tell him I said so." Mr.
Field winked. Laura, still hiding her amusement, agreed not to
tell.

"Now you wonder what you can do for me," Mr. Field
continued. "I don't exactly know myself. I'm looking for something different. Unusual, so to speak."

"You said in your letter, off the beaten track."

"That's right. Got anything in mind?"

Laura hesitated. "I can't give you an immediate answer. I
would have to do some shopping."

"That's it. Shop around. Pick out some things and bring them
here for me to look at. Then we'll talk business."

"I suppose you only want objects that are extremely expensive?"
Laura said tentatively.

"Don't be a bloody fool, woman. I don't shop by price tag.
I'm cleverer than that."

"I can see you are. I apologize."

"I may act the buffoon, but don't be deceived. I don't miss
very much."

"Mr. Field, when I observe this house and these antiques, I
can have no doubt of it."

"And remember how I got where I am."

"Using this"—Laura tapped her forehead—"and these." She
held out her hands.

He laughed. "That's right. But you can forget about the hands. I don't do hard labor anymore."

"Very well, Mr. Field, I'll keep it in mind."

He stood up to signal the end of their talk. "Thank you for coming, Mrs. Valentine. I'll look forward to seeing you again." He shook her hand. "And wear something like that dress," he added. "And that hat. It's a pleasure to look at you."

CHAPTER 5

Laura felt she had been backed into a corner. She wanted to make a sale to Nathan Field, but where, she asked herself, could she find something good enough to show him? Any of her dealer friends in Chapei would lend her an art object on consignment, but she could not think of anything suitable for that mansion on Hungjao Road. She discussed the problem with Mike, who was leaving for the North in the morning.

"You'll just have to give up," Mike said finally, covering a yawn. "It isn't that important."

"I don't want to give up," Laura objected. "I said I'd go back to show him things, and I want to keep my word."

"Sleep on it."

Sleep would not come to Laura. She lay open-eyed in the dark beside her sleeping husband and pondered her dilemma. She remembered an auction catalog she had had mailed to her from Peking. She arose, put on her robe, found the catalog in her bureau drawer and took it into the kitchen. She spread it out on the kitchen table. Just as she was studying the first page, she heard a familiar wail.

"Oh!" she murmured aloud. "Poor David! I forgot all about him!"

Plum Blossom appeared in the doorway with the crying baby in her arms.

"He is hungry, missy," she announced reproachfully.

Laura held out her arms. "I'm sorry, Plum Blossom, I forgot."

"Such a good baby," Plum Blossom said. "How can you forget such a small precious one?" She placed the baby in Laura's arms.

When she had finished nursing David and he was tucked back in his cradle asleep, Laura returned to the catalog. She had glanced at it casually before, but now she studied each item with care. She forgot about the lateness of the hour as she began to grow excited. Finally she got to her feet and went into the bedroom.

"Mike," she said softly at his bedside. "Mike, wake up."

He groaned and turned over. "What time is it?"

"The middle of the night. But I need your help."

"Now?"

"Yes, now. I'm sorry to wake you like this, but we have to talk tonight. There's no other time."

"Mother of God." He sat up. "Okay, I'm coming."

When they were seated at the kitchen table, Laura explained her idea.

"It's about my sale to Nathan Field," she said.

"I figured that out for myself." His voice was wry but Laura was intent on her own train of thought. "Instead of my buying from an antique shop," she said, "and taking a commission from the purchaser, why don't I buy on my own and resell at a profit? Just like a dealer?"

"It requires investing your own money."

"Well, I still have some set aside."

"Okay, but where would you buy?"

"At an auction."

"Is that why you woke me up in the middle of the night? To tell me about auctions?"

"Yes, Mike, because the best auctions are in Peking, not Shanghai. Peking is where the really beautiful old things are put up for sale. It's such an ancient city. Shanghai is just a nouveau riche seaport; it's a place to sell, not buy." Laura came to the point. "You're leaving for Peking tomorrow, Mike. Would you have time to go to an auction?"

"Sure, I'd have time, but I wouldn't know what to bid on."

"I have a catalog here. We could go through it together, right now, and decide what we want and how much we can afford to spend. Then it would be up to you to get something. How does it sound?"

"A little like a poker game. Anyway, better than selling cigarettes."

They heard a sound in the doorway, and both looked up. Chen was standing there in his robe decorated with scarlet dragons, looking rumpled and sleepy. He had observed the scene at the table and noticed the open catalog.

"I make you tea," he announced.

He shuffled to the stove and put on a kettle of water to boil. Laura and Mike returned to the conversation as he made the tea.

"The auction will be held on the premises of the Antique Dealers Association in Peking," she told Mike. "The most expensive pieces will be bought by international dealers like C. T. Loo and T. Y. King. Some of the small dealers will band together and bid collectively on the others. But you may have a chance at an individual piece here and there." She gave Mike an anxious glance. "I've picked out certain things, though. Don't bid on anything but what I've chosen, all right?"

"Aye aye, sir," Mike replied with a ferocious scowl.

"Take it seriously, Mike!"

"Okay. I'm serious."

Chen set steaming cups of tea on the table. Laura explained the pieces she had selected and indicated their pictures in the catalog. She marked each with a check as she spoke.

"These two vases are Sung Dynasty," she said. "This one is covered in green-gray crackle glaze called *tung*. It comes from the north of Honan Province and was made in the eleventh century. This other is celadon from the Lung Ch'uan district, and it's monochrome, all one color, that makes it valuable to collectors. Both vases are bottle-shaped, as you can see in the pictures."

"Which is better?"

"It doesn't matter; they're both lovely." She turned the page. "Here is a bowl made of *chien yao* from Fukien Province. That's a lustrous black glaze starred with irregular marks called oil spots. The flat shape of the bowl is known as *temmoku* but you don't have to remember that.''

"Thank you, dear."

She ignored his teasing tone and pointed to another picture. "Oh, Mike, this is the kind of thing Nathan Field might like! It's Ming Dynasty, seventeenth century."

He peered at it. "A little woman, lying down?"

"Yes, of patinated ivory. They were figures made for a doctor's examination, because the women were too modest to undress. So they used these ivory statuettes to indicate their problems." Laura turned another page. "Here's an ivory Buddha. His throne is cut from a solid block of turquoise. That might go too high. But this bowl—spinach green jade decorated with dragons chasing the sacred pearl—that's Ch'ing Dynasty, not very old. It might be possible. It's unusual, and it's very pretty."

Chen had washed up the teacups and gone back to bed by the time they had finished.

"Maybe I'm wrong to do this," Laura said worriedly, handing Mike the catalog. "We'll be using Eileen's school fees for next year."

"Then you'll just have to sell whatever I buy."

"Do you trust me, Mike?"

"If you trust me to do the bidding, sweetheart, I'll have to trust you to do the selling."

"Maybe we're crazy."

"Maybe you're a gambler and just beginning to find it out."

Laura wondered if she wanted to be a gambler. Then again, maybe she had no choice. She was what she was. Fate was unavoidable. Oh, how Oriental she was becoming! she told herself with a half-frightened, half-amused little laugh. Still, the wheel of fate was spinning and it would stop where it pleased. She had to strive for serenity. The Middle Way, as Mr. Fu had taught her. The Chinese way! She repeated to herself the words of Chuang-tze, the great Taoist scholar: "The man of character lives at home without exercising his mind, and performs actions without worry."

Very well. She would do that. She occupied herself with household tasks, and played with David, and discussed school-work with Eileen. The days went by. It was almost time for

Mike's return from the North. Laura found herself listening for footsteps and voices in the road and knew that was not the way of character, for she was being impatient, but she had not achieved Taoist perfection yet.

Then Mike was home. He was in the kitchen with a laugh and a hug and presents for Eileen and David and a kiss for Laura. Chen had tugged away Mike's suitcase, eager to unpack the clothes and sort out the laundry. There were no other packages to be seen. Laura felt a wave of disappointment so sharp it was almost anger. She tried to calm herself, reminding herself of Chuang-tze and his counsels of wisdom. She closed her eyes and pictured serenity. A lotus pond with glinting golden carp. A rock garden beneath lacy willow leaves. A blue sky with slowly drifting clouds. The voice of Mr. Chow, loud and real, startled her into opening her eyes.

"Where would you like these, Honorable Valentine?"

Mr. Chow was holding two large brown-paper parcels under his arm.

"On the table," said Mike. "Be careful, they're fragile."

"Mike!" Laura cried. "You bought things at the auction!"

"Sure," he said casually, "didn't you expect me to?"

"I guess I wasn't sure. . . . I was worried about how you would manage."

Mike shrugged. "It was a big poker game. Nobody shows any expression; the Japs call it 'keeping-the-face-like-wood.' There were a lot of Japanese there, buying like fury. They were the toughest competition. Everything's done with little move-ments. . . ."

"Unwrap the packages, Mike! And tell me about the auction!"

She gazed in delight at the two unwrapped objects. One was the *temmoku* bowl, a deep and glowing black with a lustre like polished black marble, spotted with irregular stars, more beauti-ful than its picture. The other was a bowl as well, the spinach green jade with its dragons pursuing the sacred pearl.

"Wonderful! They are both wonderful!" Laura threw her arms around Mike. "Now," she cried happily, "on to Nathan Field!"

Mike frowned. Something was happening here regarding the auction, and Laura, and Nathan Field. It was heralding a change in their fortunes, and he wondered if he would like it. He had enjoyed the auction, and yet it was Laura's project.

He remembered the day of the auction in Peking. He had been approaching the auction building in a rickshaw when he saw soldiers standing guard along both sides of the road, rigidly at attention. Mike's rickshaw had been forced to the curb. Three carriages had suddenly appeared, surrounded by outriders, drawn by horses at full gallop. Mike had leaned forward and asked the rickshaw coolie if he knew what personage of importance was traveling the streets.

Yüan Shih-k'ai, came the answer. *The Empress's general.* He was returning from an audience with his empress in the Forbidden City.

Ah. Yüan Shih-k'ai. Could it be that the Manchus feared revolution? To attach such importance to a general?

It could be. It could be.

Mike had wondered to himself what effect this would have on foreign trade in China. Good or bad. Was it sensible, he had asked himself in the rickshaw, to bid for antiques at an auction, in a nation that was about to be ripped apart by change?

But after all, Mike had wrecked his steamer at the bottom of the Yangtze. It was buying antiques, or selling cigarettes, or going home.

Still, looking now at Laura's excited face in Shanghai, Mike wondered if Laura's new career would shut him out, sunder their unity, that oneness that was so important to him.

CHAPTER 6

Laura was seated once again in the library of the mansion on Hungjao Road. Her host, seated opposite her, was attired in a brocaded smoking jacket and was puffing on a silver-inlaid pipe. Laura wore a duplicate pattern of the dress she had worn on the previous visit, made up by the same dressmaker. This version was black with a waistband of goldenrod yellow, and she had changed the feather on the hat to one of pale citron. The ensemble looked completely different from before but just as striking.

On a low table between them stood the two bowls from Peking.

Laura was uneasy. The sale was not progressing. Mr. Field had given the bowls only a casual glance and was now making small talk. He was discussing the recently ended Russo-Japanese War.

"Little Nips surprised the world, didn't they? First time in history that a yellow nation's beaten a white one. Imperial Russia defeated by Japan! Think of that! Now they've got their eye on Manchuria. Watch out for Japan, dear lady."

"Everyone seems to say that," Laura remarked with difficulty. "It's hard for me to believe." Her mind was on the bowls. She wished she could think of a way to turn the conversation from politics to porcelain.

"Free for dinner?" Mr. Field inquired.

"I'm afraid not. I have a three-month-old son at home, and he requires my presence for *his* dinner."

"Well, the afternoon's been pleasant, anyway."

Laura couldn't contain herself any longer. "Mr. Field—you haven't said a word about these bowls!"

"I haven't?" He looked surprised. She couldn't tell if it was real or affected. "Bloody sorry. They're nice. Excellent taste. Fine quality, especially the *temmoku*. This Ch'ing stuff is a little too recent for me." He indicated the green dragons.

"But you're not really interested in either one," Laura said, swallowing a bitter taste of disappointment.

"Not really." He gave her a winning smile. "Try again. Perseverance is the key to success, isn't it? I ought to know."

"Yes, you should." Laura rose to her feet. "As you pointed out last time, you're a very successful man."

"Now you're ruddy angry."

She was angry. She had a sudden powerful desire to even the score between them, for she had lost a battle, but she realized it was a tactical error to display it. She smiled. "No, Mr. Field, not at all. I am a businesswoman. I can't expect to make a sale with every piece of merchandise.''

"That's the attitude to take! Friends?''

"Certainly.'' She paused thoughtfully. Her desire to pique his interest was stronger than ever. Too strong to resist. An idea struck her and with it an impulse that carried its own momentum. She disguised it, but the impulse was pulling her on, quick and powerful. She yielded to it. "You may be making a mistake about Ch'ing Dynasty,'' she said in a pensive tone. "Then again, you may be right. I have some objects of great antiquity at home, a match for the Shang water jars in your entrance hall, but they are not things *off the beaten track*. And besides, the pieces are my own personal property.''

"Oh? Not for sale?''

"I don't believe so.''

"But you're not sure?''

"Not quite.''

"Let me take a look.''

"The price would be extremely high, Mr. Field.''

"Playing little games, are you? I can't be caught out that way.''

She laughed. "Of course you can't. Let's just be friends. I'll continue to shop for you, and if I find something, I'll let you know at once.'' She bent to the table and began to pack the two bowls back into their boxes. "I won't take any more of your time, Mr. Field. I know you're busy.''

"Now, now, my girl, not so fast. You started this game, let's play it, and observe the rules of cricket. What is this personal property of yours?''

Laura straightened and raised an eyebrow. "Cricket rules?''

"That's right.''

"Very well. They are Chou Dynasty libation vessels.''

"Lidded?''

"Yes.''

"Damn it, woman, that's my period! Shang and Chou bronzes are my specialty!''

"Are they, Mr. Field?''

He burst out laughing. "You bought them at auction especially for me! Clever little baggage, aren't you?''

"As a matter of fact, Mr. Field, I did not. They were a gift to me from one of the oldest families of Szechuan Province."

It was Nathan Field's turn to make a thoughtful pause. "I believe you're telling the truth," he said at last. "The straight truth. I would like to see them, Mrs. Valentine. I really would."

"Now I will tell you the truth. I swore to myself never to sell them."

"But you've changed your mind. Why is that?"

"I don't know," Laura said slowly. "You made me angry by refusing the bowls, but that's not the only reason. Perhaps I am a somewhat different person than I was before. Maybe I can no longer afford the luxury of sentiment."

"Balls," said Nathan Field. He grinned. "Don't be so bloody dramatic. You're no romantic heroine, you're just acquiring common sense. If you're going to be in business, be in business. Forget the moonlight and roses. Never mind sacrificing the family heirlooms and posing in a gauze gown like a Victorian martyr. Keep your mind on the balance sheet and the cashbook. This is the twentieth century, dear lady. Grow up. It's high ruddy time."

"That advice may cost you money, Mr. Field!"

"Let me worry about that. Just bring over the damn bronzes and let me see if they're as good as you say!"

In Peking the Dowager Empress T'zu Hsi initiated a series of reforms aimed at bringing China into the modern world. She had been shocked by the Russo-Japanese War and its startling outcome. She allowed her chief adviser, Yüan Shih-k'ai, to create a new army against the menace of Japan. She sent Chinese students to study abroad at government expense. She ordered fourteen new divisions to be recruited for the army, and they began to train with foreign instructors under the direction of the very able Yüan Shih-k'ai. the Dowager Empress didn't intend it, but she was preparing the way for civil war.

While, in Shanghai, Laura sold her bronzes to Nathan Field.

"They are gone, Mike," she said in amazement, at home on Stealing Hen Street. "I was sure I'd never sell them, but I did." She took a breath. "Mike, he paid an enormous price. I'm dazed. What shall we do with the money? Put it in the bank? Buy new furniture?"

"We'll invest it," Mike said, frowning thoughtfully.

"In what? Real estate? Shares of stock?"

"You."

"I don't understand."

"We still have the two Peking bowls, don't we?"

"Yes, but I think I can find buyers for them."

"Exactly. In our own gallery."

"Mike!" Laura was startled. "Do you think we should open a gallery?"

"Why not? You've got some capital now, thanks to Nathan Field. We can risk it. I've still got my job."

"It sounds . . . exciting. And reckless. The idea scares me."

"But your eyes are shining. I can tell you want to do it."

Laura did. The notion seemed to have been with her for a long time, for the details were suddenly falling together in her mind like clanging metal rings. She could see the storefront. The Valentine Gallery. It would have to be in the French Concession, not Chapei, in order to attract tourists from the cruise ships. Pierre-Marc would send her customers. She could sell things to Nathan Field; she understood him now. She said to Mike a little breathlessly, "We would have to find good things to sell. We would need agents in the countryside who know the old and wealthy families with treasures to dispose of. And I would have to go to auctions. . . . Mike, would you help me? I'm scared to death."

"What have you got to lose? Get your dress muddy, sweetheart. You can always buy another one."

She laughed shakily. He was obviously right.

They discussed the project until Laura fell silent, her mind racing with plans. After a while Mike asked, "Are you tired enough to go to bed?"

"I don't think so. I'm too excited about this new idea."

"That's good." He stretched comfortably. "Maybe you're awake enough to go to bed."

Laura blinked, recognizing the look on his face. "Let's talk some more."

"We've talked ourselves hoarse. Let's do something else."

"Mike, how can I concentrate on anything but opening a gallery?"

"Yes, that is a problem." Mike reflected on it with folded arms. Then he said, "I believe I can show you a way to solve it."

Laura gave him a dubious glance.

"Could you manage to keep your mind on taking your clothes off?"

"Don't be silly."

"Without tangling yourself up in your stockings?"

She didn't bother to answer that.

"If you do," he said, "you'll have taken the first step."

"Mike, you're being ridiculous." Laura started to smile.

"Think of me as your doctor. Trust me. After you've taken that first step, disrobing, the rest of my treatment will be easy."

Laura found herself laughing, and rising to her feet, and moving toward him. Very shortly the plans for the new gallery took second place in her mind.

Later, when they were both about to fall asleep, Mike said with sleepy approval, "That was an excellent suggestion you made."

"What suggestion?"

"Coming to bed."

"Oh. I didn't realize I'd made it."

"Take credit anyway. You deserve it."

"If you insist," Laura murmured. They curled up in one another's arms, mutually worn out and happy, and fell asleep.

CHAPTER 7

Mike sat over lunch in a restaurant off the Bund with George Henderson.

"Do you get any time off, George?" he asked.

"A few weeks. I haven't taken a holiday since I started the job. They owe me a vacation."

"Good. Because I have a little trip in mind."

George looked suspicious. "It's something lunatic, knowing you."

Mike shook his head in sorrow. "You're forgetting that I've changed. I'm a family man and a breadwinner now. I have a steady job with a salary. I'm on the water wagon." Then, at George's expression, he laughed. "Okay, you're right. It is lunatic. It's the craziest thing yet, as a matter of fact. But it's worth a try, for Laura's gallery. Did you know she's rented a space?" George nodded. "How's your gun?"

George looked blank.

"The one you used to carry on the steamer, in case of accidents."

"I thought we were talking about Laura's gallery."

"Now we're talking about your gun."

"It's in my bureau drawer." George's tone turned sarcastic. "I didn't figure I'd need it at lunch."

Mike ignored the sarcasm. "Well, clean it and load it, George. We're about to look for treasure in Shansi Province."

"What the hell are you talking about?"

"I met a down-and-out Australian in Peking a while ago who sold me a treasure map. It's supposed to locate a cave in the mountains of Shansi Province, stuffed with loot from the Summer Palace, stolen by a British soldier during the Opium Wars."

"What a whopper of a story."

"That may be so, George. But suppose it's true. Think of the lucky break for the Valentine Gallery. Think of the expression on Laura's face when she sees the loot." Mike had decided to test the map. He wanted to share in the excitement of Laura's venture, and this would be a chance to do it. He would add the treasure hunt to his business trip, so Laura wouldn't know. If he found anything, it would be a surprise. His own surprise.

"There isn't any loot, you hot-air merchant," George exclaimed.

"Are you positive of that?"

Mike gave George a mischievous glance. George sighed and shook his head in exasperation. "You do it every time. I must be nuts."

"Go home and oil your gun, old scout. We'll leave next week."

*   *   *

Mike had business to transact in Shansi Province. Now, with the prospect of a treasure hunt, he considered it irksome and disposed of it as quickly as possible. He visited interior towns with general stores, tacked up his advertising posters on the ramshackle wooden walls, distributed his cigarette samples to the inevitable crowd of gawkers, checked the inventories of the merchant as usual, and wrote up new orders. He planned his itinerary to conclude in Pingyangsien, a town high up on the flat plateau of the southern Shansi mountains. He and George had traveled by train to the end of the railway line, and then by wooden wagon up to the town.

"Now, George," he said with satisfaction, as they prepared to spend the night in Pingyangsien's one inn, "we're free."

"To go treasure-hunting," George said glumly. "Like a couple of birdbrains on a wild-goose chase."

"That's it," said Mike. "Sancho Panza, meet Don Quixote." He laughed. His mood was high. "Now we can hire pack mules and coolies and be on our way."

"I remember the town drunk where I grew up," George remarked. "He used to be a schoolteacher before he took to whiskey. Then he spent all his time in the barbershop drunk as a loon, yammering about a lost gold mine." George paused. "He had a map too."

"A kindred spirit. What happened to him?"

"He died in the barbershop, getting a shave."

"God rest his immortal soul," Mike said with a pious expression. George sighed. "How far is this famous cave?"

"Halfway down the mountain."

"And if there is this well-known loot, do you think we can make it back to Shanghai?"

"Goddamn right," said Mike. "Or die trying."

George nodded thoughtfully. "For once I agree with you. I don't feel like making bandits rich on my sweat and struggle. We paid enough squeeze on the Yangtze."

"It's nice to be in the presence of a man with principles," Mike said in the same pious tone. "It makes a person feel righteous. Don't forget to say your prayers before you go to bed."

"I won't. And I'll be sure to include you." They prepared for sleep.

The mountain country of Shansi Province was a place of brilliant sunshine and eerie silence. Hawks wheeled far up in the cloudless sky, for this was the Chrysanthemum Moon and there was no rain. Below on the trail the only sounds were those of the small mule train: the steady *clop-clop* of the mules' hooves, the crack of the mule drivers' whips, and yells of "yi-yi-yi" to the animals.

No vegetation grew along the miles of ragged cliffs, which were broken by rocky ravines. The soil was loess, soft yellowish-brown earth windblown from the north, drenched by rains in the spring and the fall, baked by the summer sun. The loess was unstable and shifting and liable to slide at any time, bringing with it the side of a mountain.

"George," said Mike, craning his neck to look at the sky, "this place is doing things to my mind. It's too quiet. I'm hearing ghosts from the Opium Wars. Or maybe it's the ghost of Kublai Khan."

"I'll be glad to get back to civilization myself," George muttered. "I'll even be happy to see one of those broken-down resthouses. I think I'm getting spooked."

"Not you, George. You're supposed to be the levelheaded member of this team."

"All I want to know is, where's that cave?"

"According to the map, only a few miles farther on."

"The map better be right. I have a feeling this mountain is preparing to fall on our heads."

They edged their way down the sloping trail.

Laura gazed with pleasure at her new gallery. It was empty, but the walls were freshly painted a soft apricot. The sign was in place outside, white on gray, discreetly lettered: THE VALENTINE GALLERY.

She needed to stock it. Laura pictured beautiful objects in glass cases, on stone pedestals, along teakwood shelves, objects of ebony and porcelain, ivory and jade, lacquer and gold and silk. Treasures of China. Works of ancient loveliness, mellowed with time, cherished through the centuries. She missed the presence of Mike beside her at night, as she always did when he was away, but this fresh venture was filling part of the void his absence left behind. One image of the past hovered persistently in her memory: the house of Madame Wei, behind its wall on the upper Yangtze. Everything it contained.

The house of Madame Wei. Laura grew thoughtful. She was recalling young Mr. Wei in his Western business suit and polka-dot necktie, at the riverfront in Weichang.

"In order to build my new house, I must sell the treasures my grandmother left me."

Hadn't he said something like that? It had been eighteen months ago.

Perhaps he had not yet sold his inheritance. Perhaps he had installed his telephones. Perhaps he would deal with Laura. Perhaps, perhaps. The Wei family treasures might be waiting for the Valentine Gallery at the head of the Yangtze River. *Lord, lord,* Laura whispered to herself, *imagine the house of Madame Wei!*

"Lord, Mike," breathed George Henderson, "look at that."

They were standing in a Shansi cave. Both held torches made of sticks smeared with burning pitch. Bats flapped around their heads, then disappeared into the darkness beyond. At the mouth of the cave in the daylight stood the mule drivers and coolies, smoking their daily opium allowance. Opium was part of their wages. They had refused to enter the cave.

Mike and George were staring at a huge bronze turtle, half revealed in the flickering torchlight.

"That's the ugliest thing I've ever seen," said Mike.

"I think it used to hold up the column of a *p'ai lou.* You know, a memorial arch at the entrance to a tomb."

"I believe it." Mike squatted down and peered at the enormous turtle, lowering his torch for a better look. "On second thought," he remarked, "she's got a nice smile."

"So there was a Tommy soldier after all," George said musingly. His voice cast echoes off the damp and glistening rock all around them.

"I told you not to be such a skeptic." Mike stood up, gazed about and started. "What's that?"

"What's what?"

Both of them were on edge. There were even more ghosts in the cave than there had been on the trail.

"That . . . thing in the shadows."

George squinted through the torchlight. "It's another animal. A bird; a bronze crane. See its silhouette against the wall? The long neck and the beak?"

"Yeah, I see it." Mike squared his shoulders. "Well, let's take a look around. Farther in. Maybe there's more."

Forty-five minutes later, deep inside the cave, they were surrounded by open packing cases and shredded paper. Their torches were wedged into crevices and burning low. George stuck his screwdriver back into his tool belt, next to his loaded gun.

"I think this is it, Mike."

"I think so too. Now we've got to make some choices. We can't get all this junk onto the mules."

"That's your department. I'm no art critic."

"But you know what you like?"

"Don't be funny."

Mike surveyed their find with a frown. "There must have been more than one looter, George. Probably got picked off by bandits on the trail and never made it back to Peking. That yarn about the soldier was a lot of romantic hogwash."

"Where did the map come from?"

"Well, one guy must have made it back. But I'm sure there was more than one to begin with. A single man couldn't have handled all these boxes. You remember reading what it was like at the Summer Palace. Everybody grabbing with both hands. Still, all this?" He waved at the objects on the cave floor: a dinner service for eighteen, of cobalt blue and gold; temple jars with enamel lids; tureens and covered bowls on matching porcelain stands; beakers on ormolu bases decorated with designs of court ladies in exotic coiffures.

"Somebody liked dishes," George remarked.

"I wish I knew what was worthless and what was valuable." Mike thought of the auction. It seemed to him that the decorated beakers had been disdained, and so had the colorful tureens. "I have a feeling," he said, "that Laura will like the turtle and the crane."

"My God, we can't handle those. They're enormous."

"If we leave some of this other stuff, we can. We'll wrap them up in paper and tie them with ropes and load them on three mules each. Of course we'll take that." He indicated the blue-and-gold dinner service. "Those dishes are pretty. I wouldn't mind eating off them myself. And some of the jars."

George took a deep breath. "Okay, let's get started. Call the coolies."

"First they'll have to do their mumbo-jumbo, to exorcise the demons of the cave."

"At this point I'm ready to help them."

They both unwedged their torches, now very dim, and started back for the cave mouth and the welcoming daylight.

Laura was struggling with the telephone. She was calling Weichang from the lobby of Nathan Field's hotel on the Bund. She was shouting through whistles and static.

"Mr. Wei, is that you?" she called.

"Yes, it is I." A tiny, far-off voice.

"This is Mrs. Valentine, in Shanghai. Can you hear me?"

"Yes, I can hear you." The voice was calm, even through the static.

Laura breathed deeply to relax. She lowered the pitch of her voice. "I am calling about your inheritance. Have you sold it?"

He had not. Would he deal with Laura? He might. Would he deal with Laura's agent, since she could not leave her nursing infant? That would depend on the person Laura sent.

"You will hear from me, Mr. Wei!" Laura called into the flowerlike speaker. She replaced the receiver on its hook and wiped her damp palms on a handkerchief. So far all was well.

That night, over cups of tea, she sat across the kitchen table from Chen, who wore a stubbornly unwilling expression.

"If I go to Weichang," he said, "who will cook?"

"I will cook."

"That is unsuitable."

"We can manage for a short while," Laura said firmly. "I will keep the door closed. No one will see me in the kitchen."

"I know nothing about bargaining for treasures," Chen objected.

"You will communicate with me by telephone every night."

"Telephone!" He looked even more frightened.

"You will take Plum Blossom with you," Laura said as an added inducement.

That shocked Chen out of his obstinacy. "Certainly not, missy!" he exclaimed. "You cannot be alone in the house without the master, and with a young child to tend!"

"Chinese women do it all the time."

That was so silly he didn't even bother to answer.

"But that means you'll have to travel alone," Laura said after a moment.

"I am not afraid," Chen declared. He lifted his chin. "I have traveled before. I am no country bumpkin."

"Good. I was sure I could count on you."

Chen looked abashed. "You have tricked me, missy."

"Only a little." Laura smiled in apology. "For my gallery."

After a pause he smiled back, and they sipped their tea in a spirit of understanding.

Mike and George had reached the foot of the mountains with their loot intact. They were spending the night at a Chinese inn, a one-story mud-walled structure at the bottom of a hill covered in scrub oak. The courtyard of the inn was surrounded by a flimsy-looking fence made of willow and oak branches. George was conspicuously oiling his revolver. He and Mike were seated on the k'ang in the common room; the k'ang was a brick platform heated by a flue in the winter. Tonight it was where they would sleep.

"This is a good place for a bandit attack," George muttered. "They've got plenty of trees for cover."

"We've got the Empress's soldiers for protection."

A few Chinese soldiers were sharing the inn with them, along with a dramatically bearded Russian in a belted tunic, who had informed George and Mike in bad English that he was a fur trader looking for dogskins.

"Some soldiers," said George. "Did you see their weapons?"

"Yeah. One Winchester repeater and a bunch of old muzzle-loaders. I wonder where they got the Winchester?"

"Probably from Teddy Roosevelt's Rough Riders. As a foreign loan."

Mike laughed.

At that moment a bullet exploded into the room with a whistling whine and buried itself in the back wall, scattering mud all over the floor.

"Jesus!" said Mike. "Was that what I thought?"

"Bandits!" cried the Russian. He sprang to his feet with an excited yip. "Bandits are attacking!"

Mike grabbed the innkeeper's arm as the man passed. "Who's shooting?"

"*Hung hutze,*" said the innkeeper. "Bandits."

Mike stood up and withdrew his own revolver from his belt. "They don't get my property," he said grimly.

He and George joined the milling group of soldiers in the courtyard. Bullets were whistling haphazardly over the inn roof. The soldiers were firing at random into the trees. They didn't appear to have an officer. No one seemed to be hitting anything.

Mike and George stationed themselves on either side of the gate in kneeling positions.

"What is this, a comic opera?" George said after a moment.

"I don't know, but somebody could get killed. Those are real bullets."

They squinted into the trees. Here and there was a gray-clad back. Mike aimed carefully and fired. Someone yelped. The Russian, by the fence, shouted in glee. "Good shot!"

"Take this," said George, getting to his feet. He shoved his gun into Mike's left hand.

"Where are you going?"

"The guy with the Winchester hasn't fired it once. I don't think he knows what to do with it."

The confusion increased. The soldiers fired without aiming, and so did the bandits. Bullets ricocheted off the trees, the gate, the wall of the inn. Within the mud structure the innkeeper and his helpers were continuing to prepare the evening meal; they were visible through the open door. Mike found himself next to the Russian by the gate.

"That innkeeper doesn't seem very worried," he remarked.

"They are all in—how do you say? Cahoots?"

"I wouldn't be a bit surprised."

Then came the bark of the Winchester, sounding fast and accurate. George had taken it away from the soldier, who had raised no objection. He was using it to good advantage.

After that the fight ended quickly. The bandits melted into the trees, apparently not liking the sound of the opposition. They filed back into the inn, putting away their weapons, and were served boiled noodles and roast pork.

"Tomorrow we reach the railroad," said Mike, stretching, once again seated on the *k'ang*. "Shanghai, end of the line."

"I'll believe it when I see it."

"Same old skeptic."

On the railway platform they had a violent argument with the stationmaster before they boarded the train. Mike and George announced that their packing cases and two huge parcels were accompanying them in the passenger car. The stationmaster said absolutely not. Baggage had to go in the baggage car. Faces grew red. Voices were raised. Fists were clenched and shaken.

Mike and George ended up in the baggage car seated on their packing cases with their revolvers across their laps. They'd lost the argument.

It was three o'clock in the morning. They were keeping one another awake. The train jolted and bounced; Mike glared at the box with the dinner service. "I think I'll go and break the engineer's neck. This is worse than the mules."

George yawned. "I hope Laura appreciates all this when we get to Shanghai," he said sleepily.

"She will. And stop complaining. You haven't had so much fun since Yellow Cat Gorge."

George was too tired to deny it.

Laura was thrilled with the crane and the turtle. "You never told me about a map!" she exclaimed in their kitchen.

"I try to tell you everything, sweetheart," Mike said virtuously, "but sometimes a detail escapes me."

"And this dinner service is absolutely beautiful!"

"I thought it was kind of pretty myself."

"Did you have trouble getting it here?"

"Oh, no," he said. "No trouble. Easy as pie."

Laura sighed happily. "I'm expecting many shipments from Weichang. They're coming by rail. Mike, I spent all our money! I bought like a drunken sailor! Over the telephone, with Chen and Mr. Wei!"

"So we have a start."

"Yes, but it's not like money in the bank." A worried look crossed her face.

"Sure it is. Better." Mike glanced around the kitchen. "I have a hunch we'll be leaving this dump pretty soon, and I can quit that boring job."

"Do you, Mike?"

"I surely do, baby. I'm good at hunches. That's the Irish in me. And I have another one as well."

"What is that?"

He unbuttoned his jacket and threw it over the back of a chair. Then he unloosened his tie and reached for Laura's waist. "I have a feeling," he said with a happy, cocksure grin, "that I'm going to like being rich. What time is it?"

"Late."

He buried his face in her hair. "Let's celebrate."

CHAPTER 8

The Dowager Empress of China died in 1908, at the age of seventy-three. Her death signaled the end of the Manchu Dynasty. Sun Yat-sen's Sworn Chinese Brotherhood became the foremost revolutionary organization of the country and was shortly to achieve its goal: ridding China of the Manchus. Without the Dowager Empress the Peking government was confused and drifting.

Then the worst crop failure in forty years struck the Yangtze provinces, and the farmers grew desperate. The army garrisons in Szechuan and Hupeh stirred restlessly. The wealthy were already angry over increased taxes, the result of the military reorganization and building of the railways.

On October 10, 1911, the revolution began in Hankow, a Yangtze city, as troops of a garrison calling themselves the "Modern Army" rose in rebellion against Peking. Uprisings spread to the west and south.

October 10, double ten, subsequently became a holiday in China, for it marked the birth of Sun Yat-sen's republic. The tyranny of the North was destroyed. The future looked radiant, at least to the young and radical. Older, more conservative men and women were fearful. Was this good? Could it endure? Was it according to the teachings of Confucius? No. It was an upset of the established order. That was always a bad thing. Always.

America was happy to acknowledge the new republic, for America was a republic herself. As recognition ceremonies took place, Chinese bands played "The Star Spangled Banner" and Chinese schoolchildren waved tiny American flags on bunting-draped platforms all over the country.

Just after the famous date of double ten, a fifty-horsepower, six-cylinder Rolls-Royce limousine, painted silver gray, driven by a Chinese chauffeur in a dove-gray uniform who sat high up on the open seat, braked to a halt in front of an office building on the Shanghai Bund.

Mike Valentine stepped out of the backseat without waiting for the chauffeur. After him came George Henderson. George had gained weight and lost hair. He was now the head engineer of the shipyard where he worked, but his face wore a familiar expression of exasperated disapproval. They paused on the sidewalk.

"Did you have to buy this limousine?" George inquired.

"It's the latest thing. Straight off the docks from London."

"Does Laura like the idea?"

"I don't need Laura's approval for every move I make. That may come as a surprise to you, George."

Mike looked splendid. He wore a black cashmere coat with a white silk scarf and a black derby hat at a rakish angle over his eye, and he was smoking a rich-smelling cigar.

"Sure you won't have a cigar?" he asked.

"You know I don't smoke."

"You don't do much of anything these days, do you? Why don't you get some new clothes? And get rid of that paunch?"

"Why, so I can look like you?" George frowned. "You look like a Tammany Hall politician in that derby."

"It's a bowler, you chump."

"Where I come from we call it a derby."

Mike let it pass. "Come up to the office for a minute. I have to check some invoices."

Mike used the office as a convenience, since he now supervised the export dealings of the Valentine Galleries. Six years had gone by since the opening of the first gallery. There were three galleries now in Shanghai and a branch in San Francisco, managed by a Chinese-American dealer who made frequent trips to Shanghai. There was correspondence and there were invoices, shipping orders, and profit-and-loss statements. None of it took up a full day, however. Mike had plenty of leisure. He had joined the Shanghai Club, meeting place for all the successful foreign businessmen of the city.

Laura did the buying for the galleries and supervised the employees. The Valentines had moved from Chapei to a spacious home on Bubbling Well Road. They had a new circle of friends in the close-knit, gossipy English-speaking community of the International Settlement. Laura did not have time for the long luncheons at the Palm Court of the Astor House Hotel, as some of the other women did, but she and Mike entertained in the evening.

David had begun day school. Eileen was in boarding school, for the sake of discipline. She had started to be a problem, for her long-buried resentment of Laura was beginning to surface. It was almost as though she were competing with her mother for her father's attention. Mike and Laura had agreed that Miss Haverford's School, with its strict regulations, might be the answer. She was allowed to spend alternate weekends at home.

Inside the office Mike went to his desk. He removed his derby and scaled it across the room to the hatrack in the corner. It landed neatly on a hook.

Mike lifted an approving eyebrow at his own skill. "That calls for a drink." He pulled open his bottom desk drawer and removed a bottle of Scotch and two glasses.

"Mike, it's only eleven thirty."

"Practically lunchtime. I thought I was buying you lunch?"

"Okay, but wait until we get to the restaurant before you start drinking."

"Lay off me, George. I get enough nagging at home." Mike poured himself a double shot and swallowed defiantly.

Same old story, thought George as he watched. *Gradual but steady. Back to the old habits.*

Mike sat down behind his desk and put his feet up. "Do you ever miss the old days, George?" he asked. "Running the river rapids? Fighting off bandits in Shansi?"

"Sometimes I do."

"So do I." He sipped his Scotch.

"Don't you enjoy being a man of property? Spending your afternoons at the Long Bar of the Shanghai Club? Playing high-stakes poker? Riding around town in your fancy motor car?"

"Sure, it's okay." But it was not all he had expected.

The trouble was, thought Mike, he was Laura's husband. He didn't like the role. She ran the Valentine Galleries, and Shanghai knew it. He didn't even go to auctions anymore; she did the bidding and the purchasing. She traveled on the train to Peking and Tientsin with a specially hired bodyguard.

And those employees of hers! That simpering little fairy she'd hired off the boat from San Francisco! The last time Mike'd visited the main gallery, he'd heard a meant-to-be audible whisper from behind him.

"Doesn't she look smashing!" hissed the voice.

There were no women visible. Mike whirled. "You," he said in a hard tone, "come over here."

The young man approached half fearfully, half expectantly.

"Are you trying to get fired?" Mike said ominously.

"N-no, Mr. Valentine."

"Then what are you looking for? A punch in the nose?"

The young man didn't answer. Maybe he was, thought Mike in disgust, seeing his expression. He turned and started toward Laura's office in the rear.

"Rough trade," murmured the young man under his breath as

Mike departed. "And she's so chic and refined. I just don't understand it."

Mike finished his double Scotch. He felt it warming the pit of his stomach, relaxing him a little. "Okay, George," he said, "I think I'm ready for lunch."

"You were going to look over some invoices. That's why we stopped."

"It can wait."

"In other words, you stopped for that belt of Scotch."

"Is the Shanghai Club all right with you?" Mike said evenly.

"Sure. I can't afford the membership anyway." George paused. "But you'll stay there all afternoon, won't you? Drinking at the bar."

"I told you to lay off me, George."

"It's your funeral. I'm through giving advice as of today, Mr. Valentine, you're a big boy now."

I'm almost a woman, Eileen thought breathlessly. She peered at herself in the mirror in her room at Miss Haverford's School. Whom did she resemble? Mary Pickford? Mae Marsh? No. Lillian Gish in *Musketeers of Pig Alley,* so far Eileen's favorite movie. She didn't much care for the pie-throwing slapstick comedies shown in Shanghai's one movie theater, although Chinese audiences loved them. But *Musketeers of Pig Alley* was exactly to her taste.

Yes, she decided, Lillian Gish, fragile and ethereal and lovely, courageous in the midst of horrible circumstances (like Eileen herself at Miss Haverford's School). Arousing all a man's protective instincts. Suffering! But brave!

She was not quite fourteen, but Eileen had already blossomed. Round and perfect breasts swelled beneath her school uniform. Her hips curved gracefully from a slender waist. Her face was radiant, full-lipped and wide-eyed, her eyes a melting blue, her mouth a soft pink, her face framed by honey blond hair.

If only she didn't have to pin her hair back! The style was so ugly! So was the uniform!

Eileen thought everything about Miss Haverford's School was ugly, including Miss Haverford. The gray brick building (like a prison). The dark oak walls. The framed Bible texts hanging

everywhere you looked. Even if it was, as everyone informed
her, the most fashionable school on the China coast for Western
young ladies. What of that? She detested it, she felt pent-up,
handcuffed, shackled. Her mother had sent her here! Daddy
would never have consented if she hadn't forced him! She nagged
him! No wonder he escaped into a bottle of whiskey! She,
Eileen, would do exactly the same in his position!

Eileen grew depressed when she thought of her parents. Once
she had come upon them embracing in the kitchen and retreated
hastily, feeling sick to her stomach.

She'd flung herself across the bed in her room. How could he!
How could he! She felt betrayed, deceived. Cheated. He didn't
love her! How could he kiss her that way? It was disgusting! She
wanted to cry.

Now she glanced at her schoolbooks piled on her desk. She
had pages and pages of Latin to translate. Cicero's *Orations*. *The
Musketeers of Pig Alley* was still being shown at the movie
theater; in Shanghai they always showed the same movie for
weeks, sometimes months, it took so long for a new one to arrive
by ship. But she couldn't go; it was against the rules. She
couldn't leave the building. There were thousands of rules at
Miss Haverford's School.

She went to the window and leaned out. It was a beautiful
October day, damp and mild with fleeting sunshine, typical of
this season in Shanghai. The gardener's boy was raking the lawn.

Eileen bent over the windowsill. She could speak to the
gardener's boy, for his parents were from Szechuan, and he
spoke the same dialect as Plum Blossom.

"Hey there! Kiang!" she called softly.

He looked up. "Yes, Honorable Student?"

"Want to take me to the cinema?"

He looked startled. "I cannot do that."

"Don't be a turtle's egg, of course you can. I'll pay for it. I
still have my allowance."

"I must rake the lawn."

"Finish raking the lawn and then meet me by the back door.
I'll sneak out."

He straightened indignantly. "You are breaking the rules,

Honorable Student. If you wish to do that, go to the cinema alone. Don't entangle me in your disobedience to your elders.''

"Oh, what an old-fashioned prude! Don't you know there's been a revolution?" Eileen pouted prettily. "You can stay home and read Confucius if you choose, like an old graybeard, but you don't know what you'll be missing. The world will be passing you by. You could be sitting in the dark with me, holding my hand. Being modern.''

He was only a Chinese gardener's boy, and not very good-looking at that, but he was the only male available at the moment.

He was wavering. She was not only enticing him, but she had challenged his style. She had used the most provocative word of the day: *modern*. All young Chinese desired ardently to be modern, especially in Shanghai. Eileen smiled to herself. Boys were so easy to manage. Grown men might be more difficult, but right now there was only one adult man she cared about, and he was already taken. By her mother. That thought made Eileen too angry and ill to dwell on; she dismissed it.

"Well, Kiang?" she asked. "Are you coming?"

"I will come," he said anxiously. "Let me finish the lawn." He bent and began to rake with quick movements.

Eileen laughed and withdrew to comb her hair.

Chen approached the house on Bubbling Well Road with shame and anguish. His body was trembling. The market basket on his arm was shaking with the force of his emotion.

Ai ya! How could he go inside like this? How could he face his wife? He was unmanned, humiliated, lower than the dust! A terrible thing had happened to him. As he reached the kitchen door, he put his hand to his head and began to weep.

Finally he collected himself, pushed open the kitchen door, and went inside. He prayed the room would be empty, postponing the moment of facing anyone. But Plum Blossom was there, sipping tea at the kitchen table.

She glanced up, then her face changed.

"Chen?" she said wonderingly. "My husband? What has happened to you?" She rose to her feet. "Your hair! Your beautiful queue!"

Slow, hot tears ran down Chen's face. He bowed his shorn

head. "Soldiers were in the marketplace," he said. "Soldiers of the revolution. They seized us and some held our arms and others cut off our queues with sharp swords. They said we must no longer wear them, for they are symbols of bondage."

"My poor husband!"

"I am no longer a man," said Chen in sorrow. "I can no longer be a husband to you. Leave me and find someone more worthy."

Plum Blossom sprang away from the table, ran to him, and flung her arms around him. "You are a man," she said fiercely. "You have proved it in the best way possible. I was going to tell you tonight. Husband, I have wonderful news."

"What news could there be to take away this shame?"

She whispered in his ear. A radiant smile spread across Chen's face. "Is it true?" he said, drawing back and gazing into her eyes. "After all these years?"

"Yes, it is true. Kwan-Yin has answered my prayers."

"When will our child be born?"

"During the Budding Moon."

Chen sighed deeply. "You have erased my shame," he said. "You have given me back my life."

"Our child will do that," said Plum Blossom. "He will be handsome, strong, and wise."

"Perhaps it will be a daughter."

"Then she will be beautiful, strong, and wise. The child of a new age." Plum Blossom's voice grew husky with feeling. "Forget your queue, my husband. We are living in a new China. We are bringing forth a new life to join the sweep of destiny. Should we not rejoice?"

They embraced again, both too moved to speak.

Laura was about to hold an auction. In her office at the rear of the main gallery she studied a printer's proof of the first page of the catalog. She wore a simple black frock, artfully constructed from a sketch by Paul Poiret, who had indeed become the rage of Paris. His designs suited Laura perfectly. Her early promise of beauty had been fulfilled; at thirty-three she had matured into striking womanhood. She read the opening catalog page, absorbed in her work and unconscious of herself.

THE VALENTINE GALLERIES. An illustrated catalog of a collection of antique Chinese bronzes, beautiful old porcelains, amber and stone carvings, and fine old carpets, rugs, and furniture from ancient palaces and temples of China, composing the private collection of a Chinese nobleman of Tientsin, and other objects procured by Mrs. Laura Valentine during a recent visit to ancient cities of China. To be sold at public sale at The Valentine Gallery in the French Concession of Shanghai. 1911.

"How does it look?"

Laura glanced up. Ronald, her salesman from San Francisco, was standing in the doorway.

"Passable," she said. "It's a rather long sentence in English, but it reads well in Chinese."

Ronald made a face. "I wish you didn't know so much. It makes me feel nervous."

"I don't know much at all," Laura said honestly. "I keep expecting to be exposed as a fraud. I try to learn faster, but there's always more and more to know."

"I would be satisfied, if I were you." Ronald grinned. "Mrs. Owen of the cruise ship bought the wide-mouthed pot. You know, the one in enamel and cloisonné."

"That's good news. I didn't think she'd buy anything."

He rolled up his eyes. "She's going to use it as a planter in her upstairs hall in Philadelphia."

Laura laughed. "You should be used to American tourists by now."

"What would we do without them?" Ronald said piously. "But when are you going to let me wait on Nathan Field?"

"He's stubborn; he says he only deals with owners, in any establishment."

"Oh, well." Ronald paused. "I have a telephone message for you. It came in just before you arrived."

"Who was it?"

"Miss Haverford."

"Oh, no." Laura groaned to herself. Eileen was in trouble again. And Mike would not discipline her. It would be up to her, Laura. And she and Eileen were not getting along at all. Mike was drinking heavily; that upset her too. They were heading for another crisis. Only six-year-old David was no problem. He was a sweet, obedient little boy, anxious to do the right thing at all times. Maybe that was a problem. Maybe he was too passive; maybe he should be more of a fighter; was he a mama's boy? Life did not get easier: it grew more complicated.

"Ronald, would you close the door behind you?" she said. "I'd better telephone Miss Haverford right away."

For a moment, with her hand on the instrument, she thought wistfully of Stealing Hen Street. They'd been so happy. Mike had been sober. David had been an adorable baby. Eileen had not yet reached troublesome adolescence. They'd been poor, but it hadn't seemed to matter. Most of all she and Mike had been happy together. Now they were sometimes close in bed, but at other times Mike was sullen and hostile, coming home later and later, always slightly unsteady on his feet. She wondered where it would lead, where they were heading.

She forced herself to think of Eileen, not Mike, as she prepared to speak to Miss Haverford.

CHAPTER 9

Laura was confronting Eileen, who had been sent home by Miss Haverford's private chauffeur.

"Did you think of what you were doing?" Laura demanded. She was trying very hard to control her anger, but Eileen was not making it easy. She was not showing any repentance, but sat slouched in a chair in her parents' bedroom with a sulky and stubborn expression on her face. She nudged at an invisible spot on the carpet with her toe.

"Will you look at me when I talk to you!" Laura cried. She

immediately regretted her tone of voice. *I sound like a fishwife.
How does she manage to do this to me every time?*

"I'm looking at you now," Eileen muttered.

"With a more attentive expression please?"

"Yes, Mother." The words were accompanied by a heavy,
martyred sigh.

There was no winning, Laura thought in despair. Whatever
you did, they had a way of putting you in the wrong. Then her
anger at Eileen overcame her again.

"Eileen," she said, "whatever occurs between us will not
have shattering consequences to you. But that gardener's boy lost
his job. Do you understand what that means?"

"I suppose I do."

"I doubt it. You are spoiled and selfish, or you would not
have behaved that way to a young man who desperately needs
employment. It was your fault, wasn't it? Not his?"

"Yes, it was mine. I told that to Miss Haverford."

"But are you sorry?"

"Oh, Mother, what do you want me to say? Of course I'm
sorry."

"What do you suggest we do about it?"

"Give him a job at our house?" Eileen said tentatively.

"I'm sure he wants nothing more to do with you or your house
or your family."

"Then let's send Daddy over to Miss Haverford's and *force*
her to hire him back!" Eileen's face had suddenly come alive.

Laura paused. She picked up a silver-backed hairbrush from
the dressing table, then put it down. "As a matter of fact," she
said, "I have already done that. I have persuaded Miss Haverford
to agree that the boy should not be punished for your bad
behavior. She's hired him back."

"*You* did it!" Eileen's eyes blazed. "Then what was all this
charade?"

"Suppose you tell me."

"To impress me with what a naughty girl I've been."

"Yes, Eileen, exactly."

"Oh, you can fix anything! You are just a perfect person!" No
longer passive, now quivering with emotion, Eileen jumped to

her feet. "You don't leave anything for anyone else, do you? You have to take care of everything yourself! Like a parazon!"

"Paragon," Laura whispered automatically.

Eileen didn't even hear the correction. She was on fire with her own rage. "No wonder Daddy hates you!" she shouted. "No wonder he drinks! To get away from you! Can't you see it? I do! I understand him better than you ever will! I always did! We are just alike!" She paused for breath. Laura was too shocked by the onslaught to say anything. "Why don't you go away?" Eileen cried half-tearfully. "Go to Aunt Julia, and take David with you, the way you were going to take me once. To get me away from Daddy! But you can't! I'll look after him after you've gone. We don't need you!"

"Eileen, what are you saying?" Laura whispered. She was trembling inwardly and felt the blood drain out of her face. She thought that she must be paper white.

Eileen was flushed, her eyes glittering with tears, her bosom heaving. "I mean it, Mother!" she cried.

"What the hell is going on here?" Mike's voice said from the threshold. "What is it?" He stalked into the room. "I could hear you shouting all the way in the downstairs front hall."

"Daddy!" Eileen turned to him with an expression of joy. She ran to him and buried her face in his shoulder. "Tell her to go home to America," she mumbled. "Tell her we don't need her in Shanghai. That's what I've been saying."

Mike took Eileen by the shoulders and held her away from him. "Are you referring to your mother?" he asked.

"Why . . . why, yes."

"Are you referring to your mother as *her*?"

"I . . . suppose so."

Eileen's joy was turning to puzzlement. Mike had never spoken to her in that stern tone before. She was his favorite, his pet, his "best girl."

"Don't do that again," he said. "I don't like it."

"I'm . . . I'm sorry, Daddy, I won't do it again." Eileen tried to give him a winning smile, to draw him into their usual alliance.

"You've been getting away with murder, Eileen," Mike said, instead of responding to her smile. "From now on you'll show a little respect to your mother and me and behave like a lady, or you will be very sorry. Do you understand?"

Eileen nodded.

"I expect to see a change in your behavior. For the better. Is that clear?"

She nodded again. Her flush had turned to pallor.

"Now go to your room. Your mother and I have private business to discuss." Mike gave her a tiny push toward the door.

Eileen went like a sleepwalker.

This was a worse punishment, Laura thought, than anything she herself could have devised. She looked down at her hands, feeling a quick stab of sympathy. In spite of her appearance Eileen was still a child.

"Thank you, Mike," she said. "I wasn't dealing with her very well."

He shrugged. "I've been too easygoing myself. What was she saying?"

"Silly juvenile accusations." Laura tried to laugh. "She claims I'm driving you to drink."

"Maybe you are."

Laura glanced up swiftly. "Do you believe that?"

"I don't know. Come out to dinner with me and we'll talk it over."

"Oh, Mike, I'd enjoy that. But not tonight—I have to work on the auction. Tomorrow night would be so much better—oh, no, tomorrow night we've invited Marie and Francis—"

She was making a mistake; she had already made it. She saw it from his scowl. Everything she did was wrong!

"On second thought I'll come," she said, rising to her feet, trying to redeem her error.

"Well, good. I'll have you to myself for the first time in weeks. No daughter, none of your chatterbox girl friends, no galleries, no auctions. Just us. I'll buy you champagne."

"It sounds wonderful, Mike." Laura paused. "Champagne instead of Scotch will be a nice change for you." The words slipped out.

"I don't know why we can't have both," he said evenly. "I will, anyway."

She had made still another mistake, a bad one. She knew him

too well. She'd seen the quick flare of anger in his eyes, heard the too-quiet tone of his response.

"How much have you had already?" she asked. *Have this out. It was too late to redeem anything now.*

"None of your business."

"It is my business, Mike. You know it is. I'm worried about you." *Mike, don't do this to us again!*

"Stay home and work on your auction, sweetheart," he said soothingly. "Stop worrying about me. And when you've finished your work and finished your worrying," he gave her a bright, hard smile as he turned to leave, "you can go straight to hell."

Late that night Mike sat alone in the lamplight in the library. He glanced at the mantelpiece clock. Late. Very late. Too late to wake up Laura: she'd only mumble about his drinking and how she had to get up early in the morning. Goddamn nag. She was too goddamn busy these days. She had time for everybody but him. Some wife. Some marriage. Nagging and neglect. No wonder he needed a shot of Scotch to get to sleep. Anybody would. He poured himself another drink.

Through the cloud of whiskey-soaked self-pity he had a clear thought: *Laura is about to leave me. Again. And once more it is my own fault.*

He struggled to keep hold of his insight. The thing to do was . . . quit. Pour this bottle of Scotch down the sink and sober up. Now. This minute. Then stay that way. He'd done it before. It wasn't so hard. Just . . . pour it down the sink. Not so difficult. He tried to rise.

Yes, it was.

"I'll do it tomorrow," he muttered, sinking back. "Shame to waste good Scotch. Paid a lot of money for it. Can't throw money out the window. Worked hard for it. Fought bandits in Shansi, didn't I?"

He was making alibis to himself and he knew it. He was thirty-nine, and if he lost Laura, his life would be ended. He'd go straight to hell like that Aussie in Peking. Christ. All over at thirty-nine. Fear washed over him, driving him back to the whiskey. It was a rotten circle, around and around, like one of those mules pulling a waterwheel. He didn't know how to get off. Alternately weeping a little, then angry, then crying again, he finished the bottle.

CHAPTER 10

Laura was in the servants' wing of the house on Bubbling Well Road. She was in the bed-sitting room of Chen and Plum Blossom, as an honored and invited guest. Chen stood proudly behind his wife's armchair. Plum Blossom sat gazing with rapture at the bundle in her arms. The baby was three months old.

"He is beautiful," said Laura. "Absolutely beautiful. May I hold him?"

"Certainly." Plum Blossom handed over her precious bundle.

Laura folded aside the blanket. The baby gazed up at her with huge black eyes. He was indeed beautiful, with a look of alertness and intelligence. His skin was like ivory satin flushed with rose. His hair was like black silk. Even beneath the round infant flesh one could see the sculptured line of his cheekbones.

Laura kissed his neck. The baby accepted it placidly. How good it was, thought Laura, to cuddle a baby again.

"What will you name him?" she asked. "It's long past time. Will you call him after Plum Blossom's hero? Sun Yat-sen?"

"No," replied Plum Blossom. "I considered it, but it seemed to me he would not want the name of a famous leader but something more original. He has an independent nature."

"You cannot tell in a child so young," scolded Chen.

"I can tell," said Plum Blossom, serenely.

"Honorable Mrs. Valentine," Chen said in a formal tone, "you would honor our humble family by becoming our son's godmother."

"It is I who would be honored by such a dignity," Laura replied, equally formally. "Your son will be a member of our household from this day on."

Chen bowed. "I will call him after you," he said. "Laurence Chen."

"Perhaps he would not like that," said Laura hesitantly. "To be called after a woman might not be suitable."

Chen looked slightly relieved. "In that case," he said, "may I have your permission to name him after your honorable father?"

"My father?" Laura smiled to herself, thinking of Mr. Canfield in Connecticut and how amazed he would be at this beautiful little Chinese namesake. "Why, yes, Chen. That would be lovely."

"What is your father's name?"

"His name is Henry."

"Hen-ree. It is almost Chinese." Chen took the baby from Laura's arms. "We will baptize him in the Christian church," he said with pride. He held steadfastly to his Christian beliefs, despite his wife's faith in Kwan-Yin.

Laura stood up, since all of them realized the purpose of her visit was accomplished. "Inform me of the day of the baptism," she said, "so that I may be sure to attend."

"Of course. It will be prior to your departure for the mountains."

Everyone who could afford it went to the mountains in the summer, to escape the stifling humidity of Shanghai. Usually Chen accompanied Laura and the children while Mike remained in the city to supervise the business. This summer, however, Laura, in a private conversation, had asked Chen to stay with Mike.

"Look after him, Chen," she'd said anxiously. "Don't let him do anything . . . reckless."

"I understand, missy. I will do my best."

"I know you will. And you can trust me to keep my eye on Plum Blossom and the baby."

She didn't want Mike to be alone in the house. Suppose he fell asleep with a burning cigar in his hand? No, not "fell asleep." Passed out. He was drinking harder than ever. Their relationship had worsened, and she was exhausted all the time, with dark circles under her eyes. She could no longer keep up with his sexual demands, for when he was drunk he did not lose his capacity to make love but instead became tireless. There were nights when she was too weary to engage in a prolonged and complicated bout of lust. Then she felt guilty for refusing.

"I'm just not the young girl I used to be," she said apologetically one night. "I'm a woman in her middle thirties."

"Don't remind me," he said cruelly.

She tried not to be hurt. He was just lashing out, she told herself, to protect his own pride. Then there was the spectacle of Eileen in the house, growing more gorgeous by the day, innocently—or not so innocently—flaunting her newly acquired charms. It could only remind Mike of Laura's inadequacy.

One night before she left for the summer, they had a moment of closeness again. It was a hot June evening, and she sat perspiring under the lamplight in the bedroom, hoping a breeze would drift in from the window. She was reading a letter. The paper was damp and sticky in her hand.

Mike came into the room, mopping his face with a handkerchief. "Well, that's pretty useless," he said, tossing the handkerchief onto the top of the dresser. He glanced at Laura. "What have you got there?" he said, scowling at the paper in her hand. "More gallery business?"

"No, it's a letter from my sister."

"Oh? What does darling Julia have to say?" He walked around the room shedding clothes as he spoke.

"Mike, she's getting a divorce!"

"No kidding. I guess poor old Charles couldn't take any more."

"No, you're wrong. It's Julia who wants the divorce. She says Charles is being extremely decent."

"That means there's another guy in the picture."

"Well, yes, there is. His name is Wade, and he comes from a very distinguished old Virginia family, Julia writes."

"Uh-huh."

Laura tried not to smile. "And he's a senior member of an eminent Washington law firm. So Julia will be moving to Maryland after they're married."

"Which will suit her just fine." Mike pulled his damp undershirt over his head. "It sounds like the winner in this deal is good old Charles."

"Mike, that's not nice. She is my sister."

"Oh, well. In that case I apologize." He came over to her chair and ruffled the hair on the back of her neck.

Laura burst out laughing. "You may be right," she said.

He laughed too. After a moment he said, "We always had good times in Weichang on hot summer nights."

She glanced up, thinking of those nights. Their eyes met. There was a moment of unspoken communication, and he took her hand and brought her to her feet. He drew off her dressing gown. They moved to the bed.

Their naked bodies were so slippery with perspiration it was like being oiled. Laura felt a surge of sensuous desire she had not felt in months and flung herself across his body in hungry lust. He responded immediately. She wanted him at once, without waiting, and he knew it without being told and rolled her on her back and gave her her wish. She groaned, as her breasts slid across his chest and waves of sensation crested within her.

They came to a long slow shuddering climax together.

Mike lay across her body, resting on his elbows, postponing the moment of withdrawal because he knew it always saddened her. "I wish it could be like this all the time," he said. "Lately you've just been going through the motions. Tonight you really wanted me."

"Mike—"

"I know, I know. It's my fault." He sighed. "Too bad we can't turn back the clock half an hour and start again. The way we used to. I hate to admit it, but I can't do that anymore. At least not every time."

"You'll be forty this year."

"If I make it."

"What do you mean?"

"Maybe I won't live to see forty."

"Mike," she whispered, "don't talk that way."

"I'm sorry, baby. For everything. Especially for making you miserable." He stroked back the damp hair at her temples. "I'll try to straighten myself out over the summer, when you're gone. Maybe I need to be alone for a little while. Maybe that's what it takes to get me straight."

"Oh,. Mike, if you only would!" She strained him close, wanting to cry.

The scene in front of the house on Bubbling Well Road was one of organized confusion. The chauffeur was stowing trunks into the Rolls-Royce in the driveway. Plum Blossom was giving last-minute advice to Chen, patting little Henry in her arms, and keeping an eye on David, who was attempting to help the chauffeur and getting underfoot. Eileen was seated moodily on the steps with her chin in her hands. Laura and Mike were saying good-bye to one another in the doorway.

Eileen was hoping he would give Laura a quick, cool peck on the cheek. She glanced behind her. No such luck. They were locked in one of those torrid embraces that always sickened and embarrassed her.

She told herself to face facts. She was only fourteen. Her mother was a beautiful, experienced, sophisticated woman of the world who undoubtedly knew all kinds of bedroom tricks Eileen could only guess at. She had learned how to enslave a man's senses. Eileen knew nothing. Only kissing, and not very much about that. Surely there was more?

"Hey, beautiful," said Mike's voice above her, "what are you brooding about?" He sat down beside her on the steps.

"Daddy," she said, unable to stop herself, "why do you kiss Mother that way?"

"Why do I?" He grinned. "It's okay, we're married. It's all legal. I have a paper signed by some stuffed-shirt minister in Connecticut to prove it."

"Is that all it takes?" asked Eileen, disdainfully. "Being married? I thought you had to love a person."

"What makes you think I don't?"

Eileen shrugged.

"There's a lot you don't understand. You will someday."

Eileen didn't care for the turn of the conversation. She changed the subject. "Are they all stuffed shirts in Connecticut?" she asked. "Like that minister? Mother's family, I mean."

Mike thought it over. ":I would have to admit," he said finally, "that they are."

"They probably don't like you for being Irish."

"They believe I keep pigs in the parlor," Mike said, poker-faced. Eileen gave him a mischievous grin. "Well, I'm Irish too."

"Only half."

"The better half."

He winked. They both laughed. Eileen sighed and took his arm and rested her cheek against it. "I'm going to miss you," she said. "I wish you were coming with us to the mountains."

"The summer will go fast, baby. You'll see."

Eileen didn't believe it. Time dripped like molasses from a spout, she thought in despair, when she wanted it to pour like a river in flood. She wanted to grow up.

CHAPTER 11

It was the Moon of the Hungry Ghosts in Shanghai. Laura and the family had been gone for almost three months. Chen stood in the kitchen of the house on Bubbling Well Road and felt himself trembling. He thought that the master had never been so crazy-drunk as he was this summer. The cause of it was being alone, without Missy Laura. The aimlessness and the loneliness made him violent. Always before he had held his liquor and reined in his temper, for Missy Laura would never stand for violence. She would leave him at once.

Perhaps she would leave him anyway, Chen thought sorrowfully, when she came home next week from the mountains and saw him in this condition. He had promised to reform, but he'd done just the opposite. All-night poker games in the library. Burnt cigar holes in the rug. Piled-high empty bottles to be carried out in the morning, and then it all began again.

Now Chen had been ordered to find Mike another bottle of Scotch. Chen had hidden all the whiskey in the kitchen cupboard, hoping desperately to discourage the master and fool him into thinking the supply was exhausted. But the master was too shrewd. When it came to his liquor supply, he knew to the last dram what he had purchased and what he had consumed.

Chen puttered randomly around the kitchen, trying to delay, hoping the master would fall unconscious in his chair and the fresh bottle could be saved. Anything was better than nothing, he told himself. Any effort Chen could make—for Missy Laura—was worth trying.

"What the hell are you doing in here, you lazy bastard?"

Chen glanced up, startled. The master never came into the kitchen. Nevertheless here he was, leaning against the doorway to steady himself, his voice slurred and angry, his eyes narrowed to hard blue slits. Chen spoke up manfully.

"I am looking for the Scotch, as you commanded me."

"What's taking you so fucking long?"

"I'm trying to remember where I put it."

"Don't lie to me!"

"No, master, I'm not lying."

He turned to the cupboard and pretended to rummage for the bottle. He heard heavy footsteps behind him, then felt a hand on his shoulder. He was spun around and a fist crashed into his jaw. Chen sprawled on the floor, blinking in pain and surprise.

"Now find it," he heard the master's voice say above him. "I'll give you three more minutes."

The heavy footsteps departed.

Chen picked himself up from the floor and brushed off his gown. The pain in his jaw did not bother him very much, but the pain in his heart was hard to bear. He considered running away from the house. Then what would happen to the master? He might set himself on fire, or fall and cut himself on broken glass. Drunken men were not responsible for their actions. He, Chen, had promised Missy Laura to keep him safe.

He had no choice. Sadly he found the bottle of Scotch and brought it to the library.

When he returned to the kitchen, he started again in fear. A figure was standing in the shadows by the kitchen door.

"Who are you?" he gasped. "How did you get in?"

"The door was open."

It was a woman. A Chinese woman.

"What do you want here?"

"I have come to see your master."

Chen knew that voice.

"Come forward into the light," he said. "Where I can see you."

The figure stepped forward. Chen peered. She was poor, by her clothing, and very thin, and no longer young. Traces of beauty still remained in her face, but they were almost obliterated by lines of grief and poverty.

"I know you," he said. "I recognize your face."

"I know you too, Chen."

"You are the concubine the master brought from Peking to Weichang, many years ago."

"Yes. I am Li-san."

Chen's eyes widened. "In the name of the Christian god, why have you returned?"

"I will tell you my story, Chen, if you will give me tea." She put a hand to her throat. The hand was thin and veined, the throat was scrawny.

"Sit down, woman! You need food as well as tea! There is some roast chicken in the larder, and a plate of cold boiled noodles. I will bring them."

"You are kind." She sank gratefully into a chair. He saw that her strength was almost exhausted.

The master would be contented with his Scotch, Chen thought. He would not come back to the kitchen. He busied himself with bringing the food and making the tea. He let Li-san eat before she began her story. She tried to control herself, but she was half-starved. Chen's eyes filled with sympathetic tears. So many people in this land were hungry. How could one feed them all?

"Were you in the famine in the Yangtze provinces?" he asked.

She nodded as pain moved across her face. He forebore to ask more questions until she was ready.

Finally she pushed aside her plate and laid down her chopsticks. "I cannot eat more or I will be sick," she said. "My stomach is unaccustomed to rich food." She smiled, and her former beauty suddenly sparked to life. "You are an excellent cook, Chen. No wonder you have kept your job."

"I am married now, and I have a son."

"That is good."

Her own tale was sorrowful and quickly told. She had borne two children, but they had both died in the famine. So had her husband. Her husband's family wished to marry her to his younger brother, but that would mean virtual slavery. She would have been a third wife. Nevertheless the family had the right to do so by ancient tradition. Li-san had run away to Shanghai to escape that fate. Now she hoped to get a job in a cotton factory.

"Many people want factory jobs," said Chen. "They crowd into the city from the Yangtze provinces, as you have done, and then they go hungry. Do you have money to sustain you until you find work?"

Li-san had no money. "I cannot even sell myself on the streets," she said. "Who would want this emaciated body?" She pressed her lips together. "I would not do it even if I were still beautiful. I will not be a slave. That's why I ran away."

"What will you do, then?"

"I bought my freedom once, from the master of this house. He said he would keep the money safe for me, if I ever needed it. That's why I've come." Li-san looked inquiringly at Chen. "I have heard that he is rich now. Is that so?"

"He is rich, but there is great trouble in this house."

Li-san examined Chen more closely. "What happened to your face?" she asked.

Chen gingerly touched the red mark on his jaw. "The master struck me in a drunken rage."

"So it is like that."

Chen got up to pour more tea. "He is married as well, but the mistress went away for the summer."

"What is she like?"

"A good kind woman, just and fair. She is godmother to my son."

"Does he strike her too?"

"No, but he treats her badly." Chen poured boiling water over the tea leaves. "She, too, lost a child, when there was cholera in Weichang. She grieved deeply."

"I have heard," said Li-san, "that foreigners do not grieve as we do at the loss of a child."

"That isn't true. She almost broke her heart."

"Alas," said Li-san. She bowed her head. "Misery comes to the rich and the poor, and even to foreigners. Especially to women. I am sorry for your mistress." Tears filled up her eyes. She put a hand on her heart. "My breasts are so empty, Chen. So empty. What can I do?"

"Find another husband."

"I know no one in Shanghai."

"My wife will help you when she returns."

They gazed at one another. Chen's promise was barren, as they both knew, for it would not be easy to find a husband for Li-san. Not in Shanghai, where modern men chose their own wives. Li-san had lost her beauty. Now that she was in her thirties, she was just another peasant woman.

"Shall I ask him for my money?" Li-san asked.

"He is drunk. His wife will leave him when she returns and finds him like that. Then she will break her heart all over again."

Li-san finished her tea in brooding silence. Then she stood up. "You have been kind to me, Chen. Perhaps I can help your master."

Chen stared at her. "How?"

Li-san moved to the kitchen door. "Do not question me," she said. "Just get rid of all the whiskey in the house. Then leave for an hour."

Chen nodded. He could not imagine what would happen. But whatever it was, it could not be worse than the present situation.

Li-san approached Mike's chair in the library. His head was on his breast. He was in a drunken half-sleep, muttering to himself. She lifted his chin with a delicate touch and stared at his face. Unshaven, unkempt. Still handsome, though, his body still well shaped, still a fine-looking man. But ruining himself. She glanced in distaste at the empty glass on the side table, and wrinkled her nose at the smell. That would have to end.

She shook him gently. He muttered and tried to lash out with his arm. She avoided the blow, then shook him again.

"Get away from me," he mumbled.

"I will not harm you," she whispered softly.

His eyes opened. He blinked in confusion. "Laura?" Then he

narrowed his gaze. "Son of a bitch," he muttered, "you're not Laura."

"I am an old friend."

"Wait a minute," he said. "I know your voice."

"Do you?" She stood calmly facing him with her hands in her sleeves. Mike gazed at her with dawning recognition.

"Li-san? Is it you?"

"Yes, it is."

"My God. It's been years."

"So it has."

"What are you doing here?"

"I have come to help you."

He glanced at her suspiciously. "What is that supposed to mean? I don't need help."

"Oh, but you do. I know all about it."

"Tell me, kid," he said in a sardonic tone.

"You have crawled into a bottle," Li-san said calmly, "and cannot find your way out. You will not allow your wife to assist you because of your pride."

He laughed angrily.

She ignored it. "But I am different. I am only a former concubine. You need feel no shame with me. Together we will fight your demon."

"What demon? What are you talking about?"

"Do not pretend to misunderstand me."

Mike was silent. Then he said, "Okay, Li-san. If you want to help me, you can start by pouring me a shot."

"That is exactly what I will not do."

"Do as I say."

"No."

He gave her a hard, threatening stare.

"There is no whiskey in the house," she said calmly. "I had Chen remove it. He has left for a while."

"You bitch!"

He flung himself out of the chair and grabbed her shoulders. She offered no resistance. "Go out and buy me some whiskey," he said through his teeth.

"I will not."

"I'll break your neck!" She didn't move. "Don't you care?"

"No. I don't care."

Mike gazed into her eyes. Moments passed. "You mean it, don't you?" he said finally in a quiet voice.

"Yes."

He took a long breath. "Will you really help me? Oh, God. I need help. I need help." He sighed hopelessly and released her. "I can't do it by myself. Not this time. I tried, but it wasn't any good. I need somebody."

She tactfully ignored the fact that he had begun to cry weak tears. "Go and shave. It will make you feel better. Then we will fight together."

"What do you want in return?"

"I came to you for the help you promised me once, and I found you needed my help. I will give it, then, and I will depart before your wife returns."

"Laura," Mike whispered. She would be home next week.

"You will be sober when you greet her. Your shoulders will be straight and your eyes will be clear and you will bear yourself like a man. You will cease to cry like a child and snarl like an animal. Your wife will be filled with joy to see how you have changed."

Mike thought of what that would mean. He remembered saying to Laura before she left for the mountains, *I'll try to straighten myself out over the summer.*

And she had replied, *Oh, Mike, if you only would!*

He had not done it. And he was going to lose Laura. He would wreck his life as he had smashed his steamer in the Yangtze River. Unless Li-san could help him sober up. Was it possible?

"If you can do that, Li-san . . . We don't have much time."

"I know."

"You may have to fight me. I could hurt you."

"Chen will aid me. Between the two of us we will manage to restrain you."

Fear, doubt, and hope moved across Mike's face. He suddenly bent and kissed Li-san fiercely on the mouth. Then he stood up. He rubbed the bristles on his jaw. Christ, he needed to clean himself up. "Okay," he said, "it's a bargain. God help us both if it doesn't work."

*   *   *

The Rolls-Royce glided up the driveway and came to a halt in front of the house. David was the first to tumble out of the backseat. "Mama, we're home!" he cried joyously. "It still looks the same! Everything looks the same!"

"What did you expect?" inquired Eileen, who was the next to emerge. "Did you think the house would disappear over the summer?"

"We've been away so *long*." He took a deep breath and tucked his hand into Eileen's. To a seven-year-old one summer was a lifetime.

She laughed. "Come on, you silly boy, we'll go and look for Daddy."

"And Chen," he reminded her.

"Yes, and Chen too."

David was anxious to check on all his familiar people and all his dear possessions, including his toy chest and his tin soldiers. He wanted to make sure everything was in place, and confirm to himself that nothing had been stolen by bandits in his absence. He knew all about bandits from Plum Blossom. They were called Red Beards and Yellow Turbans and they were desperate men. Sometimes he had nightmares about them.

Laura got out of the car. She glanced anxiously at the front door, wondering where Mike was. He hadn't been at the railroad station to meet them. The chauffeur had arrived as arranged with the limousine, but he hadn't seen Mike.

She wished she had made the trip back to Shanghai at least once during the summer. It was a long and complicated journey, though, with two changes of trains, and David had been sick with a cold for a while, and Plum Blossom had been occupied with Henry. She'd spoken to Mike on the telephone. He'd sounded peculiar each time, speaking in monosyllables and seeming anxious to hang up.

Worried, she entered the hallway with a hesitant step.

Everything was sparkling. The hallway was shining clean. She thought that seemed promising. Then Chen appeared. He was wearing a freshly ironed gown and his expression was cheerful, although there was a fading discoloration on his jaw.

"Welcome home, missy!" he cried.

"Thank you, Chen."

"Did you have a fine summer?"

"Oh, yes, with some of the usual mishaps. Not to Henry, though. He's in splendid health."

"He is a strong baby," Chen said proudly.

Laura smiled in agreement. Then she asked, "What happened to your face? Did you have an accident?"

Chen touched his jaw. "Yes, an accident. But it is healing. Everything is fine now."

Laura paused. "Is it, Chen?"

He glanced at her significantly. "Now it is."

She wondered exactly what he meant.

"The master is coming down to greet you," Chen volunteered. "He is saying hello to Missy Eileen and Master David in the upstairs bedroom."

"Oh, then he's home!"

"I've been home all along," said a quiet voice. Mike was coming down the stairs. "Hello, Laura."

She stared up at him from the foot of the stairs. He looked tired but calm. His gaze was steady. But there was something different about him. She tried to identify what it was. Then it came to her: He had the look of a man who had been through an ordeal and survived.

"Mike?" she said. "Mike? Is everything all right?"

"Yes, baby," he said. "It's all okay." He came toward her from the bottom of the staircase.

With a hesitant step she moved into his arms. "Something happened while I was away. I can see it in your face."

"A lot of things happened. But nothing you have to worry about. They're all over. The bad times." He bent his head and put his lips to her hair.

"You're sober."

"Yes, Laura. For good."

"Was it . . . very hard?"

Mike was silent. Then he said quietly, "It was a little taste of hell."

"Oh, God. I should have been here." She hid her face against his shoulder.

"I'm glad you weren't."

She heaved a long, shuddering sigh. "Oh, Mike, I'm so happy. I'm so happy."

He gazed over her shoulder into the distance. "Me too," he said. "Sometimes I think the last few days were a dream, or a nightmare. But they weren't, and now this summer is ended. We can forget all about it and go on with our lives." He lifted her chin and smiled down into her upturned face. "If anything is ever forgotten. Maybe events just keep echoing down the corridors of time."

"How poetic and Oriental you sound! You must have been wandering the streets of Chapei."

"Not exactly. But you're not far wrong."

She caught her breath. "Let's not talk about sad things any longer."

Hand in hand they went back up the stairs.

Li-san went to the rickety shelf over the stove in her shabby room in Chapei and took down the can of tea leaves. Her money was inside. She had taken it from Mike, who had been generous. Still, she would have to be very careful. The only job she had been able to find was a low-paying one in a cotton mill in the Japanese district of Hunkow. It was hard work in bad air, long hours, and pounding noise from the machines, but Li-san was content. Nevertheless the money in her tea can was dwindling.

CHAPTER 12

Laura did not go with the children to the mountains in the summer of 1914. There was too much to do. They were planning a trip to Europe and America, the whole family, and it would combine business with a vacation.

Laura sighed. "I'm so bored with this Chinese export ware

we're selling in the galleries," she said to Mike. They were in the library, beneath a slowly-turning ceiling fan that was rustling the papers on the desk: itineraries, letters, catalogs, lists, and shipping orders. "Famille rose dishes, Coromandel screens, ginger-jar lamps, all junk designed to appeal to Westerners."

Mike reminded her that they did just that.

"I know." Laura knew she could not afford to indulge only her own taste. Without the tourist business the galleries would be in trouble.

"You'll have things more to your liking in England," Mike told her.

Nathan Field had referred them to a dealer in London who was willing to open an exclusive shop for the Valentines in Mayfair. It would deal only in fine furniture and carpets, and the very best porcelains. It would be a companion to their store in San Francisco, only more expensive, more discriminating in what it would offer for sale. They were already arranging for freight haulage with the British steamship line of Jardine Matheson, and negotiating insurance coverage for their shipments.

"This trip will cost us a fortune," Laura said.

"We owe it to ourselves."

"I won't be sorry to leave Shanghai for a while," she agreed.

The Sun Yat-sen republic was in trouble. Sun's authority had been challenged. Yüan Shih-k'ai, once the Dowager Empress's general, had assembled his own army. Yüan was smart, tough, experienced, and ambitious. Sun was an intellectual and an idealist who had deep faith in the parliamentary system. His own parliament had betrayed him and elected Yüan president.

Yüan did not intend to be a president. A republic was not to his taste. He wanted power. He remembered the glittering days of the Empire under the Dowager Empress. Now it was his turn. He moved into the Forbidden City in Peking with his own splendidly uniformed personal guard to attend him.

The followers of Sun urged him to fight back. The inevitable happened: a civil war broke out. So far it was confined to the South and to Nanking, the southern capital, but a state of uneasy unrest lay over the land.

It was Mike's personal opinion that Sun didn't stand a chance against Yüan Shih-k'ai. Laura wanted only to have a breathing space. She still hated politics and its disrupting effect on people's lives. The skirmishes between the rival armies were spreading to the coast. Thank God for George Henderson, she thought, who had promised to look after their household in their absence. George, as always, was a rock of dependability.

Worse events occurred. Within two weeks Mike entered the house with a grave expression, a newspaper in his hand.

"Have you seen this?" he asked Laura.

"No, I haven't had time to read a paper today."

"Well, the trip is off."

"What do you mean, Mike? Why? The plans are all made. I already have the tickets."

"There's a war in Europe."

"A war!" She caught her breath. "But there's always a war somewhere."

"Not like this."

"Does it affect England?"

"Everybody. England, France, Germany, Austria, Italy, Russia. And Japan."

"Are the Japanese . . . against Germany?"

They were, Mike told her.

That was frightening news for China, as Mike and Laura recognized. The war would give Japan an excuse to move into Shantung Province, German-held territory by treaty. The Japanese could now invade the city of Tsingtao with righteous military power. This was their long-awaited opportunity for a foothold in China.

"What will this do to the tourist business?" Laura wondered aloud.

"Nothing good. People will imagine China flaming with war. I don't suppose they'll see us as a vacation paradise, or a lovely place to shop for antiques."

"And shipping . . . it's bound to be affected. We'll be cut off from Europe. And if America gets into the war . . ."

They both fell silent, thinking.

"We'll have to economize," Laura said finally. "On everything. Not just the trip."

"The easy days may be over, sweetheart. Are you prepared?"

After a moment Laura nodded and said she was. "We know how to drink bitter tea, Mike. We've done it before."

He took her hand. "That's my girl."

Plum Blossom was in her bed-sitting room darning socks, with the sock she was working on stretched over a polished wooden knob made for that purpose. Her fingers were quick and deft. Three-year-old Henry was seated on the floor playing with his blocks, gravely constructing a tower. He had astonishing powers of concentration for a three-year-old. In every way he was astonishing, Plum Blossom thought. He had walked at eleven months, begun to say words at thirteen months, was using the toilet before he was two, and now spoke in complete grammatical sentences in both English and Chinese, with an ever-increasing vocabulary.

His tower collapsed. He swept the blocks into a pile. "Honorable Mother," he said, "will you read me my book?"

Books were his passion. He obviously longed to decode the mysterious marks on the paper, pointing and asking what this was, what that was, but of course Plum Blossom could not help him. She made up stories from the pictures. He did not allow her to deviate from her original invention, and corrected her when she strayed, remembering every original detail.

He was a prodigy, Plum Blossom thought. He would be a brilliant scholar; that was his destiny. She decided to perform an ancient test, for her own satisfaction. She would not tell Chen, who chided her for clinging to country superstitions.

"We'll play a game first," she said. "Then I will read you your book."

He agreed readily, loving games. She seated him at the table on a pillowed chair. She laid out objects before him and sat down opposite him.

"Now choose, my son," she said. "Then I will read you your book."

Henry studied the objects carefully. His hand hovered over first one, then the other. He frowned, trying to decide. Plum Blossom waited serenely. He was going to choose the pen, of course. The selection of a future scholar.

No! To her chagrin and surprise he rejected the pen and picked up the toy sword, wielding it firmly, making feinting motions with it in the air.

A soldier! A common soldier! Not possible. She remembered her grandmother's proverb. She had heard it often during her girlhood, when they were menaced by marauding troops of the Emperor. "Good iron is not used for making nails, and good men are not used for making soldiers."

Plum Blossom rose and took the sword from Henry. "We will read now, my son. Fetch your book."

He scrambled down from the chair and ran happily to find it, forgetting the sword.

He had chosen the pen, Plum Blossom told herself. She would remember that and forget the other, and soon she would believe it.

Eileen Valentine was with George Henderson in the library. Eileen had passed through the storms of adolescence in the past year. She had abandoned the rivalry with her mother, for her life had become too absorbing. At seventeen she was radiant. She had attained her full beauty. She was slender, having lost the roundness of her growing-up years, and she moved with unconscious grace. Her eyes sparkled with love of life. When she smiled, her face lit up.

"Eileen Valentine," one young man had been heard to say at a Shanghai tea dance, "can turn a man's heart to jelly."

Eileen poured George Henderson a glass of sherry in the library. He had been invited for dinner. "Mother and Daddy will be here soon," she said. "They're worried about the business. I gather we're on the brink of destitution. I'll have to marry a rich husband and redeem the family fortune."

"That shouldn't be difficult," George said with a smile.

"Don't forget, I'm considered a wild girl. Reputation is everything in this city. At least in the foreign community. Everybody knows everybody else, and people gossip so."

George accepted the sherry. "Are you a wild girl?"

Eileen seated herself on the footstool by his chair. She put her chin in her hands. "No," she said seriously. "I'm not. It's just a pose. I've never done anything . . . bad. Just flirting, and sometimes I let a boy kiss me, but not very often." She gazed into his face. "You do believe me, don't you? I couldn't bear it if I lost your respect."

George was touched. "Yes, Eileen," he said, "I believe you. You are your mother's daughter. Laura's girl couldn't do anything bad."

"You think a lot of Mother, don't you?"

"She is a trump, through and through," George said from the heart.

"I think I've always known you felt that way. Mother doesn't know it, though. She can't see anyone but Daddy. She thinks he's the only man alive."

"There was a time," George remarked, "when you felt that way yourself."

"Oh, I know it! I must have been horrible! Poor Mother! I don't know how she put up with me!"

"I guess she has a lot of patience."

That made Eileen laugh.

"Uncle George," she said, "I think I'm old enough to stop calling you Uncle George."

"I think that's reasonable," George replied.

"After all, we're not related. You're just my oldest, dearest friend."

"I hope you'll always feel that way."

"I will. Don't forget, I'm not wild, and I'm not really as frivolous as people think."

George decided to tease her. "Don't they call you the Heartbreaker of Bubbling Well Road? Miss Eileen Valentine, the most popular girl in Shanghai?"

Eileen laughed. "Yes, isn't it silly? But it's fun being popular." She pushed back the thick blond hair from her face. "George," she said fervently, "I'm having such a good time!"

"Then enjoy yourself, dear," he said in a gentle tone.

They heard the voices of Laura and Mike in the hall outside, and the conversation came to an end.

CHAPTER 13

The hands of the Customs House clock on the Shanghai Bund pointed to noon. It was February 1915. A young man with flaming red hair, wearing the uniform of a lieutenant in the British Royal Flying Corps, stood on the pavement and gazed at the clock, then at the Whangpoo, then at the Bund and its hurrying crowds. He was only partly interested, although he'd never been in the Orient before. His name was Rory O'Connor, and his face was bronzed from the Indian Ocean sun; he'd made the long sea voyage from Liverpool. His eyes were a brilliant emerald green, startling against his tanned skin. When he moved, he walked with a slight limp. He was on leave from his squadron until he was well enough to return.

"Take all the time you need, Lieutenant," his commanding officer had said wearily. "But you understand the situation."

"Yes, sir. Only too well."

The Royal Flying Corps needed experienced airmen who were accustomed to flying in all weathers and had had long training in the air. Rory was one of those fliers. He knew he must return as quickly as he could to his squadron, but he was delaying. He'd sustained a wound in the thigh, but he'd suffered another wound that wasn't as obvious, and it was in his mind.

He couldn't stop brooding about the German zeppelin raid, and how it had ended. Triumph and then sudden shocking disaster. Needless, stupid tragedy.

He began to limp along the pavement. "Oh, fuck all," he said to himself in despair. A passerby glanced at him curiously. Rory paid no attention. He was thinking about the aerodrome in England.

Then he was forced to notice his surroundings. He was approaching a bridge at the end of the Shanghai Bund, and something was happening there. He could see a commotion involving soldiers, shouting, and fighting. Bystanders were scattering in all directions, and some were taking cover in doorways. What the devil? He heard gunfire. Bullets were starting to whine overhead. Good God! In the middle of a busy bridge, at high noon, in a commercial district! Bloody fools!

He remembered that a civil war was going on in this country. This was not Piccadilly Circus, he reminded himself.

He made another observation. A girl was caught on the bridge, between the rival soldiers. She was trying to fight her way out, without much success. She was an absolute smasher of a girl, a beautiful blonde, and she was fighting with furious energy.

It was time for Lieutenant O'Connor to take a hand. Rory drew his pistol and started to run in her direction.

"Thank you, Lieutenant!" exclaimed Eileen Valentine. She and Rory O'Connor were standing on the pavement of a side street, well away from the bridge. Eileen was still a little breathless and disheveled. Rory forced himself to appear casual.

"Bit of a sticky situation, wasn't it?" he remarked.

"Oh, well, you get used to those kinds of events in Shanghai. But not usually at such close quarters! They rushed onto the bridge from opposite directions, and there I was in the middle."

"But now you're quite safe. At least I hope you are?" he inquired politely. "No cuts or bruises? No hidden damage?"

"No, everything is fine, thanks to you." She glanced at his uniform. "Are you in the army? I don't recognize your insignia."

"It's the army in a way. A branch, so to speak: the Royal Flying Corps."

"Oh, a flier! How exciting!"

She thought he appeared extremely dashing and glamorous and very good-looking. And *mature*. What a change from the callow young men she knew in Shanghai. What good luck to have been on the bridge at exactly that moment! To have been rescued like Lillian Gish, a damsel in distress! Now to extend this acquaintance without appearing forward or foolish.

Rory was wondering about exactly the same problem.

"I suppose I should introduce myself," Eileen said hesitantly.

"That's absolutely in order."

"My name is Eileen Valentine."

"Rory O'Connor."

"Oh, then you're Irish."

"Only half. My mother was English."

"Me too. Only half. On my father's side."

"We have a lot in common," he said gravely. "I think that calls for a cup of tea. Or a glass of sherry. Or is it too early? I'm afraid I don't know the form in China."

"Tea would be fine," Eileen said demurely.

They began to walk.

"Have you lived here long, Miss Valentine?"

"All my life."

"But you're not British."

"No, American."

"Oh, that accounts for the curious accent."

"Curious!" She glanced at him indignantly. "You're the one with the funny accent."

He laughed. "Let's wait until later to argue it out. When we're sitting down."

After half a block Eileen said, "You're limping. I'm sorry. Perhaps we should find a taxi."

"No, exercise is good for me. I need to keep the leg muscles from contracting. Doctor's orders."

She stopped in front of a restaurant on the next block. She'd never seen it before, which was fine; she didn't feel like sharing her new acquaintance with any gossipy friends. THE CORONET CAFÉ, it said on the window. PIANO BAR. LADIES WELCOME.

"Do you suppose this is respectable?" she murmured.

Rory peered through the window. "It looks as cozy as a tea shop on Oxford Street," he reported. "Not a sinister Oriental in view. Just the waiter, and he seems peaceable." He glanced at Eileen. "Shall we try it?"

"Yes, let's."

With the sense of an adventure about to begin, Eileen preceded him through the door.

"Do you have a family?" she asked over cups of tea.

"Just my brother James. Sir James, if you will. My parents are dead."

"Oh, Sir James! Then your father was a peer of England!"

"Not quite," he said dryly. "Just a baronet."

"If I married you," Eileen exclaimed, "I would be Lady O'Connor!"

"I'm afraid not. My brother inherited the title, and he has a wife and son, with another baby on the way, so my chances are dim."

Eileen leaned forward with her chin in her hands. "What would I be, then?"

"Just Mrs. O'Connor." Rory paused. "Shall I propose now or later?"

"You might as well get it over with now. Swear eternal love and devotion and so forth."

"Is that the regular drill?"

"Yes, all my suitors do it."

"It must get rather sickening."

"Oh, no," she said seriously. "I adore it."

He started to laugh. "I think I'm not used to American girls," he said. "You're the first I've met."

"An American girl who's never been to America."

"You seem very American to me."

"I suppose I am," she said thoughtfully. "We have Thanksgiving dinner every fall, with duck instead of turkey, and water chestnut dressing, and we display the Stars and Stripes on the Fourth of July and Mother gives a big party with fireworks and everyone comes. We're very patriotic." She started to laugh. "Last summer my little brother got drunk on rum punch and had to throw up in the garden. He was mortified. He hates to do anything wrong."

"Why did he drink the punch?"

"He didn't know it was spiked with rum. No one told him. He just thought it was a pretty pink color. Poor David. He'll probably never touch alcohol again."

"So there's you, and your little brother, and your patriotic mother who gives Fourth of July parties—"

"And founded the family business and runs art galleries and speaks Mandarin Chinese and wears Paris fashions—"

"An impressive person. And who else?"

"Well," Eileen said, "there's Plum Blossom, who used to be

my amah, and is married to our head butler, Chen, and has a three-year-old named Henry who's a genius.''

"A three-year-old Chinese prodigy called Henry?"

"He's named after my grandfather, who lives in Connecticut."

"Whom you have never seen."

"No, but Mother sends him photographs and things."

Rory sat back. He was vastly amused. "There seems to be one family member you haven't mentioned."

"Who?"

"The Irish half of your heritage."

"Oh. Daddy." Eileen gave Rory a dazzling smile. "He's a roughneck."

"A what?"

"You know. A whiskey drinking, poker-playing, bar-brawling daredevil from the Wild West."

"Oh, a *roughneck*," said Rory. "Why didn't you say so?"

Eileen laughed. "But he couldn't handle the alcohol, so now he's on the water wagon."

"The water wagon," Rory repeated carefully.

"That means he doesn't drink whiskey anymore," Eileen explained. "Or any liquor at all. He stays sober."

"I gathered that," Rory said. "What about his family?"

"I don't know," Eileen said in slight surprise. "He never talks about his family. I just know he has a grudge against the Catholic Church, but he won't say why. But he was an altar boy when he was small, he told me once. Are you a Catholic?"

"Yes," said Rory, "every now and then."

"We go to the Presbyterian church, because there aren't any Congregationalists in Shanghai. Daddy doesn't go to church at all. He just stays in bed and sleeps late on Sunday morning."

"Why do I get the impression," Rory said, "that your father is your favorite person in the household?"

"Because it's true." Eileen sat back and studied Rory. "You know, you're a lot like him. Except for the uniform and the English accent."

"I'm a roughneck, I suppose."

"No, hardly. But I'll bet you were a bad little boy when you were small, and got into a lot of trouble."

"Very astute, Miss Valentine. Right on target."

"Daddy is redheaded too. You do resemble him. Height and build and so forth."

"I'm not sure I care for that comparison," Rory said.

"You should. Daddy is very good-looking."

"But I'm not feeling very paternal toward you at the moment."

Eileen leaned forward again. She batted long curly eyelashes. "Are you falling madly in love with me," she asked in a husky undertone, "and fighting an irresistible urge to sweep me into your arms and kiss me until I gasp for breath?"

Rory regarded her with disapproving amusement. "What an outrageous flirt you are."

"Everyone says that," she agreed.

"Well, I think we'd better order something to eat, and postpone the discussion of my romantic feelings until later. I haven't had lunch, and neither have you, and it's already past teatime. You can join me for supper?"

"Why, yes," she said. "I haven't heard about Ireland yet. I've just been talking about me."

"I'm afraid it won't be as entertaining as the fascinating Valentine household."

"I won't mind," she assured him. "I'm a very good listener."

The sun had set, and the sky was filled with purple-blue clouds that now hid, now revealed, a quarter moon. Rory and Eileen sat on a bench facing the river, in a little strip of park along the Bund. A junk glided past their view, its square sails silhouetted black against the clouds.

"I can hardly believe it's February," Rory murmured. "I'm used to northern winters."

"It never gets very cold in Shanghai. In Chapei, where the Chinese people live, the poor don't even have stoves. They can't afford coal. They just pile on more padded jackets. But it gets stifling hot in the summer. We go to the mountains."

"It never gets very hot in Ireland. Not even in August."

"Tell me about it, Rory."

"Shall I take you on a trip to County Donegal? The way I used to do it when I was a schoolboy home on holiday?"

"Yes, do."

"Very well." Rory paused. He mused for a moment. "Picture

it. You are with me. We've traveled on the night mail to Ireland. Then we've voyaged to the north on a little cargo steamer that makes the trip once a week up a silver river. On the quayside when we dock, old Sean is waiting for us with a dogcart. We rattle through the town, up a steep cobblestone street that runs along a causeway by the river. The town is quiet because it's so early in the morning. We can see a thicket of trees across the river, and an old gray bridge, and if we listen hard we can hear the singing of the water in the shallows.''

"Yes,'' Eileen breathed, "I can hear it.''

"We're at the top of the hill now. The road is running between low stone walls. On our left is a stretch of open fields, on our right is a wood of oak and beeches. We're almost there. We pass through the stone gate and we're on the avenue leading to the house. There it is, a long gray stone house that's crumbling to ruins. But very slowly. Nothing hurries in Donegal.''

"Whom will we meet?''

"Since we're going back to my schooldays, we'll see my father riding out on his big white horse, seventeen hands high, with his collie dog, Kerry, running beside him. Sir Liam is on his way to the house of his priest friend, Father Brian. Later on the two of them will drink a special brew of toddy made with an oyster simmering in the saucepan.''

"What will you and I be doing later on?''

"We'll be salmon fishing in the river.''

Eileen sighed. "That means we'll have fresh salmon for supper. I know we'll be very successful at our fishing.''

"Unquestionably.'' After a moment Rory regarded her gravely. "So ends our holiday. Did you enjoy yourself?''

"Oh, Rory. That was a lovely trip.''

"I'll take you there in reality someday. After the war.''

The two short words destroyed the dream. *The war*. They were both silent, watching the clouds scud across the moon.

"You must describe Weichang to me,'' Rory said, breaking the silence.

"Our house in Weichang was beautiful. It had a courtyard with weeping willow trees, and a Chinese temple. We had a gate, too, set in a high wall, a lacquered gate with an old bronze knocker . . ." Eileen faltered. "After . . . after the war I'll take you up the Yangtze to Weichang."

"There's so much to see, isn't there?"

"The whole world!"

Eileen's words quavered in the air, then died away.

Rory put his arm around her shoulders. "Will you meet me tomorrow, Eileen?"

"Yes," she said simply.

"I'm afraid I can't take you dancing. Not with this leg. I wish I could."

"I don't mind. We can talk. You haven't told me yet about flying an airplane."

"That's a whole day's conversation, at least."

"There, you see?"

He laughed. Then he took a deep breath. "You smell so good."

"It's . . . it's French perfume. Mother has a friend named Pierre-Marc, who visits us from Paris every couple of years and brings me presents. Gloves and perfume and silk lingerie."

Eileen blushed then, wishing she hadn't mentioned the lingerie. There was a sudden desperate tension between them.

"I must go now," she said. "I'll have all kinds of explanations to make at home."

"Shall I come with you?"

"No, don't. I'll take a taxi."

He stood up and held out his hand to help her rise. "Shall I call for you tomorrow?"

"No, not yet. It's too soon for you to meet everyone and . . . you don't want to meet Daddy until I prepare the way. He can be difficult." Eileen took a breath. "Meet me on the bridge, as we did today. Three o'clock by the Customs House clock."

"Very well."

The tension was still there, born of yearning and sorrow and anger and the knowledge that they might not have much time. Whatever they might experience together had to be compressed into days or weeks, for a lifetime might not exist for them because of the war, and both Rory and Eileen were aware of it. Neither of them dared as yet to speak it aloud.

*   *   *

They began to meet every day. They walked. They explored Chapei and Hunkow. They sat in restaurants and little parks. They lingered in the lounge of the Astor House Hotel amid the potted palms, while a string orchestra played teatime music. They went to a Chinese restaurant for a fourteen-course meal including Peking duck, and Eileen taught Rory to eat with chopsticks. By the end of the meal he was as skillful as she. They talked. They had endless conversations and never ran out of things to say. Eileen told Rory about Miss Haverford's, and he commiserated and told her about his own wretched schooldays. Eileen told Rory about the Boxer Rebellion in Weichang, and how Madame Wei had sheltered them while the mob howled outside the walls. She inquired about airplanes.

"You must tell me how you became a flier."

"It was all due to Nigel."

"Who is Nigel? Oh, I remember. The friend whom you're visiting in Shanghai. Because you were too restless in Ireland and getting on everyone's nerves, and came to China for a change of scene."

"Yes, I've known him since we were schoolboys in England."

Nigel, Rory explained, was the heir to a British shipping line, one that had bases in Liverpool and Shanghai. Rory was only the younger son of an impoverished Irish baronet, but they'd become fast friends at the age of nine.

At that age they'd both been outcasts at an English public school. Rory's mother had been English, from Devonshire, and his father had attended that school. Now Rory would do the same. He would learn to be an English gentleman.

Nigel had a club foot. He also had poor eyesight requiring thick spectacles and was small for his age: a natural target. Rory was an outsider from the wilds of the Irish countryside, another object of scorn. They were ragged, teased, tormented, and finally ignored. They formed an alliance out of desperation.

Rory found to his surprise that Nigel was funny, clever, and good company. Even when Rory was accepted at school thanks to his athletic prowess, he preferred Nigel's company to anyone else's.

At the age of seventeen Nigel told Rory of his new passion—flying machines. The year was 1908. Nigel had fitted up a machine shop on the family estate and borrowed a mechanic from the shipyard, and they were building an airplane.

On a visit Rory watched in boredom as Nigel and Albert tinkered endlessly with their toy. They were stretching fabric over the struts, testing the propellers, trying out the engine, putting in and taking out parts.

"Will that thing ever fly?" Rory inquired at last.

He found out for himself. He was persuaded to be the test pilot.

"Do you expect me to go up in that crazy toy?" he demanded at first.

"Only if you want to."

Rory finally sighed. "Lead me to it. It will never get off the ground."

In the beginning he was right. On the day, however, that it did get off the ground and he was soaring over fields with the wind in his face and a great rush of air in his lungs, he laughed in excitement. "This is bloody marvelous," he cried to no one and everyone.

He took the machine to the international air races in France the following summer, financed by Nigel, and lost. The prize was won by an American in a Curtiss biplane. In 1910, however, the U.K. won with a Blériot monoplane, and Rory came in third. He had become an airman.

"Are you still?" asked Eileen after she'd heard the story. "Is there no turning back?"

"One wonders. I'm in rather a funk at the moment."

"What does that mean?"

"Let's not discuss it now, Eileen. There are too many other things I want to find out, so much to discover about you. I don't want to talk about the war."

Eileen and Rory laughed together, that day and other days. They developed private jokes; it was not long before they were kissing desperately when they said good-bye, clinging to one another and oblivious to the world. They were falling in love. It was wrong, it was hopeless, for Rory had to rejoin his squadron. Somewhere far to the west were the skies of France. They imagined they could hear the artillery of the Western Front calling Rory back to war with deep far-off booms. But they didn't speak of it. China was a neutral country. For a moment beyond time here in Shanghai, on the other side of the world from France, they were out of harm's way; they were safe.

CHAPTER 14

"Nigel complains he hasn't seen anything but my back since I arrived," Rory said to Eileen.

"Well, my family doesn't miss me. They're used to my coming and going. They gave up trying to keep track of me long ago."

They were in the Coronet Café. It was "their" restaurant, the place where they had first been together. Tables lined the center of the room, with the piano bar at the rear in a horseshoe. This time it was evening and the piano player was offering a tinkling rendition of a ragtime ditty. Eileen was supposed to be at a performance of the Peking Opera, which lasted for hours. Laura had been pleased to hear it. At last Eileen was becoming interested in Oriental culture, she'd remarked, instead of a career as a social butterfly.

Rory took her hand across the table and laced his fingers in hers. "I'm never so happy as when I'm with you."

"I feel the same," she said. "I didn't know it was possible to be so happy without parties and tea dances and . . . other people."

They were quiet. The ragtime piano filled up the silence, along with tiny bursts of other conversations from other tables.

"Rory," Eileen said, "tell me something."

"What, darling?"

"Are you scared when you go up in your Blériot?"

Rory stiffened. "You mean in air races?"

He knew she didn't mean that.

"No," she said, "in your squadron."

"I thought we weren't going to discuss that."

"I want to know, Rory. I want to know the worst. Otherwise I'll imagine things, and they'll give me nightmares."

He took a breath and made a visible effort to be casual. "Well, it isn't so bad. Mostly we do reconnaissance, spotting troop formations from the air and then making reports to the strategy officers. They're planning to give us cameras, and then we'll do aerial photography."

"But is it dangerous?"

He didn't answer.

"Tell me, Rory!"

"They throw shrapnel at us with guns," he said bitterly. "It can be dangerous. And sometimes the planes crash because of poor maintenance."

"Often?"

"Quite often."

"Oh, God!"

"I . . . I sing to myself when I get scared. All alone in the cockpit. I must look an idiot, but no one can see." He grinned shakily. " 'It's a Long Way to Tipperary,' that seems to be my favorite."

"Why do they let you crash!" Eileen cried fiercely. "That isn't fair! They should take better care of the machines!"

"They do their best." Rory's expression became distant. He withdrew his hand from Eileen's. "The last time—when I hurt my leg—my two best friends were killed. Jack Brandon and Philip Farnum. They were burnt alive on the landing strip. They were good chaps too. We were all set to stand drinks at the officers' club. What a damn shame. Pity. Rotten luck and all that. But you made it, Rory. One out of three isn't bad. That's what they told me."

"Rory . . ."

"Don't say anything. Keep quiet, please."

To Eileen's concern Rory began to shake. Within seconds he was trembling violently. He couldn't seem to stop. She reached out to take his hand again.

"Don't touch me," he said through his teeth, snatching his hand back. "Leave me alone. Just leave me alone."

"I want to help you."

"Nobody can help me." The shaking was growing worse. He closed his eyes. His face whitened, and sweat beads broke out on his upper lip.

Eileen began to grow terrified. She couldn't reach Rory; she didn't know what to do. Suppose he fainted? She glanced around the restaurant but no one was paying attention to them. Rory's teeth were chattering. *Oh, God.*

In desperation she leaned forward across the table. *I sing to myself when I get scared.* She started to sing. She had a sweet, strong voice, inherited from her father. It carried into the room. "*It's a Long Way to Tipperary.*" Above the murmur of conversation, above the tinkling piano. "*A long way to go.*"

The piano player heard her, and paused. After a moment he picked up the melody. Eileen's voice with the piano behind her quieted the room.

The piano player crashed into another chorus. Rory's eyes opened. His breathing slowed. Some people at the next table sat back in their chairs and smiled and began to join in. Eileen's voice led them.

Everyone was singing. The restaurant was filled with voices and thumping piano chords. Another voice joined in, a strong, vibrant baritone. Rory was singing. He threw back his head and led them, taking over from Eileen.

The song ended on a joyous note and held, and then the room dissolved into laughter and applause. The piano player began to tinkle "They Didn't Believe Me" and people returned to their own conversations. Eileen slid out of her side of the booth and into Rory's, edging close to him.

Rory took her face between his hands. "You are an absolute smasher of a girl," he whispered softly. He bent his head and kissed her on the mouth. Her lips trembled under his.

"Rory," she said, "I love you."

"Yes, darling. Yes. I love you too."

"What are we going to do?"

"Nothing," he said. "There's nothing we can do. Until the war is over, and I can come back to Shanghai and marry you."

"Do you want to?"

"More than anything in the world."

"Would you take me to Ireland?"

"Probably not, except for a visit. The estate is James's, not mine. I expect we'd live in London."

Eileen sighed happily. "And I'd be just plain Mrs. O'Connor. It sounds like heaven."

They sat close and silent, feeling the warmth of each other's strong young bodies.

Eileen stirred. "I wish we could be married now," she murmured. "But Mother and Daddy would never consent. They think I'm too young." She brooded. "Mother was no older than I am when she got married. It doesn't seem to matter, though. They're so stubborn. Or maybe they've just forgotten what it's like to . . . feel this way."

"There wasn't a war when they were young. They didn't have to say good-bye in a matter of days, not knowing if . . . when they'd ever see each other again."

"Days!" Eileen gasped. "You didn't tell me!"

"I have to go back to France, darling. I've put it off too long."

"Suppose something happens to you! Suppose you're hurt again! How will I know?"

"I'll leave word with Nigel to keep you informed. James will know to tell him."

"And you'll write to me?"

"Of course."

"I'll write to you, too, Rory. Every day." Eileen took his arm. She was the one who was shaking now. "Mother of God," she whispered. "I hate this war."

"We're not the only ones. People are suffering all over the world. And parting, just as we are."

"I don't care about them! I can't. I love you too much. There's so much we haven't done." She caught her breath. "We haven't been together in the most important way of all."

"No, Eileen," he said at once, betraying the fact that he had been thinking the same thought.

She gazed up at him. Her eyes filled with tears. "Rory, I want to be with you. I don't care about being married. I want to be with you completely."

"No, darling. No. It isn't fair."

"To me?"

"Yes, to you."

"You're wrong. The unfairness is not being together, not ever knowing . . . just in case . . . Rory, don't you want me?"

He groaned. "Don't ask idiotic questions."

"Then make love to me, darling! Leave me with a memory to live on while you're gone, a lovely memory to sustain me until you come back! Don't leave me empty!"

"Eileen, you're making it so hard for me." He put his head into his hands.

"Because I'm right and you know I am," she whispered.

He raised his head. His face was anguished. "For God's sake let's get out of here. I think I'll go mad if I sit here another minute."

They went out into the night. It was raining, a misty rain that shimmered on the pavement and beaded shop windows and glistened in the glow of streetlamps. They started to walk. They found themselves on the bridge where they had met, near the stone railing on the pedestrian walk. They stopped in the center of the bridge.

"Eileen, I want you so," Rory said. Eileen lifted her face. He couldn't tell if the drops sliding down her cheeks were tears or rain. "I don't know if it's right or wrong. I only know I must have you, whatever the cost."

Eileen went into his arms. "You will be my first love and my last," she said against his shoulder. "I think I have been waiting for you all my life."

CHAPTER 15

Mike and Laura were worried about Eileen. She was quiet and withdrawn. Ever since she had come back from a weekend visiting a school friend in a town near Soochow, she had been a different girl. No, not a girl, Laura thought. There was something womanly about Eileen now. She seemed to have grown up overnight. She was no longer interested in parties and young men and refused all her invitations. She spent hours alone in her room writing long, long letters; Laura could see the envelopes bulging when she went to mail them. Eileen wouldn't entrust them to Chen. Eileen, who had had to be nagged to write a thank-you note! Sometimes she sat in the library pretending to read, but she was only turning pages. Her eyes were distant; her mind was far away.

Laura couldn't keep silent any longer. She went into Eileen's bedroom one night. As usual Eileen was writing a letter.

"Am I disturbing you, dear?"

"No, Mother, of course not. Sit down." Eileen set aside her pen and paper. Laura took a seat in Eileen's slipper chair.

"I'm a little concerned about you. I don't mean to pry, but you seem so changed lately."

"I suppose I am."

"Is something wrong, Eileen?"

"Not exactly. Maybe the world is wrong, but we can't help that."

"What an odd remark for you to make. You never worried about the state of the world before."

"I never worried about a lot of things before. I'm growing up, I guess."

"It seems to have happened so fast." Laura felt anxious. "And sometimes you seem so troubled. Eileen, what is it? Can't you tell me?"

Eileen regarded her tenderly. "Someday I will. If there's anyone I can talk to, Mother, it's you, and I know you'll understand. But not just yet. Let me have a little time to myself first. You see, I have some wonderful memories, and I don't want to lose them. I want to fix them in my mind, so they will be there forever, and I need to be alone to do it."

"You met a young man," Laura said.

"Yes. Someone handsome and brave and good."

"Is it someone I know?"

Eileen shook her head. "You've never met him. You will when the war is over. I know you'll like him and he'll like you."

"So he's away at war."

"Yes, in his Blériot over the skies of France."

"What is a Valerio?"

"Blériot. It's an airplane."

"Oh, Eileen. A flier."

"In the Royal Flying Corps," Eileen whispered.

They gazed at one another in sudden fear, no longer mother and daughter but two women sharing a common dread.

Laura rose. "You'll want to finish your letter," she said, trying to sound casual. "If you should ever need me, I'll be here."

"I know that." Eileen smiled. Laura thought she'd never looked so beautiful. "I think I've always known it."

Laura brushed her lips across Eileen's hair before she left.

"What the hell's wrong with Eileen?" Mike demanded roughly. He was striding around their bedroom getting undressed. He yanked at his necktie. Laura sat in the bedside chair.

"Eileen is all right. She's just maturing, that's all."

"Horseshit. She floats around here like a walking mummy."

"Let's forget about Eileen for now. It's David's future we have to settle."

"Oh, Christ. Can't we drop that subject? You know I don't like that crazy notion you cooked up with your sister Julia."

"It's important, Mike. For David. I don't want him to go to school in China. We didn't do that well with Eileen—she detested school—and David has a right to learn about his own country. Firsthand. He's an American boy; he should go to school in America. Julia is willing to supervise him and take him for school holidays."

"I'll bet she is. She's been dying to get her hands on our kids from the beginning."

"That's not so. She's already enrolled him in Lawrenceville Prep, and she says when the time comes she'll get him into Princeton."

"Lawrenceville! Princeton! Jesus, Mary, and Joseph! We'll send over a normal kid and get back a stuffed-shirt Eastern Seaboard snob!"

"Maybe a gentleman. Your prejudices are showing, Mike."

Mike sighed. "I suppose you're right. But I hate to give him up. It seems so cold just to ship him over to Julia. He doesn't even want to go.''

"He's eleven years old. He doesn't know what he wants. And maybe he clings to me a little too much.''

"Okay,'' Mike said, "okay. But I still don't like it.''

Laura explained it to David the next day. He sat huddled on his bed with his hands between his knees looking small and scared.

"What if they don't like me?'' he said. "What if they make fun of me and call me Chink or something?''

"They probably will,'' Laura said calmly. "In the beginning. But they'll get used to you and accept you after a while. If you're brave.''

"I'm not too brave,'' he said. "I'm only eleven.''

"You have more courage than you realize. You'll never learn it, though, unless you test yourself.''

"It's . . . it's so far away.''

"Aunt Julia will look after you.''

"Can I come home in the summertime?''

"Of course, David. Every summer. Daddy and I will look forward to it.''

He nodded. "Okay. I guess it will be fun. Seeing America. Meeting new kids.''

"It will.''

"I guess Lawrenceville is a very nice school.''

"It's beautiful. I've seen pictures.''

Suddenly David's bravado deserted him. His eyes filled with tears and he leaped off the bed and rushed to Laura, throwing his arms around her. "Mama, I don't want to go!'' he cried. "Don't make me go!''

Laura clasped him tight. She had a wrenching moment of weakness. *Keep him here. Don't send him away. My son. My only son.* She knew she would be making a mistake by keeping him, though. David needed to learn independence. He needed to cut the family ties; he was too timid, too home-loving. And one member of the Valentine family needed to come of age in America. David must be the one.

She stroked back the hair from his forehead. "I know it's

hard,'' she said gently. "Daddy and I aren't happy either. But you'll thank us someday.''

He didn't believe her. Nevertheless he gulped and nodded, knuckling away the tears. He did his best to be manful. "Okay, Mother,'' he said, trying to control his quaver. "America, here I come.''

It was early May, the time of the Peony Moon, on a quiet Sunday evening. Laura was passing through the downstairs hall when the telephone rang. No one seemed to be around, so she answered it. It was for Eileen. She inquired who was calling, then set down the telephone and called softly up the stairs.

"Eileen? Are you there?''

Eileen appeared at the top of the staircase. "Yes, Mother, I'm here.''

"It's the telephone for you, darling.''

"Who is it, do you know?'' She received few telephone calls these days. Not like the old days.

"Someone called Nigel.''

Eileen went white. She grasped the banister for support.

"Eileen, what's wrong?''

"Nothing. Nothing. I'm all right.'' Eileen came down the stairs like a somnambulist. She approached the telephone, with its receiver upended on the table. Then she just stared at it.

"Eileen, I'll tell this person Nigel to ring back.''

"No, Mother. I'll talk to him.''

She picked up both parts of the telephone and put the speaker to her mouth.

"Hello? Yes, this is Eileen Valentine. . . . No, you needn't introduce yourself, I know who you are. . . . No, I'm not alone. My mother is standing here with me; she answered the telephone. She's . . . she's staying; you needn't worry.'' Eileen glanced at Laura, who was hovering in the hall, wondering if she should go away and not eavesdrop. No, she must stay; Eileen wanted her. Eileen was speaking in short phrases now. "Yes . . . yes . . . I understand.'' She was nodding. Her face was ashen. Her lips were absolutely white. "I know that, Nigel. He considered you his dearest friend. He spoke of you so often . . . No, please don't cry. He wouldn't want you to. . . .'' Eileen's voice broke. "He faced it. He knew it might happen, and so did you and so did I; I'm sorry too. I'm sorry for all of us. . . . I realize you can't talk anymore. Thank you for ringing me, Nigel; don't try to say good-bye if you can't speak. . . . Perhaps we'll meet someday and compare our memories. . . . Thank you for telephoning.''

She replaced the receiver. She stared at Laura with her face a mask.

"He is dead, Mother. He is dead.''

"Oh, Eileen . . .''

"And I'm so calm! Look at me, I'm as steady as a rock!'' She held out her hands. They were trembling like aspen leaves. Eileen regarded them with amazement, as if they belonged to someone else.

She is in shock, Laura thought. *It won't last*.

"Why don't I cry?'' Eileen asked wonderingly. "Why don't I feel anything? I thought I would feel pain. But it doesn't hurt. I don't feel anything. Isn't that odd?''

"Eileen, come into the library.''

Laura led her into the library and locked the door behind them. She sat Eileen on the sofa. Eileen's skin was icy to the touch. She was obeying like a child and murmuring to herself in amazement about her lack of feeling. Laura poured a glass of sherry. She brought it to Eileen.

"Drink this.''

"No, thank you. I'm not thirsty.''

"Please, darling. Just take a sip.''

Eileen sipped obediently. She could barely hold the glass to her lips, her hand was shaking so. Laura steadied it with her own.

"I thought I would be crying and hysterical,'' Eileen said in the same childish wonderment. "Nigel was crying. He broke down and couldn't say good-bye. He was so embarrassed. He's English, you know; they believe in a stiff upper lip and not letting down the side. He was Rory's oldest friend.''

"Was that his name? Rory?''

"Yes, Rory O'Connor. Oh, Mother, you would have liked him so much! He was going to come back to Shanghai and marry me after the war. He was so handsome. He had red hair, like

Daddy, only even redder. It was a beautiful red color all over his body, under his arms and on his chest and . . . everywhere.''

So they had been lovers, Laura thought.

"He had such a beautiful body. But it was all burned up. On the landing strip, like his two best friends. There was nothing left." Eileen shook her head. "I wouldn't want to see him that way, all burned up. Would I, Mother?''

"No, Eileen. No."

She turned her face to Laura, and Laura saw that the shock had suddenly worn off.

"Mother!'' she screamed. "He's dead! Rory is dead!''

She burst into anguished tears and threw herself into Laura's arms. Laura held her tight. Eileen was sobbing bitter, heartbroken sobs, the weeping of a bereaved woman, not a girl.

Oh, darling, Laura thought with tears running down her own cheeks, *you have grown up so fast. Just as you always wanted. But not like this. Not like this.*

When Eileen was calm enough to speak, she began to pour out the story of her days with Rory. Those pitifully brief days. How close they had become. How much they loved one another. How gentle and tender he had been as her lover, and how glad she was that they had been together.

"You weren't staying with your friend near Soochow, that weekend in March.''

"No, I was with Rory." Eileen raised her tearstained face. "There's something else I haven't told you, Mother. I'm pregnant.''

"Oh, God, Eileen! Are you sure?''

"Yes, I saw a doctor. A Chinese doctor, who doesn't know us."

"Dear heaven.''

"Don't be sorry, Mother. I'm not. I am glad.''

"But the baby, Eileen . . . without a father . . . in Shanghai, where everyone gossips . . .''

"Let them.''

"You feel that way now. But what of the child, when it gets older? Children grow up. Do you want Rory's son or daughter to be stigmatized as a bastard?''

"I . . . I don't know.''

Laura sat thinking. Then she said, "We will send you to

America with David. You'll stay with Julia. We'll have to change the tickets, so you can both leave next month instead of waiting until July. David will have to understand. Then when you return with the baby, we'll think of a story to tell people."

Eileen rose. She paced restlessly around the room. She shook her head. "No. That's not the solution."

"It's the best way, darling."

"No. I don't want to be six thousand miles away when I have my baby. I want to be here, right here, with you and Daddy. Just in case anything goes wrong."

"Nothing will go wrong!" Laura cried.

"It could. You almost died when you gave birth to me. George told me how he prayed for you, with Reverend and Mrs. Peterson."

"That was eighteen years ago!"

"I want to be here," Eileen insisted stubbornly. "Upstairs, in my own bedroom, in my own bed. Not in a hospital with nurses. Not somewhere in Maryland with Aunt Julia, surrounded by strangers."

There was an aura so calm, so fatalistic and unafraid about Eileen's expression when she spoke of her coming childbirth and something going wrong, that Laura felt a sensation of dread. She resolved to take her to Dr. Fortescue at once. Tomorrow.

Eileen came over to Laura and knelt at her feet. She put her head in Laura's lap.

"Mother, do something for me?" she asked.

"Of course, my love."

"Tell Daddy."

"Oh, Eileen! He loves you! More than anyone!"

"That's why," she said. "I can't tell him. I just can't. Please tell him for me. Please. You'll know what to say."

Laura felt her tears rising again. "All right, Eileen," she said. "I'll do my best."

Eileen sighed. "I knew I could count on you."

"If I could get my hands on that bastard," Mike said between his teeth, "I'd kill him."

"You can't kill a dead man, Mike. And from what Eileen tells me, he was a fine young man. He was going to marry her after the war.''

"And she believed him! A cheap wartime romance! Goddamn it, I thought she had more sense!''

"I don't believe it was like that, Mike.''

"Are you sticking up for her? Are you trying to defend her?''

"Yes,'' said Laura quietly, "and so should you. She needs us both. You above all. She's afraid to face you, afraid of what you'll say. And please don't forget, she's had a terrible shock. Go to her, Mike, and give her some comfort.''

"You're asking too much, Laura.''

"Mike, I'm begging you. Don't turn your back on Eileen. It wasn't hard to be her father when she was an adorable little girl and thought you were the sun and the moon. Now it isn't easy because you're angry and disappointed. But now is when it matters most. Please. For her sake.''

Mike stood breathing hard. He put his hand over his eyes. "I'll try,'' he muttered finally. "Give me a little time.''

Laura nodded. She left the room.

Eileen sat in her bedroom. She was reading over Rory's letters. She wished she had a photograph. How stupid of them not to think of it! Maybe Nigel had one she could borrow and copy. She kissed the letter she was holding.

Someone knocked on the door.

"Come in,'' she said absently. The door opened. She glanced up. Her heart gave a painful thump. "Daddy?'' she said hesitantly.

"Hello, Eileen. Are you busy?''

"No, I'm not busy, I . . .'' Her throat went dry. She tried to swallow. She turned her face away, afraid she would cry. She heard his footsteps coming into the room. She couldn't look at him. "Daddy,'' she whispered, "I'm sorry.''

"Yeah, I know. So am I.''

"Are you . . . very angry?''

"I was. But I guess I'll get over it.''

She sprang up from her chair and threw herself against him. "Don't be angry,'' she said, her voice shaking. "Please. Just love me, the way you always have. I need to know that. So much.''

Mike put his arms around her. He bowed his head. "You're still my baby. Still my little girl. No matter what you do, or how mad I get, we'll never be able to change that."

"It's all I wanted to hear," Eileen said with a trembling sigh. "I was so worried." She rested her head on his chest and closed her eyes. "Now I have nothing to worry about."

CHAPTER 16

George Henderson and Laura were in the library. It was August 1915. David had sailed for America and arrived safely; the Valentines had already had a letter from Julia. She was pleased and delighted with her nephew and impressed with his manners. So unlike rowdy American children! They were going to be great friends; Mike and Laura could put their minds at ease.

"I'm not so sure," Mike had said upon reading the letter. "She's all set to take over."

"Oh, no, Mike." Laura had hesitated. "Besides, he'll be away at school next month, so Julia's influence will be weakened."

Now Laura and George were discussing Eileen, not David, and Mike was not present.

"I don't think anyone knows," Laura said. "She hasn't left the house for four weeks. Dr. Fortescue came here to examine her."

"You can't keep it a secret forever."

Laura nodded worriedly. "George, it's twins!" she said. "Dr. Fortescue heard two heartbeats with his stethoscope."

"Good lord. What are you going to do?"

"We can't seem to reach a decision. Eileen won't help. She just accepts each day placidly and leaves the whole matter in the lap of the gods. Mike and I are at a loss." Laura glanced up and saw George's face. He was leaning against the fireplace watching her.

His expression was filled with concern. Her own features crumpled. "Oh, George, I can't pretend with you! I'm not just at a loss! The truth is I'm frightened and miserable! I don't know where to turn or what to do! Eileen hasn't the slightest idea of what's in store for her, or how the children will suffer without a name in the years to come! How will we protect them? I can't sleep at night thinking about it!''

"I wish I could protect *you*," George muttered.

"You've always been so kind. But it isn't your burden."

To George's helpless consternation Laura covered her face with her hands and began to weep.

He cursed his position. George had always been an outsider, on the fringes of Mike and Laura's life, though he'd been a "family friend." That was a status he had understood and felt comfortable fulfilling. Now it was not enough. He had been watching on the sidelines for too many years; it had grown too painful.

He knew he was completely accepted by Laura and Eileen and David—knew also that Mike distrusted him a little with regard to Laura and kept a wary eye on him. That had never been necessary. George had never overstepped his boundaries with Laura; he had always been honorable.

In one important respect, however, Mike was correct. George was in love with Laura and had been for years.

He stepped away from the fireplace and went to the sofa where Laura was weeping. He put his hands on her arms and raised her to her feet. "Laura dear, don't cry. We'll find a way out, I promise."

"I can't think of anything to do. . . ."

He had folded his arms around her and she was weeping against his shoulder. He was comforting her unthinkingly, and she was accepting his embrace in the same spirit. George was happier and more miserable than he had ever been in his life. He began to say soothing, foolish things to calm her down, and he felt her grow quiet against him; he closed his eyes and smelled the wild-flower fragrance of her hair. Neither of them noticed Mike enter the room and were not aware of his presence until Mike offered George a drink.

"Sorry I can't join you, George," said Mike's voice, "but you know how it is with me. I'm better off not drinking."

George released Laura and stepped back. He felt startled and embarrassed. "Why sure, Mike. I guess I'll have a brandy."

"Why don't you help yourself? You always seem to make yourself at home in this house."

Mike's double meaning was plain. Laura began to look tense again.

"Laura, why don't you go upstairs and lie down?" Mike said. "You look tired."

"I'm not tired."

"I think you should take a nap."

Laura swiftly weighed the merits of remaining or leaving the room and decided the better choice was to depart. Her presence was disturbing to both men. She excused herself and went out.

"If you have any stupid ideas about me and Laura," George said immediately, "you can forget it."

"I'm not stupid, George."

"I didn't say you were. I said your ideas might be."

"I'm thinking pretty straight, as a matter of fact. Here's your brandy." Mike had poured it himself. He handed the glass to George. "We've been friends for a long time, and I know what you're likely to do and what you're not."

"Then you understand what was going on just now."

"Sure." Mike shrugged. "I understand how you've always felt about Laura too. You've always thought she was too good for me."

"Maybe," George said quietly.

"Thanks for the compliment."

"Maybe I was wrong, though."

"Okay, George. I'll accept that as an apology. What I wanted to say to you was, let's not quarrel. Not now. We need all the friends we can get at this moment, and I'm willing to forget the little scene with Laura. If you are."

George sipped his brandy and nodded. But he couldn't really forget it. He knew it was time for him to go. To leave Shanghai. To remove himself from the outskirts of the Valentine family. He thought he had known it for a long time.

As he and Mike made small talk, covering over what had

happened, George began to think. He was examining a notion in his mind. He came to a conclusion at last, and when he was ready, he cleared his throat and told Mike he had an idea.

"What sort of idea, George?"

"I'm thinking about leaving Shanghai."

"Mother of God. Leave Shanghai? Where would you go?"

"India. Darjeeling. I have a job offer there."

They discussed the possible job for a while until George got Mike to agree that perhaps it was an opportunity for George.

Then George steeled himself and spoke of his other idea.

"Before I go, Mike, let me do one good turn for the Valentines," he said. He paused and looked into Mike's eyes. "Would you do that?" he asked. "Would you let me accomplish something for you and Laura and Eileen?"

Mike asked what he wanted to do. Tersely, with total sincerity, George told him.

Mike was silent for a long time. "It could be undone if need be," he said at last.

"Of course. At any time. Just a request by letter."

"Christ, George. It's a lot to ask of you."

"No, Mike. It doesn't seem that way to me."

Again Mike did not speak. He turned his face aside. Then he said in a low voice, "I may want to take you up on that offer, old scout. If Eileen consents."

George Henderson and Eileen Valentine were married in the parlor of the Valentine house. Only the minister was present, and Laura and Mike, and Plum Blossom and Chen. Eileen was calm and radiant, George sober and steady, supporting her elbow with his hand. A notice was put into the English-language newspapers, saying only that Miss Eileen Valentine had become the bride of Mr. George Henderson in a private ceremony.

A week later George said good-bye to Laura in the library. He was sailing to India on a freighter.

"Will you write from Darjeeling?" Laura asked with a troubled expression.

George said he didn't think so. "It will be better for Eileen and the children if I remove myself from their lives," he told her quietly. "And from your life too."

"You belong here, George," Laura said. Her lips were trembling.

George shook his head. "Eileen will tell the children when they're old enough that their father was an engineer who disappeared in India. In a sense it will be the truth." He paused, and then added, "I'll see to it you always know where I am, in case Eileen ever wants a divorce to marry someone else."

So long, Shanghai. Good-bye, Laura dear.

He was peaceful about leaving, George thought. Now he was reconciled. Of course he would miss China. He would miss Eileen and David. He laughed ruefully to himself. He would even—although the damn fool would probably never believe it—miss Mike Valentine.

"George, you were always a man of your word," Mike had said. He'd added with a sardonic grin, "You've made yourself a big hero in the eyes of the women. I suppose you know that."

"I guess that's why I did it, Mike." It was the old teasing relationship, to cover up their emotion.

Mike's expression had softened. "I'll look after Laura; don't worry about it. You've helped us out of a bad jam, and don't think I'm not grateful."

"Sure. Take care of yourself, Mike."

"You, too, old scout. Don't forget your gun when you leave for India. What the hell, you may run into bandits."

They had laughed, a sad laughter that mingled affection, nostalgia, and regret, and then they had pressed their hands together and parted.

Now Laura was holding out her hand in farewell. *The last time, Laura.* George rose to his feet. He took her hand and raised it to his lips.

It's time to go, George. Say good-bye like a gentleman. Say good-bye to Laura.

It was okay, though. Eileen's kids would be named Henderson, and that would be fine. Laura wouldn't have to worry about gossip, and that was fine too. George could walk out with his shoulders straight. And he did.

The weeks slipped by after George's departure. The summer ended, and damp misty autumn gave way to cloudy winter. One evening Eileen decided to go for a walk. It was raining, a gently misty rain, the kind she had walked in with Rory. She was growing more awkward every day and soon she would be forced to give up her walks, so she must go now if she wished to.

She wanted to think about Rory. Alone, in the rain. She felt so close to him. Lately she had been dreaming about him, and she heard his voice in her mind even when she was awake, so gentle and tender, saying again those loving things she would never forget. She felt his strong arms around her and his warm breath on her cheek.

It came to her that they would never be parted, she and Rory. *My babies,* she thought. *They will live for us and strive to stop people from suffering. They will be wonderful children. And then Rory and I can be together always.*

People passed her on the sidewalk carrying oiled-paper umbrellas. Eileen put up her rain hood. She smiled to herself and hummed under her breath. ". . . good-bye, Piccadilly . . . farewell, Leicester Square . . ."

People would think she was crazy, she thought, singing and smiling to herself in the rain. She was not crazy, though. She was simply . . . sure. For the first time since Nigel's telephone call she was contented. She was even happy. She understood a little bit about life and death, and she knew there was nothing to fear. There were no endings. There was still Rory and there was still Eileen.

She was passing a weaver's shop and became aware she was near the walled Chinese city. Inside the shop a hand loom was rattling, she could hear its sound. The weaver was Chinese and worked late, for he was poor. Eileen could see the light of his lamp through the rice-paper window. She sighed deeply, hoping he would rest soon, and lifted her face to the gentle rain.

There was nothing to fear. There never had been, and there never would be. Eileen wished she could tell everyone. She wished she could stop people on the street and tell them. Perhaps her babies would understand that profound truth when they grew up, and be wise and strong enough to explain it to the world. She willed them wisdom, compassion, and courage. Then she knew it was time to go back home; she had walked far enough.

*   *   *

Henry Chen was standing at the window of his mother's sitting room. He was just tall enough to look out. Plum Blossom was sewing baby clothes.

"My mother," he said thoughtfully, "why do we live in this house?"

"It is our home, my son."

"Why do we not live with the other Chinese people?"

"Because the honorable master and his wife are our employers." Plum Blossom bit off a piece of thread. "We are fortunate to have this employment. Others are not so fortunate."

"I see others when we go to the market, asking for spoiled fruit. Are they hungry?"

"Many of them are hungry."

"Only in Shanghai?"

"No. Everywhere in China."

"That is wrong, my mother."

"Yes, it is wrong. When you are grown and teaching at the university, according to my hopes, you will speak against such evils."

Henry nodded. He turned from the window. "May I read my book now?" he inquired politely.

"Very well. Perhaps the book that Missy Eileen gave you, about the naughty rabbit." Eileen had given Henry her Beatrix Potter books.

"No, I would like my Chinese book." He fetched it from his bookshelf and sat down with it on the floor. Plum Blossom glanced over. It was his favorite: a cheaply printed, garishly illustrated child's biography of Sun Yat-sen.

After a while he raised his head and inquired, "Honorable Mother, what is the word for two babies at once? I have been trying and trying to think of it, but I cannot."

"Twins, my son."

"Oh, yes, twins!" Henry's face cleared. "When will they come?"

"Soon."

"Will I be allowed to play with them?"

"If Missy Eileen permits it."

"I will like not to be the smallest person in the house any longer."

"You will have only a short time to wait, my son. The time is near."

CHAPTER 17

Eileen was drifting, floating above her bed in a state of pure spirit, detached from her body but with one overwhelming thought: *The pain and struggle are over, all over; there will be no more pain, not ever. How lovely.* And she had brought the babies into the world, that was lovely too. Now she could rest.

Dr. Fortescue was covered with blood, and so were the two nurses who had assisted him in the delivery of Eileen's twins. The bedroom looked like a slaughterhouse, white and red: white for the color of Eileen's face, red for the color of blood.

"More towels," whispered the doctor urgently as he hunched at the foot of Eileen's bed. "Lord help me, I can't stop this hemorrhaging."

His arms were splashed with scarlet up to the elbows. Eileen lay terrifyingly still against the pillow, her face like an ivory cameo.

"The babies are fine, Doctor," whispered one of the nurses.

"More towels," he hissed furiously.

Laura gazed at Dr. Fortescue in dread. He had just come out of Eileen's room. The two nurses were still inside. Laura had sent Mike out of the house, finding his nervous pacing unbearable, and he had gone unwillingly, promising to return in half an hour.

"The babies, Martin?" she asked, searching the doctor's face.

"They are fine. Two perfect babies, not identical, a boy and a girl. She had no trouble with the delivery."

"Then what is it? Something is wrong! Tell me!"

The doctor sighed miserably. "Nothing that could be predicted, here or in a hospital. It is what we call a hidden, accidental hemorrhage. Massive bleeding from the womb."

"Can't you stop it?"

"We've tried. I think we've stopped it. It may be too late."

"Too late! Oh, my God! Do something! Can't you do something?"

He shook his head in wretched weariness. "There's a technique of blood transfusion. . . . It's never worked before, but they're trying something new on the Western Front . . . matching blood types so the body won't reject the blood . . . maybe in a year or two we'll know how. . . ."

"It will be too late for Eileen!"

The doctor put his hands on Laura's shoulders. "Laura, only one force can save her now. Nothing scientific, nothing I can put in a test tube or examine under a microscope. . . . It's called the will to live. I've seen it pull people back from the brink of certain death; don't ask me how." He paused. "Eileen is not fighting, Laura. She's not struggling to live. She's just drifting away. Make her fight."

"Oh, God!"

Laura wrenched herself out of his grasp and entered the room. The nurses were just leaving with the babies in their arms. Laura didn't look at the blood-soaked towels on the floor. She saw only her daughter. Eileen was lying against the pillow, calm and peaceful, deathly pale. For a terrifying moment Laura thought she was dead. Then Eileen turned her head. She saw Laura and smiled.

"Hello, Mother," she whispered. "I'm glad you're here. Come and talk to me."

Laura knelt by the edge of Eileen's bed.

"Eileen, you've been bleeding," she said softly. "You're very weak."

"I know."

"You must fight back, darling. Dr. Fortescue says you haven't been fighting."

Eileen ignored that. "There's something I want to say before it's too late."

"Don't talk that way!"

"Do you remember," Eileen whispered, "a few years ago when I was a horrible spoiled child, and I said dreadful things to you about Daddy and how he didn't love you?"

"No, I don't think I remember—"

"Yes, you do. They weren't true, Mother. I didn't mean any of them. I was just being a brat." She smiled at Laura. "Daddy loves you and so do I. I have always loved you, with all my heart."

"I never doubted it, Eileen, not for a moment."

"Oh, that's good." She sighed weakly. "I'm glad David isn't here; he's too young to understand. Tell him I said good-bye. Tell him to grow up strong and brave."

Laura struggled not to sob. "Don't let yourself drift, Eileen!" she cried. "Fight back!" She reached for Eileen's hand and clutched it desperately, trying to bring some warmth to her fingers.

"Daddy understands how I feel. He's forgiven me."

A strangled sob escaped Laura's lips.

"Don't cry, Mother." Eileen said. "Don't be sad. I'm not."

"You mustn't let yourself slip away!"

"I have to; don't you understand?" Eileen sighed. "Rory is waiting for me."

"Oh, my God!"

She raised herself from the pillow. "I can see him," she said, and now her face was radiant. "I can see him so clearly. He looks so handsome. He's wearing his uniform. He's calling me. He's holding out his hand. He says there's nothing to be afraid of." Eileen sank back. "We're going salmon fishing in the Lennon River," she whispered dreamily. "Sir Liam is there, too, on his big white horse, seventeen hands high, with his collie dog Kerry running alongside."

"Eileen don't . . . don't . . ." Laura was crying too hard to speak.

Eileen sat up again. Her voice was strong. "Mother!" she cried. "I can see Michael! He is there too! He looks lovely, with pink cheeks, just the way he did before he got sick! Do you remember? My brother Michael?"

"Oh, God . . ."

"Take care of my babies, Mother," Eileen whispered. Her voice was weak again. "You and Daddy. I know you will."

Laura's head was bowed and she was pressing Eileen's hand when she heard a gurgling sound. She looked up. Eileen's lips were parted, her jaw had dropped, and her eyes were staring wide but she saw nothing.

Laura struggled to her feet. "Martin!" she screamed. "Martin!"

The doctor was with her, holding her back from Eileen's bedside. "It's too late, Laura. She wasn't in any pain. She didn't feel any hurt at all. Bleeding to death is a very gentle way to die. Console yourself, my dear."

"Leave the room, Martin," said a hollow voice from the doorway.

"Mike!" Laura gasped.

"Leave the room," Mike said to the doctor. After a moment Dr. Fortescue sighed and left. Laura gazed at Mike in horror. He paid no attention to her. He went directly to Eileen's bedside and knelt down. He crossed himself. Laura saw in grief-stricken pity that he didn't even know he had done it. He leaned forward and gently closed Eileen's eyes with his thumbs. He lifted her jaw, restoring the sweet curve of her mouth. He folded her arms across her breast. He pulled up the coverlet to her waist and arranged it neatly. He straightened the pillow so that Eileen's honey blond hair fanned out across it.

She looked so calm and peaceful and beautiful with her eyes closed, Laura thought, taking a breath in pain.

"Go out now, Laura," Mike said in a strange, distant voice without turning his head. He kissed Eileen's forehead, then knelt again, putting his hand over hers. "I want to be alone with my little girl."

With her knuckles pressed to her mouth to keep from crying out, Laura ran from the room, closing the door behind her.

She leaned wearily against the wall in the corridor outside Eileen's bedroom. Mike was still inside with the door closed. He had been there a long time. The doctor and the nurses had departed. Laura couldn't leave. She had to wait for Mike.

The door opened and he came out. His face was ravaged but composed. He had come to some sort of peace with himself, Laura thought painfully. Thank God. Thank God.

He was silent. Then he said, "I think she knew, Laura. I think she knew all along. That's why she was always in such a hurry to grow up. She knew she wasn't going to have much time."

"Maybe you're right. . . ."

He raised his chin and his jaw tightened. "I want her to have a special casket," he said. "The most expensive one in Shanghai. Ebony, with silver fittings. And an ivory satin lining with French lace edges."

"All right, Mike. If that's what you want."

"And she'll wear her blue dress. The one that matches her eyes. The one your dressmaker made for that big party last year where she danced all night and came home at dawn."

Laura nodded silently.

"And we'll order wine and champagne and food for the whole city. Enough for a week. We'll keep the doors open, the front door and the back door, and anyone who wants to can come in and eat and drink. And there'll be music, all the time. Eileen's favorite songs."

He's going to create his own version of an Irish wake, Laura thought. *If it helps him, that's fine.*

After a moment she asked, "Would you like me to invite . . . Monsignor Monaghan?"

"I told you, anyone can come."

"Would you like to . . . speak to him privately?"

He glanced at Laura with the old hard anger in his eyes. "Why would I want to do that?"

He still didn't realize what he had done at Eileen's bedside, Laura thought. Somewhere within Mike was the faith of his boyhood, deep and unchanging, but he would not recognize it. Perhaps he would someday. In his own time. She took his hand and raised it to her cheek. They were both silent. The house was quiet. So quiet.

A shrill wail suddenly split the silence. It was joined in seconds by another. Within moments the air was filled with shrieks.

"The babies!" Laura gasped. "We forgot all about them!"

Plum Blossom appeared from the guest room at the end of the corridor. She held a screaming infant in her arms. "We have sent for a wet nurse, missy," she said distractedly. "She is on her way. They are hungry."

She approached Mike and Laura.

"Which one is that?" Mike asked over the din.

"The little girl."

The infant had bright orange-red hair and was waving enraged balled-up fists. It was impossible to see the tiny face, so contorted was it in anger.

"Mother of God," said Mike. "A redheaded scrapper."

Plum Blossom nodded. "She has a temper."

Mike turned aside and passed a hand over his eyes. "I can't think about this yet. Babies. Infants. Starting all over again."

Maybe the children would take their minds off their sorrow, Laura thought, pain moving in her chest. When their grief was healed a little, they would have the twins.

Laura wrote painful and difficult letters. To George. To her sister Julia. To David at school. To Sir James O'Connor in Ireland, explaining what had happened, feeling that as Rory's nearest relative and the twins' uncle he had a right to be informed.

When she received an answer from Sir James, his letter was compassionate and understanding, extending his condolences to the Valentines on the loss of their daughter. These were wretched and miserable times in which to live; it affected everyone, pray God the war be ended soon and the slaughter be over. Rory had indeed intended to marry Eileen; he had written as much to his brother. He had loved Eileen very much. As for the future of the infants, he, Sir James, had no objection to the Valentines assuming responsibility. If ever they felt it was wise to tell the children the truth, he would be happy to welcome them to Donegal. If not, he would understand. He would not interfere in any way; it would be the Valentines' decision to make.

The letter was signed, "Her respectful servant, Sir James O'Connor."

That was settled then, Laura thought.

She found Henry Chen hanging over the twins' cradle one day.

"Are you paying a visit, Henry?" she asked.

"Honorable Godmother," he said plaintively, "I thought they would play with me."

"They're too small."

"They can't even talk!"

"They will, when they're bigger."

He nodded. What a remarkably handsome little boy he was, Laura thought, with those thick black eyebrows and sparkling black eyes and high cheekbones and perfect ivory skin. He would be a dramatically attractive man someday.

Little Amy awoke and started to scream.

"She has bad manners," Henry observed.

"She doesn't know any better."

"I will teach her." Henry touched the baby's flaming hair with his fingertip. "It's too bad that she has such funny hair. But I'll teach her anyway. When she can talk."

"Will you teach Andy too?"

"Oh, yes. But he isn't crying."

He will be any moment, Laura thought ruefully. When one cried, the other cried. These days the house was bedlam.

CHAPTER 18

Yüan Shih-k'ai was dead in Peking, and Sun Yat-sen was in exile in Japan. It was the summer of 1916. Yüan had died under mysterious circumstances, just before he'd been about to crown himself emperor. Some said he'd been poisoned; others said he'd died of chagrin because of an uprising against him in Yunnan.

China was now without a leader. The effectiveness of the republic was destroyed, and there was no more dynasty. The provinces were dissolving into local feuds, skirmishes, corruption, and violence. Shanghai and the other Treaty Ports remained under firm Western control, but the rest of the country was drifting into chaos.

There was an inevitable filling of the vacuum of power. Local bandits in some places, renegade military officers in others, began to assemble their own armies and mark off private territories.

Some of them, it was rumored, were financed by Japan. One after another these men move moved into the *yamen*s: official residences of the provincial governors. The Age of Warlords was beginning.

By 1917, when America entered the war, Mike and Laura had had to close two of the galleries. Laura had regretfully dismissed all her employees except Ronald and a girl named Violet Wang.

"I may have to go back to that cigarette company," Mike said, "if the San Francisco store closes too."

"I would hate to see you do that," Laura said.

Laura was forty and Mike would be forty-five on his next birthday. The cigarette company would mean constant traveling for him, drafty trains, hotel rooms, poor food . . .

They would struggle on as best they could. Many of Laura's customers now were Japanese, flushed with triumph over the success of their Twenty-one Demands, an agreement that they had forced on the weakened Chinese government. The Japanese were establishing an economic monopoly on the Chinese interior. Laura was beginning to believe the warnings she had heard for years about Japan's limitless ambitions, military and economic. They were hard-eyed, arrogant people, at least in Shanghai. Maybe, Laura thought, the Japanese were different in their own country. More likable. People usually were. Those who came as conquerors to China were not likable at all. They took themselves so seriously.

The "dwarf bandits," as the Chinese called them, never seemed to laugh. They preferred to give orders, and the ones in uniform preferred to clank their swords.

Mike and Laura struggled to keep David in school. One night Laura announced she'd received a long overdue letter.

"It's about time," said Mike. "I thought he had paralysis of the hand."

David's first letters, when he'd just arrived at school, had been miserable and tear-blotched. He hated school. The kids hated him. They jeered at him and called him stupid names. They made fun of his silk underwear, lovingly hand-sewn by Plum Blossom, so now he was wearing American cotton underpants, and they itched.

Mike had read the letter incredulously. "His drawers itch? What the hell's the matter with him?"

"He's lonely, Mike."

Mike had flung down the letter. "That's it. That is it. We're booking passage on the first ship across the Pacific and getting him out of that goddamn school and taking him home. I'm not having him walking around crying his eyes out, wearing itchy underpants."

Laura had been half inclined to agree. Then she decided they were being too hasty. "Let's give it a little more time," she said. "Maybe he'll learn to like it."

"Not too much time," Mike said darkly.

The letters had improved. After the summer in Shanghai he'd been willing to return to Lawrenceville. Now Laura smiled as she turned the page.

"He's really pleased with himself, Mike. He says he made the varsity."

"What team?" Mike said sarcastically. "Polo?"

"No, baseball."

"No kidding. He made the baseball team? What position?"

"Third base."

"Let me see that letter." Mike took the pages from her hand. "Son of a gun. He did make the baseball team."

"I told you things would improve."

They did not improve at the gallery. Not even when the war ended in the fall of 1918. It was growing increasingly difficult to bring antiques out of the Chinese interior. Even train travel was dangerous. Julia volunteered to pay David's school fees, and they were forced to agree.

By the start of 1919 Mike had had to give up his membership at the Shanghai Club. They had a household to support, with two small children. "We'll have to sell the house," Mike said, "and I'll look for a job."

"There must be another way. We'll be back where we started when we left Weichang."

"You said you were prepared."

"I know, but . . . that was before."

Before Eileen died. Before the twins were born.

Like the cavalry arriving just as the Indians attacked, two

letters arrived from America. One was from Julia, informing Laura that their father had died. The other had the return address of a law firm in Hartford. In grief and shock Laura thought about the loss of her father. Finally she faced Mike, wide-eyed and dazed.

"Papa is dead," she whispered. "Isn't that strange. I thought he would live forever. He was quite old." She took a deep breath. Then she gazed down at the letter she was holding. "There's something else, Mike. This letter from the lawyers' office." She held it out. "Papa left me money."

Narrowing his eyes, Mike took the letter. He scanned it. "Holy Christ," he said, "I didn't know your father was that rich."

Laura nodded.

Mike suddenly grinned. "Saved by the bell."

"We can reopen the other galleries now. Maybe we can even carry out those plans for a shop in Mayfair, in London, remember? Now that the war is over." Laura sank down in a chair with a breathless little laugh that was half a sob of grief and regret. "Thanks to Papa, I feel like the Count of Monte Cristo. The world is mine."

"Not quite. I think we should forget about reopening the galleries. This time we'll have to be a little smarter."

"In what way?"

"Antiques are all right, but the supply is too uncertain. I don't like the looks of these warlords. They're petty little dictators, and they can close off a province or confiscate a train or do whatever they please. They have their own armies. Concubines. They like antiques too. They're furnishing those *yamen*s like the Empress's palace. With stolen treasures. Let's not depend on antiques." Mike considered for a moment. "Let's make our own."

Laura was shocked. "You mean cheat? Be dishonest?"

"No. I guess I didn't mean antiques, I meant curios."

"Cheap little knickknacks and vases and ashtrays? They do that better in Japan."

"Okay, think of something. Dishes. Plates. Porcelain."

"That sounds interesting," Laura said slowly.

"All those Chinese export wares you say tourists love . . . we could imitate that, in sets of dishes. Reproductions."

"Like Blue Willow."

"Sure."

"I like that idea, Mike. I like it very much." She paused. "Do we have enough money to start a porcelain factory? We need workers and kilns and machinery and a factory building. . . ."

"No, but we can borrow. We've got your inheritance. We can use the house and stock in the gallery as collateral. We'll keep one gallery open. . . ."

They gazed at each other with growing excitement.

They decided to take action. Letters began to travel back and forth to the lawyers in Hartford, fat envelopes bulging with papers to be signed and notarized, then arrangements were made to transfer Laura's inheritance to a Shanghai bank. They drew up plans. They studied the building and designing of kilns, the best materials for firebricks, and the most efficient heating for the firing of the pottery. The kilns would need constant high temperatures. Their choice was between electricity and natural gas, and they chose electricity as more efficient. Laura studied the composition of glazes and began to investigate a pattern for the dishes. Mike was out every day inspecting factory sites. They wanted light and air and spacious work surfaces for the throwing process in which the clay would be molded, and the glazing process, and they needed a large outdoor area for the firing kilns. They had to find suppliers of kaolin, the basic clay ingredient.

Mike located an unused factory in Hunkow which could be converted. The next step was seeing about the loan.

"The bankers are going to ask us one question we haven't discussed," Laura said. "The most important element of all. Customers. We need orders in advance. This isn't like a gallery."

Mike agreed. "We'll need some sample dishes first."

"I can have them made up at a pottery in Chapei. It's just a small workshop, but they're good craftsmen. Then what?"

One of them would have to go on a selling trip, they realized. Abroad, now that the war was over. Laura's designing work was completed; she was the logical choice. More letters were exchanged. Finally arrangements were settled. Pierre-Marc would meet her in Paris. Then London, then Julia would meet her in New York. She would visit David at school, then she would see their Chinese-American dealer in San Francisco, and at last she would voyage back to Shanghai.

"I hope I have a full order book," Laura said one morning half to herself.

Mike rose from the breakfast table. "I'm going downtown to close up that office," he said. He would be moving to an office in the factory when everything was settled. Meanwhile he would work at home. "That'll take a few hours. After that I'll be at the club for a while."

He had reinstated his lapsed membership at the Shanghai Club, where he played cards and billiards and sipped tonic-water with lime.

Late that afternoon Chen brought in a stack of papers to the library, file folders and old ledgers. They had been delivered from Mike's office. The twins were playing outside with Henry, who was home from school. Henry was a nine-year-old benevolent dictator where Amy and Andy were concerned. He was stretched out on the backyard lawn with his head propped in his hands, reading a book that was open before him in the grass, and at the same time keeping an ear cocked for the children. He heard two pairs of feet approaching. As usual they were making an inspection visit to see what he was doing.

They stood one on either side of him.

"What are you reading?" Amy asked.

"Just a book," Henry answered.

"It has pictures," Andy observed.

They squatted to look at the pictures.

"Who is that?" Amy asked, pointing.

"Nikolai Lenin."

"And who is that?" inquired Andy.

"Leon Trotsky."

"Why do they have such funny names?" Amy asked.

"Because they're Russian."

The twins were silent. Henry turned a page.

"Those people are shooting guns," Andy commented.

"They're fighting a revolution. And don't ask me what a revolution is," Henry added hastily, "because you wouldn't understand the explanation."

Amy's combativeness was aroused. "Read us this book," she demanded. "Explain it."

"No."

"Why not?"

"Because your grandparents wouldn't like it."

"How do you know?"

"I just know."

Amy glanced over at her brother. "Henry Chen," she announced, "thinks he knows everything. He thinks he's the smartest person in the world."

"No he doesn't," responded Andy at once. He usually followed Amy's lead, but he would not agree with criticism of Henry.

"Yes, he does."

"Maybe he is," declared Andy.

Amy made a fist and punched Henry in the upper arm. "Are you the smartest person in the world?" she demanded.

"It's possible," he said absently without looking up.

She punched him again as hard as she could. "Does that hurt?"

"Does what hurt?" he asked innocently. He glanced up at the sky. "Did a leaf fall off that tree just now on my arm?"

Amy burst out laughing and the twins ran off.

Laura entered the library after dinner and saw the stack of papers from Mike's office on the desk. She sighed. They'd have to be sorted. What a job. Maybe they could throw away a lot of it. Mike would have to consult with their accountant. She pulled out a ledger near the middle of the stack and browsed idly through the entries. Recurring expenses, a record of months and years. Payments to steamship lines, freight forwarders, insurance companies . . . She frowned. A payment to Chen? Here was another, exactly a month later. And another. The same amount. Not a large sum, but paid steadily.

Her curiosity aroused, she began to go back in time. They extended back, every single month. She found another stack of old ledgers and went through them. The same story, for eight years.

She asked herself what was going on. *They began in 1911.* The year Mike stopped drinking, so the money had not gone for liquor. What, then? She could inquire of Mike, but something told her not to; she had a foreboding. Mike could be difficult when cornered; he lost his temper. There was an easier way. She picked up the little bell on the desk and rang for Chen.

Chen buried his face in his hands. "I promised, missy. I promised never to say a word. I cannot break my promise."

"It is too late, Chen," Laura said. "The matter has been revealed to me. Partly revealed. Your promise is no longer valid. You must tell me the meaning of these payments in the ledgers."

Chen shook his head miserably.

"Is there a terrible secret you have discovered about the master? Does he pay you to keep silent?"

"Oh, no, missy!"

"What do you do with the money? What do you spend it on? Have you begun a hidden bank account for Henry's future?"

Chen straightened. He regarded her with dignified reproach. "You should not accuse me of such a thing, missy."

"What am I to think? You have been receiving this money for eight years. Eight years, Chen! Do you know how much that amounts to?"

"No."

"Perhaps you have given it to Plum Blossom."

"She knows nothing about it."

"You are in disgrace, Chen!" Laura cried in frustration. "You have been stealing money from your employer!"

"It is not for me!" Chen cried, goaded beyond endurance. "I do not keep it! I have not stolen anything, ever! The money is not for me!"

They stared at each other, wide-eyed, as the words died away. Chen turned his face aside.

"Sit down, Chen," Laura whispered. "You must tell me now. Everything. I will protect your secret."

Trembling, Chen lowered himself into a chair. "It was the summer you were away in the mountains, missy," he said. "When the master and I were alone in the house. Li-san came back."

The summer of 1911.

"Who is Li-san?"

"The concubine from Peking, who lived with us before you came."

The beautiful Chinese girl on the bridge with Mike when I first came to Shanghai. It must be.

"This money is for her?" Laura asked quietly.

Chen hung his head in misery. "She is very poor. Her husband is dead. She helped the master when you were away that summer, and he is grateful to her."

Laura felt a hollow in the pit of her stomach. *All that time. Eight years. Mike still loves her. He sends her money every month. Does he visit her in Chapei? Yes, of course. She is his mistress. What a fool I've been.*

"All right, Chen," she said quietly. "Thank you. You may go back to your work, and I will forget who told me this story."

"What will you do?" he asked in a quavering voice.

"I have not decided."

It was a day and a half before Laura could confront Mike with her knowledge. She was too deeply angry and insulted to speak immediately; she needed time to collect herself. The betrayal she had suffered was too profound. She could not stop thinking about Li-san, her beauty, her allure, the passion they must share. Perhaps Mike spoke of her, Laura, to his mistress when they were in one another's arms. Perhaps they both pitied her and longed desperately to live together as husband and wife.

She shook with outrage. This humiliation was too much to bear.

Finally she confronted Mike in the library after dinner. She entered quietly. Mike was seated at the desk going through the papers. A cigar was burning in the ashtray beside him, and he had his usual cup of coffee at his elbow.

"Mike, may we talk?" she asked.

"Can't it wait, sweetheart? I'm in the middle of something."

"No, it can't wait. In fact, I'm going to close the door."

"Oh, like that. I recognize the tone of voice." Mike swiveled around and put the cigar between his teeth. "You're upset. I can always tell."

"As usual your instincts are right." Laura closed the door. Then she turned to face her husband. She paused, and then she said, "It's about a certain house in Chapei. And a certain woman who lives there. And receives monthly payments from you."

She watched his face change. She watched the shock and surprise, and waited for the anger, the defensiveness, the counterattack, perhaps the unconvincing denial.

None of those things happened.

Mike just sat quietly, smoking his cigar. He said finally, "How did you find out?"

"How I found out is not important. It has no bearing on the situation."

She expected him to pursue the question, to deflect attention from the real point. She knew all his tactics. He did not do that, however. He simply nodded.

"That's true," he said, "it doesn't."

"Then you admit it? You are supporting a woman who lives in Chapei?"

"Yes."

That calm, simple answer was infuriating to Laura. Where was the shame, the guilt? Why was he sitting there so quietly, puffing on his cigar?

"What do you intend to do?" she said.

"Nothing."

"You can't just say *nothing*, as if you were throwing in a poker hand!"

"It looks like I've been dealt some pretty lousy cards, Laura. I'm not going to try and bluff."

"Don't, because now I know everything," she said icily. "Much to your relief, I am sure."

"Why should I be relieved?"

"Because now you can do what you've always wanted! Leave me and go to your true love."

"My true love?" Mike regarded her with a quizzical expression.

"I know her name—it's Li-san!" Laura cried. "I saw her once when I first came to Shanghai!" She drew an angry breath. "My congratulations, Mike, she is very beautiful. And I'm sure she is passionate and loving or this affair would not have lasted so long."

"For Christ's sake, Laura. Don't be an ass."

"Does she still wear silk gowns and a flower in her hair? She must wear jasmine perfume. Perhaps she bathes in it before you come to visit.''

Mike looked at her in amazement. ''What are you picturing,'' he said, ''some kind of Oriental vamp?''

''Am I so far wrong? I don't think so.''

Mike set his cigar in the ashtray. ''You are so far wrong,'' he said, ''that I don't know whether to laugh or cry.''

Laura ignored that. ''You and Li-san,'' she went on. ''What a handsome couple you must make.''

Mike displayed annoyance for the first ime. ''Stop talking about Li-san, will you? Stop using her name.''

''Oh, am I intruding on something very private and precious?''

''You're talking about something you know absolutely nothing about. You're making a fool of yourself.''

''*I'm* making a fool of *my*self?''

He was putting her in the wrong, but Laura didn't understand how. This was a new Mike. He rose from his chair and she took a step backward, intimidated by his sudden look of quiet anger.

''Now listen, Laura,'' he said. ''I'm going to make one explanation to you, and that's all. You're not my prosecutor and I'm not on trial.''

His voice was so . . . contemptuous. So biting. As if she were the guilty one and not himself.

''I'm going to tell you about Li-san,'' he said, ''so you can have it clear in your mind. She's no raven-haired beauty in a silk gown. Maybe she was once, but no longer. She's had a hard life. She's gone through experiences you've never had to suffer, times of shame and disgrace, and she's lived through them with dignity. She works in a cotton factory in Hunkow, and she's just getting by. She lives in two miserable rooms in Chapei. If you passed her on the street, you would never notice, except to see a worn-out Chinese factory worker in a padded blue coat and cloth slippers, too weary to lift up her head, too tired to do anything but shuffle along the pavement. So don't tell me about Li-san and our beautiful romance.''

Laura struggled with guilt and shame. She didn't know how to react. She was not accustomed to feeling guilty. Nor did she know how to respond to this changed Mike, with his quiet contempt and self-control. Their long-held positions had suddenly been reversed. She was floundering in her own confusion and attempted to put the conversation back on course.

"The fact remains," she said, "that you are supporting this woman. How do you explain that?"

"I told you before, I don't have to explain anything. These payments have nothing to do with you or our marriage. If you don't trust me or believe in me or have faith in me, then you're creating your own problems and jumping to your own conclusions."

"If I'm such a troublemaker and so insensitive," she said, trying to bring back the old Mike, "then maybe you want a divorce."

He shook his head. "The usual weapon, the sword hanging over my head. You bring it up every few years." After a moment he walked over to the window and drew aside the drapery, turning his back.

"Do you, Mike?" she asked.

"Whatever you like. It's your decision." Distant. Tired. Uninvolved.

"Apparently you don't care."

"I'm willing to go on. You're the one who keeps talking about a divorce." He sighed. "All right, Laura, let me tell you about Li-san. She stopped me from drinking that summer. Something nobody else was able to do. She gave me a new life. I owe her more than I can say."

Laura felt another surge of jealousy. "So she's better for you than I've been. Maybe you should be married to her."

"You are my wife. I love you and I always have. But my gratitude to Li-san is very real. If small payments can help her survive, why not?"

"If it's all so pure, why didn't you tell me?"

"Because I was afraid you wouldn't understand."

"Maybe I have every right to want a divorce."

"Maybe you do."

Laura stood with her chest heaving. Mike still had his back turned, looking out of the window. The silence thickened. Mike was the first to break it.

"If you decide on a divorce," he said, "let me know so I can see a lawyer. We should go on with our plans for the factory.

There's no reason why our personal lives should interfere with the business. Other people are involved.''

"Yes, that's . . . sensible." Laura spoke with difficulty. She knew the lawyer he would consult. Peter Sanders of Hamilton and Sanders, one of his friends at the Shanghai Club. Whom would she retain? She would find someone.

"Let me know what you decide," Mike said. He moved from the window, picked up his cigar from the ashtray and relit it, then went to the door.

"Where are you going?" Laura asked.

"To the club. Isn't that the traditional move to make in situations like this?" He shrugged. "Besides, I feel the need for a little change of scene."

"Mike," Laura cried as he started to leave, "you're not going to start drinking again, are you? That isn't what you mean by a little change of scene?"

He turned. He took the cigar from his mouth and smiled in rueful amazement. "You'd like that, wouldn't you? The good old days. You playing the noble, suffering martyr and me groveling at your feet and begging forgiveness and pleading to be taken back. The way it used to be." He paused. When he spoke again his voice was steady. "No, Laura," he said. "I'm sorry to disappoint you, but I'm not going to start drinking again. And as I told you, you can thank Li-san for that. Believe or not, as you choose."

He departed quietly, leaving the door open behind him.

CHAPTER 19

Laura vacillated between righteous anger and uneasy self-doubt. How could she possibly believe his story? After all, if it was true, why had he kept it a secret? He was darn right she didn't trust him. No other woman in her position would either. She had good reason to file for divorce. But the thought of the twins, of breaking up their home, was very hard to cope with.

Mike was no help. She kept expecting him to apologize, admit how wrong he had been, and then they would be able to reconcile and she could save face. He showed not the slightest sign of doing that, however. He was courteous and distant, making polite conversation at mealtimes about the children, the household, or the business, and then departing for the evening. At night he was careful to keep to his side of the bed, not touching her. She would lie awake and listen to his steady breathing, knowing he was asleep, and grow infuriated. Mike ought to be the one with insomnia! To her own disgust she missed sleeping close to him at night.

Plans, meanwhile, went ahead for her trip abroad. Visas, tickets, itineraries, a sample kit of Valentine dishes with four different patterns (looking lovely, Laura thought, except for one called Red Peony, which was garish and probably a mistake). The day of her departure grew nearer.

At the dinner table one evening she told Mike she still had not reached a decision about a divorce.

"No one is involved but you and me," he said politely. "There isn't any hurry."

"Perhaps I won't decide until I come back from abroad."

"That might be a good idea. You'll have plenty of time to think about it on the trip."

"Don't you have anything to say one way or the other?"

"I've already said it. I'm willing to go on as before."

"That's impossible, Mike."

He shrugged. "Suit yourself." He rose from the table, wished her a pleasant evening, and departed.

She was furious all over again. She stormed up to the bedroom to check last-minute items in her steamer trunk. The shoes with silver heels to match the evening gown sewn with silver bugle beads! Had Plum Blossom forgotten to put in those shoes? No, here they were. Her walking suit, in wine-colored wool, to be worn with the marten-skin fur wrapped around her throat, and the wide-brimmed hat! It was not here! Oh, yes, it was.

She rummaged angrily, destroying most of Plum Blossom's neat packing. Then she began automatically to repair the damage, folding blouses and skirts and jackets and fitting them back, though a running tirade was streaming through her mind.

Why should Mike get away with this! Why should she allow it! Maybe he was trying to trick her into a divorce. Maybe it was all a cagey waiting game, and she was playing right into his hands.

Well, she didn't need him. Not for anything. Let him play his stupid games. She'd get on with her life. She was a mature woman, and she could find someone else. There were other men in the world besides Mr. Michael F. Valentine. Oh, yes, there were!

She paused with a silk and lace slip in her hands. She realized she had been married for almost twenty-two years, and had never thought of someone else. She, Laura Canfield Valentine, was forty-three years old and had never glanced outside the confines of her own bedroom. What a lack of curiosity! They ought to engrave it on her tombstone. *She lived and died an idiot.* Because now it was too late.

Or was it. She went to the mirror. She tried to be critical and objective. What would a man think, meeting her? A strange man.

Her figure was still good; she hadn't gained weight. She squinted at herself, standing in profile.

But it was the face that counted. That was where your age showed. Were there lines, wrinkles? She leaned closer to the mirror. Not too many, actually. Just those parentheses around the mouth, and they weren't very deep. She plucked a gray hair from her temple and looked for others, but didn't find them.

Oh, this is ridiculous. She was going on a business trip, and she would be businesslike. There were only two side trips, an extra week in France for sight-seeing, and the visit to David's school. She could see Julia every night in New York, and call on store buyers during the day. The same applied to Pierre-Marc in Paris. He had promised to entertain her every evening. He would meet her on the dock at Le Havre. She told herself she couldn't wait to leave.

Laura found Paris a city of excitement and delight. The war was over, and it was spring, and soon it would be a new decade, 1920, and Paris was everything she had heard and read about, only a thousand times more beautiful. Chestnut trees lining the Champs-Élysées. Sidewalk cafés. Boats along the Seine. The Place de l'Opéra. Honking taxis. Gorgeously dressed, impossibly chic women swaying along the pavement with poodles in their arms. Men who winked at her as they passed by, and tipped their hats. Gendarmes wearing capes and blowing whistles.

"Do you like my city?" said Pierre-Marc with a laugh, seeing her expression.

"It is perfectly lovely. No secondhand description does it justice."

"I knew you would feel so. I am enormously glad you're here."

They were sitting in a sidewalk café. They seemed to have been there for hours. Laura didn't mind. She could have sat for hours more, gazing like a child. She was a girl again, the girl who had gone west on the train in 1894 and met a young man in Oregon. This time she had come by sea to Paris.

She had to laugh at herself when she thought of her dream of a shipboard romance. She had been adopted on the first night at sea by a group of elderly bridge players, and spent the rest of the voyage in the ship's lounge playing auction bridge. It didn't matter. Here she was in Paris, and here was dear Pierre-Marc, as small and merry and autocratic as ever, prepared to take charge of her entire visit. Maybe her life.

He was now inspecting the dishes in her sample kit. She was already installed in her hotel, a small residential hotel on the boulevard Haussmann, chosen by Pierre-Marc, who had instructed her to bring the dishes with her to the café.

She lost herself in watching the passing crowd.

Finally she noticed Pierre-Marc holding one of the dinner plates up to the sun. Light streamed through it.

"Fine porcelain," he said, "and the pattern, charming *chinoiserie*."

"I'm glad you approve."

"No, Laura. It will not do."

She paused. "Not good enough?"

"Good enough, but that is not sufficient. Do you realize your competition? Chinese porcelain from an unknown factory? The great days of Chinese pottery ended in the eighteenth century.

Everyone knows it. The famous names are in Europe now. Were you intending to challenge Limoges and Havilland in France, Spode and Wedgwood in England?"

"I suppose I was."

"My dear, you will fall on your pretty face. Here, this is the one you must concentrate on manufacturing." He took up the plate called Red Peony.

"I wasn't even going to show that to anyone. It seems a little vulgar."

"Precisely. Just the sort of thing that will sell. Not, of course, on the rue de Rivoli or in the expensive shops around the Madeleine. You must produce it in stoneware, not porcelain. And then undersell everyone."

"As they're starting to do in Japan."

"Are they so stupid in Japan? No. They are clever," he announced before she could answer. "You must be clever too. You will take advantage of cheap labor. You will make very inexpensive dishes and ship them everywhere. Tomorrow I will take you to the district where my great-uncles started in business, selling gloves from a sidewalk table. The rue St.-Antoine and the boulevard Beaumarchais, in the third *arrondisement*. There you can buy hardware, tin knives and forks, cotton undershirts, work clothes . . ."

"And cheap dishes."

"Exactly. In New York you will see the buyers for . . . Woolsworth?"

"Woolworth's."

"Do you agree? You must agree," said Pierre-Marc when Laura hesitated. "You know my advice is always good. Did I not start you off in business with Nathan Field?"

She laughed. "Yes, Pierre-Marc, I admit it."

He made a face. "How is my dreadful cousin?"

They discussed mutual friends for a while. Then Pierre-Marc sat back in his chair and studied Laura. "So, *ma chère amie*. You look extremely well. Maturity agrees with you. Now at last you are interesting, in a physical sense. A woman of a certain age, not so?"

"I suppose."

"Are you contented with your handsome husband?"

She toyed with a salt shaker. "*Contented* isn't exactly the word."

"Has he lost his dashing good looks?"

"Oh, no. Maturity agrees with him too."

"Still, you are ready for an adventure."

She paused. "That's an impertinent comment, Pierre-Marc."

"Aha! No blushes, no denials. I sense there have been some changes in the life of my friend Laura."

"Please don't jump to any conclusions. . . ."

He paid no attention to her demurral. "But how exciting! I must arrange something for you at once!" He was already musing aloud with his finger on his lips. "Whom shall I find? Gilbert Chambray? A banker, very rich. But too stuffy, not your style. There are some artists I know in Montmartre . . . No, too fast for you, they would strip you naked in the first five minutes and insist you pose for pictures."

"That is definitely too fast for me. . . ."

"I have it! A Bulgarian gigolo of my acquaintance, with certain specialities that drive women wild! He has been given gold wristwatches, diamond studs—"

"Pierre-Marc, I am not prepared for a Bulgarian gigolo!"

"No? Too bad. The things you could learn. However, I will think of someone."

"You don't have to think of anyone, actually. I'm here to do business, and then a little sight-seeing. That's all that's necessary."

"Nonsense. You must have an affair while you're in Paris. At the very least it will enliven your marriage."

Pierre-Marc was giving a party at his apartment in Montparnasse. Laura had expected his apartment to be filled with cubist and expressionist paintings and clashing brilliance of color. It was not; it was furnished with taffeta-striped chairs, silk-covered couches, swagged draperies, gilt mirrors with convex glass, bisque figurines, all in quiet good taste. Pierre-Marc was not everything he appeared to be, Laura thought. People so seldom were.

She was wearing a Paul Poiret creation of V-necked black velvet against which her skin looked creamy white. Her only jewelry was a pair of tiny garnet earrings and a garnet-and-old-gold bracelet, and her hair was an artfully careless pouf at the crown of her head with wisps falling around her cheeks.

"Terribly Belle Époque," Pierre-Marc declared with satisfaction upon seeing her. "We have banished Shanghai and all the Orient, according to my instructions, and now you are a Parisienne. Not modern, of course, but tonight that is not your type. You are Maxim's and the Moulin Rouge."

"I certainly am not. I am an American. And a grandmother."

"You certainly do not look it," Pierre-Marc said with a sly twinkle.

Now the party was at its height, filled with smoke and food and liquor and groups of people in every room, most of them arguing heatedly about art, philosophy, or politics.

Pierre-Marc seemed to know every intellectual in Paris, Laura thought. She was intimidated by the conversation and wished she were not the only American present. She felt a little stupid. The French had a way of doing that to a person, even when they were not trying. She wished everyone were not *quite* so brilliant. Most of the women were terrifyingly intelligent, and some had mannish haircuts and were wearing trousers and neckties. Others were swathed in shawls, with earrings dangling to their shoulders; they were in a group discussing the dance theories of Isadora Duncan. For all Laura knew, Miss Duncan might even be present.

"What are you thinking, madame?" asked a quiet voice by her side. "You seem so pensive."

"I was listening to that conversation about Isadora Duncan. I was wondering if she were here."

"Why, no, I believe she is in Berlin, running her dancing school."

"Oh, you see, I am quite out of the swim here in Europe."

Her companion smiled. He was a dark, rather homely man in his forties, but he had a pleasant smile. His eyes were kind—they were dark brown—and his complexion was olive.

"You are an American who lives in China, in the city of Shanghai," he said.

"Yes, how did you know?"

"I made an inquiry of Pierre-Marc. I asked about the charming lady in black velvet, and discovered you are the guest of honor."

He extended his hand. "Let me introduce myself. I am Claude Delarbre."

"Laura Valentine."

"Are you in the arts, Madame Valentine?"

"Only the fringes. I sell Chinese antiquities in a gallery. I don't create anything myself."

"I, too, am in that position. I am an editor in a publishing house."

"How interesting, Monsieur Delarbre."

"It is to me, I must confess."

"What sort of books do you edit?"

"Belles lettres. Nothing very exciting, I'm afraid. Poetry, for the most part."

"I find that very exciting! I love poetry."

His face lit up. "Do you? Have you read French poetry?"

"A little."

"Whom have you read?"

"Oh, you know, the easy poets, Alfred de Musset, Paul Verlaine . . ."

"Verlaine! Wonderful! Have you read any of the *Romances sans paroles*?"

"Some of them."

"Come, we must discuss this. My father knew Verlaine in the cafés, and Rimbaud too. Sad men, both of them, with wretched lives, like so many poets of that day. . . ."

He led her to a conveniently empty sofa and they both sank down, already absorbed in discussing the lives of French poets from Villon to Baudelaire. Time passed.

"Laura, may I borrow you from Claude for a moment?" asked Pierre-Marc.

"Of course." She excused herself and accompanied Pierre-Marc to a secluded corner of the room.

"*Ma chère amie*, why are you occupying yourself with Claude Delarbre? He is so boring. There are so many fascinating types here for you to meet."

"I don't think he is boring at all."

"Oh, he is very nice, I agree. Claude is a pleasant fellow. And quite eligible. His wife died five years ago and left him a packet

of money and a château in the wine country. But he lacks . . .
flair. You know. Dash. Sex appeal."

"You and I do not have the same taste in people," Laura said
firmly.

"I am only judging by your original selection."

"That was twenty-five years ago. I may be ready for a change
of pace."

"What are you discussing? Poetry?"

"Yes."

"But of course." Pierre-Marc sighed. "Good old Claude. His
favorite subject. He lives for his work. And to think of the
exciting activities you could be engaged in with my friend
Rakovski."

"Your Bulgarian gigolo?"

"Yes. However. Go back to your safe little companion Delarbre;
he will never harm you, he is too gentle."

"I will," said Laura. "We were in the middle of a very
interesting conversation."

"Would you come to dinner with me tomorrow?" asked Claude.

"Well, I . . . I'm not sure I should." Laura hesitated. "You
know that I have a husband in Shanghai?"

"I have been trying very hard to ignore that fact. And Shanghai is a far distance away." He paused. "It will not harm anyone
for us to dine together. I would like you to look at a manuscript I
am working on. A young poet who has never been published
before."

"Do you think my opinion would be valuable?"

"Yes. To me, especially. Intensely interesting."

"I think you are trying to flatter me."

"No," he said seriously, "I am not skillful at such games. If
Marianne had not been so determined, I would probably not have
had the courage to speak."

"Marianne was your wife?"

"Yes. She did a great deal to bring me out. So now I can
introduce myself to you and ask you to dinner."

Laura smiled. "I think you're right; it can't do any harm."

"Good! Where shall we go? Do you like music while you dine?"

"Do you?"

"No," he said, "I prefer not to be distracted from my food."

"I don't like it either."

He smiled. "How kind you are. I will call for you at your hotel."

Claude and Laura were seated in a quiet restaurant after an exquisitely prepared and superbly served dinner. Laura realized that she would never have found a place like this on her own. It was hidden away on a side street, behind a plain façade and curtained windows. Claude was reading poems as she lingered over a dish of tiny raspberries sprinkled with powdered sugar. It was deliciously sweet and tart, as fresh as a spring meadow. She listened as she finished the dish.

He had a beautiful speaking voice, deep and resonant. It was one of his most attractive qualities. *So does Mike. With a husky, whiskey-roughened edge that always makes me shiver at intimate moments. I must stop thinking of Mike. I am with someone else tonight.*

Claude, she realized, had his own reticent charm, concealed beneath a shy exterior. Like this restaurant, she thought. One found hidden surprises.

The poem he was reading was simple and lovely. It described Paris at the lavender hour, the time of twilight. A car on a deserted street. Footsteps echoing on cobblestones. Rain on window glass. The distant chime of cathedral bells. Tranquillity mingled with sadness.

"It is like Paul Verlaine," she said when he had finished.

"Yes, of course. That's why I wanted you to hear it."

"It's a little like Chinese poetry too. Images combining into a mosaic until a scene comes to life. Chinese poets prefer to describe nature rather than cities, though. Gorges, lakes, trees, mountains, rocks."

"Do you read Chinese?"

"A little. It's easier to speak than to read."

"And do you really enjoy to live there? In China?"

"Yes and no, Claude. It's a fascinating and frightening country. I have had some bad experiences. We . . . lost our son when he was small and our . . . daughter five years ago."

"But how sad for you, my dear." He took her hand across the table. "Does it heal a little?" he asked gently.

"Oh, yes, a little. Never completely. We are raising our daughter's children. She died giving birth to twins."

"Then you have a memory of her."

"Two very lively memories, Claude!" She laughed and the tension was broken.

They spoke of other things. After a while Laura became aware that Claude was gazing at her with a strange yet familiar expression on his face. She grew conscious of the neckline of her dress. She was wearing the silver gown with bugle beads, and it was cut very low, exposing the tops of her breasts. She recognized his look: It was the look Mike always wore when he wanted to take her to bed. How unsettling to see it on someone else's face. She resisted the impulse to tug up the top of her dress.

Claude blinked. "I'm sorry," he said. "I'm embarrassing you."

"Yes, a little."

"But you are very beautiful."

She blushed.

"I don't wish to offend you or make you unhappy, so we will talk of something else. Even better, we will go somewhere else. Would you like to hear music? Shall we find a gypsy café?"

"If that's the proper thing to do in Paris after a delicious dinner."

"It is completely appropriate."

"Then let us do it."

As he escorted her to the door of her hotel at the end of the night, with his taxi waiting at the curb, Claude took her hand.

"Since tomorrow is Sunday, Laura, you cannot make business calls."

"True enough."

"Therefore I will call for you at noon, with your permission. We will spend the day as French *bourgeois* families do, enjoying a picnic in the Bois de Boulogne. Will you like that?"

"I think I will."

"Excellent. Hope for a sunny afternoon." He kissed her hand. "I will have my cook prepare a picnic hamper."

*   *   *

Sunday brought mild weather. The Bois de Boulogne was leafy and dappled with sunshine. Far off beyond a rise children laughed. Claude's picnic hamper had been filled with pâté and artichokes and hearts of palm, chicken and small tomatoes, cream pastry, cheese, and grapes, but now it was almost empty. Claude and Laura were settled on a blanket beneath an oak tree. Claude was lying on his side, nibbling on a blade of grass. Laura sat with her skirt spread around her and her hands in her lap.

"If my last name were Monet and not Delarbre," he said, "I would paint you as you are now. Alas, I am the wrong Claude, I have no talent."

"You have the talent for creating a lovely afternoon."

"Do you believe that, or are you only being Laura?"

"Who is that, I wonder?"

"Someone very charming and very kind and beautiful. I ask myself if you are appreciated."

Laura didn't answer, understanding what he meant.

"You have not discussed him, you know," Claude said after a moment. "He is Irish-American, is he not? Your husband?"

"Yes. Pierre-Marc must have told you."

He nodded. "And so does he get drunk and knock you about?"

"Certainly not. Where did you get an idea like that?"

He was uncomfortably close to the truth, Laura thought. Mike had never actually knocked her about, but in his drinking days he had come near to it. She had no intention, however, of confirming that to Claude.

"One tends to think in clichés," Claude remarked. "It is always a mistake, of course."

"Yes, it is. Like the cliché that Frenchmen are fanatically concerned about their food."

"A *canard*," Claude said solemnly. "A base lie." He cut her a slice of cheese from the hamper and offered it to her on the knife with a grape on top. She accepted it and put it into her mouth.

Claude sighed. "Laura," he said, "I wish you could stay longer in France."

"My schedule is all arranged. It can't be altered."

"But you still have another week. Pierre-Marc told me that too."

"Until next Sunday. Then I must take the channel steamer to London."

"Will you come with me to the country?"

"I . . . I don't believe I could do that, Claude."

"I would like you to see my château. We could leave on Wednesday. I often do that, and take my work with me."

She was silent.

"After all," he said, "there is more to France than Paris. It is not so vast an expanse as China, but the countryside is very beautiful."

"Claude, you must relaize—"

"I understand," he said. "You believe I am inviting you to share my bed. I am, of course, but only if you wish to. If not, there will be no reproaches. We are not children, to indulge in tantrums when our desires are opposed."

"Why have you never married again?"

"So, you change the subject." He laughed and rolled over to look up at the sky. "Well, let me examine why. At first I was too wounded at losing Marianne and didn't wish to be close to anyone. Perhaps I was afraid. After that I simply drifted, and time seemed to race by without my noticing."

"It does that," Laura said. "You must miss her very much."

"At first, yes." He shook his head. "She was a hellion, Marianne. The devil's temper. Such fights we used to have!"

"I cannot imagine you fighting."

"I didn't, of course. When she began to break the dishes, I left the house. In the country, I would go into the village and sit in the local café with the farmers and talk about cows and crops and vineyards. Then I would return home, and Marianne would be calmed down and sorry and we would go to bed and make up and everything was very nice."

"I'm glad you have good memories."

"One only remembers the pleasant things after a while." He glanced up at her. "Are you considering, Laura?"

She realized she was, indeed, considering.

The château belonging to Claude Delarbre was set on a hilltop, overlooking a distant expanse of vineyards. The winding driveway was lined with poplar trees. Claude and Laura were walking the dogs, who frisked and barked around their heels in an ecstasy of high spirits. Claude carried a gnarled wooden stick. Laura had taken off her wide-brimmed straw hat and swung it in her hand as they strolled. They were discussing opera. It was Thursday morning.

Laura had reached her decision to accompany Claude to the country on Tuesday afternoon. Tuesday morning she had had a stroke of success.

She had been in a large dry-goods store on the rue St.-Honoré, talking to the owner's son, a plump young man in his early thirties. He'd held the Red Peony plate up to the light.

"Porcelain," he said. "This is too delicate for our customers. They need something sturdier."

She'd been speaking to restaurant suppliers, and heard the same objection. She had overcome it. Her order book was filling.

"We will manufacture it in stoneware, not porcelain," she said. "It will be very sturdy."

"And cheap," he said. "Quite a bargain. Can you make a profit at these prices?"

She didn't really know; she was taking a risk by deciding herself. Mike always wanted her to be a gambler, she thought defiantly. Well, she was gambling.

"Without a doubt," she said in a firm tone. "You have no idea how cheap materials and labor are in the Orient."

"Well, madame," he said, "there is one drawback. I don't care for the design."

"Oh? What do you consider wrong?"

"I would prefer marguerites."

Daisies instead of peonies. Easy enough to change, Laura thought. They hadn't begun manufacturing yet.

"That would be very difficult to change," she said. "It would require a big order from you."

"Oh, I would give you a big order, madame. *Articles bon marché, n'est-ce pas?* If I could get marguerites."

She began to feel excited, the excitement that preceded an important sale at the gallery. "It might be worth it for your business, monsieur," she said. She glanced around. "I see you do a very lively traffic in this store."

"In good times and bad. It is the beauty of low prices."

"Very well," she said after a bit more sparring. "You have

persuaded me. I will take it upon myself to provide you with marguerites. A whole meadowful of them."

She took out her order book and pencil.

Afterward she considered that order a sign of good fortune. She had succeeded in Paris beyond her expectations, and now she felt free until London.

She would not hurt anyone, she assured herself, by spending a long weekend in the country.

"Be careful, Laura," Pierre-Marc had warned her. "Claude is a serious type. He is not one of your lighthearted men-about-town."

"I am a serious type too," she had replied with a smile, and kissed him good-bye. Claude would take her to the steamer.

Now she felt happy and relaxed. How wonderful it was to discuss books and poetry and music in these beautiful surroundings.

Wednesday night she had slept in one of the guest rooms at the château.

Thursday night she spent in the big canopied bed in Claude's room, lying in his arms. It all seemed as simple and natural as the sunlight, a continuation of the day, and the walk, and the good food and conversation. He made love to her with gentle tenderness. She responded with gratitude and affection. They were so easy together. There was no tension, no embarrassment.

There was not the bursting excitement she always felt with Mike, either.

Was that so important? Laura asked herself. They were not young lovers. They were mature people, and they had so much in common.

"Laura, don't go back," Claude said to her early on Sunday, while they were still in bed. He put his arms around her and kissed her hair. "Stay with me."

"I must go back, my dear. You know I must return to Shanghai. Everything is waiting for me."

"Then come back to France. Settle everything and return to Europe and marry me."

"How can I, Claude? It would be so complicated."

"Not at all. It would be exactly right. You could open your gallery on the Place Vendôme, and keep a branch in Shanghai. Your husband of course would look after the factory. Your grandchildren would go to school in France, and spend their holidays here at the château. Safe and happy. No bandits or warlords or cholera. We have not had a civil war since 1871.''

Europe, Laura thought. Museums and operas and cathedral bells and vineyards. The city of Paris. A tranquil life with Claude. Poetry. A gentle and loving husband.

''I must think about it,'' she said, wide-eyed and uncertain.

CHAPTER 20

Laura did not think about Claude on the transatlantic voyage to New York. She sat alone and gazed at the ocean from her deck chair and thought of Mike. She remembered the words he had spoken in a distant and weary tone, in the house on Bubbling Well Road. ''Do what you like, Laura. A divorce is your decision.''

He really didn't care. She was free.

Mike would be free too. What would he do?

He would marry again, just as she planned to do. It would be inevitable. She knew there were women in Shanghai who had been eyeing the Valentine marriage for years, waiting for the rift to occur. The Western community in Shanghai was small, and the wives often grew bored. The handsome Mr. Valentine was considered a prize, and many ladies were hopeful that he would become available sooner or later. They probably discussed it, Laura thought, over afternoon tea in the lounge of the Astor House Hotel.

''I wonder why he stays with her, my dear. What do you suppose they do in the evenings? Does she read him Chinese poetry when the lamps are low? Do you imagine he *listens*?''

Malicious laughter would cascade over the teacups.

One of them would marry Mike; he would not remain single. The new Mrs. Valentine would probably want to sell the house and start fresh. Maybe in one of those new apartment buildings

being constructed around Avenue Edouard VII. Would she understand Mike as Laura did? Would she insist on twin beds? He
preferred a double bed with Laura. Would his new wife know
enough to keep a pot of coffee always percolating for him on the
stove and the kitchen stocked with tonic water and fresh lemonade?
Would she realize that an alcohol problem never disappeared but
simply lurked in the shadows waiting to pounce unless always kept
at bay?

It would not be Laura's concern. She would be in France. She
would be Madame Delarbre. Mike and his quick temper and his
problems would be the burden of some other woman.

*"I'm willing to go on, Laura. You're the one who keeps
talking about a divorce."*

Mike had said that too. Did he mean it? If she told him about
Claude, would he care?

Would she ever be rid of Mike Valentine? For better or worse.
She would not know the truth until she saw him face to face in
Shanghai.

New York. America. Home.

Customs officials speaking in familiar American voices and
New York City policemen in blue uniforms. The pace, hurry, and
excitement of New York, crowds on Fifth Avenue, elevated
trains thundering overhead on Third and Sixth avenues, Wana-
maker's and Woolworth's. She spoke to store buyers and owners
everywhere. They talked fast, around cigar stumps in their teeth,
between telephone calls and shouts to assistants, appearing hardly
to listen to Laura but making decisions with such blinding speed
that they made Laura blink.

"Okay, little lady, we'll give it a try. Write it up. Got a
pencil? There's a pencil around here someplace. . . . Oh, you
have one. . . . Don't mind me, I have to answer the phone; you
just keep writing while I talk."

She was breathless all the time. She'd forgotten what it was
like to be home.

She spoke to Julia on the telephone. Julia's voice was distracted.
"I'm sorry I couldn't meet you on the dock, darling; there's a
little problem here. Why don't you go and visit David first. I'll

meet you next week at the St. Regis. We'll talk and talk. I can't wait to see you!"

She went to see David at school. He looked so tall and grown up she was amazed.

"I can't get over you, David. You look so handsome."

"You look nice, too, Mom. How's everybody? How's Dad?"

"He's . . . fine. He sends his love."

David was sitting on the edge of his bed in his room. He stared at his hands. "You know, I keep thinking every time I go home for the summer that I'll see Eileen." He gazed at Laura with pain in his eyes. "Mom, why did she have to die?"

"I . . . don't know, darling. I keep asking myself the same question, but I can't find an answer."

"I guess you and Dad depend on me now. I guess I'll have to go back to Shanghai when I'm finished with school. College and everything."

"Don't you want to?"

"Oh, sure. Sure." He got up and moved uncomfortably around the room. "Aunt Julia's been really nice. I like it here now. It's swell. It's not the way it was when I first came. Aunt Julia thinks I should go to law school when I finish with Princeton."

"Is that what you would like?"

"I can't think that far ahead. It's such a long way off."

"You have lots of time to consider."

He hugged Laura close as she left. "Tell everybody I miss them. Tell Amy and Andy to behave and not to be such little devils. Tell Chen I'll write him another letter; he likes to save the stamps."

"He'll be so pleased!"

"I . . . I can't speak Chinese anymore, Mom," David whispered against her cheek. "I forgot."

"It comes back, David. Don't worry. . . ."

She tried to sound strong and sure, to cover up her own indecision.

She sat across from Julia at a table in the restaurant of the St. Regis.

"Now at last I can look at you," Julia said. "Good lord, Laura, you look marvelous. Is that a Paris frock?" She laughed.

She spoke a little too fast and her tone was a little too brittle. She was very thin; she was still very beautiful. "It seems that unlikely marriage of yours has worked out after all. Maybe I should have married your wild Irishman."

"Julia, aren't you happy with Wade?"

"Oh, no," she said airily, "we're on the rocks. And speaking of that—where's the waiter with my drink? I finished this one ages ago."

"Don't you want to order lunch?"

"Not yet. I prefer to drink, or hadn't you noticed."

"Yes, I noticed."

"Oh, God, darling, I'm so wretched," Julia said. "The only bright spot in my life is David. Sometimes he brings home a friend for the holidays and then the house is filled with young voices and laughter instead of . . . wrangling. Thank you, Laura, for sending him to me."

"He's very happy here."

"Laura—what happened to Eileen? What really happened?"

Laura gazed at the tablecloth. "I can tell you now," she said. "I couldn't bear to put it in a letter. It was during the war, and she met a young man, a British flier. We never met him. They had a brief romance . . . a love affair . . . and then he was killed. . . ."

"Oh, sweetheart, how terrible. You needn't say any more; I can fill in the rest for myself. Let's talk of something happy. No more deaths, or my marital mistakes. And here's the waiter with my drink! Bless you, darling!" She gave the waiter a dazzling smile. "Don't take so long next time." Then she returned to Laura. "What was it like in Paris? Tell me all about it. I long to go to Europe. Perhaps I will."

"You'll adore it, Julia. It's so beautiful."

"Will I meet a handsome Frenchman and have a mad love affair in the shadow of the Eiffel Tower? They say everyone does."

"It's possible."

"Did you?"

To her own disgust Laura felt herself blushing. "No, not exactly."

Julia raised a slim plucked eyebrow. "I sense a secret here. You're concealing something, dear sister. Now confess."

"I haven't decided what to do yet, Julia, so I can't confess."

"Well, think twice before you give up Mr. Valentine, if that's your dilemma. I know that sounds like strange advice, considering my earlier opinion, but I'm older and wiser now. I suspect he has hidden talents. He must have been keeping you happy in some respects for all these years, surely?"

"Julia, I don't intend to discuss my sex life, even if you are my sister."

She laughed. "Then obviously I am right. Think carefully, my dear, before you make any sudden moves. Take it from an old campaigner in the battle of the sexes."

CHAPTER 21

In Laura's absence China was experiencing a convulsion. There were no soldiers involved, no warlords, no armies, and no politicians. A great popular demonstration against foreign interference was taking place, an uprising like the Boxer Rebellion, only this time those rebelling were boys and girls. The schoolchildren of China, from primary schools to universities, were pouring into the streets carrying banners with slogans, protesting "foreignism" and economic oppression, especially by Japan. The uprising had begun at Peking University on May 4, 1919, the anniversary of Japan's Twenty-one Demands. The students called it "National Shame Day."

The schools were deserted while the students fanned out into the streets and village squares to organize demonstrations and strikes and boycotts of Japanese goods. The government made hundreds of arrests, but the crowds sided with the children.

Sometimes the jailers converted. The movement became known as the Student Revolution.

In Shanghai little Henry Chen clenched his fists, longing to join the demonstrators, but he was only nine. His mother kept him firmly under her eye.

"Why will you not let me go into the streets, my mother?"

"It is dangerous. You are too small."

"You taught me that the students are right. My teacher of Chinese taught me that they are right as well. Are they not right?"

"Yes, my son. But you are still too small."

"When I am big enough, I will join them," Henry said.

"I'm sure the revolution will wait for you," Plum Blossom commented dryly.

At the end of June, Laura came back to Bubbling Well Road.

Mike sat in the library in his favorite easy chair, meditatively watching the smoke from his cigar curl beneath the lamplight.

Something was eating Laura. She was not simply worrying about the crisis they'd had before she left. This was different. She was nervous, tense, guilty, and evasive. It was quite clear to Mike what had happened. She'd had a love affair somewhere along the way while she'd been gone, and she was working up the courage to tell him.

He sat calmly, thinking it over. Did he or did he not want her to tell him? He decided he did not. He could confront her with his knowledge and knowing Laura she would confess at once. She was a rotten liar, except when it came to business, where it was part of the game. Otherwise her mind was as easy to see as an open meadow. No dark corners there, no hidden places, just sunlight on an open field.

So she had been unfaithful. That gave him an advantage if he wanted a divorce. Financially, anyway. She would sign away everything in a paroxysm of guilt and rush off to her lover. She could fight in court and win, using the issue of Li-san, but she would not. She'd retreat to her new boyfriend.

There was probably a marriage in the offing. Laura was not the back-street mistress type.

That would leave Mike in control of the Shanghai pottery

factory. It was going to do very well too. The business would benefit from an economic boom all over the world, a tidal wave of postwar euphoria. It would probably make him rich.

He drew on the cigar and rolled the flavorful smoke in his mouth, then exhaled and watched it billow.

He did not want a divorce. He wanted his wife. He always had. Infidelity or not. This guy, whoever he was, would have to be eliminated from the picture. Starting tonight.

He made a further decision. He was not going to say anything to Laura about her misstep. He would allow her to assume her secret was undisclosed. At least he no longer had to grovel or apologize with Laura, Mike thought. This was a brand-new poker game. In a way he'd been dealt a good hand.

He stubbed out his cigar in the ashtray, doing a very careful job, making sure it was dead, and then he rose to his feet. Reflectively he unloosened his necktie as he mounted the stairs to the bedroom.

Laura was reading in bed with her glasses on as Mike entered the room. She peered over them.

"I didn't realize you'd come home."

"I never went out," he replied.

"You always go out."

"I decided this was my night to stay home."

Laura frowned and took off her glasses. "It isn't like you."

"Honey, I haven't been alone with you since you got back from San Francisco. Don't you think it's about time we spend an evening together?"

Laura was already looking slightly tense. "Yes, I suppose we should talk."

Mike pulled off his tie. He went to the closet, removed his jacket, and hung it up. Then he removed the cufflinks from his wrists and put them on top of the dresser. He started to empty his trouser pockets.

Laura watched him edgily. "You're not planning to go to sleep, are you? It's so early for you."

"I just thought I'd get comfortable." Mike took off his shirt.

"Your robe is on the hook behind the bathroom door."

"Thanks, I know where it is. I put it there myself this morning."

He made no move to get the robe. He sat down on his side of the bed to take off his shoes and socks.

"Shall I fetch the robe for you?"

"No, stay where you are. You look very cozy."

She did not; she looked nervous as hell. She reached uncertainly for her book.

Mike glanced at her and frowned. "I hope you're not intending to *read*?"

"Why not?"

"Tonight? After we haven't seen each other for all this time?"

"You've seen me. I . . . I've been home for two weeks."

"That's what I mean." He gave her a significant glance. He stood up, unbuckled his belt, and drew it off. "You can read later."

Laura put the book down hesitantly. "Mike, I . . . I'm really not in the mood."

"You don't expect me to believe that." Mike unbuttoned his trousers and stepped out of them, then folded them and laid them neatly over the back of a chair. "I know you better. It's been months."

"I can't help it. I really am not in the mood."

"Well, what about me?" he said in a reasonable tone. "Don't I deserve some consideration?"

Laura would have a tough time answering that, he thought. She was too guilty.

"Yes, I suppose you do. . . ."

"Even if this is the last time, Laura. You owe me a fond farewell."

"Do I, Mike?"

"Oh, I think so. I think it's the least you can do. After all, you're the one who's walking out. As usual. I'm only making a normal request. I think anybody would see the justice of that."

He stepped out of his undershorts. Laura's face displayed visible anxiety.

"Christ almighty, Laura, don't look so shocked. You've seen it before."

He went over to the bedside. "Move over," he said.

"Aren't you getting in on your side of the bed?"

"No, I'm getting in on *your* side of the bed. Move over."

After a moment's uncertainty she made room for him. He climbed in beside her and pulled up the sheet. "Of course if you think I am being unreasonable," he said reflectively, "we could discuss it. What's your opinion? Should we just say the hell with it, a kiss on the cheek is good enough? And tomorrow we see the lawyers?"

"Maybe not tomorrow . . ."

"Then you'll have to take some action tonight, sweetheart, because I'm getting pretty restless."

She sighed. "I suppose it won't make any difference one way or the other."

"Don't make any sacrifices if you think it's going to kill you."

"It won't kill me."

"Then let's get rid of this nightgown, to begin with."

Mike helped Laura out of her nightgown. She was tense and unwilling.

"I hope you're not going to lie there like a martyr," he said darkly when the nightgown was in a heap on the floor.

"What would you like me to do?"

"Think of something."

She hesitated. Then she put her hand between his thighs. He was already erect. She stroked him in a tense, withdrawn kind of way. He allowed it to go on for a few minutes. Then he took her wrist. "Laura," he said, "you're not handling the gearshift of a car."

She flushed. "I'm sorry if I'm not pleasing you."

"Well, you're not. So quit it."

She snatched her hand away from him and moved aside. "I told you I wasn't in the mood," she murmured rebelliously.

Mike raised himself on his elbow. "I think I'd better take charge," he said in a musing tone, "and prove to you how very wrong you are."

Laura gave him a wary glance. Mike put his hands on her shoulders and forced her back against the pillow. "The comedy is over," he said, "and so are those inadequate little efforts you're making. Now let's get down to serious business."

"Whatever you think you're doing," Laura said, "it isn't going to succeed."

He drew the sheet covering her down to the foot of the bed, where it slid to the floor with a little slithering noise. Laura's breathing started to quicken. He lowered himself across her and kissed her very gently and thoroughly on the mouth.

After a few minutes he asked against her mouth, "How was Europe?"

"What?"

"You know. Paris. London. The palace of Versailles."

"I . . . told you."

"Not everything. Did you go to the Eiffel Tower?"

"Do you . . . really want to hear about that now?"

"What's the matter, sweetheart? Can't you do two things at once?"

Time passed. He devoted himself to particular attentions.

"Damn you, Mike! Damn you!" Laura cried. He had reached the stage of what he'd called serious business.

Mike raised himself up. He was motionless and throbbing within her. Laura was panting. Sweat puddled between her breasts. "Don't stop," she said hoarsely.

"You'll have to ask more nicely than that."

"Do you want me to beg?"

"Why not? At least say please."

"You . . . miserable sadist." Laura groaned.

He brushed strands of hair from her cheek. "You still like it, though, don't you?"

"Yes . . . yes . . . but I hate you, Mike Valentine. I wish I could kill you."

"Show me how much you hate me. Oh, yes. Like that. Never mind saying please. What you're doing right now is fine."

More time passed. Now Mike was panting too. "Come on, baby," he said. "Come on, sweet Laura. Come to Papa. Don't hold back."

"I can't . . . not again . . ."

"Yes, you can."

She shuddered to a climax in his arms.

"That's my good girl." He kissed her hastily on the mouth. "Now help me. It's my turn."

She wrapped herself around him, still in the languorous aftermath of orgasm. He was breathing hard, his face absorbed, his eyes hooded, his chest heaving. He was approaching his own climax. He always told her when, a split second before, so that she could accept him with love and joy. Tonight was no exception.

He lay across her in silence. They were both silent. She tangled her fingers in the hair on the back of his neck. Finally Mike muttered, "Christ, you drive me crazy."

"Still?" Laura murmured in bemusement. "I wonder if we're getting too old for this."

"Who the hell cares. Nobody has to know but you and me. The door's closed. This is our own house." Mike rolled over and smiled at the ceiling. "You always were a sexy little kid."

"Who, me?" Laura said. "I was?"

"Yeah. Right from the beginning. Do you remember our honeymoon on the S.S. *China*?"

"Of course."

"You really had me going. I started to worry I wouldn't be able to keep up with the demand. I figured you'd burn me out in two months."

Laura began to laugh. "That can't be true."

"Well, Christ, I'd never been married before. I didn't know the pace would slow down."

Laura smiled and sighed. "We were so young and stupid."

"Then you got that notion about me and Li-san."

"You can't blame me for that, Mike."

"There's never been anyone but you, Laura," he said seriously. "Not in my life. I've loved you from the first, and I still do." He hesitated. Then he turned on his side and gazed into her face. "Listen," he said, "no more trips to Europe by yourself, okay? Either I go by myself, or we go together."

Laura stared at him. He gazed back steadily. She felt a tiny shock in her mind. *He knows. Somehow he knows about Claude. Only he's not going to say anything. And neither will I. Ever.*

"All right, Mike," she said quietly. "I consent to that."

"Good. Then it's agreed."

They had agreed to everything, without actually saying a word.

He kissed her good night, switched off the bedside lamp and settled himself to sleep. Laura stared into the darkness, picking out shapes in the shadows. Her vanity table. The lacquered cabinet that had belonged to Madame Wei. Mike's cufflinks scattered on top of the dresser. Her bedroom. Her home. Her husband. Mike, who had loved her all along, and assumed she knew. She should have known. She would never return to Claude; she would write and tell him so, gently. She was home. Why had it taken her so long to realize it?

Growing up, Laura thought before she closed her eyes, did not appear to be an overnight process. So far she'd been struggling to achieve that goal for forty-three years. Maybe she'd never make it. Maybe she would just keep trying. She sighed and curled up against Mike's warm body and fell asleep in the quiet house.

BOOK THREE

The Rising Sun

CHAPTER 1

By 1929 the Valentine family had grown wealthy. The pottery factory had expanded far beyond Red Peony stoneware. It was called the Valentine Pottery Works and manufactured several different lines, all selling at an ever-increasing and ever-profitable rate. Mike and Laura no longer needed to make selling trips abroad; they had a staff of salesmen to do that, supervised by a sales manager. Mike was president and chief administrative officer, with two secretaries and a big office decorated in "style moderne" with a sinuously curving desk and overstuffed couches. He was not very happy about the decor, grumbling that he had been talked into it. To the decorator's distress he insisted on keeping his old hatrack in one corner of the office. Mike, in his middle fifties, had striking silver-gray streaks over his temples. His face had weathered into lines of maturity that became him wonderfully.

Luara did not involve herself with the pottery factory; she remained a silent shareholder. She was too busy with her galleries. The demand for Chinese antiques had soared in the 1920s, and so had prices. Even Chinese export ware was being regarded with respect in Shanghai, and in the London and San Francisco branches of the galleries. And Laura sold every piece of Chinese furniture she could get her hands on, some to newly rich Chinese racketeers.

Cruise ships were calling again at the port of Shanghai. In the lounge of the old Astor House Hotel couples slowly danced to gramophone records. Tawdry nightclubs offered entertainment on Shanghai's North Side. Cabarets and dance halls blared American jazz into the streets and blinked red and blue neon signs against the night, creating a glow that was visible for miles across the flat marshes to the west. THE CASANOVA. THE PARAMOUNT. THE METROPOLE. GIRLS GIRLS GIRLS. Those who wished to could purchase opium, cocaine, or morphine from street-corner dealers, even on the Bund. Chinese racketeers were getting rich. The British police in the International Settlement waged war against the drug traffic and the Chinese-run brothels and the blackmail rackets but found themselves in a losing battle.

Across Soochow Creek in the factories of Hunkow, which was now known as Little Tokyo, Japanese foremen brutalized Chinese workers. Production schedules had to be met, and power tactics were considered the most effective. The workers knew of no way to fight back. They had come to the city from the villages of the interior, bewildered and ignorant, and they were beaten and cuffed and feared to lose their jobs.

Some of them found an ally: the illegal Chinese Communist party.

A young woman from Chengtu, who had the sturdy body and square hands of a country girl, sat in a chair in a flat off the Avenue Joffre, in the French Concession. She was plainly ill at ease. She twisted her fingers in her lap and hung her head when she spoke. These were strange surroundings for her.

Bookshelves were everywhere in the flat, crammed with books. She could not read them; she had no idea what someone did with all those books. The authors would have meant nothing to her. Karl Marx. Friedrich Engels. Nikolai Lenin. Pamphlets by Li Ta-chao, once a political science teacher at Peking University, and his disciple Mao Tse-tung, once the assistant librarian at that university. These men, along with others, had founded the Communist party of China here in Shanghai in 1921, meeting secretly in a girls' school.

Their greatest opponent was, ironically, the leader of Sun Yat-sen's former party, the Kuomintang. His name was Chiang Kai-shek. He'd been the head of the national military academy, and like the late Yüan Shih-k'ai, he was an army general. He was proud and ambitious like Yüan Shih-k'ai, but he lacked Yüan's military ability.

He controlled the army and the government, however. The Communists had only their tactics and their ideology and their clandestine organization. After a brief period of cooperation with the Communists, Chiang had vowed to destroy them.

The young woman from Chengtu saw papers on every surface of the flat. On desks, on tabletops, piled on the floor. What could be written on all those papers? She stirred with unease.

A young man came and knelt before her on one knee. "Don't be afraid," he told her. "No one here will hurt you. There is only myself and my professor." He indicated an older man sitting in the corner. "This is his flat."

The young woman felt comforted by his words. Perhaps also by his appearance. Yes, truly, she was soothed by the way he looked, for the young man's face was beautiful, with huge black eyes and high cheekbones and smooth ivory skin flushed with rose. His body was slim and graceful. His was an almost feminine beauty, redeemed by heavy black eyebrows and strongly defined facial planes. He was gazing at her with a mixture of tenderness and calm that gave her courage.

"May I speak openly?" She faltered.

"Of course. We are all comrades here. I am Comrade Chen T'ieh-chang."

Eighteen-year-old Henry Chen had taken a Chinese name upon joining the party two years before. T'ieh-chang meant Iron Quarry. He desired fervently to quarry iron from his own soul, though he knew the struggle would be long. Perhaps he would not live to see the end. Many had already given their lives, and many more would die. Henry hoped he would have the courage to die if he had to.

He was still called Henry Chen on Bubbling Well Road.

"My friend was beaten to death in the factory. By the foreman," the young woman said. "I saw her lying on the metal steps behind the machine room. The back stairway. She was bleeding. Her head was bleeding. She was moaning, and he kicked her. Later we learned she was dead."

"This was in Hunkow?"

"Yes."

"The foreman was Japanese?"

"Yes."

Henry lowered his eyes with a sweep of eyelashes and took a long angry breath. Then he glanced over at his professor, who shook his head slightly. Henry got to his feet. "Foreigners," he said in a low voice. "Japanese, French, British. Doing as they please. Maintaining their own police. Their own armies. Their own gunboats. Governing Treaty Ports. It's bad enough having to fight our own greedy countrymen. Must we bear the burden of foreign oppression too?''

"It has always been that way," the professor said. "From Kublai Khan to the Manchus. You know that, T'ieh-chang."

"No longer."

The young woman had understood only part of this. "Comrade Chen T'ieh-chang," she said hesitatingly, "do you hate all foreigners?"

Henry turned to her and smiled. He had perfectly straight white teeth. He spoke gently, slowly, in what Amy Henderson referred to as his "teaching voice."

"As foreigners help us, we honor them; as they love us, we love us in return; but as they despise us as inferiors, we hate them."

She nodded; she had understood that.

"We will take action against the death of your friend," Henry said. "Go home. Go back to work tomorrow. Wait for word. You will see a poster on the wall. If you can't read, someone will read it to you. This shameful death will be remembered, as all the deaths will be remembered, and the shame will be erased."

The woman got to her feet and squared her shoulders. "I am glad I came," she said. "It was good to tell someone."

"Tell us," said Henry. "Always tell us. We'll be somewhere. You'll find us."

After she had gone, Henry turned to his professor. "We'll call a strike," he said. "A general strike. Not just the Hunkow workers, but the city employees too."

The older man nodded. "Yes, it's justified. A strike and a demonstration."

"If we take to the streets to demonstrate, they'll call out the police. There'll be bloodshed."

"There will."

After a moment Henry nodded in turn. "I'll start to organize tomorrow on the campus."

"Those phrases about foreigners were your own composition, weren't they? You wrote them last year in a paper. You let me read it."

"I remember," Henry said with a smile. "You corrected my rhetoric."

The professor smiled back. Then he gazed at Henry thoughtfully. "T'ieh-chang," he said, "sometimes I fear you have a divided soul. You live in the house of foreigners. You were educated in American schools in Shanghai. You speak their language like a native."

Henry was silent. Then he said, "No, Comrade, my soul is not divided. I am Chinese. I belong to China and the party."

"What of your American godmother? Her husband and her family?"

"They are not our enemies."

"Suppose they were our enemies someday? How would you choose?"

"I would have no choice," Henry answered. He turned his face aside to conceal his sudden anxiety.

His professor was not deceived. After a moment he said in a stern voice, "For your sake, T'ieh-chang, I hope you are sincere."

David Valentine had arrived in Shanghai with his new wife, the former Kay Burnside of Washington, D.C. Kay's father, a United States senator, had not wanted his daughter to live in China. David himself had experienced anxieties about his return.

"I have an offer to join a law firm here in Washington," he'd said to Kay after the wedding. "Aunt Julia arranged it."

"David, don't be so stuffy! Washington is so dull! Imagine— Shanghai! It gives me chills just to think about it!" Kay had tossed her sleek bobbed head and pursed her lips, which were beestung like those of Clara Bow. Kay definitely had *It*. She was small and slender and lively and she could Charleston as well as Joan Crawford in *Our Dancing Daughters*. She'd been the most popular girl in Washington. David sometimes asked himself worriedly if she'd married for the "glamour" of Shanghai (in which he didn't believe) or perhaps the Valentine money.

Now they were standing in the entrance hall of the house on Bubbling Well Road. Everything was so strange and still so well remembered to twenty-four-old David. He had not been home for two years. Yet even the faint smell of furniture polish mingled with sandalwood was bringing back memories. He had already greeted his father, who was looking husky and handsome and prosperous. A taxi driver was carrying in armloads of suitcases through the open door. Kay was standing demurely to one side.

Now David was gazing into the radiantly happy face of his mother.

"David, you're here . . . you're really here! I can hardly believe it."

"Mother, it's so wonderful to see you." They embraced, Laura reaching just to the top of David's shoulder.

"I've missed you so," Laura murmured.

"Me too. . . . Where are the twins?"

"They're at school."

"Sure, they would be." David stepped back with a deep breath. He took his wife's hand. "Mother, Dad, this is Kay." His parents had been unable to leave Shanghai to attend the wedding in Washington but had consoled themselves with the fact that they would see David and Kay soon after. This was their first meeting with David's wife.

Laura smiled warmly. "Hello, Kay. Welcome to Shanghai."

"Well, hello! I just know I'm going to love it here!"

The new Mrs. Valentine was enveloped in a cloud of gardenia perfume. Bracelets jangled on her wrists. Her bangs peeped out from beneath her cloche hat, which hid the rest of her shingled bob. Her skirt barely brushed her kneecaps, and her stockings were rolled.

Mike was looking both incredulous and amused as he surveyed his new daughter-in-law. Kay caught his glance and batted her eyelashes. Surely they weren't real, Laura thought.

"David," Kay said with a pert little grin in Mike's direction, "is this your *father*?" Her grin grew wider. "You didn't tell me your daddy was a *bearcat*!"

That seemed to stop conversation, Laura thought. Mike was looking even more amused. Finally David said with a slight effort, "I guess I didn't."

Kay went up to Mike and took his arm. "Maybe you'd better show me around the house," she purred. "So I don't get lost looking for the bathroom."

"David can do that," Laura said. "I thought we'd have tea first."

"Oh, I don't know," Mike said with an amiable grin. "We don't want Kay to get lost looking for the bathroom."

Laura could have killed him. David reddened slightly. Kay giggled.

At last David said stiffly, "Go ahead, Kay. You and Dad explore the house. Mother and I have a lot to talk about."

Laura thought they wouldn't discuss Kay. Not yet.

But that night as they prepared to go to sleep, Laura couldn't wait to ask Mike his opinion of the new family member.

"What do you think of her?"

He yawned. "She's a high-class little tart."

"Mike!" Laura sat up, shocked. "What an awful thing to say!"

"You asked me and I told you."

"But . . . if you're right . . . and I would hate to think so . . . what are we going to do?"

"We're not going to do anything. It's David's problem."

"But he's our son!"

"And she's his wife. He married her. Let him keep her in line."

"You're being callous."

"And you're still trying to treat David like Mama's boy."

What *could* they do, Laura thought, after Mike had fallen asleep. Nothing. Poor David. Well, maybe Mike was wrong.

CHAPTER 2

Amy Henderson sat in her own room, at her own desk, nibbling the sharpened end of her pencil. She was creating an unsightly black smudge on her lower lip, but she didn't realize it. It was nearly noon on a gloriously sunny Saturday but she was too absorbed in what she was doing to notice. And she was beginning to get angry. Her flaming mop of red curls was in a complete tangle, and she pushed some of it off her forehead in preoccupied frustration.

She was attempting to write a short story. It was to be about a heroic young Chinese peasant, slim and muscular and fearless, with a remarkable physical resemblance to Henry Chen, who was trying to rouse the local farmers against an evil landlord and his even more wicked bailiff, known as the landlord's "dog's leg."

She considered the idea to be excellent. Two things bothered her. One was the ending. The logical climax, she thought, would be to have the young hero die in the service of his cause, so that he could become a martyr and an inspiration to his people. Somehow, though, that didn't appeal to her.

The other problem she had was actually writing the story. She could get the words down, but when she read them back they sounded . . . silly. No, worse than that. Callow. Adolescent. Like herself. Not powerful and moving, which was her aim.

"Jesus, Mary, and Joseph!" she shouted aloud, sounding eerily like her grandfather. "This writing is . . . *atrocious*!"

She swept all the penciled pages onto the floor with one arm, and then she sat furiously, rumpling her already tousled hair.

Stupid. She'd only pick them up again and try it over. Not today, though. She knew what she was going to do today; she'd known it all along and tried to talk herself out of it, but now she realized she was going to do it.

She went into the bathroom and peered into the mirror. What on earth were those black marks on her mouth? And how in *God's* name was she going to get a comb through that mop?

She made an attempt and gave up. She went into Andy's room and borrowed his military hairbrush, scrupulously neat like all Andy's things, and brushed her hair. She tried to pick all the red hairs from the bristles, so that Andy wouldn't complain, but she had an uncomfortable suspicion she hadn't completely succeeded. She replaced the brush on his dresser. She and Andy never really quarreled; they depended on each other too much.

She put on a plain brown skirt and a belted jacket. She wished she could wear trousers. Maybe she could take a pair of Andy's. Amy started to laugh. What a scandal *that* would cause! If this little excursion of hers were discovered, she'd be in enough trouble.

She was going to do it anyway, in her skirt.

She slipped out of the house and ran at top speed to the next block, where there was a tram stop. When the streetcar finally came, Amy boarded at the rear. The motorman came for her money. He held out his change container.

"Why are these trams running today?" Amy demanded before she paid him. "Why aren't you on strike? There's a strike of city employees, or didn't you know?"

He gave her a hostile look. "Fare, please," he said coldly, rattling the container. She dropped in her coins and glanced around the car with a defiant expression. She caught a few approving eyes, but others avoided her gaze. That was to be expected, Amy told herself. It was a long, slow process, educating the people. Henry had told her that. Two years ago, before he'd stopped discussing politics with her and Andy.

The twins knew why. They'd talked it over between themselves, but never told anyone because Henry wouldn't want them to. He'd never actually said so, but they understood. It was an unspoken secret among the three of them.

Once Amy had brought it up obliquely.

"When are you going to tell your mother?" she'd asked.

"Tell her what?" said Henry.

"Where you go on Tuesday nights. And all the rest of it."

He'd been silent. Then he said, "I'll tell her in my own way, Amy. When the right time comes."

Nanking Road was a shopping street. Ordinarily on a sunny Saturday it would be crowded with traffic, pedestrians, and shoppers. Today it was thronged with young marchers who were carrying placards and chanting slogans. They were protesting the death of the factory worker in Hunkow. Some of them carried flags smeared with blood, to symbolize the woman's martyrdom.

The British police were enraged by the demonstration. They considered the strike and the demonstration Communist-led and Communist-inspired. The selection of Nanking Road, they felt, was a deliberate insult, because Nanking Road was in the heart of the International Settlement.

They sent in Sikhs to break it up, on foot and on horseback. The Sikhs were big, tough, and fearless; they made superb soldiers and policemen. If they felt qualms about moving against young people and students, they didn't show it.

The chanting, singing demonstration turned into a scene of terror, blood, and screams. The street became a shambles. The police began to make arrests and drag the protestors to police vans. Blood slicked the pavement.

A pockmarked young man known as Huai, cool in the midst of the uproar, called a companion to his side.

"Where is Comrade Chen?" he asked.

"Somewhere in that direction. I saw him a few moments ago."

"Find him. I want to talk to him."

Within minutes Henry Chen appeared. He wore an ordinary student's jacket, trousers, and necktie. He was panting, but like Comrade Huai he was in control of himself.

Comrade Huai tapped Henry's shoulder. "Look over there," he said.

Henry glanced into the milling, struggling crowd. He saw what Huai had seen, and his face changed. He exclaimed angrily under his breath, instantly recognizing the flaming mop of red curls amid the sea of black hair.

"Your Little American Sister?" Huai asked.

"Yes."

"Get her out of here. You, too, Comrade Chen. Don't get arrested, either one of you. Under any circumstances."

Henry nodded. He took off, running. Within seconds he had reached his Little Sister.

Amy felt a powerful grip on her upper arm. She began to struggle furiously, balling her fists, trying to get free.

"Miss Henderson," said Henry's low, angry voice, "I'd like a word with you."

"Henry!" Amy gasped. She stopped trying to knee him in the groin.

"Where's Andy?" Henry demanded. "Is he here too?" He scanned the road for a glimpse of Andy's blond head.

"No, he went to the racecourse with Grandpa."

"That's where you ought to be."

"Andy's betting for me. I gave him my allowance; he said he'd triple it because he and Grandpa have a foolproof new system."

Henry shook his head. "There goes your allowance. Don't come to me next week to borrow money."

"Will you let go of my arm, Henry?"

"No, I will not let go of your arm. I don't trust you. Come on, we're leaving. Right now."

"I want to stay!"

"Don't argue."

Still holding Amy fast, he began to drag her through the tumult of Nanking Road.

They sat across the table from one another in a coffee bar near Peking Road, far away from the scene of disorder and screams. Henry had composed himself and straightened his tie. Now he looked like any normal, respectful, and well-behaved Chinese student. Amy sat breathing hard, still rebellious. They had ordered coffee.

"What did you think you were doing?" Henry asked calmly.

"I'm joining the party," Amy said through her teeth.

"Don't be stupid."

"I am. You can't stop me."

"Oh, yes, I can."

"Oh, no, you can't."

He could, though, in any number of ways, and Amy knew it. He could employ the simplest method of all and inform her grandparents.

"Why are you being so obstinate?" she said. "Why shouldn't I join the party?"

"Keep your voice down."

"Well, why?" she insisted more softly.

"For a million reasons, which I don't have to explain because you already know them."

Amy glared at him sulkily. He probably wouldn't tell the family, she thought, for fear of jeopardizing himself. He'd use another method. Knowing Henry. "You need a haircut," she said.

He ran an absent hand through the hair at the back of his neck. "I was supposed to get one yesterday but I forgot."

He always forgot, Amy thought. Half the time his mother had to remind him. He was too busy being an intellectual and a revolutionary to bother about his appearance. He didn't care at all about how he looked. What a waste. Other people would sell their souls to the devil to be that good-looking.

She became aware of nasty stares being cast in their direction from other tables. The atmosphere seemed oddly thick with tension. Hostility.

"What's wrong with this place?" Amy said. "Why do I get a funny feeling that people don't like us? Do you think they know we were in the demonstration?"

"No," Henry said. "It's because you're not a little girl anymore. You're growing up. And you are white and I am Chinese. And we're in the International Settlement."

Combativeness flared in Amy's green eyes. "They can go to hell!" she exclaimed. "One more dirty look and somebody gets a punch in the jaw."

Henry sighed. "Some conspirator."

The waitress, a buxom blonde, appeared with their coffee. She banged Henry's cup down so hard in front of him that the coffee slopped in the saucer. Henry appeared not to notice. The waitress stalked away.

Amy seethed. "Doesn't that bother you?" she demanded.

"Yes, it bothers me. But I know what to do about it and you don't."

"I'm willing to learn."

"That subject is closed, Amy."

"Collective action," she suggested.

"All you know are slogans. You haven't even gotten through Engels."

She stirred her coffee after dumping in sugar. "Why do I have to read all that boring stuff?" she muttered.

"To give yourself a background, so you can understand what's happening in capitalist and industrial nations. You want to write, don't you?"

She nodded.

"Well, read first. Get a grasp of the issues. Comprehend the basic forces of the class struggle. You're bright enough to understand it. You're just lazy."

She was silent. Then she said, "Do you know something,

Henry? I may be lazy, but there are times when you are a pompous ass.''

He started to laugh. "Oh, Amy. I can always trust you to puncture my pretensions. What would I do without my little sister?''

Amy didn't laugh. She stared at him fixedly. *I am not your little sister,* she thought. *Someday I'll make you admit it.*

But she didn't believe it. Once he made up his mind, she couldn't budge him. So what was the use? She was in love with Henry Chen, and he regarded her as his Little Sister.

In addition he probably considered her ugly. She didn't blame him. Red hair, green eyes, and freckles. What could be worse? What could be further from black almond eyes and perfect ivory skin like Henry's. She'd been born in the wrong body.

"Henry," she demanded suddenly, "are you a virgin?''

He blinked. "How did we get from Engels to sex?''

"I want to know.''

"I hate to point it out, Amy, but it's none of your business.''

"You've always answered our questions. Whenever Andy or I asked you anything, all our lives, you've given us an honest reply.''

"Well, that's true," he said. "I've always felt you were entitled to the truth as I've seen it.'' He paused. "Yes.''

It took Amy a moment to realize he'd answered her question.

"Haven't you ever wanted to?'' she asked. "Aren't you curious?''

"Wanting and curiosity have nothing to do with it.''

Amy sighed. She sat back and rolled her eyes. "Now I'm going to get a lecture on the correct socialist attitude toward man-and-woman relationships in a classless society.''

"I was just preparing that very lecture in my head.''

"Never mind, Henry. It's probably in one of those books you recommended.''

"If you ever get around to opening them," he said, poker-faced, "I'm sure you'll find it.''

This time Amy laughed.

CHAPTER 3

Kay Burnside Valentine was disappointed in her Chinese adventure. She and David were still living in the house on Bubbling Well Road, and although they had a lovely bedroom–sitting room suite, it wasn't like a place of their own. She hoped she would remedy that situation before very long.

And the social life in Shanghai was so dull! Respectable! David had only respectable friends; he could be such a stuffed shirt at times. Kay's father-in-law was a bearcat, that was true, but after all, how much flirting could you do with your own father-in-law? Especially when he was so boringly interested in his own wife.

Kay wistfully remembered seeing nightclubs on a daytime street one afternoon when her taxi had gotten lost on a shopping expedition. They had ended up on Yu Yuen Road, on Shanghai's North Side. The area had been shabby in the daylight, its tawdry attractions stripped of all their glamour. The street required flashing neon, goodtime crowds, and shrieks of drunken laughter to exert its lurid appeal. The names of the clubs were almost faded by the sunlight: The Fantasia. The Cosmo. The Bolero. The Roxy. The Arizona. Beside a board wall pasted with advertisements for Gold Flake Cigarettes and Ma Ling Tomato Catsup stood a poster with a cartoonlike depiction of the "Ruby Queen."

Kay could sense that life and excitement and fun lived here, when the sun went down. She wanted to be a part of it.

She was in her sitting room. She got up from the sofa on which she was reclining with a fashion magazine and went to the gramophone. She could never sit still for very long. She put the needle on a brand-new record, "Am I Blue," and as the tinny, sultry music filled the room, she began to dance slowly by herself in the middle of the floor, singing the words aloud.

David had a newly created title at the Valentine Pottery Works: Head of Personnel. All the offices were on the upstairs floor of the factory building: sales, production, payroll, and the office of the president. Only Mike's office was new and comfortable. Everything else, thought David in anger and disgust, looked like something left over from the Industrial Revolution. Dark wooden walls. Old wooden desks. Ancient typewriters. Scarred wooden filing cabinets. The head payroll clerk had a clanking adding machine that stood on the floor because it was too big to fit on the top of the desk. He also had, David noted without much surprise, an abacus, which he used very frequently. David could hear the *click-click* of the wooden balls from his own cramped little office next door.

China! David thought in despair, sitting back in his seat, which was an ancient wooden swivel and creaked when he moved. Dirt, disorder, floods, bandits, warlords, and Communists! Old furniture! Illiteracy! A head of payroll who figured with an abacus! Why the *hell* had he returned to this backward country?

It must have been for Kay, he told himself in slight desperation. She'd wanted a taste of the exotic East.

Still, he could have refused. Insisted it was out of the question. Taken her on a round-the-world cruise instead, and simply visited Shanghai. He sensed there was another reason.

There was something in himself that was drawn to this country, and the colorful, corrupt, stinking city of Shanghai. This mongrel seaport, part Chinese, part everything. Shanghai was his birthplace.

Oh, no, David told himself, oh, no. He detested Shanghai. Hadn't he always been frightened as a child by tales of bandits and demons and chopping off of heads by the Emperor's soldiers? He never even spoke Chinese. Only English. He insisted to himself that he'd forgotten the Chinese language completely. He was here like a vacationing tourist who'd made a bad mistake in choosing a holiday hotel, and as soon as he could decently check out, he would do so.

Meanwhile he would see about these repulsive surroundings.

He went into the payroll office, next door. The head clerk and the girl and boy who assisted him looked up inquiringly.

"I am going to consult with the Honorable Taipan, my father, about brand-new furniture and office machines," David announced. "And a coat of paint for these walls. White paint."

An identical expression of horror passed over all three faces. It was quickly masked.

David waited for the formal head-bows of assent before withdrawing. He was unaware of his own observation of Chinese etiquette in his speech and manners. He thought of himself as thoroughly American. China had been erased, he told himself, from his mind and his behavior.

"Dad, this is ridiculous," he said to Mike later that afternoon, sitting in Mike's luxurious office. "Look at this place," he waved around, "and then go out and look at the other offices. Are we going broke? Can't we afford a couple of new typewriters?"

"I'm the Taipan," Mike said mildly.

"What is that, some kind of feudal lord? You live in the castle and the peons huddle in the village?"

"It's a little bit like that. There are some medieval aspects to the situation."

"Oh, come on, Dad! I'm too old for folk tales."

"It's also a question of face. The head man has to put on a good show. You should understand that."

"And you're just rationalizing."

"Try and change these offices, David, and we'll be looking for a whole new staff. They'd think we were crazy. No sensible Chinese businessman spends money where it doesn't show, and we won't either. To them it's smart thinking. Only a fool wastes money on useless overhead. What's wrong with the old typewriters? They work fine. The employees are happy, and I'm happy."

David was not happy at all. He'd been brushed off and made to feel like an ass. He really couldn't stand it here. His father was no help either, he muttered to himself. This country wasn't part of the Industrial Revolution, it was part of the twelfth century. On the other side of the ocean people were living in the twentieth century, and that was where he belonged.

*   *   *

Kay was looking for an apartment for herself and David. As she entered the lobby of a newly constructed building on the Avenue Joffre, she felt a pleasurable little tingle in her spine. This place had *It*! Steel and chrome and frosted glass—very "style moderne"! She was already deciding to decorate the bedroom in white with a white telephone, like in a Gloria Swanson movie. Maybe they would make some new friends here. Exciting ones!

By the time the rental agent had ushered her into the hall on the eighth floor after showing her the flat, Kay had made up her mind to take it.

"Are you going to take the flat?" said a childish voice. Kay saw a girl standing in the open door of another flat. She was a sleepy-looking blonde in a peach-colored negligee, and she had a champagne glass in her hand.

"I'm not sure," said Kay, although she was.

"Do take it," said the girl. "Then we'd be neighbors. You look nice. My name is Sarah, but they call me Honey."

"I'm Kay."

"Are you American? So am I. I got stranded here a couple of years ago without any money. My boyfriend pays the rent. But I have other boyfriends too. Want some champagne?" At Kay's hesitation she said, "Come on in and help me wake up. I never really wake up until it gets dark. Then the fun begins."

"I haven't noticed much fun around here after dark."

"I guess you don't know the right people or the right places. I know lots."

"How did you get stranded in Shanghai without any money?" Kay inquired curiously.

"Oh, it was easy. I started smoking opium."

"Did you really?" Kay's eyes widened.

"Sure, don't you know how?"

Kay shook her head.

"Keep me company and I'll tell you all about it."

Kay dismissed the rental agent with a nod. "I don't know about opium," she said, edging toward Honey's door, "but maybe I'll have one small sip of champagne."

"Good! I've been dying for a girl friend. Men, men, men— they get on your nerves after a while."

"How many men do you know?" Kay asked in fascination as she entered the flat. This was definitely her lucky day, she thought.

Kay and David moved into the new flat on the Avenue Joffre three months later. David struggled to make an adjustment for himself at the pottery works and attempted to withdraw himself from the teeming Chinese world all around him. Kay, three years younger than David, plunged into a whole new life, one without her husband. Upon meeting Honey she'd found herself a "crowd." A fast one. They visited all the cabarets and dance halls of Shanghai smoking heroin-tipped cigarettes and drinking themselves insensible, night after night. David tried to slow her down, but she only laughed. They still met on an intimate basis in bed from time to time.

David suggested returning to America. Kay refused. She loved Shanghai. She was having a marvelous time. David veered back and forth between anger and depression.

He joined his father one day in Mike's office in a discussion with the sales manager and chief designer of the firm. They were considering the introduction of a new line of pottery aimed at the Chinese market. China was their weakest-selling area. Chinese customers were extremely conservative; Mike had learned that working for the cigarette company. Once a Chinese had formed an attachment to a certain product or brand name, he clung to it. Novelty was no allure.

Therefore, should the Valentine Pottery Works design a line of stoneware adapted from a familiar old Chinese pattern? Or was the attempt doomed before it began? The sales manager was optimistic. The chief designer was gloomy. Mike was wavering; he wanted to hear more discussion.

David was the one who suggested concentrating on the Chinese market, using designs that were faithful imitations of best-selling patterns. He thought it would do no good to strive for originality, or even to adapt old Chinese styles. To succeed, he felt, they should stay with what was popular today.

Mike admitted with grudging admiration that David's thinking was sound.

David felt a flush of pride at the praise. He noticed his father's hands as he glanced downward shyly. There was a gold signet ring on Mike's left hand inscribed MFV. There were red hairs on the backs of his fingers. David inspected his own hands, spreading them out on his knees. Did he have tiny reddish hairs on his fingers? Yes, he decided that he did.

Someday when he could afford it, he told himself, he'd buy a gold signet ring. And he'd learn to smoke cigars.

CHAPTER 4

The stock market had crashed on Wall Street, and the Great Depression had begun all over the world. In January 1930, however, the Valentine Pottery Works in Shanghai was still operating at full capacity. Their prices were low and their stoneware was cheap, durable, and attractive, and so they continued to receive orders. Pierre-Marc's advice to Laura ten years before had proved to be valuable. The Valentines had no need to change their way of living.

David was having lunch with a newly hired employee of the pottery works at a restaurant on Shanghai's Bund. He was an American called Bill Chandler, a maintenance engineer who would be in charge of the electric kilns. Chandler had been working in Manila. He was troubled about the Philippines.

"They won't allow any Caucasians to come in," he said to David. He was speaking of the Japanese, and their administration of the Palau Archipelago. Japan had been given a mandate over the area in 1922 by Britain and America, when those nations signed the Washington Naval Treaty.

"There are rumors in Manila," Chandler went on. "Filipino and Chinese fishermen say the Japanese are building fortifications on Palau. But that's against the terms of the treaty. They're not supposed to fortify their part of the islands."

"What do the Japanese say?"

"They claim they're only doing repair work on the docks. But they won't let anybody in to see for themselves."

David shrugged. "I don't know, Bill. They wouldn't violate an international agreement. It doesn't seem likely."

"Maybe not. But they're touchy. They think Americans consider them racially inferior, and that could lead to trouble."

"With Japan? America and Japan?" David smiled and shook his head. "Ask anybody in Shanghai, they'll tell you you're crazy. Maybe they have designs on China, but that's as far as it goes."

"Okay, I'm probably imagining things. You get that way in the Philippines; there's nothing else to do. I'm glad I'm in Shanghai. This city has great nightlife."

David tried to discuss nightlife, although the topic reminded him of Kay and the changes that had taken place in her. Kay's personality seemed to have deteriorated in the last months. She had always been restless. Now she couldn't concentrate at all. She laughed at nothing, and her laughter had a note of hysteria. She was taking drugs, along with Honey and her crowd, and he couldn't do anything about it. Kay wouldn't listen.

David kept his worries to himself. He had to cope with his wife on his own. The only course he could take was to pretend to himself that nothing was wrong. She would snap out of it. Kay was all right. Just a little wild. She had to get some things out of her system, that was all.

"Is it true that racketeers in Shanghai kidnap people right off the sidewalk?" Chandler asked.

David admitted that it was true.

When the lunch was over and he'd said good-bye to Chandler, David walked to his car, moving along the sidewalk to the curb. He climbed into the front seat of the car and brooded for a moment before starting the motor; he was thinking about his marriage.

Suddenly a face thrust itself into the open window. A tough young Chinese kid was addressing him. Asking him if he was Mr. David Valentine. Wondering if he would like some advice.

"What are you talking about?" David demanded at once.

"Mrs. Valentine."

David flashed with anger. "My mother?"

"No, the other Mrs. Valentine."

The words were like flinging a match into a puddle of oil where David was concerned. "What do you know about my wife?" he cried.

"She's spending a lot of time at the Ruby Queen," the boy answered, "with a man named Sandor. She's going to get into trouble. He's a blackmailer."

"Who are you? What's your name?"

"I'm just a friend. Or maybe an enemy of Sandor who wants to ruin his scheme."

"Get out of here! Don't come back!" David shouted.

"Tell your wife to stay away from Sandor and the Ruby Queen. If she knows what's what." The boy touched a hand to his head and disappeared, running across the street.

David started the motor of the car and drove off fiercely.

He brooded for the rest of the afternoon. A miserable heaviness had settled in his chest, accompanied by a burning sensation around his heart. He wondered if he were having a heart attack. Maybe he should go to the doctor.

It wasn't a heart attack. It was indigestion.

No, not that either. It was fury at Kay. He couldn't dismiss the memory of the Chinese kid on the sidewalk. *Jesus. What if he told the truth? What if he really does have information about Kay? What is the . . . Ruby Queen?*

David left the office early and went home.

He found Kay in the bedroom reclining on the bed with moist pads over her eyes. She was wearing her bathrobe. He contemplated her with disgust and fought it down.

She is my wife. Who am I going to believe? My own wife? Or some unknown young thug on the street?

The boy's face rose up in his mind.

"Kay, what is the Ruby Queen?" he asked abruptly.

"What are you doing home so early?"

"I came home to ask you a question. Now, answer me, damn it."

She sighed and removed the pads. "It's probably a nightclub, David. It wouldn't interest you in the slightest. You'd think it was dull."

"Would I?"

"Yes, cutie pie, you would. People laugh and dance and drink in nightclubs, and there's entertainment. . . . Oh, you'd be bored to death."

"But you like it."

"Mmm," she said with a smug little grin, "I do."

"Have you been in this particular club?"

"Oh, I don't know. I may have. There are so many."

Lies, lies, David thought. *What's been wrong with me?*

"I was told," he said, "you know someone named Sandor at the Ruby Queen."

Alarm flashed over Kay's face, which she quickly hid. "Sandor? That's an odd name. A man or a woman?"

"Who is Sandor, Kay?"

She flung herself on her side. "Don't badger me. I need my rest."

"Who is Sandor?"

"I don't know."

"I think you're lying."

Kay sat up in a spurt of anger. "If Honey has been jabbering to you," she said through her teeth, "I'll pull her hair out."

"So you *are* lying."

Kay's eyes narrowed. "Who told you this story?" she said after a moment. "It wasn't Honey."

"It was a Chinese friend of mine," David said calmly.

Kay smiled in relief. "Oh, well, you certainly won't take that person's word against mine."

"Why not?"

"David, *sweetheart,* I know how you feel about Shanghai and everything Chinese. And you're right, of course. The only *decent* place in this whole country is Shanghai. The only decent *people* are in Shanghai. It's the only city where you can really have a good time. Everything else is a dead loss." She closed her eyes again and reached for the pads.

There was a long pause.

"You cheap bitch," David said.

Kay's eyes opened wide in shock. The pads fell on the pillow.

"What do you know about China?" he went on. "You don't understand the country or anything about it. As far as you're concerned, it's an exotic playground, a place for cheap thrills, a fun-fair. But you're pretty shallow, Kay. People live here, work here, suffer and die here, just the way they do all over the world. This is a vast nation. Why don't you get to know it?''

Kay glared at him maliciously. "Like you, David dear?''

"Yes, like me.''

"And how do you come by this enormous understanding?''

"I was born here,'' he said. "Remember?''

Kay laughed incredulously. "Civic pride!''

"Maybe.''

"Don't make me laugh! You hate Shanghai! You've said so ever since I've known you!''

"I was probably wrong.''

Kay stared at him. David gazed back calmly. Then Kay put her hand to her head. "Oh, God!'' she moaned. "This is the most tedious conversation!''

"I won't burden you with it any longer. You can start packing.''

She gave him a suspicious glance. "Where are we going?''

"I'm not going anywhere. You are.'' David paused. "I'm staying in Shanghai and you're going back to Washington.'' Suddenly, with a jolt of surprise, David made a realization: He had changed.

Kay leaped off the bed. "You bastard! Are you throwing me out?''

He gazed at her reflectively. "Yes, Kay,'' he said with an air of quiet amazement, "that's exactly what I'm doing. I wonder why it took me so long.''

CHAPTER 5

In the autumn of 1932 Mao Tse-tung's peasant army was quartered in Kiangsi Province. Chiang Kai-shek had already launched three unsuccessful "Campaigns of Annihilation" against Mao. All three times Chiang's soldiers had been beaten back, defeated by ragged men armed with sticks and spears.

The Communist party itself was divided on the subject of Mao Tse-tung. In the flat of Henry Chen's professor, Henry and his friend Comrade Huai were debating the controversy.

For argument's sake Henry had taken the conservative position. Mao was a "romantic bandit" who put his faith in the peasants of the countryside. Hadn't Marx himself insisted the revolution would arise from the urban proletariat?

"Dogma!" cried Comrade Huai. "Marxian dogma! You know what Mao says about dogma!"

" 'Dogma,' " Henry quoted with exaggerated style, " 'is more useless than excrement.' "

"That's right! And remember his comment about the peasants!"

" 'The peasants of China,' " Henry quoted elaborately, " 'constitute seventy percent of our population. If all they did was sneeze in unison, they would blow away the other thirty percent.' "

"Tell me, Comrade Chen. Is he really organizing a 'rifle movement' and not a revolutionary army?"

Henry sighed. "No," he said, "you're right. The future is with Mao in the countryside, not in the cities with us."

Comrade Huai brooded for a moment. "I'm going to Kiangsi," he said finally, "to join Mao. He needs everyone he can get. I'm leaving next month. Will you come, Comrade Chen?"

"Soon," Henry murmured, averting his glance.

He had been told to stay in Shanghai until further notice.

Alone in his room later that night Henry endured a lonely crisis of self-doubt. For the first time in his life he experienced a crumbling of confidence in himself.

Henry had always been lucky, and he knew it. He had been born to adoring parents who treated him like a precious gift from the gods. He had been brought up in a comfortable home and given books and encouragement from his earliest days. Most fortunate of all, he had been endowed with quick intelligence and humor, and those qualities had ensured his happiness with himself, even when he was alone. He was never bored, never empty, never at a loss for diversion. There was always something to think about, an idea to ponder, a book to read, a problem to solve, an argument to work out, sometimes a flash of wit to provide his own amusement. He tried to be humble, realizing that these gifts had come to him without any effort on his part, but Henry was young, and doubt and fear of failure were unknown visitors to his mind.

Now they were knocking, pounding on the door of his dwelling place, the residence of his innermost soul, his secret sense of himself. They were demanding to be let in, and he feared they would destroy him.

It is the autumn of 1932 and I am still in Shanghai.

Such a simple fact to be so frightening. His Communist cell leader said Henry's presence was required in Shanghai. When the time was correct, he would leave for Kiangsi Province to join Mao Tse-tung, as many of his friends had done.

Perhaps not. Am I a coward? Is that the truth? Am I glad to be out of the shooting war? Henry shuddered with anxiety as he examined his motives and his life and found them wanting.

He remembered a person he had met not long ago, a young men he thought of as the Manchurian Warrior. What a romantic sobriquet for a coarse youth, Henry thought half in despair and half in disgust with himself, what a typically intellectual city-bred point of view regarding a rough, illiterate son of the soil. But the Manchurian Warrior was brave. He had a crude sense of humor and he'd made it clear that Henry was an object of ridicule.

"What do you do?" he'd demanded of Henry at a recent meeting. "Never mind—I can guess. You read books."

"Sure," Henry had replied with an easy grin. "All the time."

"Books!" The Manchurian youth had thrown his head back and boomed with laughter. "Nice! Easy! Simpler than fighting, eh, Comrade Chen?"

"Well, I—" Henry had faltered and stopped. The Manchurian Warrior was teasing him, Henry told himself nervously. But somehow he didn't feel like laughing.

"I can see that you don't want to spoil that pretty face," the Manchurian Warrior had remarked. His own face was scarred and pitted, darkened and weatherbeaten by the sun and the wind, and his hands were like slabs of pork. "You ought to be in the Peking Opera, Comrade Chen. You'd make a beautiful princess." He'd chuckled crudely.

All the parts in the Peking Opera were played by men, including the girls' roles. The actors made slender, willowy, and astonishingly feminine girls with delicate faces and pretty soprano voices. But they were actors! Not soldiers of the proletariat! Henry had received a cutting insult, probably unwittingly. He'd flushed with humiliation. He couldn't rebut the teasing, for this peasant was a genuine hero. He was a member of the Red Rifle Society, a group of men who fought the Japanese in the Manchurian countryside with stolen rifles and farmers' pitchforks. The Manchukuo government called them bandits and criminals, but the Chinese regarded them as patriots battling for their land.

Manchuria had been invaded and annexed by Japan in September 1931. It was now the Japanese-controlled state of Manchukuo. There were two enemies now for the Communist party: Japan and the Kuomintang.

Two enemies against whom to battle at the risk of one's life, Henry thought. While he remained in Shanghai, risking nothing. With shocking suddenness he was attacked by self-loathing.

The Manchurian Warrior was beyond attack. He could not argue ideology with Henry and his university-educated friends. He was the son of a farmer. He'd been an itinerant boxer and a vagabond and a waiter and a wandering acrobat and a millstone pusher in a bean-curd shop and now he was a guerrilla soldier fighting the Japanese. He could not quote passages from Engels, but he understood why he was fighting. Henry had to take him seriously, had to question himself with trembling anxiety and sudden self-hatred.

The Warrior had brought with him a handwritten manuscript for the comrades in Shanghai to read. It was the beginning of a novel about the guerrilla war, written by a fellow soldier. Henry had started to read it in his room on Bubbling Well Road, but he'd been forced to stop by the surge of his own emotions. The book was too moving, too shaming.

Never before had he been unable to concentrate on his reading. *Who am I?* he cried silently, the pages of manuscript trembling in his hand. *What is happening to me? Who is Comrade Chen?*

He rose from his chair and went to the mirror and gazed at his own pale features in the silvered glass.

. . . you don't want to spoil that pretty face. . . . You ought to be in the Peking Opera . . . You'd make a beautiful princess . . .

By all the gods of China and all the Sons of Han, was it true? Henry buried his face in his hands.

Andy Henderson was questioning himself as well, wondering as Henry did about his own manhood. Andy didn't like to gaze at his own reflection. Henry seldom concerned himself with his own appearance, but Andy worried about it often.

He resembled his mother, Eileen. Amy looked like Rory O'Connor, with Rory's red hair and strong bones, but Andy had inherited Eileen Valentine's blond beauty. His face was sculptured, his lips were a graceful curve, his hair was like gleaming corn silk. He detested his looks. For that reason he made his features into an impassive mask. He showed no emotion except to those he loved: Amy, Henry Chen, his grandparents. The rest of the world saw an alabaster statue, a fair-haired god with an expression of aloof disdain. Girls sighed romantically when he appeared and vied with one another for his attention.

In the Shanghai Club with his grandfather Andy had met a paunchy gentleman with bloodshot eyes who seemed old to Andy but was actually not yet forty.

"So you're the son of Eileen Valentine," the man had said. "I might have guessed. I courted Eileen once, in 1914. Along with a million others. Did you know they called her the Heartbreaker of Bubbling Well Road?"

"I hadn't heard that, sir."

"Well, you look like your mother."

So his fate was sealed, Andy thought. He had no choice but to become a male version of Eileen. The Heartbreaker of Bubbling Well Road. *Oh, Christ.*

If only he possessed a direction as Amy did—or Henry—his problem would be solved, Andy thought despairingly. He would be able to pursue a goal, and forget his hated appearance. Amy had already started on her path: she'd been hired as a copy girl on the *Shanghai Mirror*. After graduation she'd begin as a cub reporter.

Henry, Andy thought, had always understood himself and known where he was going. His politics and his love for China consumed him.

Andy only loved . . . people. He concealed his grief and pity and tenderness for humanity behind the alabaster façade of his face, but the sight of suffering tore at his emotions. He wanted to help those who suffered, but he didn't know how. Working for a political cause like Henry or writing articles like Amy was too impersonal an activity. Andy wanted to sweep the sufferer into his arms and comfort him amid the dirt and stench and sound of weeping. He wanted to feel warmth and touch hands. He thought it must be a strange quirk in himself; sometimes he thought he was crazy.

He would probably go into the Valentine Pottery Works like his uncle David and simply drift. The idea made him heartsick and angry, but he didn't know what else to do.

Last week he had met Amy on the Bund, where she had been shopping, and they'd been on the pavement when a woman had been run over in the road by a taxi. After the horrid screeching of brakes, the policeman's whistle blew. Traffic stopped and a crowd gathered. The woman lay crumpled in the middle of the street. Blood puddled under her head, sticky scarlet against the black tar.

Andy rushed unthinkingly to her side, although Amy didn't follow. He elbowed aside the gawkers and knelt beside the injured victim, careful not to jostle her. The woman, who was Chinese, gazed at Andy in a daze of bewildered pain. A tiny gold cross hung around her neck.

Andy took the woman's hand and she squeezed back gratefully with astonishing strength. She mumbled something. He bent his gleaming fair head to listen. Then he raised his face and said to the hovering policeman, ''She wants a priest.''

"There's one coming."

The priest arrived as the ambulance siren howled on another block, halted by the traffic. Andy got to his feet, allowing the priest to take his place by the woman's side. The clergyman was gray-haired and shabby, his cassock none too clean, his face frowning. He began to administer the last rites. The woman smiled at him as though he were an angel. She died on the pavement in a gurgle of blood, still smiling. The priest got to his feet wearily, shaking his head; he began to wipe his spectacles on his handkerchief. Another job done. The amubulance arrived in time to take the body to the morgue. Andy stared after it with a somber expression. He seemed to have no emotion, but inside he was aching with hurt. So much pain in the world, so much anguish, so much fear, so much death . . . and so little human comfort. The priest had comforted the dying woman without even trying. But what of Andy? What could young Andrew Henderson accomplish in this universe brimming with misery?

Amy was quiet and thoughtful on the tram going home, tugging one red curl over her temple.

"Andy, I could never have done what you did," she said at last.

"What was that?"

"Rush over to the woman in the road and kneel down in her blood. I was too cowardly. Oh, lord. And I'm planning to be a reporter. . . . Andy, you were so brave. I was proud of you." She paused, then glanced away. "There's blood on your sleeve."

Andy brushed abstractedly at the dark stain. "I wish I could really do something to help. All those people . . . needing some-one . . ."

"Study to be a doctor," Amy suggested after a moment.

"I'm no good at chemistry and science. You know that."

"You could be a teacher," Amy said uncertainly.

"And hide behind a wall of books?"

"Or a minister . . ."

"That would be fine," said Andy bitterly, "if I believed in God."

"Oh, Andy! I don't know what to tell you!"

He gave her a lopsided grin as the tram rattled on. "I'll settle it somehow. It's not your problem."

"I worry about you." Amy placed a hand on his arm and looked questioningly into his face.

"I'll be okay."

He was not. He was flailing in confusion, an idealist adrift in a dark sea with no sense of direction, no landmark, no horizon. He hid behind his mask. Others saw only the beautiful alabaster face. "Andy Henderson is very handsome," they said, "but what a cold fish. He's not like his sister at all."

CHAPTER 6

Henry Chen was in his room, struggling once more to read the manuscript from Manchuria. It was called "Village in August," and it was written by a man named T'ien Chün. As before, he couldn't concentrate. Unhappy with himself . . . miserable alone . . . he was undergoing a new and painful experience. When would it end? There must be a way to reason out a solution, but reason was not helping him. He was trying to cope with his emotions, but it was so difficult to do alone, dialectical arguments were so sterile, so useless. . . . *What was he saying!* All the foundations of his belief were cracking! For the first time Henry was understanding that psychic pain was more terrible than the physical sort. For someone like Henry, who lived in his mind, it was almost insupportable. He had lost his sense of perspective.

With relief he heard a tap on his door. He set down the pages of manuscript.

"Come in."

Amy entered the room. "Am I interrupting?" she asked a little shyly.

"No, I'm glad to see you."

Amy was wearing gray slacks and an emerald green sweater

that was exactly the color of her eyes. She was still coltish and tomboyish, but there was now a new womanliness about her as well. Her sweater was belted at the waist, in the fashion of the day, bringing out the tiny roundness of her breasts, and her face had softened with maturity. She would never be pretty, for her face was too strong, but that very strength gave her a radiance. Intelligence and kindness shone in her eyes. Her coloring was different from Laura's and her features were different, but she resembled her grandmother in many ways. Henry wondered why he had never noticed before.

Because Amy is my Little Sister. She is American and I am Chinese, but that makes no difference. Amy is the other part of myself. I never noticed myself before either.

Henry felt a little comforted.

"We haven't talked in a long time," said Amy.

"I guess we've both been busy. How are things at the newspaper?"

Amy's shyness seemed to increase. It was a new and unexpectedly feminine aspect of her nature, Henry thought. Two-fisted Amy, the fighting redhead, acting shy? A tender sympathy for her began to drive out his own anxiety. He wanted to protect her.

"That's what I'd like to talk about," she said. "I think it may be a turning point for me."

"Oh?"

She sat down on the edge of the bed. "I need to discuss it and you're the one who will understand." She paused. "You know how many years I've been trying to write short stories."

Henry nodded.

"Well, I think I'm going to give it up. Permanently. I've decided I have no talent."

"For God's sake, Amy. That's a stupid thing to say."

Her expression became earnest. She leaned forward.

"It isn't, though. It's realistic. I've been kidding myself all this time, and going in a wrong direction, and I think I understand it clearly now."

"At seventeen?" Henry tipped his chair legs back and smiled at her teasingly.

"Go ahead and laugh, but I may be right."

They slipped back effortlessly into their easy give-and-take,

their relaxed and happy-serious kind of conversation, this time
with more mature issues to discuss and a more equal basis on
which to meet.

At last, thought Henry, *something to take my mind off me!*

He saw only his Little Sister; he did not see the new pitfall
they were approaching. It was too soon.

Eventually, as the quarter hours passed, he was even able to
translate aloud some of the Manchurian manuscript for Amy to
hear, and this time he paid attention to the words himself:

" 'It had been a hot summer day full of the chirping of crickets
and the cackling of hens. In the evening we heard the long sad cry
of a steam whistle. Along the railroad tracks came the insistent
singing vibration of train wheels. A lookout in the tree began to
wave his signal flag. Mountains stood on either side of the
railroad pass. It was the tunnel to a grave, there was no escape.
. . . A roar burst into the cool beauty of the evening. There came
a shrill whistle. The train rolled on its side like a great stricken
snake, its free wheels still turning helplessly. We took our guns
and ammunition . . .' "

"Read more," Amy said when his voice stopped.

"All right." Henry turned pages. "This is the part where they
come across the Japanese troops in the village." He began to
read again, translating into English as he did so.

" 'The enlisted men not on duty sat in the temple courtyard,
each with a towel wrapped around his neck, talking, cursing,
telling lewd stories. Seki Moto, playing a slender reed flute, was
beating time with his hobnailed boots. His bayonet was correctly
in his scabbard at his belt. He took his cap off to wipe out the
sweat around the band. His steel helmet hung from a strap around
his neck. Little bronze bells at the corner of the temple roof
sounded in the evening wind. . . .' "

Amy heaved a long sigh when he stopped again. "Do you
understand why I believe I can't write fiction? How can I measure up to that?"

"But, Amy, it isn't exactly fiction. It's written like a novel,
but it's really more like a diary of last summer's fighting."

"A diary," Amy repeated uncertainly. "What could I put in a
diary except my own foolish moods? You said it yourself. I'm
seventeen. I have nothing to write about."

"I thought your new goal was to be a journalist."

"It is."

"Then you'll have plenty to write about. Once they give you assignments."

"I suppose so." She brightened. "At least I'll have good models. You'll see to that, won't you?"

"Sure."

"Henry, do you think I can do it? Do you think I can be a good reporter?"

"I was never so sure of anything."

She clasped her hands together. "If you say so it must be true!"

Henry grinned at her with his old wry humor. "Such confidence. What did I ever do to deserve it?"

"Nothing," she said, "except to be your usual smug and complacent self." She grinned back, his bantering opponent once more. His other self, his Amy. He realized with a surge of relief that he was halfway to being normal again. Amy was a miracle worker.

"Do you think you'd like to go to the Peking Opera some night?" he asked impulsively.

"I'd love it!" she exclaimed. "A night when they're playing *The Water Margin*."

"You've only seen *The Water Margin* thirty-five times."

"Never with you." She gave him a mischievous glance. "To explain the political significance, of course. So I can fully comprehend the peasants' rebellion."

Henry cleared his throat. "I'm thinking of giving up politics and becoming an actor," he remarked. "In order to play the beautiful princess."

"Lord, Henry, you're much too ugly for the princess. You'd need ten pounds of makeup."

"Thank you, Little Sister," he said ironically.

"Don't mention it," she said with an airy flip of her hand. "Whenever you need a compliment, just call on me."

"I may just do that." Henry's face lit up in a radiant smile.

Henry and Amy spent more time together after that. They did go to the Peking Opera, in the shabby theater in Chapei, and munched sunflower seeds and ate mandarin oranges and whispered and laughed, but it didn't matter: the rest of the audience was doing the same thing. The opera lasted for five hours without an intermission. They stood on the bridge over Soochow Creek and leaned on the parapet and had heated arguments about America's historic and economic role in China. They went to the movies and saw Marlene Dietrich in *Dishonored*, which Henry declared was the most foolish picture he'd ever seen. Amy disagreed. She admired the camera angles.

"The only movies you've ever liked," she said to Henry, "have been directed by Eisenstein or Pudovkin."

"That's true."

"Isn't that a little narrow-minded?"

"No. It just means I have high standards." Henry had regained his self-confidence.

"Have you seen *The Love of Jeanne Ney*?" Amy asked.

"That's a book by Ilya Ehrenburg. I read it years ago."

"In Russian, I suppose."

Henry only grinned. Actually he had read the Chinese translation.

"Well, it's a movie too," Amy said, "directed by Gustav Pabst. It was made in Germany about five years ago and it's being shown next week. Would you like to go?" She paused and smiled. "Even though Pabst is German and not Russian?"

Henry hesitated. "I think not, Amy," he said. "I'm going to be very busy next week."

He was recognizing belatedly what was happening to them. He was determined not to let it go any further. Even now when their hands touched accidentally, a tension sprang up between them and it scared Henry. He had a sinking feeling it was too late for himself, but what of his Little Sister? She must be protected from pain; her nature was free and open and she had no defenses. There was no future for them together, none at all. He would not admit it was too late for Amy as well.

He went to his Communist cell leader and begged to be sent to Kiangsi Province.

"It is past time. I have stayed in Shanghai too long."

"Not yet, Comrade. We need you here."

"But why! The fighting is in the South!"

"You know better than to argue, Comrade. Where is your discipline?"

Where indeed? Henry asked himself desperately, accepting the rebuke. As long as he was in Shanghai, he could not avoid Amy. She was the other part of himself: a part he must someday turn his back on forever. He knew that and dreaded it and wished the leave-taking would happen soon, to have it over, but right now he was here with his Little Sister and he loved her more every day.

CHAPTER 7

In 1933 Japan's investment in Shanghai amounted to a billion yen, a fantastically high figure. The Japanese population in the International Settlement had grown from eight hundred in 1890 to thirty thousand. They were by far the biggest foreign group in the city.

Above Shanghai, in the Yangtze valley, Japanese investors owned a land company, a machine plant, a paper mill, and the power plants of twenty-four cities.

In the North, Manchuria remained Manchukuo, a Japanese puppet, in spite of an investigation by the League of Nations. The Imperial Sun was lifting over the horizon with a hard and brilliant light.

David Valentine had remarried in the winter of 1932, after his divorce from Kay. His new bride was a quiet, pretty girl named Margaret McCabe, the daughter of an American banker recently transferred to Shanghai. By the summer of 1934 the marriage was over, as Margaret tearfully declared that she could not bear to live in China another moment: it was dangerous and dirty, and although she loved David, she did not love him enough to endure this hated exile.

David withstood this second marital failure philosophically. He decided he was probably doomed to bachelorhood and moved into a new apartment. He was enthusiastically welcomed back into the social circle of the International Settlement. Wealthy and eligible bachelors were always popular.

Something of a stir in the smart set was created by David's young nephew, Andy Henderson. At nineteen Andy still had the face of a frozen angel. He seemed indifferent, with an aspect of "nothing-matters-so-why-not," and his sophisticated attitude produced romantic flutters in the hearts of young women. That was not Andy's intention. He was genuinely miserable, but no one knew it except his sister Amy, who felt helpless to assist him. Andy was baffled by his inability to right even some of the wrongs of the world. Amy was covering assignments as a cub reporter on the *Shanghai Mirror* and was regarded in the newspaper world as someone to watch: bright, ambitious, and talented. Andy pretended to work at a job at the pottery works, but more often than not he neglected to appear at his desk. Mike and Laura were worried about him, but he only shrugged off their inquiries.

"Mother of God, Andy, do you want to be a playboy all your life?" Mike demanded one evening with a mixture of anxiety and exasperation. "Is that your idea of a career? Doing the town and drinking champagne every night? Living in nightclubs and coming home drunk at dawn?"

"Why not?" Andy replied indifferently. He was not callous, as he appeared. He thought that if he pretended to be uncaring long enough, he would make it come true.

"People are starving all over the world. There's an economic depression going on."

"Not for us, Grandpa. We're still rich."

"And it hasn't done you any good, has it? Do you like the way you're living?"

No. I detest it.

"Oh, I imagine I'll get tired of it after a while."

"Why don't you go to college, Andy? Here or in the States. If you want Princeton, Uncle David will pull some strings."

"If I decide to do that, Grandpa, I'll let you know."

Wherever he went, his life would be no different, Andy thought tiredly. Whatever he was looking for—if he only knew—he would be able to find it in Shanghai as well as anywhere else.

He attended a dinner party one evening at the home of the Rex Thornhills. As the guests began to leave the drawing room in groups of twos and threes, the men in black topcoats, the women in silver fox, Andy stood by the fireplace, leaning negligently against the ornate white mantel with one elbow propped up on the mantelpiece and a glass of champagne in his other hand. He was the picture of a jaded young man-about-town. He was wearing a black dinner jacket, with a white silk shirt and silver and white muttonfat jade cuff links, which had been a birthday gift from his grandmother.

"Andy darling," Laura had said, "I can't give you anything antique because you're much too modern."

"Is that a compliment, Grandmother?"

"I don't know. I only know that you're troubled and I love you very much."

He wondered if she and Amy had been discussing him.

"I know why everyone's leaving!" cried a woman guest who still remained in the Thornhill drawing room. "We've run out of champagne!"

"The Thornhills never run out of champagne," said a thin dark man named Leo Gamsa, who looked like a spider with very hairy eyebrows. "They have a spigot in the kitchen attached to a special fountain with a pipeline that runs directly to France."

"What an imaginative fantasy, Leo," said the woman, covering a bored yawn with manicured fingers. "God, do we have to go home? Who can recommend an entertaining new place to go? Somewhere different?"

No one volunteered a suggestion. The woman shrugged and rose to collect her wrap and find her husband. Leo Gamsa glanced speculatively at Andy.

"I'm surprised that a young man like yourself doesn't know any new place to go," he remarked.

"In Shanghai? There are none," said Andy.

"Oh, but you're wrong. There are all sorts of unexpected corners and holes-in-the-wall in this city."

"I don't frequent holes-in-the-wall."

The other man laughed. "World-weary, aren't you?"

"Sorry if I'm not more enthusiastic." Andy didn't sound sorry.

Leo was not deterred by the young man's manner. He continued, "Even a gaudy dance hall would be new to you. You go only where it's fashionable, with the crowd."

"Yes, that's so." Andy still displayed ennui. He drained the last of his champagne and set the empty glass on the mantelpiece.

Leo surveyed the departing guests. "They're all going somewhere safe and *au courant*."

"And nobody's asked me along," said Andy. Actually he'd had several invitations, but none had interested him.

"Would you like to come with me?" Gamsa asked.

"Where are you going?"

"To take a bite of Eve's Apple." Leo Gamsa grinned. "It's the name of a cabaret."

"Eve's Apple. You're right, I don't know it." Andy lifted a languid eyebrow. "Shall I come?"

"You won't be sorry, if you've never been there. Petrushka might put in an appearance."

"Who is Petrushka?"

"How shall I put it, dear boy. A force of nature."

"You do have a taste for fantasy. Or is it melodrama?" Andy smiled, which made him look years younger, dispelling his veneer of adult sophistication. "Very well," he said, "I'll take that bite of Eve's Apple with you. Where is it?"

Andy drove his own car from the Thornhill home to a dark side street near Blood Alley, according to Leo Gamsa's directions. They were in the Shanghai of pulp magazines and dime-novel legends here, a place of slinking shadows, yellow-faced assassins, and the sweet stink of opium. Andy was a little nervous as he braked the open roadster. They were certainly off the beaten track, he thought. He didn't know Leo Gamsa very well. Kidnappers abounded; that was no pulp-magazine fiction or Chinatown pipe dream. But, lord, the man was a friend of the Thornhills, and Rex Thornhill was a poker chum of his grandfather's, so he must be all right.

"Where is this Eve's Apple?" he inquired. "I don't see any lights."

"Up a flight of stairs, in that building over there."

They climbed out onto the almost empty street, found the building, and entered a narrow doorway. Inside was a long, steep flight of stairs with a closed door at the top from behind which pulsed the faint sounds of music, conversation, and laughter.

They mounted the stairs and pushed open the door. Out came a blast of noise: shouting, high-pitched giggles, the blare of trumpets, the rattling of crockery, the shuffling of feet to music, the wail of saxophones and the insistent rhythm of a trap drum. With the noise billowed air that was heavy with the smells of whiskey, perspiration, and cigarette smoke. They passed through the door and the room lay revealed, dimly lit and crowded with tables around a dance floor. At its far end was a tiny stage and a five-piece band. Red wool curtains hung around the walls from floor to ceiling, casting a lurid glow across the room.

Just inside the door stood a coatrack. Andy and Leo Gamsa began to shrug off their overcoats. Beside the coatrack a table offered zakuski, small Russian delicacies: bits of smoked fish, pickled beets, cucumbers in sour cream, blini, black bread, and caviar. Attending it was a waiter in an embroidered blouse.

"You didn't tell me this was a Russian place," Andy remarked to Leo.

"You didn't ask me."

Shanghai, true to its cosmopolitan nature, had become a haven for White Russians after the Bolshevik Revolution. The Russians had remained without passports or nationality and often without jobs. They were a pitiful lot, existing on drunken dreams. Eventually the women worked. They earned money as waitresses, dance-hall hostesses, cabaret entertainers, and prostitutes. Some of them had been countesses in Russia.

"Your first visit, gentlemen?" asked the waiter. "Here, have some zakuski, fresh tonight. Unfortunately you have just missed the cabaret."

"A program of Gypsy songs, no doubt," commented Leo.

"So beautiful and sad that tears would have come into your eyes," the waiter confirmed. "Everyone in the room was sobbing."

"Tell me," said Leo, "is Petrushka here tonight?"

"She hasn't arrived. But there are other lovely ladies here to dance with. Come inside and see for yourself."

Following the waiter into the room, Andy and Leo seated themselves at a small table near the dance floor and ordered champagne.

"One drink and then we'll leave," Leo said. "Without Petrushka it seems quite dull. Sorry."

"No need to apologize." Andy spoke coolly. He was disappointed himself. Just a shabby little White Russian cabaret, he thought. No style. Not even dangerous. He made an attempt to be polite. "I hate to go straight home after a party. Can't stand the letdown."

The champagne arrived in its silver bucket, the cork was popped, and the glasses filled.

"Do they sell tickets for the dancing?" Andy inquired.

"No, not here. The ladies are employed by the management in this place. If you buy them drinks, they'll dance with you for nothing."

The women who were not dancing stood along the walls against the backdrop of the red wool curtains. They wore cheap sateen dresses and had crimson lipstick on their mouths and black mascara on their eyelashes. Most of them seemed to be Russian. On the dance floor women were pasted against their partners. Here and there a foreign tourist stared down at the dancing partner draped around his neck, half embarrassed and half fascinated by this glimpse of Shanghai nightlife. A few American Marines in dress uniforms, with square pink faces and short-clipped hair, stared impassively over their partners' shoulders as they shuffled around the floor. Andy thought it was all rather sordid. No—pitiful. He leaned back and lit a cigarette, concealing his helpless rage. He hated this, too, because he couldn't change it. There was nothing to be done. It was Shanghai, like the woman struck by a taxi on the Bund.

A throaty laugh rang out above the music. A ripple seemed to pass through the room as excited whispers ran from table to table. "She's arrived. . . . Petrushka is here."

Petrushka stood inside the doorway. She wore a bronze silk dress, *cheong-sam* style, with a mandarin collar and a calf-length skirt slit to the top of her thigh. Above the collar her throat rose in a sweep of golden-brown flesh. Her head was thrown back and she was laughing. Her face was dominated by high cheekbones and a wide mouth. Her hair, which tumbled in a thick mane to her shoulders, was the color of topaz. Her eyes were long and amber and tilted at the corners. She was a big woman, deep-chested, broad-shouldered, and long-legged. The three men who stood beside her seemed like shadows in the reflection of her brilliance.

"What a lioness." Andy, staring at her, whispered the words aloud.

"I warned you." Leo took a sip of champagne. "It's Petrushka. Marvelous, isn't she?"

No. Something is wrong. Andy caught a glimpse of her eyes as her gaze slid over his table. They were glazed and unseeing. Her laughter was synthetic; he felt it like a stab of pain.

"She's in trouble," he said. "Something is wrong."

"That sort of woman is always in trouble. Drink, drugs, what-have-you—it's the life she leads."

"She has a right to be happy. Everyone does. Everyone in the world."

Leo regarded Andy with amusement. "My dear young man," he murmured, "are you always so sentimental?"

Andy had betrayed himself, but he didn't care. Not after glimpsing Petrushka. She was a frightened little girl behind her mask of laughter. She was suffering Shanghai. She was all that Andy wanted. She had made an immediate impact on his emotions, and he felt reckless. Light-headed. Almost drunk, although he wasn't. He felt like doing something crazy.

"Let's join Petrushka's table," he said.

"You don't mean it."

"Of course I mean it."

"The lioness is a magnificent beast, I grant you, but one admires her at a distance. At close range the reality isn't so pleasant."

"I intend to join her anyway. Will you come?"

Leo Gamsa sighed. "I brought you to Eve's Apple; I suppose I'll have to. Where's the waiter?"

"Never mind the waiter. Take the bottle."

Andy held their champagne glasses and Leo had the silver bucket and half-empty bottle under his arm as the two men threaded their way across the room to where Petrushka sat with her three companions.

"May we sit down?" Andy bestowed an impartial smile on all four of them. He was light-headed. "We've brought an offering of champagne."

"What, a stinking half-bottle?"

Petrushka had spoken. She was sprawled with both elbows

resting on the back of the chair. Her voice was low and husky,
brimming with scornful amusement. "That entitles you to sit
under the table on the floor. At our feet!" She chuckled, and the
three men laughed with her.

"Then we'll order more bottles." Andy continued to smile.
He pulled over a chair and sat down, across the table from
Petrushka so he could face her. Leo squeezed in beside him. "It
seems pretty lively here tonight," Andy said in a pleasant tone.

"Lively?" one of the men snarled in answer. "The place is a
graveyard, packed with decaying corpses."

"I'm not a decaying corpse," Andy said.

"No," said Petrushka, narrowing her long amber eyes at him
across the table. "You're not a corpse at all." Her voice was
beginning to slur. "I think you're a young man, and I think
perhaps you have a very handsome face. Or maybe I'm very
drunk; I can't quite tell."

"You're drunk, Petrushka," another of the men put in. "He's
a commonplace young man with a very ordinary face."

"Shall we go?" Leo muttered in Andy's ear.

"No," Andy replied. Sitting across from her, staring at her,
he could see the bruises of experience on Petrushka's face, the
dark circles under her eyes, the grooves that ran like parentheses
from her nostrils to her mouth, the vertical lines between her
eyes. He felt a rush of tenderness and compassion for her,
mingled with a powerful surge of physical desire. He wanted to
caress and comfort her and at the same time to punish her for the
life she was leading. He had the dazed feeling he had turned into
the Reverend Davidson confronting Sadie Thompson. But he was
no clergyman. He wondered if Petrushka sensed his emotions.
He reached out and caught her hand.

She allowed her fingers to remain within his for a moment or
two. Her hand was large, warm, and dry, almost as big as
Andy's own. He stroked his thumb along her knuckles and she
snatched her hand away.

"Be careful, you haven't paid for that."

"Must I pay?"

"Can you pay, that's the question. Do you think you can get
by on your looks alone? Even pretty young men must pay for
what they want." She tossed her mane of hair, then spoke in a

deliberately coarse manner. "First you'd like to squeeze Petrushka's hand, all right. Then after a while you think she's too far gone to care and you reach under the table and put your hand up Petrushka's dress. Very well, I don't object. But first show us the color of your money."

"I don't want to buy you."

"Why not, darling? After a certain hour of the evening I'm for sale." She smiled at him; her smile was charming. "Parts of me for sale at any rate. Not to worry, you won't be disappointed."

"You needn't say that."

"But it excites you."

"No."

But it did excite him. Andy forced himself to ignore it and looked directly into her face. "You're not a whore; why do you talk like one?"

"Be careful of your language," one of the men said angrily. "You are speaking to the daughter of Ivan Pavlovitch Koubettsky, once an officer of the Imperial Guard in St. Petersburg. She is Petra Ivanovna; she may say what she pleases. You may not."

"Is that true?" asked Andy of Petrushka.

"Yes, he's right." Petrushka's expression turned sulky. "Have respect for me. I've told you that parts of me are for sale, but other parts are not. Learn to know the difference or go away."

"I know the difference."

"Where's that champagne you promised?" Her mood had changed again. Now she was restless, slouching in her chair and biting a fingernail. "We need something to drink. Why don't you spend a little money? Give me a cigarette. Somebody dance with me. For the love of Christ, are we going to sit here all night?"

Andy rose half out of his seat, on fire to dance with her, but she ignored him and turned to one of her three companions. They moved out onto the dance floor.

Leo Gamsa said to Andy in a low voice, "The woman is half mad."

"It doesn't matter." Andy watched Petrushka on the dance floor. "See how she moves."

"She's wearing nothing under that dress; it's quite apparent."

The curves of Petrushka's body were clearly visible under the tight silk dress. She moved as unselfconsciously as an animal.

Once, however, she stumbled, betraying her drunkenness, and abruptly she dropped her arms from her partner.

"To hell with this. I want to sit down."

Back at the table she threw herself into her chair and glared at Andy.

"You—pretty one! What's your name?"

"Will you dance with me if I tell you?"

"I make the bargains, not you. Tell me."

"Andy Henderson."

"American?"

"Yes."

Petrushka struck a match and lit a cigarette. Then she leaned back and blew a stream of smoke at the ceiling. "Ah," she said dreamily, "a filthy-rich, tightfisted American millionaire. No wonder he won't part with money. That explains everything."

"It doesn't explain anything."

"A filthy, thieving American," Petrushka said softly, almost crooning, still gazing at the ceiling where the smoke moved. "Growing rich and fat, like all millionaires, feeding on Russian flesh. Pounds and pounds of Russian flesh, to satisfy the greedy Americans. You see how thin we are, how poor and ill and starving, how degraded. But the businessmen grow fat."

"It's easy to blame other people for your troubles," said Andy, irritated in spite of himself.

"See him rise to the bait! See his face grow red!" Petrushka chuckled. It was a delightfully contagious sound, and her companions chuckled in sympathy.

Leo Gamsa stood up. "Come on, Andy. Haven't you had enough of this?"

Andy shook his head. His anger had died away; he was staring once again at Petrushka's face—at the lines of anguish written around her mouth; the pain and bewilderment in the depths of her amber eyes.

"Will you dance with me now?" he asked gently.

"All right, my little millionaire."

On the dance floor Petrushka seemed like a different person. She melted against Andy and crooned into his ear in a husky contralto that she couldn't give him "anything but love, baybee."

Andy was engulfed by a rush of emotion he couldn't name as he held her against him.

When the music ended, Petrushka insisted on returning to the table. The fresh champagne had arrived. She threw back her head and drained a glass at one swallow. Then she returned to the theme of thieving American businessmen. She harped on it until Andy was maddened.

"Carrion," she said, "gorging on our flesh."

"Then take mine in exchange," Andy said foolishly. At that moment the music stopped as the musicians prepared for a break, and Andy's voice rang out into the sudden quiet. "Take my flesh as a token, Petrushka. A repayment for what you've suffered." The idea appealed to him. He was light-headed again.

"Do I understand this?" Petrushka narrowed her eyes. "Are you offering me your body? It sounds amusing."

"No, not my body." Andy leaned back, withdrew a gold cigarette case from the inside pocket of his jacket, and selected a cigarette. He lit it casually. Then he looked over at Petrushka and suddenly he was taut with intensity. "Only a portion, sweetheart. A section of flesh. To repay you."

She smiled in derision. "From where will you take it? This portion of flesh?"

"From wherever you like."

"May I take it myself?"

"If it pleases you."

"Very well." She twisted in her chair. Leaning back on one elbow she bellowed to the small stooped waiter who was moving among the tables taking orders. "Dmitri! Dmitri! Come here!"

He scurried over to her side. "Petra Ivanovna, what is it you need?"

"Something special, Mitya. A special request. Go to the kitchen" —she glanced over at Andy and the corners of her wide mouth twitched in amusement; she resembled a great playful kitten— "and fetch me a paring knife. A small, sharp paring knife. It must be very sharp, Mitya. And be sure it is clean."

"Of course, lady." He went off.

Silence fell on the six people who sat around the table. Andy calmly smoked his cigarette, one ankle crossed on his knee. Having made his offer, he was prepared to stand behind it. Leo Gamsa moved restlessly in his seat, glaring at Andy from under his eyebrows. Petrushka and her three companions waited, their eyes gleaming with anticipation. Conversation and movement churned and bubbled all around them in the red-tinged room, but none of the six seemed to notice. They waited for Mitya the waiter to return from the kitchen.

"You can't be serious about this," Leo hissed into Andy's ear.

"It stopped her babbling, didn't it?"

"That woman will cut out your liver with a knife in her hands."

"We'll see."

Andy snuffed out his cigarette in an ashtray, noting that his hand was steady. One part of his mind told him that he was behaving in an irrational way. Madness must be contagious. On the other hand he felt that his madness was lucid. He would carry out his promise to Petrushka. And it *had* shut her up.

The waiter returned to the table. "Here, lady, I have brought you the knife. Do you wish some fruit or cheese?"

"No, Mitya. You may go now."

The knife lay on the table in front of Petrushka, an ordinary paring knife with a wooden handle. Its blade was short and pointed. SHe picked it up and held it to the light. The edge was razor-sharp. Andy regarded it with interest.

"Have you made up your mind, Petrushka? Have you decided where you'd like to cut? The knife seems suited to our purpose."

For the first time Petrushka's expression of mockery faltered. Her gaze flickered over Andy's body as he sat relaxed and casual in his chair. Then she stared at his face. "Suppose I take the flesh from your face?" she demanded. "From your cheek?"

"Fine. Shall I come to you, or will you come here?"

She sprang to her feet, grasping the knife. "Stay where you are."

She moved around the table to Andy and stood over him. Her companions watched intently. Leo Gamsa's mouth fell open.

Andy sat back. "Shall I close my eyes? Will it make it easier for you?"

She glared at him wildly. "Fool! Mad fool! Do it yourself!" She threw the knife onto the table.

"As you wish. From my own face?"

"Take it from your arm, what the hell do I care?"

Leaving him, she stalked back to her seat and flung herself into it. Andy picked up the knife and ran it along his thumb. "Are you sure you want to have my flesh?"

"Get on with it," she said sullenly. "Let's see what the word of an American is worth."

"Leo, hold my coat."

Andy rose to his feet, removed his jacket, and stood in his shirt sleeves and black cummerbund. His fair hair shone in the reddish light. One of Petrushka's companions reached out and took hold of his sleeve and rubbed it between his fingers.

"Nice," he said, grunting. "Pure silk."

Andy held out the jacket to Leo Gamsa, who shook his head violently and turned his face aside. "I won't be a party to this," he mumbled. "You're as crazy as these Russians."

Tossing his jacket onto the back of the chair, Andy sat down again and removed the muttonfat jade cuff link from his left cuff. Then he rolled up his sleeve to the elbow, revealing a lean muscular forearm covered with fine blond hair. With his hand palm down, he thrust the arm into the center of the table, almost within touching distance of Petrushka. She shrank away.

Andy picked up the paring knife in his right hand.

"How much are you going to cut for us, millionaire?" asked one of the men.

"Whatever she says." Andy nodded at Petrushka. Her mockery had disappeared. So, apparently, had her drunkenness. She watched Andy intently.

Holding the knife pointing downward, he drew it along his arm, halfway between the elbow and the wrist. A thin bright line appeared. He drew the knife at right angles until he had formed a square. Now four red lines were oozing blood. Petrushka watched as though hypnotized.

"Stop this," Leo muttered. He grabbed Andy by the right wrist.

"Let go of me, Leo," Andy said pleasantly.

"Do you intend to cut yourself open?"

"A small measure of justice for what she has suffered," he said in a formal tone.

Shaking off Leo's hand, Andy plunged the point of the knife deeply into his flesh. Blood bubbled up and over his arm, overflowing onto the tablecloth and staining it red. Turning the knife sideways, he began to slice. More red wetness . . . Petrushka cried out. Leaning across the table, she thrust her own hand into the bloody wound on Andy's arm.

"No! I see now what he is! A holy man! A martyr!" Drawing back her hand, she traced the sign of the cross on her forehead with her bloody finger. "Stop it now, stop it at once. Your holy blood has been spilled. It is enough."

"He is not a holy man, Petrushka," one of her companions said in disgust. "He's only an American. Let him go on."

"Stop!" She stared at Andy. Obediently he put the knife down on the table. His arm continued to flow crimson.

"I should have known," she went on, half in a whisper. "When I first saw you, I should have realized what you are. You have the face of a saint."

"No," he said, "you're wrong. I'm not a saint."

"An angel, then."

She seemed transfixed. The cross of blood was caking and drying on her forehead. Andy, too, sat very still, his bleeding arm outstretched. With a table napkin Leo began to bind up his wound.

"Well, Petrushka, have you had enough at last?"

"Yes," Petrushka muttered, "I have had enough. I am satisfied."

"It takes very little to satisfy you tonight," said one of the men.

"I'll take you home," Andy said.

"No."

"Then I'll come here tomorrow night and find you."

She made no answer. Andy rolled down his shirt sleeve over the napkin-bandage and picked up his jacket from the back of the chair. Staring at Petrushka, he said, "Leo, we can leave now."

"Take your cuff link.

"Let her have it."

Her eyes wide, her pupils dilated, her gaze on Andy, Petrushka picked up the jade cuff link and closed it in her fist.

"It's valuable," said Leo. "Don't be a fool."

"Haven't you understood yet?"

With a last brilliant smile at Petrushka, Andy turned away from the table.

Andy's arm healed, but his spirit did not. He could not stay away from Petrushka. In the months that followed they wrangled, quarreled, spat, argued, danced, embraced, and after a while became lovers, although Petrushka insisted it was a sin to have carnal knowledge of a holy man. Her conviction made their times together more obsessed and passionate. Often Andy felt degraded and enslaved. She was a whore, he told himself desperately. She still saw other men, she drank too much and took heroin, and sometimes she disappeared for days or weeks when she descended into a drug trance. Andy would rescue her from debased surroundings where she was being used by evil and leering men. He would lead her back to her room, clean her, nurse her, and embrace her tenderly. She would be pitifully grateful.

"You are a saint," she would weep against his shoulder. "A saint. I will be different, my little holy father. I will be a pure young girl again, for you. I swear it."

For a time she would be sweet and loving as she had promised, and their hell became a heaven. Then it would start again. Andy despaired, seeing only one hope for himself and Petrushka: He must redeem her permanently from her way of life. Otherwise they were both lost.

CHAPTER 8

Amy's existence was bounded by ambition and hard work on the one hand, and her time with Henry Chen on the other.

She yearned to climb up from the cub reporter cellar of society news and women's club gossip.

"Grandmother," she cried to Laura one Sunday morning at breakfast, "the Garden Club of America was visiting Shanghai last week!"

"Was it interesting?"

"It was ridiculous! One of the ladies gave a talk on civic beauty, and I had to cover it for the paper. . . . She spoke about eliminating signboards! She said they were unsightly, and at home in her town she'd persuaded the Chamber of Commerce to do away with them! Couldn't we start a campaign like that in Shanghai, she wanted to know?" Amy's expression was comically despairing.

"Oh, Amy."

Laura couldn't help smiling. They both thought of Shanghai and every Chinese city. A riot of signboards. Huge gilded characters hanging on metal frameworks along every narrow street. Neon signs flashing in English and Chinese from the second story of almost every building. Walls painted with huge crude murals depicting cigarette smokers blowing smoke rings, or happy Chinese mothers powdering their infants with Perfection Talcum Powder. Chapei, where every alley and street was thronged with swinging signs. Eliminate signboards in Shanghai! You might as well eliminate vines from the jungle!

"Well," Amy remarked philosophically, "Henry doesn't agree either."

Laura noticed once more that Amy brought Henry Chen's name into almost every conversation. Amy was not even aware of it. Amy and Henry Chen, she thought. Andy and his deep silent trouble, whatever it was. Oh, lord, when they grew up, their problems did not go away, they only became more complicated, and she felt more helpless. . . .

Amy was continuing to report Henry's opinion to Laura. "He says that someday the signs will be instructive and informative," she said, "but he doesn't talk about doing away with them. He knows better." She sighed. "I'm so tired of these women's clubs, Grandmother. I want to do something interesting. Police news, like a real reporter."

"I'm sure you'll get your chance if you're patient."

Slowly, little by little, Amy's chances came. She started an investigation of her own, of an oily little man called Mr. Suzuki who ran a camera shop in Little Tokyo. He was apparently just an unimportant Japanese shopkeeper. Amy, however, had good authority to believe that he was spying for the Imperial Government and was photographing American and British shipping in the Whangpoo. She began to accumulate evidence and cultivate her own informers. She used her own money. It was convenient having a rich family at a time like this. Mike was proud of her and advanced her whatever she needed. After a while the paper started to believe her suspicions of Mr. Suzuki, and became interested. Articles began to appear "by Amy Henderson." Her final triumph came when the camera shop closed and Mr. Suzuki disappeared—recalled to Japan. It was a small triumph, for Mr. Suzuki had not been very important, but it meant a lot to Amy. Her editor was amused and impressed.

"Tell me, Red. Do you really think this Japanese threat is going to amount to anything?"

"Yes, I do," Amy said earnestly.

"Naturally they're going to war with China. We all know that. But the U.S.A.?"

"Possibly."

"Maybe you're listening too hard to your radical buddies."

"And maybe I'm not."

"Okay." The editor grinned. "I'll listen to what you have to say, Red. On paper."

"No more women's clubs?"

"Oh, yeah. Stick with that too. Do both."

Amy didn't mind. She was tremendously happy. She felt she was really on her way.

It was February 1934, the Holiday Moon. It was time for the Feast of the Lanterns in Chapei. As children Amy and Andy had always gone with Plum Blossom to the Chinese town to watch. They'd looked forward to it for weeks. Christmas and Fourth of July and Chinese New Year and Feast of the Lanterns: all part of the Henderson twins' lives, the festive landmarks of their year. During the Feast of the Lanterns they had always made an offering of Chinese money, octagonal coins strung on a string, to the shrine of Tsao Wang in Plum Blossom's cousin's kitchen. Amy had kept up the custom.

Amy went to find Plum Blossom one evening to make her donation. She had the coins ready in her pocket.

She looked into the kitchen. Chen was seated at the kitchen table, his head in his hands. He looked small and old. Amy called to him softly. He raised his head. Amy was shocked to see tears in his eyes.

"Chen? Why are you crying?"

"It is hard, missy. It is hard."

How desolate his voice was.

Amy searched out Plum Blossom in her room. Plum Blossom was weeping, seated in her chair, staring into space, her hands folded, tears running down her cheeks like winter rain. Amy had a quick, frightening suspicion.

"Plum Blossom," she said through suddenly dry lips, "where is Henry?"

Plum Blossom turned to gaze at Amy. "Where is my husband?" she asked in turn.

"He is in the kitchen. Crying."

"Yes, he will not come to me until he is strong. He thinks it would be unmanly. Chen, that old turtle's egg. What a stupid old man. As if I didn't know him." She burst into loud weeping and covered her face with her hands.

Amy went to her chair and put a gentle hand on her shoulder. "Is it about Henry?" she asked softly.

Plum Blossom nodded, unable to speak.

"Where is he, Plum Blossom? What's wrong? Can you tell me?" No answer, only weeping.

"Is he arrested? Maybe I can help."

Plum Blossom shook her head. She found her voice. Not arrested. Worse. Gone to be a soldier. To fight and perhaps to die. Her beautiful, brilliant son, who should have been a scholar, who knew the contents of all books, with his lovely hands and long fingers that were meant to hold a pen, carrying a gun! Like a common peasant. Like a bandit. To die in the dust. To choke in his own blood. A soldier.

"Stop it, Plum Blossom. Henry needn't die. He wants to fight for his convictions, that's all. He'll come home to Shanghai when the battle is done." Amy spoke in a voice of strength and assurance, but she was lying. Inside she was horribly afraid. She wanted to wail like Plum Blossom, to weep like Chen with her head in her hands. And she was angry. How could Henry go away without saying good-bye! Without a word! How could he!

"When did he leave?" she asked Plum Blossom.

"He has not left yet. He will go in the morning, on the early southbound train."

His destination is Jui-chin in southern Kiangsi Province, Amy thought. *He's going to join Mao Tse-tung. As he wanted. At last.*

"Where is he tonight?" she asked in a low voice.

"He has gone to say farewell to some friends in Chapei."

"Will he return home?"

"I do not know. He has bade farewell to us." Plum Blossom began to weep again.

"Tell me where I can find him, Plum Blossom. Please."

"I only know the name of the street."

"Tell me that."

When she had learned the street name, Amy looked for Andy in his room. Perhaps they could say good-bye to Henry together, she thought. But of course Andy was out. He was always out somewhere these days and often didn't come home until dawn or later. Very well. She would find Henry Chen on her own. She was still deeply, furiously angry with him. She felt betrayed. *He should have said good-bye.*

She drove her own car across the Soochow Creek Bridge and into the ancient Chinese town. Then she was forced to park the car and go on foot. People thronged the sidewalks and the gutters, many of them children who were laughing excitedly and clinging to their parents' hands. Every shopfront blazed with lighted lanterns. Paper crabs with moving claws. Dragonflies with flapping wings. Birds with swaying necks. Red paper lanterns with holes pricked to spell *Happiness* and *Prosperity.* White silk lanterns that represented moons. Lanterns with riddles pasted on their sides.

How she had once loved this, Amy thought distractedly as she pushed through the crowds. She and Andy had had toy lanterns on wheels to pull along the sidewalk. Once they had bought a pair of lanterns on bamboo tripods and stuck them in the garden on Bubbling Well Road and lighted them for guests at night.

This night she had to find Henry. Once she located the street, she would knock on each door if she had to. And then she would give him a piece of her mind! She would shout until she was hoarse! She would let him know what a rotten friend he was, how careless and thoughtless! She would . . . she would . . . Amy realized she was crying. She brushed her knuckles across

her cheeks and gulped back her tears. She kept on going, turning
corners, arriving at a main road.

She needed to cross the road, for the street she sought was
facing her, but she couldn't yet. The dragon was coming. Down
the center of the road it swayed, a great dragon with cloth sides
and blazing yellow eyes. Inside it were young men carrying
lanterns, their shuffling feet moving the dragon along the road,
their lanterns glowing through the cloth sides and making the
creature undulate with light and motion.

Amy stood helplessly on the wrong side of the street, watching
the dragon through tear-blurred eyes. How slowly it progressed.
How the children loved it. Maybe the children really mattered,
and not Amy Henderson and her stupid heartbreak. In love with a
boy who was absolutely and forever wrong. Even the wrong
race. To say nothing of his politics. What a dumb thing to
happen. Only a redhead like Henderson would get into a fix like
that. What a laugh. The guys in the city room would laugh their
heads off. It was so dumb it was funny. Why wasn't she laughing?
She ought to find her car and go home. Forget this night and this
idiotic search. Forget Henry Chen. If she could just stop crying.

The dragon had moved on, carrying its blaze of light. Amy
stepped tentatively onto the road, making for the shadows on the
other side where the shops were unlit in deference to the dragon.
That narrow alley over there was the street she wanted. She
stumbled up onto the curb, brushing against a little boy with a
butterfly lantern. He giggled. She smiled through her tears.

"*Ni hao*," she said. "Can I hold your lantern?"

He nodded shyly and passed it up. She held it at arm's length
against the dark sky. "Very, very pretty," she said. She paused.
"Does your mother have a shrine to Tsao Wang in her kitchen?"
she asked.

He nodded again.

"Would you make a humble offering for me at Tsao Wang's
shrine?" She handed him the string of coins from her pocket, the
ones she had meant to give Plum Blossom. The little boy accepted them gravely. Then he took back the butterfly lantern. His
father came then and led him away.

The children matter, Amy thought. *War is coming. There may*

*not be many more Feasts of the Lanterns. Let the children laugh
tonight. It doesn't matter if I cry. I've had my happy times.*

"Oh, Amy," said a soft voice behind her, "what are you
doing here in Chapei? On the street?"

She turned to see Henry Chen, his face gently shadowed in
lantern light.

"Oh, my God, Henry," she said, "you found me."

He put out his hand and let it fall again. "You weren't . . . by
any chance . . . looking for me?"

"By some chance . . . Henry . . . I was."

"Amy, there's something I must tell you."

"I know it already. You're going away in the morning. Leaving for Kiangsi Province."

"Yes."

Amy took a deep breath, letting her anger swell. She let it rise
within her. "Well, of all the dirty tricks."

"What?"

"Of all the inconsiderate, thoughtless, cowardly, sneaky things
I've ever heard of. Leaving without saying good-bye."

Henry looked bewildered. "Wait a minute."

"I should never have made the effort to come here at all.
Because now that I see you, I realize I have nothing to say. Oh,
no. Why would I? I just want you to go to Kiangsi and get
yourself killed, so that I'll never see you again. Isn't that right?
And if you think I care, then you're crazy." Amy suddenly
pressed her knuckles to her mouth.

Henry's drawn-in breath was like a whisper. "Is that what you
believe?" he asked wonderingly. "That I was leaving you without saying good-bye?"

Amy didn't answer.

"I was leaving it till last," he said in a husky voice. "Because
it was the hardest good-bye." Amy looked at him in silent
inquiry. He gazed steadily back. "I was putting it off," he said.
"I was a coward. You're right, that's why I didn't tell you
before. Just now I was going back to Bubbling Well Road to find
you and get it over with."

Amy was silent. Then she said, "Were you really, Henry?"

"Yes, Little Sister. I've told you the truth. As always."

"Then I'm . . . sorry I said those things."

He didn't speak for a moment. Then she saw him smile tenderly. "Crazy redhead. You can't help yourself."

"Be careful how you insult my race, Mr. Chen." Amy tried to speak in a light voice. "We Caucasians are very touchy."

"Especially the ones named Amy."

"Yes, especially those."

They both fell silent. Their bravado deserted them simultaneously as words failed. They stared at each other. Children laughed and lanterns bobbed. A peddler passed hawking sweets-on-a-stick. Henry drew Amy into a dark doorway, bare of lanterns, where they could be away from the crowd.

"I'd better take you home," he said.

"I have my car."

Neither of them moved.

"Henry, don't go!" Amy cried suddenly. She flung herself against him and threw her arms around his neck. He caught her by the waist. She raised her face and their lips met. They stood locked in a long, sweet, poignant kiss, their first and perhaps their last. There was no future for them. Not for Amy Henderson and Henry Chen, who would be, tomorrow, Comrade Chen T'ieh-chang of the People's Army. His path was chosen; an American woman could not walk it with him. But just for this moment they were a girl and boy who loved each other and were saying good-bye. A long, long good-bye.

"Amy, take care of my parents," he said against her mouth.

"I will, Henry."

"Look after them; they're old."

"I will."

"I love you, my dear Little Sister."

"I love you, too, Henry. I always have."

"Oh, God, I know that. And I'll never be able to say this again. Nor will you."

They kissed passionately, the same first-last kiss.

"Will you come back to Bubbling Well Road?" Amy whispered.

"No. I'll stay with friends tonight."

"Can I see you off at the railroad station in the morning?"

"No, Amy. No."

"Henry, will there ever be a yes?"

"Not for you and me, dearest." He caught her close and buried his lips in her hair. "I am so glad you're strong."

"I am not strong! I feel like dying."

"But you won't. You are strong, Amy. Trust yourself, for you are the other part of me. I will remember you always. Whatever happens."

She ached with yearning, clinging to him, knowing he was violating every instinct of propriety he possessed by this public embrace. The Chinese believed that physical affection between a man and a woman should be expressed in private. Always. But there could be no privacy for herself and Henry. They did not dare to be alone. There could be only this, warm lips and strong arms and a dark doorway on a Chapei street.

A long, long good-bye, one long, unending kiss that had to end. Around them swirled the Feast of the Lanterns.

CHAPTER 9

"Grandmother," said Amy, "could I speak to you for a minute?" She was standing in the doorway of Laura's sitting room.

Laura looked up from the illustrated catalog she'd been studying. It was the announcement of an auction to be held in Peking, and she thought she would go. Her days still revolved around the galleries. She was deeply absorbed now in T'ang and Sung Dynasties, almost to the exclusion of other periods. She could afford to indulge her personal interests these days; she did not need to consider public taste. Ironically, because she was no longer catering to customers, the galleries were more successful than ever. Laura Valentine was a respected name in the world of Chinese antiquities among people who were scholars and connoisseurs, people who had no idea the Valentine Pottery Works even existed, or that Laura's husband was the president.

Now, however, Laura set aside the catalog. Amy needed her. That was apparent from the expression on Amy's face.

"Come in, dear. I wasn't doing anything special."

Amy entered and took a seat on the floor beside Laura's chaise longue.

"Grandmother—have you ever been very unhappy?"

"Yes."

"Of course, what a stupid question. I know you've had tragedies. Terrible things have happened in your life. But I feel as though I'm the only one in the whole world who's ever suffered. I must be very selfish." She bowed her head.

"Not selfish," Laura said. "Just in trouble and needing help."

"I don't think anyone can help me," Amy said very low.

Laura paused. "Is it something to do with Henry's going away?" she asked gently.

Amy nodded. "Everything," she whispered. She laid her head on Laura's knee. "I love him so. And it's absolutely hopeless."

Laura felt an aching sorrow for her granddaughter. "As long as you understand that, Amy. About the hopelessness."

"I do. I have no silly dreams or fancies. But it hurts so."

Laura hesitated, wondering how to be tactful, but thinking she ought to know how far this had gone. "Have you told Henry how you feel?"

"Yes, he knows."

"And has he expressed his feelings for you?"

Amy gave a despairing little laugh. "Oh, Grandmother, you needn't worry; we haven't done anything. Not that way. You know how honorable Henry is, and what a puritan he is about his beliefs."

"Henry is a remarkable young man," Laura said softly, "just as he was an extraordinary child. I often wonder what his future will be."

"I pray to God he has a future," Amy said bitterly.

"Oh, my dear, so do I."

"Even though I won't be in it. That's what hurts so. I must . . . get over this bad time. Somehow." She began to cry.

Laura stroked her hair. "You're strong, Amy. You will recover."

"That's what Henry said."

"And he's usually right, isn't he?"

"Damn him." Amy raised her face and tried to smile through her tears. "He's a very irritating person. I'm . . . I'm so glad we were friends, Grandmother. I guess that's all I have left. The memory of friendship." She began to cry again. "Will you forgive me for saying I wish there'd been more?"

"Yes, I forgive you," Laura whispered.

It was southern summer, the hot summer of 1934. Henry Chen knelt by the side of a country road in Kiangsi Province. He rested his rifle on his knee. Across the road a comrade was doing the same thing. They were covering a retreat from the village of Holung, to create a delay when Kuomintang troops appeared over the rise in the road. It should be soon. They were the rear guard of a small detachment. Henry wore the uniform of the People's Army: a plain blue tunic with unadorned buttons, a high collar, and no insignia. Everyone wore the tunic, from the youngest soldier up to Comrade Mao, and no one wore insignia. There were no officers.

Henry was thin and tired and somewhat numb. Shanghai was a dream. His parents, his home, his university professors, his love, even his ideas, were being purged into a thin, clear flame in his mind, and soon he would not be Henry at all but T'ieh-chang. He was dimly aware of it. He hoped that the flame would forge him into a steel link in a steel chain. He was still in the painful process of transformation. He was young and tired and scared, but he was resolute. The numbness helped.

Holung was just a small village in Kiangsi Province. Farmhouses, a dirt road, pigs and chickens, some scrawny yellow dogs, toddling dirty-faced children and the peasants who lived there: weatherbeaten men and women who said little and worked hard.

Now that the Communists were retreating, the peasants would have an extra burden: they would be forced to billet soldiers of the Kuomintang. Troops of the Kuomintang never paid for their food. Red Army soldiers, on the other hand, were advised to pay for whatever they consumed. They were instructed to do so by their leaders. Mao Tse-tung counseled respect for the peasants as a matter of policy. "We must swim like fish in the ocean of the people," he told his army. According to his instructions there was no raping or looting; Mao's troops paid for their food and lodging, and when there was work to be done in a village, they were told to offer their help.

In Kiangsi they were on the verge of annihilation by Chiang Kai-shek. They were encircled by a ring of iron. Their strongholds were bombed every day by airplanes from Nanchang, the provincial capital. The Kuomintang had imported a German military commander, General von Falkenhausen, who had begun what was called the Fifth Encirclement Campaign against the Communists. Artillery bombardments, aerial bombing, and a massive economic blockade combined to starve and pound the Red Army into fragments.

Chiang Kai-shek boasted to his friends that Mao Tse-tung was encircled in Kiangsi. There was no escape for the Communists, he cried in triumph. They were trapped, and now it was only a matter of time until they were completely destroyed.

Henry heard the whine of airplanes and looked up at the sky—*another bombing raid*—and then the engine whine faded and there was only the chirping of insects. He wondered if he would die on this dusty country road near an obscure village called Holung. Would he mind? Oh, yes. He was young and he wanted to live. But they all might die. They probably would.

He had a crazy thought, born of blind faith that had nothing to do with rational, intellectual Henry Chen of Shanghai and everything to do with Chen T'ieh-chang of Jui-chin, the young man he was in the process of becoming. *Comrade Mao will save us. It is his destiny to preserve us. He will lead us out of this trap into safety. We all know it.*

He wiped his sweating palms on his tunic, gripped his rifle, and rested in the sun, blinking perspiration out of his eyelashes and waiting.

September was still warm in Shanghai. By the Moon of the Hungry Ghosts the sweltering humidity of summer had eased, but moisture still hung heavy in the air. Ceiling fans still moved lazily indoors, cooling still-perspiring flesh. Outside the sky was a gray-white haze veiling a still hot sun. Often it rained, a warm off-and-on drizzle.

When Amy left the *Shanghai Mirror* office at seven o'clock one evening she realized it had been raining; the pavements were still glistening. The neon signs of the city made delicate traceries of light against the sky, spelling out messages in Chinese characters through the mist. The needles of the endless neon knitter of the Great Ball Wool Company flickered high up on the Great World Building.

Amy hesitated on the sidewalk, knowing she should go home to dinner, but she felt depressed and restless and wished she had somewhere else to go. As a delaying tactic she opened her copy of the late edition of the newspaper, which she was carrying under her arm.

The first item she read only depressed her more. The Nanking government was about to grant independent status to five northern Chinese provinces: Shantung, Hopei, Shansi, Chahar, and Suiyuan. That meant they would fall under the Japanese sphere of influence. Chiang Kai-shek's decision, Amy whispered angrily to herself.

"What's the matter, kid?" said a sardonic voice beside her. "Why the long kisser? Have you found a friend's name in the obits?"

"Hello, Mac," said Amy. "I'm not reading the obituary column. Not exactly."

The man beside her was Lloyd McNamara, the UPI correspondent in Shanghai. As usual his hat was pushed to the back of his head, a cigarette drooped from the corner of his mouth, and he looked faintly amused at the world. He was dark, with thick eyebrows and a craggy face. Amy didn't know him very well—knew only that everyone called him Mac.

"I can see you need cheering up," he said. "Come on, I'll buy you a drink."

"I don't drink."

"I forgot, you're only a child. Red Henderson, the precocious girl reporter. Okay. How about a chocolate soda?"

Amy laughed and shook her head.

"A strawberry fizz? A vanilla malted?" He paused. "An egg cream?"

"What is an egg cream?"

"Obviously you didn't grow up in New York City."

"No, I grew up in Shanghai." Amy hesitated, and then grinned. "I'll accept a cup of coffee, Mac. I think I can use it."

"Done."

They found a restaurant where Mac ordered a glass of beer, the only alcoholic beverage on the menu, and Amy a cup of coffee. Mac fortified his beer with a swallow from a silver flask which he took from his jacket. Amy peered at the glass.

"Beer and whiskey?" she inquired. "Do you drink too much?"

"I'm afraid I do, kiddo. Occupational disease."

"I wonder if it will happen to me."

"I wouldn't be a bit surprised. If you stay in the newspaper game. And if you walk around with a long puss like that." He took another swallow from his flask, shuddered, and then relaxed. "What's your problem, Red? You look down in the dumps."

"I am. But it isn't your concern; you hardly know me."

"We could do something about that." He leered at her in mock lechery.

"I doubt it," Amy said warily.

"Hey, don't take me seriously. I'm an old man. I have two ex-wives and a very checkered past." Mac paused. "Well, not so old. Thirty-one. But the rest is true. Does it scare you?"

"No. My uncle David has two ex-wives, and he's one of the nicest men I know."

"I am not your kindly uncle. Still, I've got a shoulder you can cry on if you like."

Amy sighed. "Oh, Mac. If you really want to know, I'm worried about a war with Japan—that's what I was reading about in the paper—and I'm worried about my brother, who is horribly depressed and won't tell anyone why, and I'm worried about a friend who's trapped in Kiangsi with Mao Tse-tung in that miserable ring of iron and hasn't written in weeks."

"A Chinese friend, I gather."

Amy nodded. "The son of our head manservant. We grew up together."

"Oh," Mac said elaborately, "your head manservant. Pardon me. I didn't know I was in the company of the swells."

"Don't be a reverse snob."

"Sorry, angel face. I'm just a kid from Hell's Kitchen. My old man was a trolley-car conductor. We didn't have any servants, man or otherwise."

"Well, you don't have to boast about your proletarian origins.

We're not so fancy. My grandparents started the Valentine Pottery Works from scratch, and not so very long ago either.''

"Valentine? Mike Valentine? Is he your grandfather?"

"Yes, do you know him?"

"Only by reputation. One of Shanghai's many colorful characters. Old riverboat pilot and well-known poker player. No wonder you're the scrappiest girl reporter in town."

Amy laughed. "Is that what I am?"

"Sure, I thought you knew." Mac regarded her amiably. "Do you play poker too?"

"Absolutely. I'm a demon. I learned from Grandpa."

"Oh, wonderful. Just the kind of poker player I like. A cocky redhead with a fat bankroll. I'll let you know the next time there's a game."

"I think you're the one who's cocky. But we'll see."

"Drink your coffee," Mac said, "you're looking better already."

As they were leaving, Amy did feel cheered. "Thanks, Mac," she said as they emerged from the restaurant. "You improved my mood."

He gave her a quizzical smile. "Anytime, Red. Whenever you need someone to buy you a drink or listen to your troubles, just call on Mac. I'll be around."

CHAPTER 10

It was a dark night in southern Kiangsi Province. It was the night of October 16, 1934, and the Red Army was gathering like a vast organism with a single heart, near the town of Yutu.

The road out of Yutu stretched south into darkness. For miles and miles it was crowded with donkeys and mules, horses and wagons and men. The noise was astonishingly slight for such seething activity. Muffled clank of weapons. Creak of wagon wheels. Thump of sacks on muleback. Crunch of boots on the road, as columns organized for march. Few voices; silence was essential. An army of 100,000 troops was moving out under cover of night. In the air was the faint smell of peanut oil and sweet raw sugar from the sacks, mingled with the odor of mule droppings and the sweat of horses.

Henry Chen watched from the roadside with pride and amazement. He told himself that they would escape from the Kuomintang trap. They would do it. In another moment he would return to loading wagons and then find his place in a column, but for the moment he observed the scene with a peaceful expression on his face.

A hand fell on his shoulder. "Resting, Chen T'ieh-chang?" said a husky voice.

"Yes, just for a moment." Henry looked up and blushed as he recognized the familiar tired face above him. "But I'm ready to go back and work now, Comrade Mao."

"No, T'ieh-chang, rest for a few more minutes. We have a long way to go." The reassuring hand fell from his shoulder and Comrade Mao moved on to speak to others, his tall figure soon lost in the shadows and the mass of men and mules and wagons on the road. After a moment Henry realized that someone else had come up beside him, an old Kiangsi farmer.

"Have you come to say good-bye, Grandfather?" he asked absently.

The old man nodded. "And wish you well. Me, I'm staying behind to fight with the partisans. To keep the Kuomintang off your backs for a little while. After all, it's better than having the cursed landlords come back. You know what they say about us farmers. Our feet are on another man's land, our heads are in another man's sky."

"I know the saying."

Henry thought about the way ahead as the old man left. The Communists would be moving west and south in two columns. They would be trekking into a wild country of gorges and mountains and deserts and rushing rivers, a land inhabited only by aborigines who had never seen a Chinese and would attack on sight; harsh terrain on the western border of China and Tibet. It was almost suicidal, Henry knew.

His rest period was over; he moved to a wagon and began to load sacks of sugar.

It was spring of 1935, the Budding Moon. Amy had come home exhausted from the newspaper to the house on Bubbling Well Road. She was being allowed to write more and more about the Japanese encroachment on Shanghai. The Chinese mayor of the city was cowed. The Japanese barracks in Little Tokyo was spilling over with soldiers. Armed and helmeted Japanese marines patrolled the streets of Chapei with arrogant strides. Japanese officers marched through the railroad station with swords clanking at their hips. Japanese gunboats steamed in the Whangpoo, able to lay down a barrage of shells at will.

It was war! Amy thought. Undeclared war! Shanghai for all practical purposes was a conquered city! Why didn't Chiang Kai-shek declare war and make it official? No, he was too busy pursuing the ragged remains of the Communist army, struggling toward Yenan on the trek that had come to be known as the Long March. It was rumored to be an ordeal of incredible hardship, of winding back on trails and losing six days for every one of advance, of fighting and starving and meeting Kuomintang troops, of men who were determined to reach Yenan in the North.

Oh, Henry, are you still alive . . . ?

"What will happen to us, Grandfather?" Amy had asked Mike about the Japanese war. "And the pottery works? And Grandmother's galleries?"

"So far it's business as usual. This is between the Chinese and the Japanese. The International Settlement isn't involved."

"So the Valentines will stay put?"

"Looks that way. I'm not running, and your grandmother isn't either. Neither are David and Andy."

"Good! I'm so glad! I couldn't bear to leave China now!"

Mike had glanced at her quizzically but made no comment.

Now Amy made her way wearily down to her room. She paused at Andy's door. She thought she heard the sound of muffled sobs, and she opened the door without knocking.

Andy was sitting on the edge of the bed with his head in his hands. Amy took a breath.

"Andy, you've got to talk to somebody," she said. "It might as well be me."

He glanced up. He looked dreadful. His eyes were bloodshot and his face was gaunt. Blond stubble covered his cheeks. *Andy, who is always so impeccable,* Amy thought. She concealed her dismay. She'd been so wrapped up in herself that she hadn't noticed Andy. *I should have.*

"For God's sake, close the door," Andy said hoarsely, dropping his head again.

"Will you talk to me?"

"Yes."

Amy closed the door. She suspected what this was about: the Russian woman who worked in a cabaret called Eve's Apple. That was all anyone in the family knew about her. Except that she was destroying Andy inch by inch.

"It's Petrushka," Andy said. "She's disappeared."

"Hasn't she done that before?"

"Yes, but never for this long. I've always been able to find her before. This time I can't. I don't know where she is."

Amy hesitated and then said in a low voice, "Let her go, Andy. She isn't worth it."

"Things aren't that easy. I feel responsible for her."

"Why should you feel responsible?"

Andy groaned. "God help me, Amy, I don't know. I elected myself, I guess. All I know is, if anything happens to Petrushka, it will be my fault."

"It will not. It will not."

"Help me find her, Amy. Please. If I don't find her this time, I'll go crazy."

Amy sat down and listened to the efforts Andy had made to find Petrushka. To Amy it seemed that he had tried everything. Finally she had an idea.

"In two days it will be Russian Easter," she said. "Will Petrushka go to church?"

Andy glanced up hopefully. "She might. It's very possible. I know the church she'd attend; it's in the Russian district, on a little hilltop. If I went there at midnight, when the service ended . . ."

"You might see her."

His face lit up as he nodded. "Thank you, Amy. I'll try it."

On Easter night Andy went alone to the Russian church. He waited outside on the hill, where the gold-leaf onion dome of the church was silhouetted against a dark sky, and listened to the muffled sound of chanting from within. He felt his search would be ended tonight. *I will find Petrushka, the real Petrushka, at last.*

At midnight came the holy moment of the service. The church doors were thrown open. A procession of robed and bearded priests marched out, chanting as they came. Some were swinging censers; some were carrying huge glowing candles; some were bearing icons. The worshipers spilled out with them, surging in a mass down the steps. The bells of the church broke into a peal and the priests chanted, *"Kristos Voskris! Kristos Voskris!"* Christ is arisen!

As the service ended, Andy caught sight of a familiar face in the crowd. A woman, wearing a black shawl over her hair. Thin, pale, worn, with traces of great beauty in her features. It was Madame Koubettskaya, Petrushka's mother. She had disclaimed knowledge of her daughter to Andy before, but perhaps, he thought, tonight would be different. Andy ran to catch up with her, and when he reached her, he took her by the arm.

"Madame Koubettskaya—stop a moment."

The woman halted. She stared up into Andy's face. "So, you have heard," she muttered after a moment.

"Heard what?"

"You want to express your sorrow? You needn't. She had a rotten life and a miserable death. She's better out of it."

"Death?" The chanting, the candles, and the incense were making Andy dizzy. No, they had stopped. "Petrushka is dead?"

"Didn't you know?" The woman laughed bitterly. "Well, don't grieve. She's better off where she is, in her grave, and you're better off as you are, alive and well."

He had to speak. He had to force himself. "How did she die? . . ."

"Drugs, pneumonia, heart failure, everything. It was a mess, she died in my arms in some wretched flat in Little Tokyo."

"Did she ask for me? . . ."

"She may have. I think she did." The woman paused, obviously feeling a pang of compassion at the sight of Andy's stricken face. "Yes, she asked for you. She said to forgive her, and she was sorry."

"Are you sure that's what she said?" Andy listened to his own hoarse voice, the voice of a stranger.

"If you are her little holy father, that's what she said."

"Oh, my God, Petrushka, I'm the one who's sorry. . . ."

Madame Koubettskaya shrugged, signifying that she could say no more, and she moved on, leaving Andy to his grief.

CHAPTER 11

The Communist army had reached the southern border of Szechuan Province by the summer of 1935. If they could win their way to central Szechuan, they would achieve safety. Here, near the village of An Jen Ch'ang, they were threatened on many sides. Enemy troops were racing to engage them from the north and southeast. Enemy airplanes had found their position and were attacking from the sky. Behind them were junglelike forests from which they had emerged. Ahead of them was the Tatu River.

They had to cross the Tatu Ho to get to Szechuan. They were attempting to cross by ferryboat, but it was taking too long, too long.

The vanguard of the army was on a forced march along the Tatu cliffs, trying to find a crossing. Ragged files of barefoot soldiers carrying torches marched all night along the riverbank, longing to hear the words which finally came.

"Ten-minute rest! Ten-minute rest!"

The soldiers collapsed in heaps for the ten-minute rest. They were given bowls of rice and prepared to listen with half-closed eyes to a lecture. A political worker always spoke to them at these times; tonight the speaker was young Henry Chen. He was as weary as any of them and barefoot as they were. His voice was hoarse—he had been speaking to them for days—but he tried to conceal his fatigue and his physical pain as he squatted before them to speak. He was assigned to raise their morale.

He explained that they had reached the last possible crossing of the Tatu Ho east of Tibet. If they failed to cross the river, they would have to detour a thousand kilometers and retrace their steps to Likiang on the Tibetan border. They would not survive such a detour.

"Ignore your fatigue," he told them. "Give your whole hearts to this task, for it is critical."

Over and over he urged them to keep on marching, and over and over they listened and pulled themselves wearily to their feet.

Finally there was a bridge: the Communists' last chance. It was called the Bridge Fixed by Liu. It was built of sixteen iron chains stretched across the river, each end embedded in a cement piling under the stone bridgehead. Between the iron chains were lashed thick boards that made up the span.

Only the span was partially destroyed.

Kuomintang troops had reached the bridge ahead of the Red Army. Half the boards were removed, and the iron chains swung bare to the midpoint of the stream. Below them rushed the Tatu waters, swift and silver-strong. At the opposite end was a Kuomintang machine-gun nest.

The Kuomintang had made a mistake, however. They had only removed half the span. Communist leaders marched up and down the columns of their troops, crying for volunteers. "Who will volunteer to cross the Bridge Fixed by Liu?" they shouted.

The troops could see that there was only one way. Hand over hand along the iron chains, with grenades and Mausers strapped to their backs, and an enemy machine gun chattering over their heads.

Comrade Chen was among those who stepped forward. Thirty were chosen, the youngest and the fittest, and he was chosen. They swung out above the churning river, clinging to the iron chains. Three died at once, hit by bullets. Then one of them tossed a hand grenade, which found its target, and the machine gun was silenced. Somehow twenty were across and the enemy was fleeing. The boards of the span were being replaced by triumphant soldiers, for now their army could cross the river.

Later the Communists referred to them, both the living and the dead, as the Thirty Heroes of the Tatu Ho.

There was a teahouse in the Chapei district of Shanghai called Willow Lake. It stood in the middle of an artificial moat spanned by a picturesque crooked bridge, with tables placed in the open beneath willow trees. Reed-and-string music floated from a secluded courtyard while people sipped their tea. Willow Lake was meant to be a tranquil refuge in the ancient Chinese style, far from the dance bands and brittle modern gaiety of the International Settlement.

Andy sought out Willow Lake teahouse in the summer of 1935. He came alone and sat for hours listening to the delicate Oriental music, struggling to find peace within himself, attempting to calm his troubled spirit.

He did not succeed. The Oriental way was not his way, anymore than it was Amy's or Mike's. Only Laura, his grandmother, had a true communion with the soul of the Chinese past. She surrounded herself with objects of the Sung Dynasty and understood them. Andy had been born in China but he was Western. He had to find another path.

He wandered into a Catholic church, looking for a place to go. The doors were opened and so he entered and sat down. He stayed, not knowing why. People came and went, knelt, prayed, counted rosary beads, made novenas; masses were said; still Andy remained. He didn't understand the reason. He was not a part of this. He was only an observer. Still, it was calming him more than the Willow Lake teahouse. He came back day after day. He grew more peaceful. Still he took no part.

After a while he began to gaze at the statues by the altar. He began to ask himself questions. Weeks passed. Andy continued to visit the church every day. He was amazed at himself. He was starting to accept the death of Petrushka. Perhaps it was only the passage of time, but maybe it was something else.

He could not stay away from the church. He continued to make his visits every day. Finally the day came when Andy rose from his seat in the church and went to the priest's office. Observing was no longer enough. His grandfather need not know, he told himself. This would be Andy's secret. He knocked on the door of the office, and a young priest answered.

Andy straightened his shoulders. "My name is Andrew Henderson," he said. "I'd like to learn something about your church."

The priest's eyes were puzzled. "You mean about the architecture?" he said. "We're quite proud of it. We raised money in a parish in Philadelphia for the Chinese missions in order to build this church. . . ."

"No, I don't mean the architecture. I mean about the . . . Roman Catholic religion. I'd like to know more about it."

"Oh. I see." The priest extended his hand. "My name is Father O'Halloran. Won't you come in?"

Summer passed and the Moon Year wheeled into autumn. Amy Henderson worked late at the newspaper almost every night in a cloud of blue cigarette smoke as her typewriter clacked. She had started to smoke almost absentmindedly, and had realized to her astonishment one day that it was an unbreakable habit. Well, too late now. For Amy typing and smoking were now inseparable companions. Her ashtray filled with stubs.

> *By Amy Henderson*, November 1935:
> It has been reported that survivors of the Long March have reached Yenan in Shensi Province just south of the Great Wall. Less than twenty thousand troops, it is said, have reached the end of the journey. They have passed through a dozen provinces and broken through ten enveloping armies. It has taken them a year. Chinese communism has apparently been crippled but not destroyed.

No letters were coming from Yenan, for the stronghold was hidden and isolated.

Henry, will I ever see you again?

> *By Amy Henderson*, March 1936:
> A small bomb made of a tin can containing scraps of metal exploded against the wall of the Japanese Consulate General last night. Damage was insignificant, but the cap of the

unknown bomb-thrower is said to have been found on the spot. The cap, it was reported by an eyewitness, bore the insignia of the League of Anti-Japanese Youth.

It was almost unheard of to catch cold in the summertime. Respiratory illnesses were for the winter, and it was July of 1936, the Lotus Moon.

Nevertheless Chen had caught cold. The cold had turned to pleurisy and pleurisy to pneumonia. Chen's lungs were filling with fluid, and he labored to breathe. He was dying; Plum Blossom wailed in anguish in the corridor outside his room. *You stubborn old man! How can you do this to me! Oh, don't die, old Chen!*

Chen tried to say good-bye to his beloved missy, who sat by his bedside.

"Do you remember when you first came to Weichang, missy?" he whispered weakly.

"Yes, I remember."

"You were so young and kind. I was so frightened to meet you. A strange foreign woman with light eyes. But you smiled at me so kindly I wasn't afraid anymore."

"Oh, Chen, I was frightened too."

"I found you a pretty house to live in, missy. With a temple. Didn't I?"

"Yes, you did. It was beautiful."

"I am sorry you lost Eldest Son in Weichang."

"It was a long time ago."

"I, too, have lost my son."

"No, Chen, you will see Henry again."

He shook his head feebly. "It is too late for me." He gazed at Laura beseechingly. "Even though I am Christian, do you think I will join my ancestors?"

"I am sure of it. . . ."

Laura burst into tears in the corridor, weeping into her hands. Little Michael and Madame Wei . . . Henry Canfield in Connecticut . . . Eileen and Chen . . . Henry perhaps lost . . . the years seemed like a parade of death.

Then Mike's arms were around her.

"Sweetheart, don't cry," he murmured. "Whatever happens, we still have each other."

She pressed gratefully against the comfort of his body, listening to the solace of his voice. The storms and troubles of the past were behind them now, and they did have each other. Safe harbor after the tempest. The memory of Li-san had faded in Laura's mind. She and Mike, Laura thought, were the only safety. For the world outside was more threatening every day. They had lived through troubled times. Boxers. Revolutionaries. Warlords. Now they were blinking in the rays of the Rising Sun, and maybe this was different.

> *By Amy Henderson*, January 1937:
> Japanese officers are saying in the teahouses of Hunkow that the cherry tree is the fulfillment of the destiny of the warrior. They boast that the cherry tree flowers and drops its petals, dying in full glory, rather than shriveling up into old age on the stem, just as the samurai soldier, in the pride and glory of his youth, lays his life upon the altar of his Emperor.
>
> We wonder if the Nanking government is aware of this cherry-tree symbolism?
>
> We hear that in Japanese-controlled Manchukuo, warehouses and army depots are bulging with accumulations of military supplies for the invasion of north China. The trains of Manchuria, we are told, rumble all night long. Has Chiang Kai-shek heard this too?

Amy paused and drew on her cigarette, reading over what she had just typed. She became aware that someone was looking over her shoulder. She glanced up. Mac McNamara was standing there reading her copy.

"What are you doing here?" she inquired.

"Just wandered in." Mac squinted down at the paper in the typewriter. "You're going to get in trouble with that stuff," he remarked. "You're making some of those Nipponese officers in Little Tokyo very unhappy. They don't like the things you're saying."

"They don't scare me." Amy lit another cigarette from the

burning stub of the one she was smoking. Then she sat back, stretching her spine. "Little tin soldiers with keys in their backs."

"They aren't, you know," Mac said gently. "They're real. Too real."

"Oh, Mac, I know. I'm just acting smart. Don't mind me."

"Can I buy you a drink?"

"Sure."

"Well, what do you know. Smoking, drinking, the kid is growing up. 'What's next on the list of mortal sins? asked he, with a gleam in his eye.' "

"Nothing, Mac." Amy gave him a wry grin. "This is as far as I go."

"That's okay. There are plenty of broads—I mean girls—in this town who like to play around. I can wait."

"So that's why you always lose at poker," Amy said. "Lucky in love." She stood up, stubbed out her cigarette, jammed her hat on her red curls, and picked up her pocketbook. The hat was a small black felt with a brim that shadowed her eyes.

"You look cute," said Mac.

"So do you." Amy grinned. "Except you didn't shave."

"I did," he protested, fingering his jaw. "This morning."

"You must wake up very early." Amy laughed and took his arm. "Come on, I need that drink."

It was not long after that when Andy asked Amy to meet him at a restaurant for dinner. He had something he wanted to discuss with her, he said, and he didn't want to do it at home. He chose a quietly expensive restaurant in the French Concession, free of both tourists and saber-rattling Japanese officers.

"I don't believe I'm used to being treated like a lady," said Amy with a rueful smile, as the wine steward took their order at the table. "Now that I'm one of the boys at the newspaper, I think I've forgotten how to behave."

"You're on your way where the paper is concerned," said Andy. "But I always knew you'd succeed. So did Henry. I'm proud of you. He would be too."

"Why, Andy." Unexpectedly tears came into Amy's eyes. "Thank you for saying that."

Andy looked different to her. He appeared very calm. There was something faraway about his eyes, Amy thought. Sorrowful and yet serene. *He has found himself*, she thought. then she felt scared. Maybe she was going to lose Andy too. Somehow, in some strange way.

"I'd like to ask your help," Andy said. "Will you lend me money if I need it?"

"Of course. You know I can't spend my salary, and they keep giving me raises. Aside from the car and my clothes, I have no expenses."

"Well, I may not have to ask you; I'll probably be able to manage on my own. But in case I can't—"

"You can count on me," Amy said worriedly. "Whatever it is."

"Oh, Amy." He gave her a relieved and affectionate smile. "You said yes before I even told you."

She blushed. "I know you would do the same for me."

"Yes, it's always been that way. You and I and Henry. The unbreakable threesome. It will still be that way, no matter what life does to us."

"Henry may not be alive," Amy said in a low voice, staring at her hands, which were folded in her lap.

"He is," said Andy.

She glanced up quickly. "Do you have word from Yenan?"

"No. I'm just sure of it."

"I wish I could have your faith."

Andy took a breath. "Amy," he said, "I'm going to enter a seminary."

She gaped at him stupidly, not quite taking it in. "You mean study to be a priest? A Catholic priest?"

He nodded.

She couldn't think of anything intelligent to say. "But where? How?" she stammered.

"In the North, near Peking."

Emotion rushed over her. Fear. Disbelief. "But—you can't! You can't do such a thing!"

"Oh, my dear, I can and I will. Don't you see? I'm happy. Sad and happy at the same moment. I know I'll have miserable times, lonely times, doubts, but I'm prepared for that. Haven't you ever known when something is right?"

She nodded dumbly.

"For me this is right. It's the first time I've ever known it. Truly, in my soul. It's like . . . recognizing your fate." He laughed apologetically. "I don't mean to be theatrical or mystical. I just want to tell you how I feel."

A Catholic priest. Andy, in a cassock and a Roman collar. She had time to think about what he had said as the meal was served and the wine was poured and waiters hovered. Finally when they were alone again, she said, "If this is what you want, Andy, then I want it for you. I'll help you all I can. I just wish it were something else."

"Please don't wish that." He smiled at her sadly and hopefully.

She had to ask the so far unspoken question. "Have you told Grandfather?"

"No, not yet."

"He won't forgive you. You know what he thinks of Catholicism."

Andy gazed down at his plate. "I hope he will. I'll try to explain."

"Perhaps you'll change your mind when you speak to him."

Andy shook his head. "Nothing will change my mind."

He had that far-off look again, Amy thought. *They are both so stubborn.*

CHAPTER 12

Andy regarded his grandfather with despair. *He is so stubborn,* he thought. *He has always been unreasonable on this subject.*

"I am not doing this to hurt you, Grandfather," he said pleadingly. "I'm doing it because I must. Because I have no choice. Please understand."

Mike's expression was stony. "If you take this step, Andy, you will become a priest," he said. "There are no priests allowed under my roof. Even though you are my grandson, even though you are Eileen's child, I cannot change. Not on this issue. I took a vow once not to forgive a priest, any priest, and I never will.''

"It must have been a long time ago!''

"It was.''

"Doesn't time release you from a vow?''

"No.''

"I'm not *any* priest!'' Andy cried. "I'm Andy! I'm myself! I have to follow my own path!''

"I've followed mine for sixty-five years. How old are you?''

"What does that have to do with it!'' Andy cried.

"If you knew my reasons, you would respect my wishes.''

"Tell me your reasons!''

Mike was silent. He thought that it was too late to explain. It had to do with his mother, and it had to do with betrayal, and he did not want to speak of it. He never had, not even to Laura.

"Please, Grandfather! Talk to me! Tell me why you feel this way! Perhaps we can understand each other!'' His grandson's voice was beseeching.

"There is nothing to say, Andy. I will support you in any path you choose to follow, except this one. You don't have to stay at the pottery works. I'm not that obstinate, but I won't see you become a priest. Anything but that.''

"Oh, lord.'' Andy groaned in helpless frustration.

Mike put a hand over his eyes to shut out Andy's imploring face. This argument was bringing back the past. All the grudges and bitterness. Oregon. His mother.

Nora Corbett Valentine had been a pale, withdrawn woman who had emigrated from Ireland to America as had her husband, Patrick. Mike had been born in a logging village in Oregon where Patrick Valentine had been a lumberjack.

Her small son's recollection of her was of a woman always on her knees, praying, a rosary permanently at her fingertips. As a child Mike considered her to be a saint, she was so pious. She had so little love for her son, he concluded, because everything was lavished on Christ and the Holy Mother of God. As a boy Mike tried everything to capture her affection, but his mother remained distant, her body most often at the altar rail in the one-room church tended by Father Hugh Connolly.

Patrick Valentine was at the logging camp much of the year. When he was home, Mike found it hard to like him, with his red face and loud voice and clumping feet. He was not a man to display affection, as Nora was not an affectionate woman. When he was killed in a logging accident when Mike was ten, Mike cried, but they were surface tears. He was frightened. How would they live; what would they do for money?

Nora became a waitress at the Tall Timber Café and supported them simply but adequately. Mike's respect for her increased as he grew older. She was a pure good woman; he sensed it profoundly. If she withheld her love, it must be Mike's own fault.

The one source of comfort, affection, and companionship for Mike in the years of his childhood was Father Connolly. The priest was a charming man with a warmth of manner that won Mike's trust. He seldom came to the Valentine house, but he frequently invited Mike to his own simple room. There he taught Mike to find solace in conversation and piano music, and to dream dreams of a larger world. He heard Mike's confessions with compassion and understanding. Mike thought Father Hugh was the best person he'd ever known. He began to consider the priesthood.

"Think it over, Mike," said Father Hugh. "It's a big step. You don't want to decide too young."

"You decided young."

Father Hugh's face clouded. "I had a clear vocation. But it's been a burden as well as a joy. Think it over carefully."

As he grew older, Mike temporarily set aside the idea of the priesthood and took a job on a riverboat, learning to navigate the river rapids, preparing to be a pilot. When he was twenty, he won four hundred dollars in a poker game. He wanted to celebrate at least once in his life. Some of the money he gave to his mother. But with the rest he invited Father Hugh Connolly on a trip to San Francisco.

"Just the two of us, Father Hugh," he cried. "We'll see the sights and stay in a fancy hotel and eat in restaurants like the swells. What do you say? I've always wanted to get a look at Frisco!"

Mike's enthusiasm was engaging. Father Hugh laughed. "Are you sure you want to visit San Francisco with a stodgy old priest?"

Father Hugh was in his early forties; to Mike that was old.

"Sure!" said Mike, laughing. "You can take off your collar."

"Oh, no, Mike."

"I won't tell anybody."

Father Hugh looked hesitant. His eyes shone. "It would be great fun," he murmured. "I shouldn't."

"Then wear your collar. But come along."

At last Father Hugh allowed himself to be persuaded. "Only because it's you, Mike. You and that Irish charm of yours. It's dangerous."

"You have a little of it yourself," said Mike, with a mischievous grin. Father Hugh smiled and rumpled Mike's hair. "I wish I could refuse you once in a while. But you've had little enough indulgence in your life, Michael Francis. You've deserved more."

Mike agreed silently.

Nora Valentine disapproved of the trip, but after one low-voiced objection she tightened her lips and said nothing. She took her prayerbook and went to the church.

The trip to San Francisco was carefree. They ate fresh-caught shrimp on the waterfront and strolled the Embarcadero, and ventured into the Tenderloin and wandered the streets of Chinatown and gazed admiringly at the elegant ladies on Market Street. They climbed Russian Hill and looked out to sea, past the Golden Gate.

"It's a big world, Mike," said Father Hugh.

"I'll see it. I'll see it all."

"You'll be luckier than I was. You'll do more things, achieve greater success."

"You have a lot of faith in me."

"I do, Mike. I want you to gain something better from life than a backwoods parish in a western logging town."

"Why didn't you?"

Father Hugh paused. "Maybe it's a penance," he said very low. "But you're different. You have everything ahead of you."

"You're the only one who's ever cared what happens to me," Mike said. "Not even my mother really gives a damn."

"Of course she does!" There was shocked pain in Father Hugh's voice. Mike shrugged and didn't argue.

On their last night in San Francisco, Father Hugh agreed to wear a plain suit and discard his Roman collar. Just this once. It would be a farewell dinner, and they would go to a really fancy restaurant.

"My treat," insisted Father Hugh.

"Oh, no. Not on your life."

They finally agreed to divide the bill in half.

"But I'll buy the wine," said Mike.

"As long as it's not champagne."

Mike did order champagne, over Father Hugh's murmured protests. As the waiter pulled the cork, Mike leaned forward across the table. "Don't look now," he muttered, "but the lady at the next table has her eye on you. The lady in gold brocade."

"Don't be silly."

"She does. And there are two of them. One for you and one for me. Both pretty."

Father Hugh grinned. "Is that why you lured me out without my collar? To get me into trouble?"

Mike only laughed. The lady was staring, however. As she was leaving with her companion, she paused at their table. With a becoming blush she addressed herself to Mike. "Forgive me for being impolite. But you and your father seem to be having such a good time; it's a pleasure to watch you."

"My . . . father?"

"Yes, the resemblance is striking; you must hear it all the time. You seem to be such good friends as well. How nice. I'm sorry if I stared." With a pleasant nod and a smile she departed from the room.

Mike felt fiery color rise into his cheeks. "Of all the stupid mistakes," he managed to say. He tried to laugh and glanced at Father Hugh for an answering smile. But there was none. Father Hugh's face was as white as the tablecloth.

"It was stupid," Father Hugh whispered. "The most stupid thing in the world." Then with a visible effort he recovered himself and attempted to smile.

Mike stared. He couldn't help himself. *The resemblance is striking*. Was it? Did he resemble Father Hugh? *Yes*. The same red hair and wide-set eyes and shape of face . . . the same gestures and quick laugh . . . He was looking at himself twenty years older.

Mary Mother of God it can't be. Nora Valentine and Hugh Connolly. But it would explain so much.

"Let's get out of here," Mike said in a strangled voice.

"Mike—"

"Where's the waiter?"

"Mike, don't let a foolish remark by a foolish woman prey upon your mind. Forget it!"

"We have to get back to the hotel. Where's that waiter?" Mike paused, trembling. "There are questions I need to ask you," he said, and tried to keep his voice from shaking.

Father Hugh started to protest, then subsided. His eyes were suddenly bleak. He looked old.

In the hotel room Mike sat on the edge of the bed with his hands between his knees and his head bowed. Father Hugh stood by the window, staring out.

"Tell me one thing," Mike said, gazing at the floor. "What was your father's name?"

There was a long pause. Then Father Hugh sighed. "Michael," he said wearily. "Michael Connolly."

"Michael Francis Connolly?"

"Michael Francis Bartholomew Connolly. If you must know."

"So it's true. It is true."

Father Hugh didn't answer.

"It wasn't just a foolish remark by a foolish woman."

Silence.

"Why didn't you tell me!" Mike burst out wildly. "Goddamn you, why didn't you tell me? Why did you let me believe in a lie? You and she both! I thought you were saints! And you let me believe it! Like a fool!"

"I'm sorry, Mike. . . ."

"That isn't enough!"

Father Hugh passed a hand over his eyes. "What could we do? We couldn't possibly tell you."

"Does everybody else in town know the truth?"

"I don't believe so. People only see what they want to see. They can ignore unpleasant facts."

"I can't ignore them!" Mike drew a long, shaky breath. "Why didn't you go away?" he muttered.

"God forgive me, I wanted to see you grow up. And I couldn't let Nora bear the burden of raising you alone. Her husband was an insensitive man." Father Hugh averted his face. "She was so beautiful and so lost, back then," he said half to himself, "and I was young and confused and lonely, straight out of the seminary . . . but we paid."

"I paid!" Mike shouted. "I had no childhood! I had no mother! She was too busy asking forgiveness in the church! God damn the Church!"

"Mike, don't," whispered Father Hugh. Tears came into his eyes. "Don't blame God for our sin, mine and Nora's. I tried to make it up to you. I tried to be your friend."

"You succeeded too well," Mike said bitterly. "I trusted you. I won't make that mistake again."

"Please. I hoped you would trust me. I hope you will again."

"I'll never trust anyone with a Roman collar, from now on."

"Mike, you're young, and you make harsh judgments. Try to understand."

"I understand that I was deceived and lied to and made a fool of. Don't you realize how much I respected you? And my mother?" Mike laughed hollowly. "I wanted to be like you. I wanted to be a priest. Isn't that funny?"

Mike buried his face in his hands. There was a long silence. Finally he raised his head. "There's a way out," he said hoarsely. "A way we can forget all this and start again."

Father Hugh's face lit up with hope. "There's nothing I want more," he said in an eager voice. "Nothing that would make me happier."

"Will you take my suggestion?"

"Of course, Mike."

"Anything I propose?"

Father Hugh suddenly looked anxious. "If it's reasonable."

"I think it is."

"Then tell me."

"Leave the Church."

Father Hugh drew in his breath. Mike went on steadily, "Give up the parish, and we'll go away. All three of us. Together. You can marry Nora and we'll start again, in a new place, as a family. The way it should have been from the beginning. No more lies, no more pretending, no more praying. We'll be normal happy people and try to forget the past."

"Mike—you're asking too much!"

"Am I?"

"Where would I go, what would I do?"

"Anything. Get a job. You could teach school."

"But I'm a priest!"

"You could stop being a priest."

"It's not possible!"

"If you loved me," Mike said evenly, "as a father loves his son, you would do it."

"I do love you! You are my son! But I have a vocation!"

"You love Jesus Christ more than me, is that the idea?"

"Don't present me with an impossible choice, Mike! For the love of all the saints! You or Christ!"

"I am presenting you with it. I'm asking you to choose."

Father Hugh began to cry. Mike was dry-eyed. He was too bitter to cry. He had been wronged, not Hugh Connolly. He would never set foot in another church again, he vowed silently, or speak to another priest. To hell with everything. He'd keep his memories and his grudges and his bitterness and he'd keep the name Valentine, but that was all. He would go far away, as far as possible, as far as he could get. And maybe someday he would meet somebody he could trust.

He found that somebody in a hotel lobby in Oregon. He married Laura Canfield and found what he was seeking; but he did not forget his vow.

Now his grandson Andy was waiting for an answer to his impassioned plea for understanding. Mike could not help him.

Mike took his hand away from his eyes. "Andy," he said in a harsh, heavy voice, "if you enter the seminary, I will not have your name mentioned in this house ever again."

Andy Henderson saw himself staring at certain defeat. Turning his face aside, he abandoned hope with an inward groan. *I can't change either, Grandfather. I am so sorry.* He knew he would have to leave.

Later he told his grandmother, hoping for Laura's approval, her blessing, before his departure.

"You will always belong to this family, Andy," Laura assured him with tears in her eyes. "Forgive your grandfather. He's admitted to me he's suffering from a childhood hurt so deep he can't even tell me about it. We *will* mention your name in this house again."

Andy was comforted by her words.

The "double seven" arrived that summer: July 7, 1937. On that day Japanese troops clashed with Chinese troops on the Marco Polo Bridge near Peking. The Marco Polo Bridge was a structure of gray marble with a double row of three hundred marble lions seated on small columns. The "incident" there signified the real beginning of the war between China and Japan.

In August, Japanese airplanes bombed Shanghai and Japanese soldiers invaded the city. Chinese troops resisted fiercely. Shanghai battled against the attackers. Bombs fell on Nanking Road, Shanghai's great shopping street, and blood slimed the pavements, helpless wounded screamed in pain, sirens wailed, hospitals overflowed, and death fell from the sky.

Amy worked on doggedly at the *Shanghai Mirror* as the bombs fell, her face set, her jaw determined, writing of the agony around her so the world would know.

The pottery works escaped the bombing, and Laura tried to keep the galleries open, but she wondered for how long.

In November the resistance ended and Chinese forces abandoned Shanghai and the war moved on to Chiang Kai-shek's capital of Nanking.

In Shanghai, an already-fallen city, Japanese sentries in dark uniforms and antiseptic masks stood on the bridge over Soochow Creek. All foreigners and Chinese passing the sentries were required to bow and say a polite "good morning" or "good evening."

In December the Japanese announced a victory parade along Nanking Road.

"Well," Mike demanded of his family at home on Bubbling Well Road, "shall we go to the parade?"

"*Banzai,*" murmured David in a sarcastic tone of voice.

"Is that a yes or a no?" inquired Mike.

"I suppose it's yes, Dad. We ought to take a look at the victorious Sons of Nippon in their hour of glory."

"How about one of those little Rising Sun flags," Mike suggested ironically, "so you can wave it as the officers pass by?"

"Now you're going too far."

"What about you?" Mike asked Laura and Amy.

"I think David is right," said Laura. "This is an historic occasion. Bitter as it is, we should witness it."

"Amy?"

She nodded. "I have to be there anyway, Grandpa. For the paper."

Mike glanced around the room. "All right then," he said. "We'll watch the victory celebration together on Nanking Road. And no matter how arrogant they get, we'll just observe."

But in spite of Mike's warning to his family it was Mike who lost his temper.

There were little Rising Sun flags waving like a red and orange sea all over Nanking Road as the parade went past. There were shouts of "*Banzai!*" from Japanese civilians all along the route. Many young women wore brilliant kimonos. A representative from a Tokyo radio station held a microphone into the crowd so that the cheers could be heard at home.

The Chinese and the Westerners stood silent.

Someone threw an object wrapped in a Chinese newspaper into one of the marching columns. It exploded; it was a small bomb. Three soldiers were wounded.

Confusion broke out. Screams. Shouts. The parade halted. Sentries began to shove and push in the crowd. Mike was one of those shoved. He immediately lost his temper and punched someone in the face. Unfortunately it was a Japanese officer. A sentry raised his rifle, butt forward, and rushed toward him.

"Mike!" screamed Laura, jostled away by the crowd.

A well-dressed European man who spoke Japanese joined the melee and attempted to calm tempers, separating the two sides.

He appeared to be making fluent apologies. Eventually his peace-making efforts were successful. Tempers cooled, hands were shaken, grim warnings were given by the Japanese, and Mike returned to the others.

"Oh, my God," said Laura, "were you hurt?"

Mike shook his head.

"Won't we have to leave Shanghai now, Mike?"

"We'll talk about it, Laura."

A family conference was held. To stay in Shanghai or to leave? Laura's sense of threat was subdued by the commonsense attitude of the others.

"What's the consensus, Dad?" asked David. "What are other people doing?"

"Some are pulling up stakes and running like hell for home; others are staying."

"I must stay," Amy said in a tone of finality. "I have work to do. My job is here."

"After Nanking Road?" murmured Laura. But after all, she told herself, the Japanese would never really dare to harm Americans. The episode on Nanking Road was due to extraordinary tension; it was unusual.

"I had an official apology from a Japanese colonel," Mike said. "He came to visit me personally at the pottery works. He especially asked me to remain in Shanghai. They want all foreign businessmen to stay, so the economic life of the city won't be disrupted. They guarantee the autonomy of the International Settlement, he said. We will not be affected by the change of government."

"So he said," Laura murmured.

There was a short silence. Then Mike spoke again.

"To tell you the truth, I don't care for the idea of starting all over again. And I don't feel like retiring just yet."

"Nor I, Dad," David said promptly. "I think we can get along, if others are doing it. I can live with the Japanese if I have to."

"That leaves you, Laura." Mike looked at his wife. "I'll abide by your decision."

Laura sighed. "If they'll leave the International Settlement alone, as they promised—the Chinese always did—I suppose it's to their advantage not to harass us. . . ."

Another short silence fell. No one could truly feel a sense of danger. They were citizens of the United States.

"I guess it's settled," Mike said finally. "The pottery works stays in operation, our employees keep their jobs, and for the time being the Valentines stay in Shanghai."

CHAPTER 13

By Amy Henderson, March 1938:

The war continues to go badly for China. Japanese bombing raids on all major Chinese cities take place day after day.

The Chinese government in the new capital of Chungking has recognized the Red Army in Shensi Province and created a "United Front" against the common foe. The Red Army has now become the "Eighth Route Army" and the Shensi Soviet Republic has been declared an "Autonomous Border Area."

Amy dropped her hands from the typewriter, wishing she could write more about the Red Army, but no one had any information. The Communists were still isolated in their guerrilla stronghold in Yenan.

She ought to be grateful, she told herself, that she worked for an American-owned newspaper, and that her editor steadily ignored the Japanese attempts at censorship.

"They can't tell us what to publish," the editor declared to his staff. "We are American citizens. If they don't like what we say, to hell with them."

The Japanese did not like it, but they kept a wary and smoldering distance.

Life stumbled on in occupied Shanghai. Andy wrote letters to Amy and Laura from his seminary. Existence was austere but peaceful for him. He was content with his decision. More and more he was convinced that he had made the right choice. He missed them and everyone at home.

He always sent his love and prayers to Mike, who never acknowledged them.

Plum Blossom returned sorrowfully to Szechuan Province after the death of Chen. Now that she was a widow she wanted to be in the home she had purchased for herself in the village of her birth. It seemed just the same.

She walked along the village road and saw once again the shop where Peng of the gentle smile had mended old shoes. Peng, executed so long ago by order of the landlord. That was a difference, Plum Blossom realized. The landlord was gone. Yes, the landlord's house was empty and the tiles of his courtyard were broken and scattered; she saw it now as she passed.

A young man knelt among the tiles of the empty courtyard. Plum Blossom stopped to watch. Three farmers knelt around him in a circle. The young man was teaching them a lesson with colored tiles.

The red tiles were the poor peasants. The gray tiles were the government officials. The black tiles were the landlords. The broken half-tiles were stalks of grain.

The young man added half-tiles to the black and the gray. He added none to the red.

This young man, Plum Blossom thought, standing under the hot bright sun, could be her son. He was like Henry.

With Plum Blossom's departure, Amy felt she had lost her last link to Henry. But she was a reporter. That was her life now. She worked even harder than before.

In the spring of 1939 she went to a café with Mac McNamara. Over cocktails they discussed the Sino-Japanese War.

"Chiang Kai-shek's so-called army is a mess" she said to Mac across the table. "Their morale is destroyed, whatever little they had to start with. So is their organization. The only hope in this war is the Eighth Route Army in Shensi."

"I have to admit, kid, that you are right. Just like Comrade

Mao predicted, the Reds are swimming like fish in the ocean of the people." The Communists were leading the Japanese far into the interior, away from their supply lines, and then picking them off with hit-and-run tactics. "They're waging guerrilla warfare," Mac said. "If they survive the war, and if by some miracle China wins it, the Reds will be in a very good position."

"I wish I could find out what's going on in Shensi," Amy said gloomily. "How is *their* morale?"

After a while she noticed that Mac was simmering with suppressed excitement.

"What on earth is wrong with you?" she inquired. "I know you're not drunk, because then you get mean and moody."

"Black Irishman that I am."

"Well, what is it?" she asked.

"You'll know soon enough. It's about you." He shook his head. "I wish I could change places with you, Red. Lucky stiff."

"Now you'll have to tell me!" she exclaimed.

"No, I can't. It's not up to me to tell you. Besides, it isn't definite. I only heard it as a rumor."

"*What* rumor! Mac, I'll throttle you if you don't tell me!"

"Not me," he cried dramatically. "Grill me—give me the third degree—I swear I'll never rat on my sources!"

He pretended he was James Cagney for the rest of the evening and refused to talk.

Amy was still mystified when she was called to see her editor the next morning.

"Well, Red, you're in luck," he said. "All your sniping at the Japanese seems to have paid off. I have to hand it to you, you started early with Mr. Suzuki."

"What is this about?" she said. "I've been hearing rumors, but no one will tell me anything."

"It's about the Eighth Route Army," he said.

Amy's heart leaped. *Yenan? No, too much to hope for.*

"You've been invited to Yenan," he said.

"Me?" she squeaked.

"If your name is Amy Henderson, then it's you."

"That's been my name since I was born," she said breathlessly.

"It seems that with this United Front there's a new attitude on the part of the Communist guerrillas. They've decided they want some good publicity in an American newspaper, and they're willing to have an American reporter come up and look around. They chose you.''

"What if I write unfavorable stories? What if it isn't good publicity?''

"I guess they're willing to trust you.''

"How about you?'' said Amy.

"You'll call 'em like you see 'em,'' he replied. "I trust you to use your judgment, without stars in your eyes.''

"I will,'' she said. "I promise.'' She paused. "Did you . . . did you get a letter?''

He nodded. "By special courier. It's signed by some liaison officer they've appointed for press relations. You'll meet him when you get there.''

Amy was breathless again. "What's his name, do you remember?''

"Not exactly. Mo, Po, something like that. I'll look it up for you if you want.'' He began to rummage on his desk.

"No, that's okay. I'll find out later.''

Not the right name.

"When do I leave?'' Amy asked then.

"Tomorrow morning. You'd better go home and pack your undies and a toothbrush.''

"Mother of God,'' said Amy, "I don't have much time.'' She stood up.

"I don't have to tell you, kid, that we're counting on you. Every newspaperman in China envies you right now. This is a hell of a chance.''

He didn't have to tell her.

From Amy's notebook, en route to Yenan:

The first part of my journey will probably be the easiest, and it's the least interesting: the train from Shanghai to Peking. Familiar territory. I won't meet any representatives of the Eighth Route Army until I get to Sian, the capital of Shensi. That will be two days and nights by train out of Peking.

*   *   *

Now on the train from Peking to Chengchow. The worst train I've ever seen. Totally dilapidated. I can hardly write for rattling. I hope I can read these notes.

My handwriting is greatly improved. Transferred to a new train at Chengchow, comfortable and modern. We're now climbing up into hill country, surrounded by loess cliffs. The cliffs are very weird. Geologists say loess is soil blown into China from the Central Asian desert. It creates strange formations shaped by the wind, like giant sand castles all twisted and bent out of line, and it makes the countryside look eerie.

Sian, the capital of Shensi, is an old walled city high up in the loess hills. My instructions were to check into the hotel (there's only one) and wait for my contact. Well, here I am in my hotel room after dinner (noodles instead of rice; when you come from Shanghai that seems odd) and I'm waiting. Not feeling very patient. I'm too excited. Expecting the phone to ring any minute, or a knock on the door. Wondering if this trip was a wild-goose chase. Praying not.

If I thought the Chengchow train was bumpy, I was mistaken. Nothing compared with this. I'm in the back of an army truck heading north out of Sian on a very rough road. I have a young, polite Red Army escort. We left at dawn. The huge wooden gates of Sian creaked open at sunrise with a dragging of chains, and there was a truck convoy filled with supplies waiting for us to climb on board. After we showed our military pass. I tried to read the signature on the pass, but I can't read Chinese that well—maybe it was Mao Tse-tung but I won't swear to it. Two hundred miles to Yenan. Lots of dust. Lots of ruts. I doubt we'll make it by tonight, judging from the condition of this road.

Spent the night at a Chinese inn, sleeping on a *k'ang*. Hard as a rock, and the room was not too clean, but better than sleeping in the truck on a pile of sorghum sacks. At least the food was good. Pork and vegetables. I'll have to compare

notes with Grandpa back in Shanghai; he slept in lots of
Chinese inns in the old days, when this was bandit country.
Won't be long now till Yenan.

Passed our first group of Red Army soldiers on the road.
They looked sturdy and fit. Lots of loess cliffs all around.
Also fields of opium poppies ready for harvest. My escort
says the Red Army is trying to weed out the poppies and
replant millet for food. It will take time. Opium smoking, he
says, is outlawed in Yenan. I'll try to check that for myself
if I get to tour the barracks. I know what opium smells like.
You can't get rid of that odor.

I'm glad I brought plenty of ordinary cigarettes. Much
appreciated by the truck drivers and my escort, when we
stop to stretch our legs. I offer the pack and everybody takes
one.

There are naturally no latrines. No shrubs or bushes either.
Fortunately many little hills of loess.

I can write more easily now, the trucks have slowed down.
We're approaching Yenan. It's protected all around by steep
mountains and gorges. Located on a riverbank, the River
Yen. We pass a group of blue-clad women pounding clothes
in the river. Now driving through a gate of the town wall.
Inside, a typical north China village of sun-dried mud bricks
with buzzards mewing and circling overhead and the familiar creak of carts in the road. Different, though. This is a
town of cave homes carved out of the surrounding cliffs.
The Eighth Route Army lives in the caves, which have
rooms, I am told, just like houses.

Amy tucked away her notebook in the big shoulder bag she
carried and leaped down from the truck. Before her was a little
garden and a whitewashed wall bordering the road. It was her
quarters: a cave home.

Someone would call for her in an hour, she was told, and
escort her to the community hall where she would meet the
liaison officer in charge of her visit and some other officials as
well. There would be food inside the cave.

The trucks pulled away in a roar of motors.

Amy inspected her new lodgings. The cave was honeycombed into a sandstone hill. Inside were three small rooms, the first a living room–dining room, furnished with a table bearing fruit and tea and wheatcakes, and a plain sofa and chairs. Amy grabbed an apple from the table as she looked into the next. A bedroom. Spartan but very clean, with a taut khaki blanket on the bed. Night table. Lamp. That was it. A tiny WC with a flush toilet. No bath or shower, just a sink. Oh, well. She bit into the apple. She was pleased to find the third room was furnished as an office, with a wicker chair and a table with a typewriter. A military map of China was tacked to the wall.

She finished the apple down to the core and went back to the living room and poured herself a cup of tea.

Outside the battered walls of Yenan, through a gap in the wall, wound a string of water carriers bearing buckets from the River Yen slung on their shoulders on bamboo poles. From the hillside near the river came the shouts of a goatherd to his flock. Amy heard his calls as she approached the community hall on foot, escorted by the soldier who had called for her. She had expected a delegation to be awaiting her and it was, outside the entrance. There would be handshakes and a formal welcoming speech and she would be expected to respond. She had already prepared something to say.

It was all as she had anticipated. The liaison officer introduced himself—Mo Chi-jen—and welcomed her formally to Yenan. He spoke in halting English after inquiring if she understood the dialect of Honan and she confessed that she did not. They awaited her own little speech. She tried to collect herself, confronting the polite, expectant group of faces. She was shaking inside. One of the faces, stern and handsome above his high-collared tunic, was that of Henry Chen.

She prayed she wouldn't stammer. She wondered how she would get through it. She thought she saw the tiniest ghost of a smile flicker across Henry's face and it steadied her. She expressed her gratitude at the opportunity she had been given to visit Yenan and assured them she held it in the highest seriousness. She would be fair and open-minded in what she wrote and endeavor to learn and observe as much as she could in the short time she was here. She would report everything according to the strictest standards of justice. She knew they expected no more and deserved no less.

Everyone seemed pleased when she had finished. There was the usual handshaking all around. She tried not to look at Henry. He was a boy no longer, and his adolescent beauty had matured into the hard facial contours of a man. He was still startlingly attractive. There was something austere about his good looks. Like Andy, she thought, saying he was entering the seminary.

Of course if Henry smiled, he wouldn't look austere any longer. . . .

"Miss Henderson," said Mo Chi-jen, when the handshaking was over, "I believe you are previously acquainted with Comrade Chen T'ieh-chang?"

"Why . . . why, yes. In Shanghai."

"Comrade Chen is one of the Thirty Heroes of the Tatu Ho. He is now a lecturer at our school, in political science and Chinese literature. Since my English is limited, we have considered it is best if you remain with Comrade Chen for your beginning tour. Then you will not need an interpreter. Would that be agreeable?"

She nodded, trying to keep her voice steady as she said, "That would be fine."

"Let it be done. We leave you in the so-capable hands of Comrade Chen."

They all departed. She was alone with Henry.

He was standing with his familiar easy grace, shoulders erect, face impassive.

He was thinking, *My Little Sister! Oh, Amy, my Little Sister! It has been so long since I have seen you, and I have missed you so! I didn't know how much until just now.*

He cleared his throat. "Welcome to Yenan, Miss Henderson. Would you care to start with the community hall, or would you prefer to tour the town?"

"Tour the town, please," Amy said in a faint voice.

"That's probably a good idea. It will give you a sense of the geography. Shall we go on foot?"

"Oh, yes, I need to walk. I've been riding in the back of an army truck for two days."

So this was how it was to be, Amy thought with inner trembling. Correct and distant. Casual acquaintances.

It is better than nothing. He is here. Alive and well. Handsomer than ever. Be grateful, be happy.

Henry assumed his duties as a guide and he and Amy set off.

Amy, are you still the same? he thought. *You have grown up and become a woman. But you still have your freckles; do you still care for me? Do you recall the Feast of the Lanterns and the night I left for Kiangsi? I remember.*

He pointed out landmarks in a tour-guide tone as they strolled through the narrow streets. The school with its cave classrooms. The barracks. Many cave homes of leaders whose names she recognized. Amy concentrated on remembering what she saw.

An old ambulance being used as a truck. A group of soldiers wearing red paper flowers on their tunics, drinking hot water out of rice bowls. A two-story bookshop made of stucco, surrounded by little wooden stalls.

"Don't you have questions?" Henry said.

"Many. Never fear, I'll ask questions. For the moment I'm just storing up impressions."

"I don't suppose you take notes, either. You just remember things."

She didn't like what she interpreted as his slightly sarcastic attitude. "I never write things down," she said loftily. "I have a mind like a steel trap."

Henry stopped and burst out laughing. "Oh, Little Sister, you haven't changed at all!"

Amy looked at him in surprise, taken aback by his laughter. "I certainly have changed," she said.

"Oh, really?" He was still laughing. "When will you learn not to be provoked at a moment's notice?"

After a moment Amy started to laugh too. "Never, I guess. Did you provoke me on purpose?"

"I wouldn't dream of it." Henry grinned mischievously. He was the old Henry Chen of Shanghai, Amy thought. Enormous happiness washed over her.

"There's a bench over there where we can sit down," Henry said. "Under that date tree. Then we can really talk."

CHAPTER 14

"Whose idea was it to give me the typewriter?" Amy asked, stretching beneath the shadow of the date tree. The ambulance-truck was rolling through the streets of Yenan carrying workers home from the paper-making cooperative. They were singing "The Sky of Liberation." Through the town gate carts were creaking in from a day's travel, and in counterpoint to the crying sound of their wheels came the snuffles of the mules that pulled them.

"Not mine," said Henry.

"You must have had something to do with my coming here."

"Oh, a little," he said, and folded his arms across his chest with a lazy grin. "I may have introduced your name. But we make no individual decisions, you know that."

"I don't care who decided," Amy said. "I'm just glad to be here."

They spoke of Yenan. "Do you really teach Chinese literature?" Amy asked.

"I do."

"*The Water Margin* and *The Three Kingdoms* and *The Dream of the Red Chamber*? To peasant guerrilla soldiers?"

"Mostly illiterate at that. But they're eager to learn. Half of it they don't understand—more than half—but we teach them anyway. Along with tactics and political science."

"What sort of tactics, Henry?"

" 'Know your enemy as yourself,' " he quoted, " 'and in a hundred battles win a hundred victories.' "

They were silent. Then Amy said, "I would have assumed you'd ignore literature. Except for writers like Lu Hsun."

"We're still Chinese. We're not about to throw three thousand years of culture into the River Yangtze. Maybe the Russians do things differently but we have our own methods.''

Amy took out her pack of cigarettes and absentmindedly withdrew one. Automatically she offered the pack to Henry. He helped himself and thanked her.

She was taken aback. "Henry, do you smoke?"

"Why are you surprised?"

"I don't know. You just never did."

"Neither did you."

She lit both their cigarettes. "I suppose we've grown up in a lot of ways," she murmured, waving out the match.

"Well, I hope you've grown out of asking those damned embarrassing questions." Henry shook his head. "You were a terror. I never knew what you would say next."

"You said it yourself, Henry. I haven't really changed."

He gave her a wary glance, and she laughed. They fell into a companionable silence. Finally Henry said, "Tell me about my father, Amy. Was it very bad at the end?"

She told him about the passing of Chen, and Plum Blossom returning home—he knew that—and Andy's decision to become a priest, which startled him, and about the household in Shanghai.

"It seems so far away," he murmured. "Shanghai. The university. City life."

"It is far away," Amy said. "It took me days to get here." She paused. "Tell me about tonight. What will happen? Will I get to see a performance of the Living Newspaper?"

"Tomorrow night, I think. Tonight there'll be a dance at the community hall and maybe someone will challenge you to a game of Ping-Pong, and there'll definitely be a lot of talking and you'll be able to ask all your questions."

"Do you suppose I'll get to dance with Comrade Mao?"

"Probably. He usually shows up, and he likes to dance."

"Is there anything I'm not allowed to ask?"

"No. Feel free to say what's on your mind. If we want anything off the record, we'll tell you, or maybe refuse to answer. You won't hear any lies."

"Nevertheless, Henry, I'm going to come to my own conclusions about what I hear and see. Just because we're old friends doesn't mean I'll be biased in your favor."

"That's too bad," he said dryly. "I was hoping you'd be putty in our hands. Less strong-minded than you are. You *have* changed, Miss Henderson. You've become a hard woman."

"So I have, Henry. I'm a newspaperman now."

He gave her a long thoughtful glance. "How are things for you, Little Sister?"

Amy was embarrassed. She glanced away. "All right. Perfectly all right."

"I thought you might be married by now."

"Not me. I suspect I'm a born bachelor girl. Andy and I make a good pair, don't we? But you're no one to talk, Henry. You're not married either."

"I probably will be one of these days. It makes life easier."

She felt stupidly jealous.

"How are your quarters?" Henry asked, breaking a short silence. "Aside from the typewriter."

"Fine. Much nicer than I expected. I have three whole rooms."

"That is luxury. Most people double and triple up."

"Surely you've seen it," Amy said.

"No, I didn't get a chance."

"Well, why don't you come by tonight, after the dance and so forth, and have a cup of tea with me, and yóu can see my quarters and we'll have another opportunity to talk. I mean privately, without a crowd."

She never expected him to accept. It sounded a little raffish to her, perhaps not quite respectable. She regretted issuing the invitation. She was somewhat startled when he said, "Yes, that sounds nice. I'll do that."

Not only was she startled, she realized she was nervous.

It was late when Amy returned to her quarters. It had been a long evening after a long and tiring day. She was exhilarated, however. Her notebook was crammed. She had asked questions and listened to answers, and heard stories about the war, written down biographies of Yenan leaders, tales of the Long March, explanations of strategy, plans for long-range goals. . . . In one day, Amy thought dazedly, she probably had the makings of a book.

Still ahead of her was a performance of the Living Newspaper, the theater the Red Army had devised to dramatize current events for their largely illiterate army. The actors and actresses were reputed to be talented and quick-witted, drawing on a long tradition of Chinese theater as well as their new technique of political instruction.

She sat down at the table in the living room to look over her notebook. In her absence someone had left a fresh-brewed pot of tea on the table along with clean cups and a refilled fruit basket. She wasn't hungry. She was too keyed up.

Would Henry really come? Would he actually appear?

They hadn't exchanged more than a word or two all night, and then just in passing. There'd been so much else to do, and she hadn't even thought about it. Now she had time to wonder.

The knock on the door, when it came, was very soft.

She hastened to answer it. Henry stood in the doorway in his tunic and peaked cap.

"Hello," he said, "are you too tired for that visit?"

"No, I'm not tired at all. Somebody left me a fresh pot of tea. Come in."

He removed his cap as he entered.

"I think you've dispossessed Comrade Mao," he remarked, looking around.

"Have I really?" she asked, aghast.

He laughed. "No, of course not. He's farther out, by the river."

"Let me show you around."

She felt ridiculously embarrassed displaying the bedroom. She told herself not to be such an idiot. She was a grown woman; it was about time she learned to be cool and sophisticated.

Naturally Henry noticed. "What are you fidgeting for?" he asked with a frown, standing by the bed. "What's making you so jumpy all of a sudden?"

"Me? Jumpy?"

"It must be the surroundings. You're afraid I'll seduce you."

"Possibly I am."

"Maybe I will, just to get that dumb expression off your face."

If that was a joke, Amy didn't think it was very funny. "I'm sure you won't," she said. "What about your Communist ideals?"

"I'd have to consider the question," he said. "It requires a little pondering."

"Always the intellectual."

"Not always. There are other areas of life."

She was more nervous than ever. "How about some tea?" she inquired briskly, to cover up.

"Changing the subject, I see."

"No, just giving you time to think about your great decision."

He laughed. "First let me look at the celebrated typewriter. I may appropriate it for myself after you leave."

To her relief they departed from the bedroom.

When they were seated in the living room over cups of tea, Amy found herself still a little edgy. She was overaware of Henry sitting opposite her. His physical presence seemed to fill the room. She made a determined effort to discuss the goals of peace after the war was won (they were sure they would win) and Communist plans for agrarian reform.

"Aren't you tired of politics?" Henry asked finally. "I would assume you'd had enough of that subject for one night."

"I wouldn't expect *you* to make that remark."

"You seem to think I'm a robot."

"I know you, Henry."

"Maybe not as well as you think you do."

There it was again, that ambiguous little hint, disturbing and upsetting. She grew angry. "What else can I talk about," she demanded, "with you sitting there in that damned high-collared tunic?"

"I'll take it off if you like," he replied mildly. "Except that then I'll have to sit here in my undershirt. It wouldn't be very esthetic." He paused. "It's khaki."

"I'm not interested in your underwear!" she exclaimed crossly.

"Well, I don't blame you," he said in a soothing voice. "We'll talk about agrarian reform. Or occupied Shanghai. I haven't heard all about that yet. You must have a lot of fascinating stories to tell."

"I hate that tone of voice, Henry! As if you were humoring a five-year-old child!"

"You always did."

"Then why do you do it?"

"Just to make you angry."

"You are obnoxious," she said in the same cross voice.

"I'm a terrible person," he agreed. "I haven't mellowed at all in the hardships of war."

As usual he made her laugh and she couldn't continue to bicker. They discussed Shanghai for a while, and the changes the Japanese government had made in the life of the city. She couldn't stop thinking about what he had said in the bedroom. Finally, unable to help herself, she inquired, "Are you still planning to seduce me?"

"I think so." He considered for a moment. "First I'd like to finish my tea, though. If it's all right with you."

"I wish you wouldn't tease me, Henry. Not about that. I was hoping you'd say it was all a joke and I should forget it. Because it's making me very nervous."

He gazed at her in mild astonishment. "Dear girl, I haven't been teasing."

She didn't answer. Then she said in a small voice, "You mean you're really serious?"

"Unless you have some strong objections."

"I—not exactly. But I should make a rather embarrassing confession." She started to stumble. She hated herself for it. "You may have the wrong impression of me," she persevered. "I mean, career woman and newspaper reporter and all that." She hesitated. "What I'm trying to say is—Henry, do you remember that demonstration on Nanking Road for the murdered factory worker?"

"Yes, of course."

"Do you remember you took me to a coffee shop afterward and I asked you a dumb kid question which you were honest enough to answer?"

"Very well."

"That's—that's what I'm trying to say."

"And haven't," Henry remarked. "You haven't said anything."

"Do I have to, in so many words?" she inquired desperately.

"What, admit that you're a virgin? No, I think I caught on."

Amy flushed. "I'm supposed to be clever with words, but I haven't been very clever." She paused. "Does it . . . does it make a difference?"

"My dear Little Sister, behold, I have finished my tea."
Henry placed his cup on the table and stood up.

"Are you leaving?" Amy whispered.

"Not unless you want me to."

"No, stay." She rose and moved toward him, suddenly overwhelmingly happy and overwhelmingly anxious, knowing it was
all showing on her face, everything she was feeling. She had no
way to hide it. "Please stay."

He smiled and held out his hand.

"Henry," whispered Amy, in the small Spartan bedroom of
the cave home, in the narrow bed, "I didn't know it would be
like this." She turned in his arms.

"What is it you expected, my love?"

"Everything to be . . . awkward. How to arrange yourself.
Where to put arms and legs."

"No," he said with tender amusement, "those matters seem to
work themselves out."

"Oh . . . yes . . ."

Outside the town wall came the soft chatter of soldiers making
their way up a hill path. Late travelers passed through the streets
carrying paper lanterns to light their way. They sang little snatches
of songs under their breath as they went, quietly, so as not to
wake sleepers.

"Henry," murmured Amy drowsily in their bed, "I wonder if
you were just sorry for me in my unawakened state."

"Is that how it seemed to you, dearest Amy?"

"No," she confessed, "not in the slightest. But I wanted to
hear you say it."

"Then I will tell you. Again. But not in words."

At last the streets of Yenan were silent. The last patrol had
passed through the gates. The last travelers had returned to their
homes. The carts were still, and the mules drowsed in their
stables.

It was the hour before dawn. Amy slept in Henry's arms, her
red curls tousled, her breathing steady and even. He roused her
very softly.

"Little Sister, I must leave now."

She stirred and came awake. "Oh, is it time?"

"Yes, I would rather not leave in daylight."

"All right, if you must. . . ."

"I'm glad you slept. It will be another very long day."

Amy sat up. She brushed back her hair. "Stay just a few more minutes," she said with sudden tension. "Smoke a cigarette with me. It won't be dawn for a while."

"All right, just a few minutes."

"Later today we will be our public selves again, won't we? Comrade Chen and Miss Henderson."

"I am afraid so, dearest."

"I won't betray you, Henry. Not in any way."

"I never thought you would. You are my Little Sister, the other part of myself."

She propped herself on her elbow and traced the outline of a long puckered scar on his chest. "I used to look at you when we went swimming in the summer. You were always so smooth. Like ivory satin, I thought. And now you're marked. Is this a bullet crease?"

"Yes."

"From crossing the Tatu Ho?"

"No, I came through that without a scratch. I got this later, on the grasslands."

"Tell me about it."

"Oh, my love, you don't want to hear any more war stories."

"I suppose not. I just want to keep you here." Her eyes were frightened. "Because after I leave Yenan, there won't be any other times for us. Will there?"

"No," he answered quietly.

"Only memories."

"If we meet after this visit, in another time and place, it will have to be formal," he said. "As it was last evening in the community hall."

"All right," she said bravely, "I can face that."

He bent his head and kissed her on the mouth. "At least we won't have to regret something that never happened. That's the worst regret of all."

"Oh, the wisdom of Confucius," she said with a laugh that was half a sob.

"Maybe the memories are important too." Henry leaned back

against the pillow and stared into space. "Forgive me for trying to be an oracle, dearest Little Sister. You know it's my failing. But if the war goes as we hope—no matter how long it takes— and if afterwards matters turn out as we hope for China—then I have the sense that your government and mine will be enemies."

Amy's eyes reflected pain. "That cannot happen, Henry. It must not."

"Ten years from now it may. If you and I are still alive then, we will never be enemies. We will have a bridge of memories in our hearts, of love and tenderness and respect—we will remember that we laughed together and touched one another in intimacy and love here in Yenan. And we'll keep the bridge standing— secretly if we must; you and I in our memories—so that someday people can cross over again in friendship. Surely that has to be important."

Amy bowed her head to hide the tears in her eyes.

"What are you thinking?" he asked after a while, stroking her hair.

"About what you said. And then I was seeing an army truck bouncing down the road to Sian, going to the railway, with myself in the back and you remaining here—"

"Not yet," said Henry, holding her close. "Not for a little while."

CHAPTER 15

By the spring of 1940 the war in Europe had shaken everyone. China, too, was convulsed. Shanghai was a demoralized city. Sullen gangs of Chinese youths roamed Chapei breaking shop windows and helping themselves to radios and clocks. Even more aggressive gangs of young Japanese thugs elbowed pedestrians off the sidewalks of Little Tokyo, and beat people at will with fists and knives. The population of Shanghai was uneasy and restive, even in the International Settlement. The war with Japan dragged on, far from Shanghai, Chiang Kai-shek's forces losing battle after battle, only the Eighth Route Army in the North fighting with skill and persistence as they dynamited bridges, destroyed railway tunnels, and lured bewildered Japanese troops into booby-trapped villages. The Communist guerrillas of the Eighth Route Army were losing few men. They struck and then seemed to melt into the countryside.

The Japanese held a press conference in Shanghai every week, to transmit news of the war front, they announced. All they ever reported, however, were Japanese victories. Soldiers of the Emperor were never defeated, not even in a tiny skirmish. At least if you believed Major Shogama, the press officer.

Few of the reporters did. The English-language press was openly skeptical in print. The Chinese newspapers were required to cooperate; they were part of Japan's "New Asia" policy and there were ominous tales of reprisals and torture of recalcitrant Chinese journalists at Bridge House, an apartment-hotel converted into a headquarters for the Gendarmerie, the Japanese secret police.

Not all the Chinese were cowed. Many of them continued to print what they believed to be the truth.

One of them was Mr. Tsai, a short, plump, round-faced man with merry eyes who published a daily paper in Honanese dialect.

He raised his hand to ask a question at the press conference as Major Shogama finished reading his prepared statement in his usual monotonous drone.

"Why do we come every week?" Amy whispered to Mac McNamara, who sat beside her on a folding chair. "It's such a waste of time."

"We're always hoping the good major will be embarrassed."

"Yes, Mr. Tsai will ask an embarrassing question, bless his soul."

"Is it not true," Mr. Tsai inquired, rising to his feet, "that a patrol of Japanese soldiers in Honan last week stopped to pick tomatoes from a peasant's vegetable garden? And that the entire patrol was blown to bits because the vegetables were mined? Exploded amid the tomatoes and lettuce and carrots?"

Major Shogama's face turned red. "Certainly not," he gritted. "What a stupid and disgusting story!"

Reporters were busily scribbling, "Japanese Patrol Reportedly Demolished by Booby-Trapped Tomatoes."

"Mr. Tsai always has good information," Amy whispered to Mac. "Especially from Honan. It's probably true."

Mr. Tsai was a good friend of Amy's. He was always willing to share his information with her; they had different audiences anyway.

Amy was somewhat of a celebrity now. Her long series of articles on Yenan had caused an enormous stir and made her name well known even in the United States. The articles had been reprinted in *The New Republic*. An agent in New York had written to her asking for a book, which she was trying to organize in her spare time. She had a tentative job offer from *The Nation*, which so far she had refused, not wanting to be supervised from New York. And she was doing a weekly fifteen-minute radio broadcast on a Shanghai station, *The News as Seen by Amy Henderson*.

The Japanese detested her but so far had left her alone, contenting themselves with veiled threats of harassment.

She had taken her own apartment in the French Concession, on the Avenue Joffre, needing a place to receive visitors. Some of them slipped in under cover of night from the fighting front. Some of them had even been to Yenan. She asked questions about people she had met. Occasionally, with studied casualness and a fast-beating heart, she inquired after Chen T'ieh-chang.

It would not do to have these comings and goings take place on Bubbling Well Road, she'd explained to the family. Mike had grumbled, but she promised to come for dinner at least twice a week. It was a promise she could not keep, as it turned out, but she did her best.

As the press conference dissolved, and Major Shogama stalked out with his aides, looking angry and grim, Amy caught up with Mr. Tsai.

"That was splendid," she exclaimed.

He grinned. "One does one's humble best to tarnish the glory of Dai Nippon."

"Can you come for dinner tonight, Mr. Tsai?"

"Not for dinner, no. I promised it to my wife and family." He made a comical face. "My sons have almost forgotten what I look like. I have to remind them every now and again."

"After dinner, then?"

"Yes, I would be delighted. I have much to tell you."

Amy thought she had time to stop by and visit her grandmother at the Valentine Gallery.

She had not told Laura what had happened in Yenan, except to say that she had seen Henry and he was looking well, but she suspected Laura knew something intimate had transpired. She had not confided in anyone except Andy, in a letter, and received a beautiful and understanding letter from him in return, which had made her cry.

Andy had written that as soon as he was ordained he would be sent to Hong Kong. He would be sorry to leave China proper, especially in these times of her agony, but he was immensely relieved to be staying in the East.

Amy planned to visit him in Hong Kong when he finally got there.

In the gallery office she watched Laura unpack a shipment of porcelain vases and bowls, admiring the gentleness, deftness, and authority with which Laura handled the precious objects.

"Grandmother," she said, "I wish I could be more like you."

"I like to think you are like me," replied Laura. "In many ways. Although I'm probably flattering myself."

"Oh, no. You're so charming and cultured and gracious, so ladylike and tactful, not like me at all. And you always dress so beautifully."

Laura started to laugh.

"What's so funny?" asked Amy.

"I was remembering myself as a schoolgirl. I was the least gracious, least charming adolescent anyone in my town had ever seen. My family used to shut me in an upstairs room when callers came, because they were afraid of what I'd say. It was always something terrible and gauche."

"That can't be true."

"Well, it is. And as for being beautifully dressed, if I have any taste at all, I must thank Pierre-Marc Daniel. If it weren't for him, I'd be a frump. And I was a wife and mother before I met

him, with another child on the way, who turned out to be your
uncle David.''

Amy sighed. "Such disillusion. The next thing you'll be telling me is that you and Grandpa were not always perfectly suited
to each other, like two peas in a pod, and have not had an ideal
marriage from the very beginning.''

"Oh, lord, that would take too long to contradict. But believe
me, darling, it isn't true either.''

"Someday you'll have to tell me the story of your life.''

"I doubt if you'll want to listen to an old woman's ramblings.''

"You're not old. You never will be old. 'Age cannot wither
her, nor custom stale her infinite variety.' '' Amy paused. "That's
Byron.''

"It's Shakespeare and you know it.''

Amy grinned. "Just trying to catch you out.''

As Amy was leaving the gallery, Laura's face turned serious.
She took Amy's arm. "Be careful, Amy, won't you? I worry that
you're too outspoken about the Japanese, and there are rumors
about Bridge House. They say an American journalist was taken
there last week and badly beaten.''

"I know, I heard that too. Joe Sinclair. No one has actually
seen him, though. It's all the more reason to speak out. People in
America should be warned. They don't take Japan seriously
enough, and I believe that war with Japan is coming. Maybe not
this year, or next year, but some year. We have time to make
preparations if we're on the alert.''

"I wish you didn't have to be the one to sound it.''

"I have a little bit of name now, Grandma. It has to be me.''
Amy grinned mischievously. "Besides, the Japanese wouldn't
dare touch such a famous celebrity.''

Amy stopped at her office at the newspaper before going
home. She wrote up the press conference, including Mr. Tsai's
question, and then worked on the script for her radio broadcast.
Someday, she told herself, she'd have to get to that book on the
Eighth Route Army, but there was just never enough time. She
ate a sandwich at her desk for dinner. Then she looked at the
clock and saw it was late. She had to get home. She'd invited
Mac to visit after dinner, as well as Mr. Tsai. Mac's dispatches
for the United Press were heavily cut, unlike Amy's articles for

the *Shanghai Mirror*, for China was just one part of the global picture where UPI was concerned; but Mac was conscientious and filed everything. Amy generously shared her sources.

She parked her car in the apartment-house garage and entered the elevator. She had her key in her hand as she got off on the fourth floor.

Something large and round was leaning against the door of her apartment. For a moment she thought someone had left her a melon. Then she came closer.

For the first time in her life Amy shrieked in hysteria. She clapped her hand over her mouth and fled back into the elevator, pushing the DOWN button frantically. She leaned against the elevator wall retching violently and trying not to vomit.

Mac was just entering the lobby. She rushed over to him, trying to talk.

He grabbed her by the shoulders. She was shaking all over. "For God's sake, Red, what is it? I've never seen you like this!"

"Mac—upstairs—by my apartment door—they left me something—a warning—"

"Left you what! Pull yourself together!"

Amy attempted to do that. She took five deep breaths. She gulped, but her voice came out a croak. She gazed up at Mac piteously. "Mr. Tsai's head," she whispered.

Mr. Tsai had been tortured and beheaded at Bridge House. So much was certain. Amy recovered from her shock and fear, and did what she could for Mr. Tsai's family.

She discussed the situation with Mike, who was at first enraged and insistent that she quit her job, but finally admitted she could not do that with honor.

"At least quit making the radio broadcasts," he said. "That's what really gets under their skins."

"I can't quit anything, Grandpa. Any retreat is a loss of face. I don't have to tell you that."

Mike grudgingly agreed. "However," he said, "I'm sending you a personal bodyguard, and I won't hear any argument. He'll chauffeur the car and stay with you all day and sleep in your extra bedroom at night."

"I don't have an extra bedroom. I have a little home office."

"Not anymore. It's being converted."

Amy sighed. "I won't argue. Actually I'm grateful. They've just been . . . snatching people off the street and taking them to Bridge House. Joe Sinclair lost an eye. And poor Mr. Tsai, he was so brave and funny."

Mike clipped the end of a cigar, then struck a match and lit it. "Sooner or later we're going to have to fight a war," he muttered.

"I think so, too, Grandpa. Are you making any preparations?"

He nodded. "I'm transferring assets little by little out of China, and your grandmother is sending as much as she can to the San Francisco gallery."

"Do you and Grandmother plan to settle in California?"

"Yes, and reestablish the pottery works, if we can find enough craftsmen."

"Do you think it will be soon?"

"Couple of years."

"I'll probably have to live in New York, if I join the staff of *The Nation*. God, it seems so strange."

And what about Andy? she wanted to ask. But he would be in the British Crown Colony of Hong Kong, surely that would be safe, if he had to remain in the Orient.

But I will be so far away from Henry. . . .

She saw the poster on a board fence near Nanking Road. It would probably be ripped down before evening by Japanese military police, but for the moment it stood out in bright bold colors.

She was strolling with Mac. She paused to look at the poster. A handsome and heroic young Chinese soldier with Henry Chen's face was leading a brave-looking peasant army into battle.

"Nice romantic picture," Mac remarked. "With a fairy-tale soldier some artist dreamed up out of his imagination."

Actually it was a good likeness.

"I met someone who resembled that poster in Yenan," Amy said, and immediately regretted it.

"Did you now. Who might that be, I wonder?"

Amy tried to retrieve her mistake. "I don't remember the name offhand."

"I think you're just trying to make me jealous."

"And it isn't very hard to do," she retorted.

She might have known Mac wouldn't forget the exchange. He came to see her at the newspaper one afternoon and perched on the edge of her desk.

"You're sitting on my lead article," Amy pointed out.

"Sorry." He shifted his hip.

"And you could take off your hat," she observed.

"I could but I won't. I only obey one order a day." He paused. "Hey, I found out who your Chinese friend is. The one on the Communist poster."

"Oh?" Amy tensed.

"That business about not remembering his name was a lot of hogwash. He's the son of your former houseboy on Bubbling Well Road, and you grew up together in Shanghai. He's now one of the fair-haired boys—so to speak—of Comrade Mao in Yenan. His name is Chen T'ieh-chang."

Amy was silent for a moment. Then she said, "Orchids to you, Mac. Pulitzer prize reporting."

"Shucks, ma'am, it wasn't much." He lowered his eyes bashfully.

"So now you're convinced there's a big mystery?"

"Nah." Mac shook his head. "Water under the bridge. Here you are in Shanghai, a big-shot reporter, and there he is in Yenan, a married man with a baby on the way. Nothing's going on."

Amy forgot to be discreet in her sudden shock. "Is Henry married?"

"Oh, is it Henry?" Mac inquired.

"I mean Comrade Chen."

"Sure. One of the actresses from the Living Newspaper. Supposed to be gorgeous, and very talented." He grinned. "So I finally scooped Miss Henderson. I do deserve the Pulitzer prize."

"You can have it as far as I'm concerned," Amy whispered.

Mac dropped his teasing tone. "Hey, Red, I'm sorry if I upset you. I didn't mean to."

"No, it's okay." Amy looked down at her hands resting on the typewriter. "But I do have to get back to work now," she muttered, desperately wanting to be alone. "I have a million things to do."

"Can I buy you a sandwich later on?"

"Not tonight, Mac, thanks. Maybe . . . maybe tomorrow."

"Sure thing." He tapped her lightly on the jaw as he slid off the desk. "Keep your chin up."

Weeks passed before Amy was able to speak about it to Laura.

"Henry is married," she said in a low voice, sitting in her favorite spot on the bedroom floor by Laura's chaise longue. "His wife is expecting a baby."

Laura made no comment, waiting for Amy to say more.

"I was horribly jealous at first," Amy said. "I hated her—his wife, I mean—and I had bad thoughts . . . terrible thoughts . . . and I despised myself for it but I couldn't help thinking them. It was like having an awful disease. A fever that makes you so delirious you get violent and you want to do away with a person who is your enemy. Just . . . sweep that person off the face of the earth. A woman I don't even know! But I got over it, Grandmother. Thank God. I thought of you, and Andy, and how you would feel if you were me, not violent but understanding, and now I'm glad to say that I don't hate anyone."

"If you love someone, Amy, you want that person to be happy. Even if it causes you pain."

"That's what I told myself. And now I am happy—truly—I'm happy that Henry has someone who cares for him, and will have a kind of normal life and a family. . . ."

"I'm proud of you," Laura said.

Amy smiled mistily. "I'll tell you a secret, though, Grandmother, that I wouldn't admit to anyone else. I gloat sometimes, in my secret heart, that I knew Henry for twenty-five years before she ever met him. Those years belong to me and they always will."

"I'm sure Henry remembers that, too, although he might not speak of it, any more than you will." Laura gazed into Amy's face and brushed back a strand of Amy's hair. "Now you can think of your own personal life."

"One of these days." Amy gave a shaky laugh. "Right now I'm just too busy. I'm still trying to find time to get to Hong Kong so I can see Andy!"

She took Laura's hand, and they sat in sad and peaceful silence, each lost in thought.

*   *   *

In September of 1940 Japan signed a pact with Nazi Germany and Fascist Italy, creating a sinister wheel of Axis power. The war threat deepened.

By the autumn of 1941 Amy still had not found time in her hectic and overworked schedule to leave Shanghai. The last four months had been ones of increasing anxiety for Americans in the Orient. The summer of 1941 had brought rising tensions between Japan and the United States. Everyone in Shanghai was convinced war was inevitable. Opinions differed on when it would happen.

"It's bound to be in the spring," Mike said to Amy. "No later than April. I'm making plans for us to leave Shanghai as soon after Christmas as possible. I'm arranging passage now."

When Mac McNamara took Amy out to dinner in October, she told him about the plans to leave China. She herself couldn't make up her mind what to do. "Christmas of 1941 in Shanghai and Easter of 1942 in California," she said. "That's my grandfather's schedule."

"I'm leaving, myself, in two weeks," Mac told her. "I was saving the big news for the brandy and coffee."

"For good, Mac?" She was concerned. She'd gotten used to having him around.

"It depends on when the war comes. I'd like to get back to Shanghai in three or four months. Right now I need a change of scene. I've got China fever."

"What's that, some new disease?"

"It's an intense desire to smell the Hudson instead of the Whangpoo. How about you? Don't you want to take a look at Gotham on the Hudson? Why don't you come along for the boat ride with me?"

"I don't think I can."

"I'll show you New York. Take you to the Stork Club and introduce you to Sherman Billingsley. You can say hello to Walter Winchell. Pal around with Brenda Frazier. Eat scrambled eggs at El Morocco."

"Gee, it sounds glamorous."

"Café society, kiddo."

"First I have to get to Hong Kong," she told him. "Then I may take you up on that offer."

"Sure," he said, and leaned back and lit a cigarette. "I won't hold my breath until you do."

"I'll miss you, Mac," she said seriously.

He gave her a wry grin and didn't answer.

"Don't forget to come back," she warned.

"Four months. Maybe sooner, if it looks as if the Pacific's going to explode."

"Otherwise I'll meet you in New York. That's a date."

Amy finally planned her trip to Hong Kong for just after Thanksgiving. Mike took her aside after Thanksgiving dinner on Bubbling Well Road.

"You will be back from Hong Kong in time for Christmas, won't you?" he said. "Your grandmother is depending on it."

He wouldn't mention Andy's name, and Amy was combining the visit with a story on Hong Kong's defenses in the event of war, so Mike pretended that was the only purpose of her trip.

"Oh, yes," Amy assured him, "I'll be back at least five days before Christmas."

She wasn't sure about her date with Mac in New York, but Amy knew she would be in Shanghai during the week preceding Christmas. She was always home for the holidays. That was a rule; 1941 would be no different.

BOOK FOUR

Someone Else's Sky

CHAPTER 1

Mike was in the shower, Laura could hear the water running. Downstairs in the kitchen the cook was preparing breakfast; she could smell percolating coffee. An ordinary morning? No, those deep sounds from the direction of the river were not ordinary. She listened worriedly. The noise was not rifle fire; she knew that sound all too well after the battle for Shanghai in 1937. This was deeper, louder, and more resonant.

She threw open the east-facing bedroom window, telling herself she was being ridiculous; what could she expect to see?

It was a beautiful, clear December morning with a mild breeze.

She did see something. Red flashes of light against the dawn sky. Just where the Whangpoo would be. Just where the sun was rising. *The rising sun*, Laura thought, and felt a premonition.

Mike was suddenly beside her, in his bathrobe, smelling of soap and shaving lotion.

"Don't stand by the window, you'll get chilled," Laura said. Mike would be seventy next year. He had to watch his diet and his daily routine, the doctor had told him, he had mild diabetes and must stay away from sugar and not be such a pigheaded Irishman all his life or he would need insulin injections. Mike had grumbled but obeyed, hating the idea of injections.

"Mike, what is that noise?" Laura said, after she'd closed the window. "And what are those red flashes in the sky? Are they what I think?"

"Yes," he said, frowning. "Heavy artillery. Somebody's shelling something on the Bund."

"Who? Why? Shanghai isn't at war. The Chinese lost this city four years ago."

"I don't know, but we'd better get downstairs and turn on the radio. It doesn't sound good to me."

Amy took a deep, happy breath. "Andy, it's so wonderful to see you," she exclaimed. "Even in that cassock and collar. Although I have to admit it's becoming. You always were a handsome devil. I always thought it was terribly unfair that you got all the looks. We're twins; we should look alike."

"Girl and boy twins never look alike," Andy said, and smiled. "Besides, you have seniority. Six minutes."

"Then as your older sister, I command you to stay the morning and have lunch with me."

They were in Amy's room at the Peninsula Hotel, on the Kowloon side of Hong Kong. Andy's parish was on Hong Kong Island, across Victoria Harbor. He had arrived for breakfast. They were both on their second cups of coffee.

"I don't think I can stay that long," said Andy. "You don't know how busy I am. Come to the rectory for dinner tonight instead."

"Okay. Meanwhile I'll call room service for another pot of coffee."

Amy picked up the telephone and dialed. She listened to ring after ring, but room service didn't answer.

"And this is supposed to be such a fancy hotel," she said. "They're probably busy, I'll try again later."

"Tell me about your newspaper story," Andy said. "Hong Kong's defenses."

"Inadequate," Amy replied. "If there's a Japanese attack, the British will be in trouble. I don't think Singapore's in any better shape. Andy, I wish you'd go to America with the family in April."

"Even if I wanted to," said Andy gently, "I couldn't go *with* them."

"Oh . . . Grandpa . . . blast that stubborn streak of his; he's like a concrete wall. But I know he misses you, Andy. I know he does. I see a lonesome look in his eyes sometimes, and I know he's thinking of you. Especially at holiday times. Thanksgiving and Christmas. You're like the ghost at the feast."

"Lord help me, I miss him too. Amy, is he really sick?"

"Not sick, exactly. He just doesn't have the energy he used ↘ have. He gets tired faster, and he's lost some weight."

"Don't let him smoke so many cigars," Andy said worriedly.

"Grandmother looks after him. She even nags and he pretends to complain about it, but he leans on her."

"It's always been that way," Andy said. "Haven't you ever noticed?"

"No, I haven't. Not until recently. I think you have better perception than I do. I just make more noise about things."

Amy reached for the telephone to try room service again.

David had the habit of strolling to work every day to assume his duties as head of personnel at the pottery works. He started at dawn from his apartment and then stopped to have a leisurely breakfast at a small restaurant. He resumed his journey in plenty of time to get to his desk before anyone else arrived.

He preferred his morning walk to driving his automobile. He only drove to work when the weather was bad.

On this early December morning the weather was lovely, clear, and mild in Shanghai.

He bowed curtly as he passed Japanese sentries on the sidewalk and said the required good morning. They were usually sleepy-eyed at this hour. Today as they acknowledged his greeting, they were bright and alert, with smug smiles on their faces.

What the hell are they so happy about? David asked himself.

Then he heard explosions coming from the river, deep reverberating booms. Heavy firing from artillery pieces.

They're celebrating a German victory, David thought in disgust. This afternoon victory balloons would probably float over the city, with long streamers in Chinese proclaiming the Axis success. It was the usual Japanese routine. He reached the restaurant and then stopped to listen to the sounds.

No, this was going on too long, he told himself, and the firing was too heavy. Something was happening on the Whangpoo. Something unusual.

Instead of turning into the restaurant, he directed his steps to the Bund. He started to walk faster. He would be able to have a clear view of the river from the Bund. Find out what was going on.

Once on the Bund, he stood on the grassy strip bordering the Whangpoo to look out at the bend in the river. A gunboat was anchored there and it was firing its artillery; the noise was booming across the water. From somewhere on shore flashed the reddish streaks of tracer bullets. Shells landing in the river were kicking up little fountains of water.

Two other gunboats were anchored midstream. David peered at the flags; he saw that one was flying the Union Jack, but the other was too far away for him to make out.

"What the hell," he exclaimed.

"Bloody bastards," said a bowler-hatted man standing nearby. He looked and sounded like an Englishman. He was peering at the river through field glasses.

"Can I look?" asked David.

The Englishman handed over the field glasses without a word.

David gazed out at the river. The gunboat firing the shells was HIJMS *Idzuma*, the flagship of the Japanese China fleet. David swerved the glasses. The Union Jack ship was H.M.S. *Petrel*. And the third—*my God*, David breathed to himself—it was flying the flag of the Rising Sun, but painted on its side were the words U.S.S. *Wake*.

"That's an American gunboat," David gasped. "But it's flying a Japanese flag."

"It's been captured," the Englishman said bitterly. "They had no time to scuttle her."

Just then the British *Petrel* was raked from stem to stern by shellfire. The vessel burst into flames and keeled over on its side, blazing in the middle of the river. Figures leaped overboard.

"She's sinking!" cried the Englishman. "Oh, the bloody bastards!"

David handed back the field glasses and began to run across the Bund. He headed for Bubbling Well Road.

Laura and Mike were huddled in front of their radio in the library. Mike was fully dressed. They were both sipping cups of black coffee. They could not get anything on the radio but recorded music, and Mike's anger and frustration were rising. They could see the glare in the sky from the burning gunboat in the Whangpoo, but could not tell what it was.

It had taken all Laura's powers of persuasion to keep him in the house.

"Try the radio just a few more minutes," she begged. "Surely we'll hear some news."

"You can turn it off, Dad," said David's low voice from the doorway. "I met someone with a shortwave radio, and I've been listening to San Francisco."

"David, I'm glad you're here." Laura became immediately apprehensive at the grim look on his face.

"What the hell's going on?" said Mike. "What's all that shelling?"

"The Japanese have attacked Clark Field and Manila in the Philippines and Pearl Harbor in Hawaii. They've sunk two British battleships off Malaya. And I've just been on the Bund, and they've sunk the *Petrel* midstream in the Whangpoo. That's the burning you see and that's the shelling you were hearing."

"David! My God!" cried Laura.

Mike said nothing. Savagely he snapped on the radio again. There was music, and then it stopped abruptly. They heard a Japanese-accented voice speaking English.

"Attention American and British citizens. You are at war with Imperial Japan. Forces of the Japanese Empire have achieved a glorious victory today. The United States Pacific Fleet has been totally destroyed and is at the bottom of the Pacific Ocean. It will be years before it can be raised and repaired. Britain's hands are tied in Europe and the Atlantic and Indian oceans. Surrender is imminent."

In helpless despair and rage Mike turned the radio off again.

"I don't think that's true, Dad," David said quietly. "It's bad, but not that bad. I believe San Francisco before I believe the Japanese in Shanghai. The Pacific Fleet isn't totally destroyed. Surrender isn't imminent. Although God knows they seem to have done enough damage."

"The point is," Laura whispered, "our country is at war with Japan. And we are here in Shanghai."

CHAPTER 2

Amy had wandered to the window of her room at the Peninsula Hotel. They had never gotten the second pot of coffee, but it was almost time for Andy to leave.

"Andy, that's odd," she said. "Come over here and look out the window. Isn't that the direction of the airport?"

He came to stand beside her, and then nodded.

"Why are those little planes circling and diving?"

Andy looked perplexed. "Maybe they're on maneuvers," he said after a moment.

"If they're on maneuvers, then why do I see smoke billowing up from the ground?"

"Don't they use smoke screens on maneuvers?"

"Andy—do you believe that?"

He paused. "No," he said. "Let's go down to the lobby."

The elegant lobby of the Peninsula was overcrowded with travelers. People were on the sofas, seated in the armchairs, wandering about with flight bags in their hands, but no one was checking into the hotel. They had all checked out of their various hotels earlier in the morning and boarded the airport bus. It always left from the Pan American office here at the Peninsula. A Pan American Clipper had been scheduled to depart for Manila.

Everyone had been ordered off the bus and back into the lobby but not told why. So much Amy and Andy discovered.

They waited in the lobby like everyone else, in an atmosphere of tension and unease. Then the big glass doors to the street burst open and a group of men and women in uniform tumbled in. They were Pan American employees: the flight crew. Their story spilled out in breathless gasps. Their Clipper had been dive-bombed and blown up on the ground at the airport. Luckily no one had been in it but a steward, and he had escaped through a window.

"Who was it?" Amy demanded of a crew member. "Who bombed you?"

She was about to hear a reply when a hotel employee—one of the desk clerks—mounted a leather hassock in the center of the lobby and raised his hand. He looked distraught and bewildered. "Ladies and gentlemen, may I have your attention. I have an announcement."

A baby cried and was hushed. Everyone fell silent. They listened to the incredible news. A long, whispering sigh swept across the room when the clerk had finished.

As if on cue came the whine of airplanes in the sky. Involuntarily many in the lobby flinched and ducked. The baby began to wail again. Outside the whine faded. The Japanese dive bombers were returning to their air base in occupied China. They would be back.

The silence broke, and a babble of voices filled the lobby, tense and half hysterical. One woman was staring fixedly at the roof of the lobby as if expecting a bomb to drop through it. The din increased. Amy turned to her brother, about to speak, but Andy spoke first. He drew her aside.

"Amy, you must get out of Hong Kong," he said in a low, urgent voice. "Go directly to the airport. Find a plane heading for Chungking; it's your only safety."

Chungking was still in Chinese Nationalist hands, far behind the Japanese lines in the Chinese interior, still Chiang Kai-shek's wartime capital.

"What about you?" she demanded.

"I can't leave, you know that."

"The Japanese will take this city, Andy. I swear they will. It can't be defended for long."

"Even if they do, I don't believe they'll harm a priest in his parish."

Pipedreams, Amy thought desperately. "Andy, for God's sake, they'll harm anyone! They raped nuns in Nanking, on the sidewalk, and then cut their throats with bayonets!"

"I have nuns to look after as well," he said quietly. "I'll have to find a way for us all to leave, if Hong Kong can't hold out. But, Amy, you must get to Chungking as soon as possible."

Amy wasn't listening. Her eyes were wide. "Shanghai," she whispered, ashen-faced. "Grandma and Grandpa. Uncle David. Oh, God. What will happen to them?"

"We'll ask God to protect them," Andy said, equally white. "There's nothing else we can do."

Laura thought helplessly that instead of one unruly male on her hands, now she had two. Mike and David had asked for the car to be brought to the front door. They intended to go to the pottery works and investigate the situation. On the way back to Bubbling Well Road they would stop at David's apartment and pick up his shortwave radio.

Laura considered the plan foolhardy. They had been informed on the radio that a fresh detachment of Japanese marines had arrived in Shanghai and was patrolling all the city streets. They were bound to be in a triumphant mood. Everyone knew the story of Nanking.

Mike and David insisted that Shanghai would not be subjected to that kind of indiscriminate terror. The city had surrendered to the Japanese long ago.

Finally David suggested, "Why don't I take the car and investigate on my own?" He knew his father's temper.

Mike and Laura agreed to that plan. David left swiftly.

He was back in less than an hour with news. The pottery works, like all foreign-owned businesses, had a notice affixed to the door saying the property had been taken over and was now under Japanese control. Any violation would be considered a breach of Japanese military law.

Mike swore.

The Gendarmerie, the Japanese secret police, had already taken over an apartment building in Little Tokyo for its headquarters.

"Interrogations?" Mike inquired.

"I think they'll still be at Bridge House."

"Go on," Mike ordered grimly.

American, British, and Dutch citizens were being classified as enemy aliens. Not French, because the Vichy government was considered an ally. There would be a detention camp for enemy aliens, but it wasn't ready.

"So we have a little time," Mike muttered.

To do what? Laura wondered. They were trapped. The Pacific Ocean lay between them and California. The Chinese interior and the Japanese lines lay between them and Chungking. There was nowhere to go. Would Mike survive a detention camp? What sort of food would there be? What sort of conditions?

She didn't say anything.

"An Englishman told me that certain people will be taken to Bridge House immediately if they're judged to be dangerous foes of Imperial Japan, and lord knows what will happen to them," David said. "They'll be lucky if they're just beheaded."

Heavy silence fell. Bridge House was as notorious in Shanghai as Nanking was to the world.

"Thank God Amy isn't here," Laura whispered.

"If they make the connection between us and Amy," said David, "they'll be on their way to arrest us."

"The Gendarmerie knows all about it, you can bet on that," said Mike. "They keep very complete dossiers." He paused. "Still got your gun, David?"

"What are you planning to do, Dad," asked David, "gun them down one by one as they come in the door?"

"That wasn't what I had in mind," answered Mike. "We'll only need three bullets."

There was another silence. Then Laura said hoarsely, "That will be all right with me. I don't think I'd be very brave under torture."

"Oh, Christ!" David sprang up and began to pace the room. "That can't be the answer! There must be a better solution!"

"Think of one," said Mike.

It was night in Hong Kong. Amy leaned against the outside wall of the field station at Hong Kong Airport, scribbling in her notebook by the light of a single beam coming from within, shining through the blackout curtains. All around the airport in the darkness milled refugees desperate to get on an airplane. Any airplane out of Hong Kong. The night was thick with fear, strained voices, crying babies.

"Darkness has fallen on Hong Kong," Amy wrote, "ending the first day of its war. The Japanese in formations of twelve planes have been dive-bombing shipping all afternoon in Victoria Harbor. Shells have been bursting in ever-thickening clusters on the Kowloon side of the city. No one has seen any British military planes in the air. There are reports the planes have been destroyed at their bases. Here at the airport—"

"Are you a journalist, or just keeping a diary?" asked an English-accented voice at her elbow.

Amy raised her head. The man beside her gave her a shy smile. He was thin and bald and wore spectacles.

"I don't usually accost strange women," he said. "Very un-English of me. This is a rather unusual night, though, isn't it?"

Amy smiled back. "Yes, it is," she said. "I'm not keeping a diary, I'm a journalist. Amy Henderson of the *Shanghai Mirror*."

"Peter Essex," he said. "Marine engineer for Jardine Matheson."

He was about to say more when a faint engine drone hummed in the air. They both tensed. A plane was coming in.

An improvised ferry service was operating to Chungking, with pilots and planes from China National Aviation. The rescue would only be able to operate tonight. Every plane lifted off the field was overloaded with refugees.

The blackout could not be violated for very long. When an airplane approached, the riding lights on its wings twinkled for a split second. Inside the field station a prearranged count began. The landing lights bordering the field flashed on and the plane touched down. Then the lights died.

Amy and Peter Essex blinked in the sudden glare and like a stage picture saw the little airplane with its wheels touching the tarmac. Then the curtain of blackness came down again.

"No hope of my getting on one of those flights," said Peter Essex into the darkness. "I can see that now."

Amy herself had a good chance, according to the Pan American official she'd spoken to in the afternoon. "Henderson of the *Shanghai Mirror*?" he'd said. "Okay, reporters are on a priority list; you're on it. Go out to the airport. Give your name to the field station; we'll try and get you a seat."

"What will you do?" she asked Peter Essex. "Just stay here and wait for the end?"

"Not bloody likely," he said. "Haven't got the temperament. A group of us have rounded up a lorry. If we can't get a flight we're heading out to Repulse Bay to organize a defense. At least we'll be on the perimeter of the city, not the center. Maybe from Repulse Bay we can strike out on foot for the South. Anything's better than staying in Hong Kong waiting for the ax to fall. Or should I say the bayonet."

"It sounds good," said Amy.

"I expect we could make room for you in the lorry, if you'd like to come. The more the better, actually, if they're fit."

"Thanks," said Amy, "but I think I have other plans. Good luck."

"If you change your mind, we're over there on the edge of the tarmac."

He crunched away in the shadows.

The runway lights flashed on, then quickly blinked out as the plane took off, lumbering into the air with its heavy load. Amy was about to return to her notebook when she felt a clutching hand at her leg. She glanced down. A small blond boy was gazing up at her with wide eyes, illuminated by the beam of light from the window.

"Jimmy, come back here," said a young woman. She rushed to snatch him up. "I'm sorry, he doesn't understand what's going on," she said to Amy with an apologetic smile.

"That's okay," said Amy.

"Oh, are you American too?"

"Yes, but I live in Shanghai." *Did* live in Shanghai, Amy corrected herself silently.

"We live in the Philippines; my husband's stationed there. He's an army sergeant. He went back to Bataan a couple of days ago, and I stayed in Hong Kong to shop."

"You won't get back to the Philippines, I'm afraid."

"I know. I thought if we could get a flight to Chungking we could work our way back home from there. You know, home to the States. It would be important to Jim to know that Jimmy Junior was safe. But it doesn't look as if we'll make it. You need a special priority, I guess." The girl raised her head and hugged the child in her arms. "Listen."

They both heard a far-off engine drone.

"Here comes another plane," the girl said. "I don't suppose there'll be many more." Amy saw her raised profile in the sudden beam of light. She looked like a child herself.

"No," said Amy, "probably not. This may be the last one."

A shadowy figure approached out of the darkness. "I'm looking for Miss Henderson," said the voice belonging to the shape.

"I'm Miss Henderson," Amy replied.

"Final flight, Miss Henderson. We have a seat for you. Move fast, please, there isn't much time."

"I'm not going," said Amy. "This passenger is going instead. She'll hold the baby on her lap." She gave the girl a gentle push in the small of the back.

The runway landing lights flashed on, flashed off. The plane was touching down and taxiing to a stop.

"You sure?" the man said to Amy.

"I'm sure," Amy replied.

"Okay, then." He turned to the young mother. "Get a move on, lady, if you're coming."

"I—I—" The girl had no time to say anything else before being led away at a trot, clutching the baby. Then she paused and looked back for a moment. "Thank you," she called faintly across the shadows.

Amy smiled and waved. She realized when she had done it that she couldn't be seen. She closed her notebook and tucked it away in her bag. Well, that was that. Forget Chungking. Now what? After a moment's thought she decided to try and join forces with Andy.

CHAPTER 3

The mild weather of December 8 in Shanghai had turned to a thin fine drizzle by Tuesday morning. Double sentries were already posted at all the corners of the International Settlement. Japanese soldiers worked in the rain stretching military communication lines, one man walking ahead with a reel of wire on his back, the others behind him laying the wires from post to post.

Atop the Shanghai Municipal Building flapped the flag of the Rising Sun.

Japanese officers had taken over the police, and Japanese "supervisors" had assumed control of all the public utilities, the radio stations, and the newspapers.

Everything was efficient and orderly. It had been carefully planned and there were no disturbances.

The Americans, the British, and the Dutch awaited developments with a combination of rage and apprehension with fury uppermost. They considered the International Settlement their territory. They had been Lords of the East for so long—all their lives—that they could not adjust to these small yellow men strutting about giving orders. Taking over their property. Moving into their clubs. Drinking at the bar of the Shanghai Club. Outrage could go no further.

The Japanese smiled grimly to themselves and went on with their plans. They would learn.

Laura and Mike waited uneasily on Bubbling Well Road. The Gendarmerie had made no arrests yet; they were still organizing their headquarters, but the reprieve could not last much longer. Events were progressing at too even a pace.

"They figure we have no place to run," Mike remarked, lighting his third cigar of the morning. "They can come and get us at their leisure." He sighed and exhaled a cloud of smoke. "Jesus, Laura, you know what I wish I had right now?" She shook her head. "A very large whiskey and soda. I can practically taste it."

"Mike, for God's sake."

"Is there any more coffee in the kitchen?"

"I'll go and see." She rose, grateful for something to do.

David was in his own apartment building in the French Concession. He was ringing the doorbell of the apartment at the ground floor rear. His own apartment was on an upper floor. The ground floor rear had a back entrance leading to the garden. He needed to borrow it. If the Gendarmerie made an appearance and went upstairs to David's apartment, the man at the switchboard would buzz a warning to David after they'd entered the elevator. He would have a chance to escape through the garden.

This was only a temporary expedient; it would not suffice for long.

The tenant of the ground floor rear answered her bell, saying that her maid was out. She was an elderly Frenchwoman named Madame Renier. She was very rich and very old; David hoped she would not object to the apartment-switching idea.

He declined to enter at her invitation. He explained his request very swiftly as he stood in the hall. Would Madame Renier mind very much moving upstairs for a few days?

"It would only be for a short time," he said.

Madame Renier didn't answer. She regarded David thoughtfully. Then she said, "I know your mother, she is a most charming woman. Cultivated, with artistic taste. One can hardly believe she is American."

David concealed his impatience at her irrelevant remarks.

"Therefore," Madame Renier continued, "I will accede to your request."

David felt ashamed of himself.

"I will trust you to look after my possessions," she said. "I know I can depend on you to do so with care."

He could see beyond her into the apartment. He recognized some of the antiques; Aunt Julia had collected French furniture. Savonnerie carpets. French Empire clocks. Louis XVI porcelains.

Boulle writing desks. Aubusson tapestries. Lord, lord. It would be like living in a museum.

"You can trust me," he said. "I'll only stay for a little while and then make other arrangements and you can move back in."

Madame Renier's face changed. Concern moved across her features. "Not Bridge House, I hope," she whispered.

"Not if I can help it."

By three o'clock the Valentines were all together on Bubbling Well Road.

"After we're safe the chauffeur will come back and get as much stuff as he can," David told Laura and Mike. The Chinese chauffeur, Christopher Ho, was a trusted employee. "You won't need clothes. Maybe Dad's cigars . . . and Mother's jewelry—you'll certainly need that."

"I'll cram as much as I can into my handbag," Laura said.

"No," said David, "the sentries may search you on the bridge."

Laura flushed.

David explained more of what he had learned that morning from employees of the pottery works. The Gendarmerie was going to confiscate all automobiles, firearms, and radios and require that they be delivered to Gendarmerie headquarters personally by the owners. Receipts would be issued.

"Hah," said Mike shortly.

They would see to it that queues were long and slow-moving, David continued. They planned to take motion pictures of the frustrated and miserable people waiting in line, and then create newsreels.

"That should cheer them up in Yokohama," commented Mike.

"Anyway," David said, "we'll just be a little early fulfilling the order. We'll tell the sentries we were given advance notice at the Gendarmerie because they want the Packard."

The current Valentine automobile was a new black Packard sedan.

"Do you suppose the sentries know about this order?" asked Laura.

"I'm sure they do. They have instructions to snarl traffic as much as possible when the automobiles start crossing the bridge.

That way they can increase the misery." David paused. "Never mind about that. The important thing is to get over Soochow Creek and across the bridge to Chapei as Dad suggested."

Christopher Ho would chauffeur them in his uniform across the bridge. Once they were in Little Tokyo, he knew backstreet routes into the Chinese town.

Mike had made the suggestion moments before, with a meaningful glance at Laura.

"I know a place in Chapei where we might be able to stay," he had said. "It belongs to a woman called Li-san. I took care of her once when she needed help. I'm sure she'll do the same for us if she's still there. Besides—it's about time you met her, Laura. So you can see how silly you were once."

David had been a little confused by the conversation, but he had agreed that the area was the only hope; the Chinese town was a narrow impenetrable maze where humanity overflowed the alleys.

If anywhere was safe for the Valentines, it would be Chapei.

Amy had not been able to reach her brother. She had hitched a ride on Peter Essex's lorry at Hong Kong Airport, hoping to make her way to Andy's church if they dropped her off nearby. It had not been possible. The streets were barricaded, some littered with rubble from bombing, some blocked with trucks and vans carrying British soldiers and Hong Kong Volunteer Guards, some alive with police trying futilely to arrest looters who were running wild in the night. Amy and the others had wasted time driving around and around, taking detour after detour.

"Why don't you try it tomorrow?" shouted the lorry driver to Amy at last. "I'm driving back to Hong Kong for food supplies in the morning. It'll be easier in daylight."

"All right," Amy agreed wearily. "Let's get out to Repulse Bay."

The lorry left the city streets and they headed along a straight road to the beach; the resort area of Repulse Bay, where the beautiful and expensive Repulse Bay Hotel had always been a center of activities for the Hong Kong social set. The hotel, with its wide verandas and flowered lawns, faced the sea. It could be defended like a fortress, they agreed in the lorry. Surely the Japanese would attack from the sea.

The hotel manager, a brisk and competent woman named Miss Matheson, greeted them in her bathrobe and found them rooms in spite of the late hour and despite the fact that the hotel was crowded. Others had had the fortress-on-the-sea idea.

In the morning they all discovered how wrong they'd been.

They were surrounded by snipers. The Japanese had not come in from the west by sea. They had crept through the mountains and ravines of the east during the early dawn. Now the road was cut off. Rifle fire cracked and whined all around them. The riflemen were invisible in the surrounding underbrush. They were wearing netting in their helmets stuck with twigs and foliage.

"I'm sorry, old girl," Peter Essex whispered to Amy as they peered through the dining room window, crouching by the windowsill. "You won't get to Hong Kong now, I'm afraid. They've outwitted us. We're worse off here than in the city."

"I should have known," Amy muttered. "They're trained, experienced soldiers. They've had four years of fighting in China, they're seasoned troops, and we're just a bunch of civilians."

"Out of the frying pan," said Peter.

"I hope we're not going to surrender without a fight, though," said Amy. "We still have possession of the hotel. We can hold them off for a little while, surely?"

"That's the ticket," said Peter Essex. "We have plenty of ammunition and rifles and grenades and even a couple of machine guns. That beach road is important. It leads to the army post on Stanley Peninsula." He looked pale. His face was drawn. "If only they'd come by sea, we'd have been waiting for them."

Amy sat back on her heels and smiled tiredly. "Can you show me how to use a rifle, Peter? I'm pretty good at changing a typewriter ribbon, but guns are a little out of my line."

"You'll be all right, old girl." They stared bleakly at one another. "We all will," he added in a stout voice.

Neither of them believed it.

The black Packard sedan was ready in the driveway on Bubbling Well Road. The chauffeur sat behind the wheel. Laura and

Mike climbed into the backseat. David opened the front door on the passenger side.

"You'd better get in back, David," Mike warned. "It will look better."

"Yes, you're right." David shrugged, angry at himself. "You're the only one thinking straight around here."

He got into the backseat next to Laura.

Christopher Ho turned the ignition key and started the car. Laura glanced back once at the house. Then she looked away determinedly. She would not be Lot's wife. She could not turn into a pillar of salt. Mike needed her.

She felt his hand warm over hers and they linked fingers. They sat in silence.

The Packard began to roll through the streets of the International Settlement.

How strange to see no one on the streets except men in Japanese uniforms, thought Laura.

I wonder who is sitting in my office at this very moment, thought David. *In my swivel chair. At my desk.*

Those bastards never even warned us, thought Mike.

They were approaching the bridge over Soochow Creek. They rolled a few feet onto the bridge. The sentry halted them with an upraised hand. He walked over. Christopher Ho wound down the window.

Only a few yards now. They could see the other side.

I have crossed this bridge a hundred times, thought Laura. *When we lived in Chapei. And never thought twice.*

I have crossed this bridge a thousand times, thought Christopher Ho. *My hands never sweated before.*

He's only a son-of-a-bitching kid, thought Mike, glancing at the sentry. *Eighteen years old at the most.*

Dad, control yourself, thought David. *Don't say a word. Don't move.*

The sentry gestured at Christopher Ho, asking for a pass. Everyone needed a pass to cross the bridge. The Valentines didn't have one.

Christopher Ho explained their errand in Chinese, informing the sentry why they didn't require a pass. The sentry looked blank. He didn't understand Chinese. Nor did he understand English.

He spoke only Japanese. He wanted a pass. No pass? They couldn't cross. He gestured to Christopher Ho to back up.

Why hadn't they thought of this? Mike asked himself desperately. Such a dumb, stupid obstacle. He pointed to the other sentry at the far end of the bridge. Get him over here. Maybe he could speak English or Chinese.

The Japanese boy understood the gesture but he looked stubborn. This was his responsibility, his decision. Back up.

The chauffeur sat equally obstinate. No. Get the other man.

The sentry, losing his temper, reached through the window to turn on the ignition himself. Christopher Ho pulled out the ignition key and stuck it in his pocket.

Impasse.

The sentry stepped back, squared his shoulders, and raised his rifle. He spoke a short sentence in Japanese. No need for translation. Back up or I'll shoot.

No one in the Packard moved a muscle.

Shoot us now and get it over with, thought Laura, closing her eyes. *It will solve all our problems.* She was instantly ashamed of herself. *The chauffeur didn't have to die.*

She opened her eyes, hearing a new voice, older and deeper. The other sentry had come over to investigate the problem. He ordered the first sentry to change posts with him. The youth moved sullenly to the far end of the bridge.

The new sentry understood Chinese. He listened impassively.

Keeping-the-face-like-wood, David thought. It was a Japanese technique.

The chauffeur was explaining in slow, clear language why they wished to cross the bridge. Mike was concentrating on remaining calm. He considered lighting a cigar and decided against it. The idea was to appear firm but not cocky.

Sons of bitches. Treacherous bastards.

Keep cool. Easy does it.

The sentry was going to make them sweat it out, Mike observed. He was strolling back and forth, occasionally pausing to look up at the sky. Asking advice from heaven? Mike wondered.

Finally the sentry strolled back to the Packard. He jerked his thumb. Forward, across the bridge. They could continue. After all, what lay ahead but Hunkow, Little Tokyo?

Christopher Ho took the ignition key out of his pocket and started the car. They rolled forward across Soochow Creek.

Ten minutes later after byzantine twists and turns through the back streets of Hunkow with everyone drenched in nervous sweat, they were negotiating the narrow alleys of Chapei. Laura sank back against the seat. Only the first danger was past.

"I'm too old for this," she whispered.

"It's just the beginning," said David somberly. "The problem now is survival."

For the first time Laura was able to think of the strange meeting that lay ahead.

She was about to meet Li-san. Finally, after all these decades. Her ancient rival. The beautiful young woman in the silken robe who had been speaking to Mike on the bridge. The woman he had been supporting all these years. Laura could not imagine what it would be like to confront that woman face to face. And in circumstances of such humiliation. How would she, Laura, be able to comport herself?

She wondered miserably what thoughts were passing through Mike's mind.

Mike was not thinking of Li-san at all. He was thinking about the war. How long it would be before the enemy was defeated. How long it would take for America to mobilize and fight back. How long to end it? A year? Two years?

And did Amy get out of Hong Kong? He knew Laura was trying to suppress that terrifying question in her own mind.

Amy and . . . Mike groaned to himself. *Amy's brother . . .*

"I am Loo Li-san," said the soft Chinese voice after Mike had explained their situation. "Welcome to my house in this time of great trouble. May it be a shelter from those who wish to harm you." She bowed.

Tears came into Laura's eyes. This careworn woman with the soft dark eyes and gentle voice, this elderly woman with the compassionate mouth, this stocky figure in her peasant tunic and trousers—was this Laura's dangerous rival? What blind foolishness.

"I am Laura Valentine," she said. She extended her hand.

Li-san took it hesitantly, with as much anxiety and fear, Laura saw, as she had been feeling herself.

"I want you to know—" Laura began. Then she stopped. The tears in her eyes spilled over and rolled down her cheeks. "How kind you are to do this," she said brokenly. "How very kind."

"I am happy to assist you," Li-san whispered back. She raised her eyes and smiled timidly at Laura. "Do not be ashamed to accept help. Sometimes it is a mark of strength. Sometimes women comprehend that better than men."

They gazed at one another in understanding.

"I will try to be as courageous as you," Laura said after a moment. "You must aid me."

"There is terrible danger," Li-san replied. "Honorable Mrs. Valentine, I will aid you in any way I can." She bowed as Laura thanked her.

David wondered again who this woman was who was being so kind to them.

"Mother," he said in a low voice to Laura a few minutes later, "who is she?"

"Just an old friend of your father's," Laura replied simply, looking at Li-san.

CHAPTER 4

Amy slumped wearily to the floor in the east wing of the Repulse Bay Hotel. Peter Essex dropped down beside her, holding his rifle. They were by the French windows on the second floor of the hotel. The once elegant resort was a grimy wreck from veranda to roof. It was the morning of December 22 and the occupants had been besieged for two weeks. They were running out of food and water and they were sleeping in snatches. Air raids never ceased.

Amy, sitting with her back to the wall, began to laugh.

"What's so funny?" Peter asked her.

"I was just thinking that it's three days before Christmas."

"Best joke I've heard all day."

"And I promised my grandparents I'd be home in Shanghai for the holidays."

"Even more of a thigh slapper."

Amy kept on laughing. "Oh, Peter, do you suppose I'll make it home for Christmas?"

He sighed. "Now listen, Amy old girl, don't go round the bend. The only two sane people left in this place are thee and me."

"And sometimes I wonder about thee," Amy finished.

They were no longer defending the hotel alone. British soldiers of the Middlesex Regiment had arrived from Stanley Post to protect the beach road. Now some of the soldiers were dug into pillboxes on the hillside, trying to hold off the Japanese approach. Others manned machine guns by the roadside.

Japanese snipers, however, continued to creep through the hillside brush. The rifle and machine-gun fire went on and on, back and forth, with the hotel caught in the center. People inside were living on canned goods, supplemented with extra supplies brought in by the soldiers.

They had no doctors. The wounded were lying on cots in the main-floor lounge. Amy had managed to reach Stanley Post by telephone a few days before. She had spoken to a weary-sounding major.

"We have critically wounded men here, and we have no doctors!"

"Sorry, all our doctors are on twenty-four-hour duty."

"Can't you even send one?" she'd cried.

"Sorry, we can't spare anyone."

They were forced to listen to the piteous groans of injured men and rip up sheets for bandages. There was little else they could do.

Back and forth went the gunfire.

Amy and Peter had taken spyglass duty. One of the hotel

residents owned a spyglass with which he'd watched sailboats on the bay from the veranda in happier days. Now Amy used it to look out at the lawn from the front door, trying to spot a Japanese sniper wriggling through the grass. Very often she did. Peter would take aim with his rifle to drive him away. So far none of the snipers had reached the veranda.

They were both off duty now and had come to the east wing to rest.

"Would you like a cigarette?" asked Amy.

"Yes, thanks."

"I wonder if our cigarette supply will give out before we will."

"I'm afraid not," said Peter. "It's just a matter of time. It won't be long now."

They smoked in silence.

"Those poor devils downstairs in the lounge," Peter said after a while. "Begging to die."

Amy had no answer for that.

From outside came an unfamiliar crumping noise. They both alerted.

"Got the spyglass?" asked Peter.

"Right here beside me."

"Sounds as if someone's established a mortar on the hillside." He paused. "Ours or theirs?"

"We'd better take a look," Amy said. She started to rise.

"I'll do it," said Peter. "You finish your cigarette."

"Put your helmet on, Peter."

They had all been issued steel helmets and wore them before opening doors or windows. Peter put his helmet on and went to the window holding the spyglass. He opened the window, raised the spyglass, and peered out.

A shell looped directly onto the roof of the east wing where he was standing. Simultaneously a sniper's rifle cracked. Huge chunks of the roof crashed to the floor. Amy, crouching, flung up her arms to protect her head. Wreckage settled. Dust swirled. Amy moved her arms and legs, discovered she was unhurt, then cried, "Peter, are you all right?"

She heard no answer. Then a faint voice replied, "Still got my helmet on."

Hugely relieved, she crawled toward him. He was lying on his back on the floor, covered with rubble, and he did have his helmet on.

"Get out of that dust, Peter," she said jokingly, "we don't have any bathwater to wash it off."

"Sorry old girl, I'm afraid I can't move."

Her relief turned to fear. She scrabbled at the wreckage with her hands until she got him clear. Then she settled on her heels, fear turning to despair.

It had not been the shell but the rifle bullet. He had been hit in the abdomen. The wound oozed dark-red blood. Amy felt sick. She'd seen that kind of wound before.

"We'll get you downstairs to a cot," she said. "I'll go for help."

"Yes, and tell them the position of that mortar. On the northeast slope of the hill." Peter tried to smile. "I guess it's theirs all right."

Amy tried to smile back. "I guess it is." She began to crawl away.

"Amy," Peter called.

She turned.

"Carry on, old girl. I won't make it, you know."

She started to reassure him and say that was nonsense, of course he would, but the words wouldn't get past her throat. It was too late for lies. She made an effort not to cry. It was too late for that too.

"I'll carry on," she said thickly.

She was afraid that Peter no longer heard her.

David was leaving Shanghai. The apartment of Madame Renier in the French Concession was too dangerous a place to remain, and Li-san's small flat was too tiny to accommodate four. He could not jeopardize another Chapei resident by asking for shelter. There was only one alternative.

He must make his way to Chungking.

Others had set out on the dangerous journey to Chungking, using one mode of travel after another as they went, sometimes on foot, other times by train or on a farm cart, slipping through the Japanese lines and up the Yangtze valley to the Chinese interior. Only the strong and healthy could attempt it. David spoke Chinese; that would help him.

He would disguise himself as a Chinese peasant wearing a padded tunic and wide straw hat. He would have to remember to keep his eyes lowered and his face hidden by the hat brim.

Mike went into the small back garden of Li-san's house on the morning of his son's departure. Laura, seeing the stony anguish on his face, wanted to go after him. David stopped her with a hand on her arm.

"No, Mother, leave him alone. I don't think he wants to speak to you now."

"He feels so powerless, so . . . shackled. We are trapped here while you are going off into God knows what, but at least you are attempting something. . . ."

"That's why."

"He could never survive a journey like that. Nor could I. We must stay here. David, let me explain."

"Mother, he knows it."

"I suppose you're right. It's so difficult to know what to do." Laura covered her face with her hands. "I can't think clearly. What has happened to the twins in Hong Kong? What will happen to you on the way to Chungking? David, how will your father and I bear this?"

"You will, Mother. We all will. We'll have a reunion in Shanghai someday, and move back to the house on Bubbling Well Road and reopen the pottery works and resume our lives, and everything will be just the way it was."

"Nothing can be just the way it was." Laura raised her face. "Do you suppose that is how it was meant to be?" she asked in a trembling voice. "We can never go back. Everything must change. The wheel of life must turn and turn."

"I'm no philosopher. I can't give you an answer."

"Oh, darling, just be safe. Live through this. Come back to us, and we'll try to wait and survive."

David stood with his straw hat in his hands. He wore his blue Chinese tunic, and his face was stained an unfamiliar brown. His fair hair was dyed black. But his eyes, thought Laura, were David's eyes.

He was thirty-seven years old, she thought. He had been born only a few months after they had moved to Shanghai from Weichang. Now he was leaving, and when would she see him again? *Mrs. Valentine you have a son,* said a long-forgotten voice in her memory. A hospital nurse? When he had left, she would have nothing but the rags of courage. She must cling to them, for herself and for Mike.

David went out to the garden to say good-bye to his father. There was no grass on the small plot of land, only brown earth. Mike sat on a splintery wooden bench under a tree.

"Dad," said David softly, "I'm leaving now."

Mike glanced up. "I have half a mind to come with you."

"Somebody's got to stay and look after the women."

Mike grinned crookedly. "Sure," he said, "that's one way to put it."

"Hell, it's the truth."

"It's horseshit, son, and you know it. I'm an old man and I'd never last the course."

"Okay," said David, "you're tough enough to face facts. You wouldn't make it to Chungking. So what? I'll be an old man someday, too, if I'm lucky. Then I'll sit on a bench and watch the young guys break their necks. Today it's your turn. Just be here when I get back, because I'd kind of miss you if you weren't."

Mike laughed. "Think you'll get to Chungking and back?"

"They can't kill me; I'm too stubborn." He put on his straw hat and tilted it over his eyes. "See you after the war, Dad. I'll bring you a present from Chungking. A big kiss from Madame Chiang Kai-shek."

"Just bring yourself," Mike said, suddenly somber, revealing the bleakness of his mood. "That will be enough."

In the main-floor lounge of the Repulse Bay Hotel the improvised hospital was abandoned. The cots for the wounded were empty. On the veranda lay discarded ammunition belts and useless rifles.

The siege was ended. All the British soldiers had surrendered to the Japanese hours before. They had been marched away down the road. Now it was dark, and an eerie quiet surrounded the hotel.

The civilians remained within. They had no electricity. Some lay on their beds in the darkness of their upstairs rooms. A small group of men and women sat in a circle around flickering candles on the floor of the lounge. Amy, her face white and strained in the candlelight, was one of the group.

"Shall we go out and hoist a white flag?" someone asked hoarsely.

"Is anyone out there?" said another. "It's so horribly quiet."

"Listen," said Amy.

A dog barked outside. A rifle cracked, and the bark changed to an agonized yip, then ceased.

"They're out there," said a grim voice. "The snipers are there."

"No white flag," said Amy. "It's too risky, going outside. They may shoot us on sight. Like the dog."

"What then?" asked another. "Wait till they come and get us?"

"I can't wait that long," Amy said desperately. "This is deliberate. They're trying to drive us crazy."

"And succeeding," someone muttered. A candle hissed and died, making them all jump.

Amy sprang to her feet.

"Where are you going?" a man demanded.

"Just to the door. Put the candles out."

She went to the dark door leading to the veranda. She opened it a little and shouted into the ominous waiting blackness.

"There are no soldiers here! Only civilians! No soldiers! No soldiers! All the soldiers are gone!"

Rustle of trees. Lap of water.

"No soldiers!" Amy cried. "No soldiers!" Her voice echoed in the night.

No answer. *They were there*.

Amy closed the door and returned to the circle on the floor. Someone relit a candle. They waited.

The door opened very, very quietly and only a fraction. A bayonet slid through, head high. Seconds later another bayonet appeared, knee high.

Two Japanese soldiers leaped into the room, both crouching, holding the bayonets.

"Up! Up!" one of them screamed. "All up!"

The members of the group struggled to their feet.

"Hands high! Above heads!"

Arms rose into the air.

"Keep hands up! Do not lower hands!"

The group stood with raised hands as the two soldiers trotted around them in a circle, still crouching. Amy felt her arms and shoulders aching while the inspection went on and on.

Finally they were allowed to go upstairs and collect their possessions. Everyone, they were told, would be required to appear at sunup on the front lawn.

"What will they do with us?" a woman whispered to Amy as they mounted the stairs.

"Take us to an internment camp, I suppose," Amy said wearily. "We'll find out in the morning."

At sunup on the front lawn, before the wrecked hotel, they were forced to form a line and hand over their jewelry and watches. A Japanese officer halted before Amy. He reached into the sack of her belongings which was at her feet and yanked out the spyglass. He glared at it with fury, then broke it over his knee and hurled it to the ground before moving on.

At last the process was finished. Another officer stood in front of them and made an announcement.

"You will now march to Victoria Harbor. We have no trucks. You will go on foot. Back trails will be followed. No one must fall behind."

It was twelve miles to Victoria Harbor by the back-trail route. Some of the group were elderly. It did not matter.

In a straggling line the survivors of the Repulse Bay siege began their trudge to captivity.

CHAPTER 5

They were the years of war. From Pearl Harbor to Hiroshima, four years of anxiety, tension, fear, death, bravery, cowardice, and boredom. Was it another world war—or the same war as 1918, continued after an intermission? The days of the historian were still to come.

David reached Chungking in 1942, after a long and weary journey. Eventually he went to work on General Wedemeyer's staff, handling liaison and personnel as a civilian employee. And he worried about Shanghai.

Once every six months or so a letter reached him from Shanghai, smuggled through the Japanese lines. His parents were still alive. He learned that Amy was in prison camp in Hong Kong; she had sent word through the International Red Cross to her aunt Julia in America, who had written to David in Chungking, who had sent word to Laura and Mike in Chapei. There was no news of Andy.

The years of the European Theater. The years of North Africa. The years of the Pacific. The years of strategy and invasion, bombing raids and beachheads and Four Power Conferences. The years of concentration camps and internment camps. The years of hope and despair. No one would ever forget them; no one who had lived through them would ever be able to erase them from memory.

For Laura and Mike they were blurred, strange times. Their universe narrowed to the roof and walls of Li-san's little house in Chapei, and the open sky over Li-san's back garden. The gray-misted sky of Shanghai's winter, the heat-dazzled sky of summer, the thick rain-dark sky of early spring, the bright blue sky of early autumn. The same patch of sky, changing with the seasons, how well they knew it, Laura thought with a combination of weariness and numb surprise. She was worn down and yet sometimes she was hopeful. The war would end. Surely it would end.

They ventured outside onto the street to watch the Chinese New Year celebration as 1942 changed to 1943. Firecrackers and lanterns and a snaking parade; no one paid attention to Li-san's "relatives." Those who knew the secret, those who were trusted neighbors, kept it to themselves; there were informers even in Chapei.

When the weather became fine, Laura and Mike spent most of their time in the garden. Li-san kept her job at the cotton mill, and so Laura and Mike were alone most of the day. Li-san saw to it that they had books to read. Laura planted a patch of vegetables in the yard and raised tomatoes and cucumbers. Mike struck up an acquaintance with the old man in the next yard. He taught Mike to whittle, bringing him a supply of wood and a knife, and after a while a Noah's ark of little animals appeared in Li-san's house.

The months passed.

Amy's existence was bounded by walls and barbed-wire fences. Twice a day, in the morning and the evening, the prisoners in the Hong Kong internment camp were lined up in the exercise yard and counted. They were all thin and sickly, for the food was poor. Sentries stood in watchtowers around the walls, guarding them with guns and bayonets, observing them with field glasses.

They had been obliged to sign a paper upon arrival, pledging not to try to escape, or to do anything against Japan. If they did so, they would be shot.

The prisoners governed themselves, forming their own camp administration. This was by order of the camp commandant, Colonel Tsubaki. Amy wore an armband designating her chief of the Women's Sanitation Department.

The prison was actually a set of former tobacco warehouses near the waterfront converted into living quarters by plywood partitions and canvas-and-iron cots. Each prisoner was assigned a tiny, individual room.

On the Fourth of July, 1942, the American prisoners organized a softball game in the exercise yard. The sentries and the officers, including Colonel Tsubaki, observed through field glasses.

They played a doubleheader in 1942. The next summer no one was healthy enough to endure two games. Their energy was exhausted after one.

The days passed and the months passed. The war dragged on.

Will there ever be another life? thought Laura. She sat back on her heels in the patch of garden in Shanghai and wiped her face with her arm beneath the wide straw hat she was wearing. She had an unbearable longing to see Amy and Andy, hear their voices, embrace David, look into his eyes, return to a time when they were all together. A Thanksgiving dinner on Bubbling Well Road. A Fourth of July party when the twins were small. This was a bad day, she thought. Please God it would pass, as everything did.

Mike was sitting on the back steps in the sunshine. He was not whittling or reading or even making conversation. He was simply sitting. He was brooding about something, Laura thought, for he had an inward expression on his face. He had grown much calmer in the past year and much more thoughtful. He seldom lost his temper now or raised his voice. He had not been ill, although she and Li-san had both had the flu during the winter. So it was not poor health, she thought. Something else. This strange, isolated, solitary existence? Perhaps it did queer things to a person's mind. Laura suddenly felt worried.

"Mike," she said, "do you want to talk?"

"If you do."

"I just thought you seemed lonely."

"No, I'm not lonely."

"But something is wrong. Isn't it?"

"Not exactly."

She gazed at him helplessly.

"Laura," he said, "I have been doing a lot of thinking in the past year. About myself and my life."

She didn't say anything, wanting him to go on.

There was a long pause. Then, "Laura," he said, "I was wrong."

"About what, Mike?"

He didn't answer directly. "It's been hard for me to admit that to myself. I guess I can be a stubborn son of a bitch from time to time.''

"I won't deny that."

He smiled faintly. "I've had a lot of time to think things over, and it's pretty clear to me that I was wrong. I only hope to God it's not too late to make amends."

Tears came into Laura's eyes. She knew now what he meant. "You're speaking of Andy."

Mike nodded. "Yes, Andy, and two other people who probably died a long time ago, God rest their souls. It's too late now to make it up to them—it all happened fifty years ago—but if Andy is still alive . . . Dear lord, what I wouldn't give to tell him I am sorry."

Laura bowed her head. "He would be so happy," she murmured. "He was never angry with you, Mike. Never."

"I think about him all the time."

"Maybe he knows it. Somewhere."

Mike raised his face to the sun. "Do you suppose there's a purpose to all this, Laura? What do you think?"

"I think there may be," she answered quietly.

"When I see Andy," Mike said, "I will ask him."

From far away, on the other side of the city, came the deep tones of the clock on the Shanghai Customs Tower, striking noon.

In the Hong Kong internment camp there was a shed containing a battery of seven showers. This building was known as "the baths." The Japanese had supplied the building materials and the showers had been constructed by local labor. The "baths" were open twelve hours a day. Women were lined up, this late spring afternoon of 1944, in a huddled queue, all wearing wooden clogs on their feet, waiting for a turn at the showers.

Amy, however, was in the office of the camp commandant, Colonel Tsubaki. The commandant was seated behind his desk, gnawing on a corner of his thumb and contemplating Amy. She stood on the other side of the desk wearing her prison smock, her red hair, grown long, tied back from her face with a length of ribbon. Her cheekbones were prominent in her gaunt face; her green eyes were blazing like emeralds. She was angry. She was representing the Internees Grievance Committee.

Colonel Tsubaki, a well-built man in his late forties who spoke passable English, stopped gnawing his thumb and glared up at Amy.

"Miss Hen-dra-son, you are not a good prisoner."

"I am not here to be a good prisoner, Commandant. I am here to defend the needs of the internees."

"We are aware of your needs."

"Then do something." Amy leaned forward across the desk. "The food is inedible. We cannot live on buffalo meat and dried fish."

"We give you rice and vegetables."

"Not enough! We need milk and fruit and cheese. . . . People are suffering with vitamin deficiencies. . . . You feed us like animals. . . ."

"Miss Hen-dra-son! We do the best we can!"

"It is not good enough, Commandant!"

The colonel rose to his feet. "You are impossible!" he said through his teeth.

"I am doing my duty for the prisoners!"

"I too!"

"You are starving us!"

The colonel banged the flat of his hand on the table. "You are eating," he suddenly shouted, "better than Japanese soldiers in the field!"

Amy's eyes widened. She stared at the colonel in silence. Then she said quietly, "Is that true?"

The colonel sat down again. He gave a weary sigh. "I will see about more vegetables," he muttered, and shuffled some papers on the desk. "Perhaps powdered milk. Fruit will be out of the question."

Amy stood thinking. He had given her a clue as to the progress of the war. The prisoners were starved for more than food; they were starved for news. They were allowed only one newspaper, a Japanese-controlled Hong Kong daily that told only of Japanese victories. The paper's favorite headline read, NIPPON'S WILD EAGLES SMASH AMERICANS.

Now Colonel Tsubaki had given her a hint that all was not

going well for Japan. If the troops were living on short rations
. . . She tucked the information away in her mind to repeat at
dinner.

She returned to her agenda. "We need a new priest, Commandant," she said. "Since Father Malloy was repatriated, the
Catholics have had no services."

"Yes, yes, I know." Colonel Tsubaki lit a cigarette. He
glanced up and caught Amy staring hungrily at the smoke. He
sighed again and pushed the cigarette pack across the desk.
"Take one and go," he said. "You have ruined my morning.
You are the worst prisoner in the camp."

"Repatriate me. Send me home."

"Not possible. You are classified as a dangerous enemy of
Japan. How many times must I tell you?"

She knew that. She went back to the former subject as she
groped for a match in her smock pocket. "What about the
priest?"

"The Catholics will have a new priest; he is being sent from
another camp." Colonel Tsubaki leaned back, puffing on his
cigarette. "Are you satisfied? Now will you go?"

"Yes. Thank you, Commandant." Amy performed her ritual
little half-bow and left the office.

CHAPTER 6

The Japanese were conducting their usual military ceremonies at
the internment camp. They lined up in the exercise yard facing
Tokyo and the Emperor. Bugles blew as the commanding officer
began his inspection. There was the customary bowing and click-
ing of heels and standing at attention. Some of the prisoners,
Amy among them, watched from an upper window of their
building, to relieve the tedium more than anything else.

A conversation went on behind Amy. She listened absentmindedly as she watched the familiar ceremony in the yard below.

"We were supposed to have a new priest," said one man, "but I understand he was taken to a hospital instead of coming here."

"A prison infirmary, you mean?"

"No, a municipal hospital in Hong Kong. He was bayoneted in the leg, trying to protect an old man from being beaten by a guard." The speaker paused. "At least Tsubaki isn't a sadist; he doesn't order beatings. We can be grateful for that, at any rate. Things could be worse. They are at other camps."

"What will happen to the priest?"

"They say he may lose his leg. If he lives. You know how infection spreads in these places. No one's healthy."

"God."

The first speaker turned to Amy. "His name is the same as yours, Amy," he remarked. "Maybe he's a relative? Father Henderson?"

Amy grasped the windowsill with straining knuckles. Her face whitened. She couldn't answer.

"But you're not Catholic," the man went on. "So I guess not."

"He is . . . my brother Andy," Amy whispered after a moment. She bowed her head, feeling faint. *They say he may lose his leg.*

After all this time! Three years without a word! Andy!

If he lives . . . you know how infection spreads. . . .

She went again to the commandant's office.

"Please, Colonel Tsubaki!" she cried. "Please! Father Henderson is my brother. I haven't seen him since December of 1941! Please let me visit him in the hospital!"

"It is against the rules to let you leave the prison grounds."

"If I were ill, you'd let me go to the hospital!"

"Seriously ill. You are not ill at all."

"I will be, if I have to!"

"What would that accomplish? You would be guarded in the hospital ward like a prisoner."

"Then send a guard with me as an escort, so I can visit my brother!"

"Do you think I have nothing better to do with my soldiers than send them junketing about on errands of mercy?"

"Please, Commandant! Please!"

They stared at one another, Amy standing, twisting her fingers together, the colonel sitting behind his desk, drawing deeply on a cigarette.

"I will be a model prisoner from now on," Amy whispered, "if you grant this request. I give you my word."

"You will cease to plague my life?"

"Yes."

"You will not come bursting in here day after day with impossible demands?"

"No."

The commandant was silent. Then he murmured, "I cannot imagine what that will be like, Miss Hen-dra-son." He shrugged and waved a dismissing hand. "Very well. I will order a guard to escort you to the hospital."

Amy's face was radiant. "Thank you, Commandant."

"I suppose I have made worse bargains," he said dryly.

"There was a time," Laura said to Li-san in the kitchen of the little house in Chapei as they prepared the evening meal, "when I thought you were my enemy." They were speaking Chinese, so that Laura could stay in practice.

"Yes? But you did not know me," answered Li-san.

"I was jealous. What a foolish emotion."

"Exceedingly foolish," agreed Li-san.

"My granddaughter Amy once confessed she was jealous of a woman she had never met," Laura continued. "But she recovered from her folly by thinking of me, and how I would behave, and concluded that I, her grandmother, would never be so stupid."

Li-san laughed. "Of course you did not correct her."

"I believe I did not," Laura said thoughtfully.

"It is not always the path of wisdom to reveal unpleasant truths."

"I am just beginning to learn that," said Laura. "It is taking me a very long time. I am sixty-six."

"May you live to be a hundred," Li-san said piously, "and attain the mountaintop of wisdom."

"I think that mountaintop is out of reach," said Laura. "At least for me, in this life."

Li-san patted her on the arm as she passed by. "We will keep climbing, you and I," she said with a mischievous smile on her lips.

Andy was dimly aware of where he was. A hospital ward somewhere in Hong Kong. He could hear sounds. Rubber soles padding on the floor. A clatter of metal instruments. Someone groaning in another bed. Why was he here? Something was wrong with him. He was shivering and burning at the same time. He was lying on his back in a hospital bed, and somewhere far away in the region of his leg there was pain.

A glittering silver bayonet flashing in the sun. Terrible pain. Blood.

When was that?

Yesterday. Last week. That guard had been beating Mr. Tarbush. That hadn't been right. Somebody'd had to stop him. The guard must have had a bayonet and he must have used it. *On me.*

Andy hoped Mr. Tarbush was okay. Such an irascible, outspoken little man, a defender of prisoners' rights; such a peppery little guy with that fringe of reddish-silver hair around his head. If he hadn't lost his hair, Andy thought with a dreamy smile, he'd be a pint-sized version of Grandpa. Always ready to take a poke at somebody.

He thought of Grandpa teaching him to box, a million years ago in Shanghai.

"Jab with your left. Your left, Andy, your left! Keep that right hand cocked in front of your face! Don't throw your right until you're sure you'll connect! Keep it up to protect your face! Keep jabbing with the left, Andy, and keep moving! Don't stand still or I'll pop you one . . . like this . . . you dropped your right, kid, try it again. . . ."

Oh, Grandpa, I never really learned. I tried, though. . . .

He thought of Petrushka, so beautiful and confused and unhappy. . . . *I'm sorry, Petrushka; why couldn't I have saved you? I did love you but it wasn't enough. . . .*

He still had a scar on his arm, a reminder of the first night he'd spent at Eve's Apple. Now there would be another on his leg. Or would there? Maybe he wouldn't have a leg. Then there wouldn't be a scar.

Hello, Pollyanna, he whispered to himself. He realized he was feverish and delirious. It wasn't so bad to be delirious. Now that he'd stopped shivering and his teeth had stopped chattering. He . . . floated and burned.

Maybe he would die. Not frightening. Death was not an end but a beginning. Still, he felt he had a lot more to accomplish before he died. He wanted to do so many things. . . . And he would like, Andy thought, to see Grandpa just once more. Grandpa . . . and Grandmother . . . Amy and Henry and Uncle David . . .

"Andy," said a soft voice above him.

He opened his eyes.

"Oh, Andy, it's really you! I almost didn't believe it!"

His sister's face was floating above him, looking thin and pale and incredibly happy and beautiful. Two Japanese soldiers with guns stood behind her.

"Amy," he said, and smiled. It was all he could manage. "Amy."

There was a confused time for a while, as they struggled with emotions and greetings. Then Amy dropped to her knees beside the bed. She placed her palm on Andy's forehead. "You're burning up."

"Tetanus, I think."

"Andy, are you strong enough to hear the truth?"

He nodded.

"They say your leg will have to come off above the knee."

He licked his parched lips with the tip of his tongue. "Okay," he said.

"Is it okay? You won't just give up and die?"

He shook his head.

"I wouldn't if I were in your place," Amy said seriously.

"I won't either."

"We haven't had a chance to talk, Andy . . . and I have so much to tell you. . . ."

"I won't die. I don't think heaven is ready for me yet."

"It's not. Oh, it's not. . . ."

After a while Andy made an effort to sit up and speak. "I

would have written . . . but the camp commandant wouldn't allow letters . . . Red Cross . . .''

"Never mind. You're coming to our camp. Colonel Tsubaki isn't so bad; he's our commandant. He's allowing me to visit you at the hospital.''

"Do you think the people at your camp . . . will object . . . to a one-legged priest?''

"If anybody objects," Amy said, swallowing hard, "I'll sock him right in the kisser.''

Andy smiled and closed his eyes. "That makes me feel a whole lot better,'' he said, and rested his head against the pillow.

CHAPTER 7

The Second World War was over. Laura and Mike Valentine emerged from the streets of Chapei blinking and bewildered. This was their city. Shanghai. Once more they could cross the bridge over Soochow Creek. Once more they could return to their house on Bubbling Well Road—empty, dirty, full of broken furniture and soiled linen, denuded of treasures, the valuables stripped, the wallpaper hanging in rags, the curtains torn, but theirs, the walls still standing, the ceilings intact, the front driveway just the same. . . . The pottery works, the galleries: they had to put their lives together like the pieces of a broken vase.

Shanghai, Mike thought. *My God, Shanghai.* It had been there all along, while he and Laura sheltered in Chapei. But had it been like this? He didn't remember it like this. The skyscrapers on the Bund padlocked and empty. The streets silent. The air clear, free of industrial smoke. The factories quiet. The clamor stilled, even the cries of the street peddlers gone from the alleys. The traffic vanished except for a few rickshaw men pad-padding along the roads, their footsteps strangely resonant in the quiet. What city was this?

Shanghai, thought Laura. *I do not know it.* Where was the glare of neon against the night sky, lighting up the horizon for miles across the flat marshes? Where was the throb of jazz music? What of the harbor with its bustling wharves and crammed shipping and shouts of stevedores along the jetties? *Empty.* Only an occasional junk bobbed in the lapping water. The river could have been a remote stream of inland China . . . not the Whangpoo. And the city. The streets. Where was the rush-hour traffic, where were the crowded trams, the chattering shopgirls, and the overflowing restaurants?

Gone with the Japanese army.

Surely this was a new Shanghai, and perhaps a new China, and the old might never return. . . .

The war was over. Amy, in Hong Kong, said good-bye to Colonel Tsubaki in his office at the prison camp, where he was completing his last administrative duties. The camp was a prison no longer. Amy was free. She wore her own clothes, tightly belted at the waist to gather up the excess folds of cloth that hung about her.

"You must gain weight, Miss Hen-dra-son," Colonel Tsubaki observed, "now that you are returning to your normal life." He stood erect and square-shouldered behind his desk. He no longer wore his sword.

"It is first on my list of activities, Colonel, I can assure you. I am dreaming of a certain restaurant on the Avenue Joffre." Amy paused before she inquired, "And what of you? Will you return to your wife and children in Osaka?"

"Yes," replied the colonel.

"What then? What will you do?"

"I do not know. I am a professional soldier in a country which no longer has an army."

"There will be a place for your skills at home, I'm sure. You are an administrator as well as a soldier."

Colonel Tsubaki shrugged.

"If I or my family can be of any assistance, please call upon us."

"Thank you," he responded formally, "you are most kind."

Amy extended her hand. "It has been interesting to be your enemy, Commandant."

Colonel Tsubaki smiled for the first time. "Yes? You believe so? I too." He took her hand and bowed over it. "I have thought sometimes," he murmured, "it is a pity there are national and racial barriers between us, Miss Hen-dra-son."

Racial barriers. Amy thought for a moment of the strong and handsome face of Henry Chen, and not knowing whether to laugh or cry, she wondered what Colonel Tsubaki would say if he knew.

Laura and Mike hired a taxi, for as yet there were no private automobiles in Shanghai, and they went to the railroad station. A train was arriving from the west. Out of a cloud of steam on the railway platform came David, laughing and healthy, from the staff of General Wedemeyer.

"Mother!" David cried, "you look wonderful!" He picked Laura up in his arms and swung her around. "My God! We can start our lives again!"

"Almost, darling. We still have some waiting to do. . . ."

Five days later another train arrived in Shanghai, this time from the south. The twins were coming home.

The train pulled in from Canton and Hong Kong. Passengers spilled onto the platform, porters piled suitcases onto carts or tucked them under their arms, cries of greeting and squeals of joy rose from embracing groups, and other travelers hurried alone toward the big clock in the central waiting room. Steam puffed, brakes hissed.

Mike stood a little apart, scanning the faces of those who were still disembarking from the train. He felt both anxious and humble. He had been given another chance to make amends to someone he loved, and he wondered if he deserved it.

Perhaps the chance was withdrawn, he thought miserably; he saw no one familiar. He was to be punished after all. He tried to resign himself. Patience and resignation were practices he was just beginning to learn, and it had taken him four years of wartime disaster to start to teach him.

No. Not withdrawn.

A gaunt young man with shining fair hair was beginning to descend the train steps. Slowly, for he leaned on a cane. He wore a black suit with a clerical collar: a priest. He was being assisted by . . . *Amy, Amy, red curls and all, bless you dear heart, you have brought him home. . . .*

"Grandpa," Amy said in a strangled voice. Her arms went around his neck.

She and Mike did not speak for a while. Then Amy whispered against his cheek, "Andy is here. He came with me."

"I know that, Amy. Mother of God, I can see it for myself."

"He has a wooden leg, but he manages with the cane. He does wonderfully."

Mike released Amy and looked over. Andy had been embraced by Laura and David. Now they were turning to Amy, and she was running toward them. Mike was facing Andy, who was standing alone resting on his cane. Waiting. Uncertainty and hope written on his face.

Mike did not hesitate. He strode over to his grandson. He said nothing at first, not trusting himself to speak. Instead he held out his hand.

Andy flushed deeply. "Hello, Grandpa." He extended his left hand, needing his right for the cane.

"Hello, Andy."

Their fingers gripped.

"I . . . missed you," Andy said.

"Yes, I . . . missed you too."

Moments passed. Then Mike said huskily, "You know, don't you, that I've been a damn fool?"

There was a little silence as Andy swallowed. Then he gave Mike a shaky grin. "I'd like to hug you, Grandpa, but I'd need two hands. And I can't let go of this cane."

Mike didn't speak for a moment. Then he said, "We'll get you something better than a damned wooden leg! We can't have you limping around with a son-of-a-bitching cane!"

"Watch your language, Grandpa," Andy said gently. "You're speaking to a member of the clergy."

"So I am," Mike said in a soft voice. "So I am. Forgive me, Father, for I have sinned."

Andy gave him a startled glance to see if he was joking, and realized that Mike was not. He took a deep breath. "I guess we have a lot to say to each other." He paused and looked into Mike's face. "Shall we join the rest of the family, Grandpa?" he murmured. "Will you help me?"

There was only one answer. Mike put his arm around Andy's shoulders and slowly they approached the others, who were waiting. The Valentines were together once more.

CHAPTER 8

It was civil war again in China. The Communists in their northern stronghold denounced the Kuomintang "clique" for corruption and inefficiency. They demanded to share in the government. Chiang Kai-shek refused. He and no one else was the head of the government, he maintained.

Only a very few, like Mac McNamara in New York and Amy Henderson in Shanghai, both writing for newspapers, thought the Communists had a chance to prevail. Except for the Reds themselves, who had reason to believe they would win. Chiang Kai-shek had every apparent advantage. More manpower. More weapons. Better transportation. All the big cities. All the arsenals. All the rich provinces.

The Communists were confined to the poverty-stricken areas of the North. They had no air force, no gunboats, few railways, no big cities, only primitive industry and trade.

What they had was training. They knew ways to reach the peasants in the villages, through political workers and performances of the Red Theater. They had well-informed troops and the carefully cultivated support of the university students. They also knew hit-and-run military tactics. They had acquired their knowledge through hard experience.

At the end of the war the Japanese officers in the North had surrendered their swords to the Red Army officers who had defeated them. Not to Chiang Kai-shek.

The Communists, selecting their spots, established guerrilla bases through the countryside between the Yellow River and the Yangtze. They chose areas well in the rear of Chiang Kai-shek's armies. Then they sent well-trained political workers into the villages to rally support. They did not overlook women in their propaganda effort.

Henry Chen and a coworker from Shensi called Yuan were in a Honan village in the spring of 1946. It was evening and they were attending a meeting of the newly organized Women's Association, a group that they had helped create. They sat in folding chairs at the back of the little meeting hall; they were present only as observers. Tonight's function was being run by the women themselves.

Another man was present, but he was on trial: Chu, a "tyrannical husband." He stood before the women with his eyes lowered. He was a wife-beater. His wife led the accusers.

"We are no longer slaves!" Chu's wife cried. "You cannot beat me any longer! You cannot kick me like a dog!"

Chu raised his head and glared but didn't answer.

"Women hold up half the sky!" cried another woman. "Don't you know that? Admit the truth of how you treated our sister! Confess your brutality!"

Chu curled his lip but refused to speak.

"We will beat you ourselves with our fists," shouted another, "unless you do as we say! This is a new society, and you must apologize to our sister! Publicly, in front of us all!"

"Never," Chu snarled, finding his voice. "I will never humble myself in front of an association of women!"

"Beat him!"

"No, lock him in a room until he's hungry enough to confess his crimes!"

"Leave him," said Chu's wife in a low voice, turning her face aside. "I will pay for this later."

"You will not," said another woman, comforting her. "You can do nothing alone. But you are not alone. We are with you; we are against all bad husbands as the comrades have taught us;

we hold up half the sky and we stand together. So much we have learned.''

When the meeting was over, Henry and Comrade Yuan strolled outside into the mild spring night for a cigarette. The sky was full of stars.

"Do you suppose Chu will confess?" said Yuan.

"I doubt it," replied Henry. "He is stubborn and reactionary and believes thoroughly in the old ways. We must have patience."

"Ah, patience," said Yuan. "It's so easy to get angry with people, isn't it? Sometimes you feel like banging their heads together to knock some sense into them."

Henry laughed. "Yes," he said, "but sometimes, Yuan, I feel like shouting with joy when I think of the glorious opportunity that's almost within our reach. Do you realize we are on the brink of grasping all of China?"

"No one but us seems to think so."

"It's true, Yuan. Consider it!" Henry looked up at the star-filled sky and laughed again. "This whole country, from the Great Wall in the North to the rice paddies of the South, from the China Sea to the borders of Tibet, this China, with all its stubborn, aggravating, tradition-bound marvelous people, ours to teach and rebuild! Doesn't it excite you?"

Yuan looked at him and shrugged. "It won't be so simple. There won't be a common enemy like Japan. The troublemakers will be our own peasants, like Chu."

"Don't you think I know that? And not just peasants. There'll be resistance in the cities too. I grew up in Shanghai and I know. If my own father were alive, he wouldn't understand the new China. He wept with shame when the soldiers of Sun Yat-sen cut off his queue. My mother told me. Still, the adventure! The opportunity!"

Yuan gazed at Henry with a faint smile. "You look like a boy when you speak this way, Comrade Chen."

Henry gestured apologetically. "I am thirty-five years old. My eldest son will be six on his next birthday. I have been in this struggle for nineteen years. And yet you are right; these thoughts do make me feel like a boy."

"Where do you go from here? Back to Yenan?"

"Not yet." Henry dropped his cigarette to the ground and

stubbed it out with his toe. "Comrade Mao," he said thoughtfully, "has given me permission first to visit Shanghai. There is a friend I haven't seen for many years. I have a feeling I may not have another chance."

The war is over, thought Amy, composing an article in her mind, placing the words in orderly sentences so they would be easier to write down later, *but not in China. Here in Shanghai, almost a year after the Japanese surrender, the streets still echo with gunfire.*

She stood up and peered into the distance, shielding her eyes with her hand. She was on the rooftop of a hotel called the Broadway Mansions, just across Soochow Creek in the Hunkow district. She could see the bridge, and the park beyond it, and the shipping in the river. In fact she could smell the river water, that rancid odor peculiar to Shanghai that she would never forget, no matter where she went. She was most interested in the gunfire. A street battle was in progress on either side of the bridge. Kuomintang troops were opposing a group of Communist insurgents on Mission Row. The firing was coming in short, aimless bursts, first from one side of the bridge and then another, sending up little puffs of smoke. Both groups of soldiers were young and inexperienced. The seasoned Communist cadres had not yet reached Shanghai. This was by way of a preliminary encounter. Amy had come here to observe it from the roof; she could smell the odor of hot sticky tar whenever she moved.

She had no doubt how the war would end, eventually. That was why the Valentines were going home to America. They had decided as a family. There would be no place for the Valentine Pottery Works in the new China, and they all agreed that the new China was on its way. When it arrived, foreigners would no longer be welcome. They would be living under someone else's sky.

The plans were all made for their departure. This time there would be no Pearl Harbor; they were really sailing for home.

Was America really her home? Amy wondered as the gunfire subsided on both sides of the creek.

She had accepted a job on the staff of *The Nation*. She was a "heroine of Japanese brutality" since the internment camp, as well as a celebrated journalist. China, Japan, and the Orient would be her speciality. She would live in New York.

Andy was already in San Francisco, in residence in his new parish, where he was assistant pastor. Laura and Mike would join him, and David as well. David was planning to set up the new pottery works, and he was organizing plans to begin production. Li-san had reluctantly agreed it was no longer safe for her in China; she, too, would move to San Francisco. Mike had decided to retire. Laura would supervise her San Francisco gallery. They would live in Marin County; Andy had written that he had already seen a house he considered would be splendid for his grandparents.

So they were all accounted for, Amy thought. She felt melancholy and depressed, although she knew she shouldn't be. She had an exciting new job awaiting her, and a proposal of marriage. By mail. From Mac McNamara.

He sounded almost tearful in the letter. He had been worried sick about her for four years. They had a date in New York, had she forgotten? "Jesus, Red, don't do that to a guy. It's not polite to stand somebody up without notice. But I'll forgive you if you'll just show up with all your freckles. Even if it's a little late. Do you think you could put up with a guy like me for the rest of your life? I've been crazy about you for years—don't ask me why—but I guess you've always known. . . ."

It would be a funny kind of marriage, Mac admitted in the letter. She would be working in New York, he would be traveling as a foreign correspondent for UPI; they'd have to tip their hats in passing most of the time. But they'd get together every once in a while, and then it would be great, and they sure as hell understood one another. . . .

Amy hadn't decided what to do. She would make up her mind when she saw Mac in New York, she told herself.

She had a poignant sense of unfinished business in China. It would always be that way as long as she lived. Yet there was a yearning she couldn't stifle, a good-bye she wanted to say and could not. Henry was far away, out of her reach. They'd said good-bye in Yenan in 1939.

Amy peered from the roof across Soochow Creek. A soldier with a megaphone appeared on the sidewalk opposite the Embank-

ment Building. He waved his arms, then shouted through the
megaphone.

"*T'ou hsiang, t'ou hsiang!*"

His voice sounded tinny and faraway. He was calling to the
Kuomintang to surrender. A short burst of gunfire answered him.
He ducked out of sight.

Soon all foreigners will be gone from China, Amy composed
in her mind. *There will be no more International Settlements or
port concessions or treaty rights. Those days will end when the
gunfire stops. It will be both good and bad for the world when
China closes her borders. In the long run this huge nation cannot
live in isolation.*

The gunfire seemed to Amy to have stopped. She felt she had
seen all she had come for on the roof, and the article was half
written in her mind, so she prepared to leave.

Walking along the sidewalk to the place where she had parked
her car, two blocks away from the Broadway Mansions, Amy
thought of the fighting. The soldiers had called off their hostili-
ties for the day. They would resume again tomorrow, for this was
a desultory kind of skirmishing until the real battle for the city
began.

Amy had lived through one battle for Shanghai, in 1937,
between Japan and China. She would not be present for the next,
between the Kuomintang and the Communists.

How strange it would be, she thought, reading and writing
about Shanghai from the other side of the Pacific. Still, she
would remember. You never truly lost anything, not while it was
still locked in your memory. She would remember the sounds of
Shanghai, she told herself. The clang of trams crossing Soochow
Creek. The rumble of derricks and cranes in the Whangpoo. The
cry of peddlers in the alleys of Chapei. The factory hooters
calling lunch hour and quitting time for the cotton-mill workers
of Hunkow. The chime of the big clock striking noon on the
Customs Tower. She would bring them all back to her memory
after she had left.

A taxi pulled up beside her at the curb. "Need a lift, missy?"
said the driver.

"No, thank you," Amy replied. "I have a car."

The taxi continued to cruise in the road beside her as she walked.

"I told you I don't need a taxi," Amy said finally. She turned her head, intending to dismiss the driver once and for all.

"Are you sure you're not making a mistake?" The driver braked the car.

Amy gasped. She saw him for the first time.

"My God!" she whispered, and put her hand to her mouth.

Henry Chen gave her a delighted smile. He reached behind him into the backseat and opened the rear door. "Get in," he said. "Tell me, Little Sister, did I fool you with my disguise?"

In Chapei, Li-san was trying to organize for the Great Move. The packing was only half done but she was flitting from one task to another, picking up objects and putting them down, making aimless moves. David was trying to help her.

"You're not accomplishing anything, Li-san," he said. "Why don't we make a list and we'll check things off?"

"What sort of method is that? A list! Am I a scribe, to make pretty brushstrokes on a sheet of paper instead of working?"

"I'll write the list."

"You'll do nothing of the kind. I wish you would go on about your business and let me pack."

"If you were packing," said David meaningfully, "I would go on about my business."

She'd stopped listening to him. "I must take this," she cried. She swooped to the stove and picked up her big iron rice-pot, clasping it to her breast with both hands.

"You certainly won't take that," said David. "We have pots in San Francisco."

"Not like this."

"Better. You won't need your pots. Or the rice bowls either."

"They are from the Valentine Pottery Works!"

"We're starting a new pottery works. I'll give you a prettier set of bowls."

Li-san's face crumpled. She set the pot back on the stove, caressing it with her hand before letting her arm drop to her side. "I won't be able to cook anything in that place," she whispered. "They won't have Chinese vegetables."

"Certainly they will. You can live on Grant Avenue, surrounded by Chinese people and Chinese food."

"There won't be anyone from Szechuan. They'll all be from
Canton."

"That is not true," said David. "You'll probably meet someone from your very own village the very first day."

"Oh, you," said Li-san, smiling mistily through her beginning
tears. "All right, let us not waste any more time." She looked
around the kitchen. "First of all," she declared, "I will not
need that iron pot. They have many many pots in San Francisco."

Henry had parked the taxi on the Bund. He and Amy were
walking in the little park that bordered the river.

"You've taken a chance by coming to Shanghai," Amy said,
glancing at him anxiously. "If the Kuomintang knew you were
here and took you prisoner, they'd have a big propaganda victory."

Comrade Chen T'ieh-chang was known to be a trusted aide of
Comrade Mao, and already he was a valued and respected voice
on the Central Committee.

"They won't know I'm here," said Henry, "and they won't
take me prisoner. If I cannot outwit the Kuomintang after all
these years, I don't deserve to be free anyway. Besides"—he
laughed and gazed out at the river—"this is my native city. The
Whangpoo. Bubbling Well Road. Scenes of my childhood. You."

In his disguise as a Shanghai taxi driver Henry was wearing a
loose woolen jacket and trousers, and a shirt with a band around
the neck instead of a collar. The shapeless clothes, however,
could not hide the lithe gracefulness of his form. His brilliant
black eyes and arched eyebrows were concealed by the peak of
his chauffeur's cap, which made Amy feel a little easier. At least
that unmistakable face would not be completely visible, she
thought.

They leaned on the iron railing by the water. There was no need
yet to talk or exchange greetings or declare emotions. It was as
though they had never parted, Amy thought. Something tight and
miserable seemed to dissolve in her chest. She sighed and inhaled
the Whangpoo.

"It always smells of oil and garbage, doesn't it?" Henry
remarked. "You actually miss that smell in other cities."

"Only if you were born in Shanghai."

They leaned on the railing in companionable silence. After a while Amy said, "How long do you have?"

"Just a little while. I'm on my way back to the North."

"Where you'll give a report on conditions in Shanghai. And that's why you've come." Amy spoke matter-of-factly, but she was half hoping he would deny it.

"That's not why I've come," Henry said. "We have ample reports on conditions in Shanghai from many other sources."

"Oh." Amy gazed at his face, studying his features. "Did you really come to . . . say good-bye to me?"

"Why, yes." Henry looked back at her gravely. "It has been seven years since I've seen you, Little Sister. You have suffered hardships. Oh, yes, I know all about Hong Kong; you see, I have kept track of you. And I know you are leaving China. I'm sorry I was too late to meet Andy—give him my love when you see him. But you, Amy. I need not have worried, for how beautiful you have become."

"Beautiful!" Amy put her hands up to her face. "I've lost my youth, Henry. Those four years have aged me."

"No. Not really. You only imagine it. Yet something has changed in your face. Your spirit is visible now. Such a strong and loving spirit, Little Sister. How courageous. How lovely to me."

"Henry, you have become more . . . Chinese since I've seen you last. Even the way you express yourself. You're losing your American ways of speaking."

"I suppose that's natural. I have been living among my own people almost exclusively for the past twelve years."

"It's done your career no harm." Amy gave him a thoughtful glance. "Are you ambitious, Henry?"

"Shall I tell you the truth?"

"Please."

"Then I am, a little. But I don't think I'd confess it to anyone but you. Personal ambition isn't considered admirable. Still, I have my dreams."

Do you tell your wife? Amy wanted to ask. She suppressed the question. She didn't ask, nor did she inquire after his family. Nor did she tell him about Mac and the proposal of marriage. Those were separate parts of their lives; they had nothing to do with Henry and herself.

He understood that perfectly, she knew. They didn't have to discuss it.

If we meet again in forty years, when both of us are old, it will be just the same. We will have no need of words, Henry and I.

"What will become of our house on Bubbling Well Road?" she said after a little while.

"We have thoughts of turning it into a school," Henry replied. "A school for crafts, where youngsters can learn calligraphy and pottery and weaving and jewelry making. The downstairs could be the display hall."

"I would like that," Amy said.

"I supposed you would." Henry paused. "And my godmother . . . she would like it too."

"Of course. You know that. I will tell her."

"So the Valentines will not actually leave Shanghai. Not in spirit."

"No, Henry."

He moved close to Amy and lifted her chin with his finger. "Keep the bridge built, Little Sister," he said softly, looking into her eyes. "Do you remember?"

"You said that in Yenan. Yes, I remember. You can trust me." Amy blinked back tears.

"I always have. I always will." Henry leaned forward and kissed Amy gently on the cheek. "That is why I came to Shanghai," he whispered. "To hear you say it. And that is all we need to speak of good-byes."

Laura was packing photographs, books, and letters in the library on Bubbling Well Road. She was kneeling on the floor emptying a bookshelf. Big cardboard cartons stood all around the room, some already filled, some still half empty.

The accumulation of a lifetime, Laura thought.

No, not quite a lifetime. But almost.

She told herself she would never finish this task if she didn't stop daydreaming and reminiscing over everything she saw.

Oh! A photograph album from Weichang! It had pictures of Eileen. That must be kept. She placed the album on the pile of things-to-bring-to-San Francisco, although the pile was already teetering. She found a wedding picture of Eileen and George Henderson. They had lost touch with George in the last years. It was as though he'd fulfilled his role and left them. She kept that too.

She told herself sternly to settle down, tend to business, and certainly be more selective about packing.

But photographs . . . she couldn't throw away family photographs.

"Laura, you haven't made much progress since I saw you last."

Mike had come into the room.

Laura settled back on her heels. "I know. I keep getting nostalgic; it's like cleaning out an attic only worse. Just think, though, suppose that Japanese officer who lived here during the war had destroyed the library. Then we wouldn't have anything."

"And you wouldn't have all this packing to do, either."

"Mike, look at the photograph album with pictures of Eileen. I'd forgotten all about it. Weichang, remember?"

Mike came and gazed at the album over her shoulder. Laura noticed that he had a letter in his hand.

"Oh, did the mail come?" she asked.

"Yes. Here's a letter from Andy." Mike's face lit up. "I read it—it's addressed to everyone. He says he's really gotten his strength back."

"That's good news." Laura smiled and extended her hand. "Help me up?"

Mike assisted her to her feet. She saw how happy he was. Mike and Andy were very close now. Mike had returned to the Church. He did not attend mass every Sunday; he said old habits were too hard to break. Andy said he would settle for what he could get from an old reprobate like his grandfather: Mike's confession alone had probably taken four or five hours, and he was glad some other priest had had to listen.

Mike had finally told Laura the story of Nora Valentine and Father Hugh. It was another confession, and he said wonderingly that he had been a fool to carry that burden of vengefulness and resentment around with him all these years. Now at last the wound was healed. As they were preparing to sail for home.

Mike said softly, extending the envelope with Andy's letter,
"Here, Laura, read it for yourself."

"All right. But I can't rest long. I must get back to these
cartons or I'll never finish."

Still, they decided with a laugh and a sigh that they needed to
have a meal.

After she and Mike had had dinner, Laura returned to her
cartons and boxes, books and photographs. Now she was working in lamplight. Mike had fallen asleep upstairs. The house was
quiet. She wondered what would happen to this house when they
were gone. The Valentines had sold it to a Chinese banker who
was a heavy supporter of Chiang Kai-shek, but if the Kuomintang
lost the war, the banker would have to leave as well.

Laura made a decision about the contents of the library. She
would simply pack everything on the shelves.

Then she came across a set of old auction catalogs from
Peking, dating back to 1921. Did she need those?

Yes. Because of the photographs and descriptions. They would
go into her art-book collection.

Well, what about these children's books? An entire collection
of Tom Swift, which had belonged to David.

He might want them, she told herself firmly, she oughtn't to
leave them behind.

Another volume of Shakespeare's plays? Where did they get so
many? But this one had beautiful steel engravings. . . .

Laura sat back on her heels and started to laugh at herself. This
was hopeless. She was the wrong person for the job.

"Grandmother, what's so funny?" asked Amy from the
doorway.

"Me. I can't throw anything away. Look at this room." Laura
gestured around at the library with its cartons, boxes, and piles.

"Then we'll just pack it all up," said Amy. "Come on, I'll
help you."

"That carton over there is almost empty. You can start filling
it from this stack on the floor."

Amy looked tired but very calm, almost radiant. She looked
happier than she had in a long time, Laura thought. There was a
peacefulness about her that Laura had not noticed before.

"Something nice has happened to you," she observed.

Amy smiled. "Grandmother, I have just seen Henry Chen."

"Why, Amy! Here, in Shanghai?"

"Yes. He couldn't stay—he had to return to Yenan—but he sent his love. He said he couldn't address you as Honorable Godmother, because there will be no more honorifics in the new China, but you would understand."

Laura smiled too. "Henry was such an adorable baby," she said. "He had such fat cheeks and beautiful black eyes, and he practically never cried."

"Unlike me."

"Every time you cried, so did Andy. You can't imagine what bedlam the house was when you were infants."

"I can see this is a night for reminiscing." Amy gazed affectionately at her grandmother. Then she knelt on the floor and reached for one of the cartons. She and Laura both busied themselves with packing. Into the preoccupied silence Amy said, "Grandmother, here is a picture of a little girl in a garden." She had picked up the photograph album. "Is that my mother?"

"Yes, when she was five, in our garden in Weichang."

"So long ago. She was so pretty. Andy looks like her."

"Yes, he does." Laura paused. She surveyed Amy for a moment. Then she asked quietly, "Forgive me if I'm prying, Amy, but about you and Henry. Have you parted as friends?"

Amy set down the photograph album and nodded. "I'm reconciled, I think. In fact, I may even consider a proposal of marriage in New York."

"Oh?"

Amy abandoned the packing and came to sit beside Laura on the floor. "It's Mac McNamara," she said. "He asked me to marry him in a letter. I may just do it. I'm not exactly in love with him but . . . he's one of the few people I can picture climbing into bed with." She glanced up at Laura. "Is that such a terrible reason to get married?"

"I can think of worse."

"I guess you didn't consider such matters when you married Grandpa."

"On the contrary, I believe it was my principal motive."

"Really?"

"Well, I didn't know it. I was young and innocent and I believed I was attracted by 'vitality' and 'energy.' "

"But it was really sex appeal. I can understand that. Grandpa never really lost his sex appeal, did he?"

"No."

"Sailing for China," Amy said wonderingly, "in 1895, when you were both so young. Grandmother, what did you imagine it would be like?"

"I can't quite remember."

"Try."

"I suppose," Laura said with a distant expression on her face, "I thought it would be exotic. Strange. I thought it would be a romantic adventure, full of fantasy." She smiled at Amy and brushed back a strand of hair from her granddaughter's cheek. The years rushed in on her, full of tumbling memories, not packed in the cartons but whirling in her head like bits of colored glass in the kaleidoscope she'd had as a child, like the snow-flakes in the glass paperweight that had stood on her father's desk in Connecticut when she was growing up. "It was not, though, darling. It was not a romantic adventure at all." The lamplight glowed golden on her granddaughter's face as Laura said slowly, "It was something much better. It was life."

Fiction

GENERAL

☐ The House of Women	Chaim Bermant	£1.95
☐ The Patriarch	Chaim Bermant	£2.25
☐ The Rat Race	Alfred Bester	£1.95
☐ Midwinter	John Buchan	£1.50
☐ A Prince of the Captivity	John Buchan	£1.50
☐ The Priestess of Henge	David Burnett	£2.50
☐ Tangled Dynasty	Jean Chapman	£1.75
☐ The Other Woman	Colette	£1.95
☐ Retreat From Love	Colette	£1.60
☐ An Infinity of Mirrors	Richard Condon	£1.95
☐ Arigato	Richard Condon	£1.95
☐ Prizzi's Honour	Richard Condon	£1.75
☐ A Trembling Upon Rome	Richard Condon	£1.95
☐ The Whisper of the Axe	Richard Condon	£1.75
☐ Love and Work	Gwyneth Cravens	£1.95
☐ King Hereafter	Dorothy Dunnett	£2.95
☐ Pope Joan	Lawrence Durrell	£1.35
☐ The Country of Her Dreams	Janice Elliott	£1.35
☐ Magic	Janice Elliot	£1.95
☐ Secret Places	Janice Elliott	£1.75
☐ Letter to a Child Never Born	Oriana Fallaci	£1.25
☐ A Man	Oriana Fallaci	£2.50
☐ Rich Little Poor Girl	Terence Feely	£1.75
☐ Marital Rites	Margaret Forster	£1.50
☐ The Seduction of Mrs Pendlebury	Margaret Forster	£1.95
☐ Abingdons	Michael French	£2.25
☐ Rhythms	Michael French	£2.25
☐ Who Was Sylvia?	Judy Gardiner	£1.50
☐ Grimalkin's Tales	Gardiner, Ronson, Whitelaw	£1.60
☐ Lost and Found	Julian Gloag	£1.95
☐ A Sea-Change	Lois Gould	£1.50
☐ La Presidenta	Lois Gould	£2.25
☐ A Kind of War	Pamela Haines	£1.95
☐ Tea at Gunters	Pamela Haines	£1.75
☐ Black Summer	Julian Hale	£1.75
☐ A Rustle in the Grass	Robin Hawdon	£1.95
☐ Riviera	Robert Sydney Hopkins	£1.95
☐ Duncton Wood	William Horwood	£2.75
☐ The Stonor Eagles	William Horwood	£2.50
☐ The Man Who Lived at the Ritz	A. E. Hotchner	£1.65
☐ A Bonfire	Pamela Hansford Johnson	£1.50
☐ The Good Listener	Pamela Hansford Johnson	£1.50
☐ The Honours Board	Pamela Hansford Johnson	£1.50
☐ The Unspeakable Skipton	Pamela Hansford Johnson	£1.50
☐ In the Heat of the Summer	John Katzenbach	£1.95
☐ Starrs	Warren Leslie	£2.50
☐ Kine	A. R. Lloyd	£1.50
☐ The Factory	Jack Lynn	£1.95
☐ Christmas Pudding	Nancy Mitford	£1.50
☐ Highland Fling	Nancy Mitford	£1.50
☐ Pigeon Pie	Nancy Mitford	£1.75
☐ The Sun Rises	Christopher Nicole	£2.50

Fiction

HORROR/OCCULT/NASTY

☐ Death Walkers	Gary Brandner	£1.75
☐ Hellborn	Gary Brandner	£1.75
☐ The Howling	Gary Brandner	£1.75
☐ Return of the Howling	Gary Brandner	£1.75
☐ Tribe of the Dead	Gary Brandner	£1.75
☐ The Sanctuary	Glenn Chandler	£1.50
☐ The Tribe	Glenn Chandler	£1.10
☐ The Black Castle	Leslie Daniels	£1.25
☐ The Big Goodnight	Judy Gardiner	£1.25
☐ Rattlers	Joseph L. Gilmore	£1.60
☐ The Nestling	Charles L. Grant	£1.95
☐ Night Songs	Charles L. Grant	£1.95
☐ Slime	John Halkin	£1.75
☐ Slither	John Halkin	£1.60
☐ The Unholy	John Halkin	£1.25
☐ The Skull	Shaun Hutson	£1.25
☐ Pestilence	Edward Jarvis	£1.60
☐ The Beast Within	Edward Levy	£1.25
☐ Night Killers	Richard Lewis	£1.25
☐ Spiders	Richard Lewis	£1.75
☐ The Web	Richard Lewis	£1.75
☐ Nightmare	Lewis Mallory	£1.75
☐ Bloodthirst	Mark Ronson	£1.60
☐ Ghoul	Mark Ronson	£1.75
☐ Ogre	Mark Ronson	£1.75
☐ Deathbell	Guy N. Smith	£1.75
☐ Doomflight	Guy N. Smith	£1.25
☐ Manitou Doll	Guy N. Smith	£1.25
☐ Satan's Snowdrop	Guy N. Smith	£1.00
☐ The Understudy	Margaret Tabor	£1.95
☐ The Beast of Kane	Cliff Twemlow	£1.50
☐ The Pike	Cliff Twemlow	£1.25

NAME..

ADDRESS...

....

Write to Hamlyn Paperbacks Cash Sales, PO Box 11, Falmouth, Cornwall TR10 9EN.

Please indicate order and enclose remittance to the value of cover price plus:

U.K. CUSTOMERS: Please allow 55p for the first book, 22p for the second book and 14p for each additional book ordered to a maximum charge of £1.75.

B.F.P.O. & EIRE: Please allow 55p for the first book, 22p for the second book plus 14p per copy for the next seven books, thereafter 8p per book.

OVERSEAS CUSTOMERS: Please allow £1.00 for the first book plus 25p per copy for each additional book.

Whilst every effort is made to keep prices low it is sometimes necessary to increase cover prices and also postage and packing rates at short notice. Hamlyn Paperbacks reserve the right to show new retail prices on covers which may differ from those previously advertised in the text or elsewhere.